AGENT OF
THE CROWN

MELISSA
MCSHANE

Night Harbor Publishing
Salt Lake City, UT

Night Harbor Publishing
340 S. Lemon Avenue #9773
Walnut, CA 91789
www.nightharborpublishing.com

Cover design by Yocla Designs
North sign and shield designed by Erin Dinnell Bjorn
Ben's song appears courtesy of Jacob Proffitt

First Printing
10 9 8 7 6 5 4 3 2 1

To my parents —
In thanks for always providing me with a library
and the books to go on its shelves

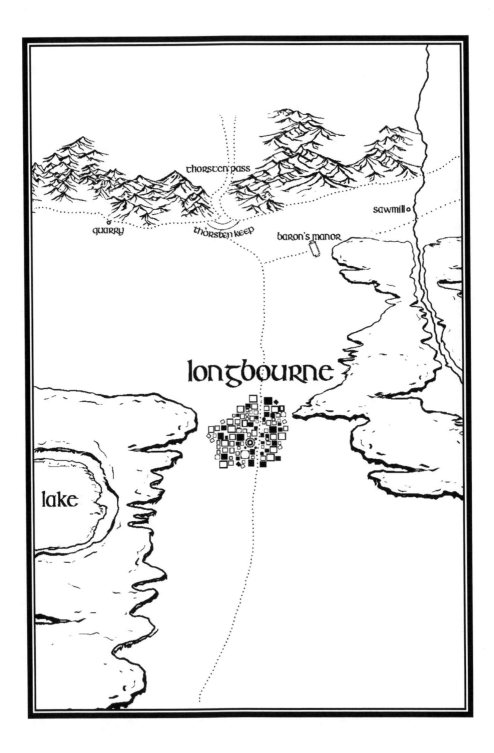

SUMMER

CHAPTER ONE

Telaine raced through the streets of Aurilien, turning the familiar streets with their tall, elegant mansions into blurs of gray stone and bright glass. Her speeding carriage hit a bump, nearly tossing her off her seat onto the cobbles flying beneath her. She screamed, and hoped the fleeing bystanders would mistake her terror for exhilaration. She gripped the reins of the horses drawing the high-seated two-wheeled carriage, her hands white-knuckled under her gloves, and prayed it wouldn't become a one-wheeler as the horses took the next sharp corner at speed. More pedestrians scattered, shouting things she was happier not understanding.

Broad Street wasn't busy at this time of day, but what traffic there was dodged quickly out of her way. Everyone knew her shining rose-lacquered carriage with its perfectly matched bays; that was the point, that everyone know who she was when she careened through Aurilien. She wished she'd thought of some way to make herself conspicuous that was less likely to leave her a bag of broken bones in the wreckage of the awful pink carriage.

She caught a glimpse of herself in the plate glass window of one of Broad Street's exclusive clothiers, her hair flying — when had she lost her hat? — like a flag behind her, and she smiled despite the terror she told herself was excitement. Yes, the Princess would be remembered for this day. She gritted her teeth, snapped the reins, and the horses responded with a burst of speed she hadn't thought they had in them.

Within the carriage, her maid Posy let out a squeak Telaine could hear over the noise of the rattling wheels. Telaine sent her a silent apology, though Posy had known what kind of ride she was in for the moment Telaine took the reins. No one ever appreciated just how good a driver you had to be to look this bad.

They flashed past the Park, men in dark suits and women in bright dresses mere splashes of color as they went in and out of its gates. Ahead, Telaine could see the vast hulking sprawl of the palace, which looked as if it had grown there on its hill instead of being built. Willow

North's tower thrust its dark gray finger high above the roofs, as if in defiance of ungoverned heaven.

Then the horses were through the never-closed iron gate with its delicate black filigree and charging up the drive. With Telaine hauling hard and desperate on the reins, they slid on the cobblestones until they came to a stop at the black granite steps leading to the palace's front door. The carriage slewed a bit, tilted, and hit the drive with a bounce. Telaine concealed her relief under a sunny mask, all smiles, and took the hand of the footman in North blue and silver who approached her. "Welcome home, your Highness," he said, as calmly as if four thousand pounds of horse and carriage hadn't just come barreling up the drive toward him like an equine thunderstorm.

"It's good to be home, Walter," she said, stepping down from the carriage and bestowing another smile on him. "Will you see to the horses? And Posy—" Telaine turned to look at the woman staggering out of the carriage and silently apologized again. "Please take my bags to my room? I have urgent business inside." That, at least, was the unvarnished truth.

She ran as quickly as she could through the mazelike halls of the palace, hobbled by her narrow pink skirt and high-heeled pink shoes, acknowledging everyone who greeted her with an airy, featherbrained laugh but not stopping to chat. In the Long Gallery, filled with portraits of the Kings and Queens of Tremontane, she paused to make her usual curtsey to the youthful image of Queen Zara North. Her great-aunt, dead at an assassin's hand nearly fifty years ago now, stared back at her down her straight, imperious nose.

The north wing was all heavy oak paneling inset with ebony, ponderous and serious. Combined with the narrowness of the halls, it seemed oppressive, as if it knew how important it was and made sure everyone else did too. Telaine had to step out of the way of men and women hurrying on errands who didn't pay any attention to her. Outside the palace, she was a well-known, popular figure. Here in the palace she was just Telaine North Hunter, another one of the North clan. She wasn't even a very important one at that, daughter of the

King's long-deceased younger sister.

She dodged functionaries, passed the curved marble-topped reception desk with a nod for the King's appointments secretary, and rapped at a door identical to all the others, ignoring the secretary's protest. At a muffled command from within, she opened the door and slipped inside.

The room had looked the same her entire life: thick gray carpeting, walls painted a pale cream color and hung with paintings depicting great moments in Tremontanan history, cupboards and bookshelves bulging with tattered tomes and unbound sheets of paper. Two of the windows, both taller than she was, looked out on the massive northern wall surrounding the palace, while a third showed the lower curve of the palace wall whose sheer granite blocks were interrupted only by Ansom's Gate. It looked impregnable in its stark simplicity, secure and cluttered and welcoming.

Telaine leaned against the door for a moment and let the tension drain out of her. There were only two places in the world where she could drop her madcap, frivolous guise, and this was one of them. She straightened her spine and crossed the room to stand in front of an enormous, highly polished oak desk with legs carved like lion's feet and a top piled high with paperwork.

A man with graying black hair and a short beard wrote something on a sheet of paper before him; the nib made a scratching sound as it crossed the page. A Device emitting a steady white light hovered over his left shoulder. The man turned the Device off and looked up. "Well?" he said.

Telaine clasped her hands behind her back. "You were right about Terence d'Arden," she said. "He's thrown in his lot with the Sudenvilles. Unfortunately, so has Lady Brightwell. She's been dealing privately with Susan Armsworthy, pretending to be an ally, but she intends to cast her vote for the other side at the last minute. Armsworthy has been foolishly listening to Brightwell about who's supposedly on their side and hasn't done any recruiting on her own. She's going to be unpleasantly surprised."

"Good work. I take it cutting your visit short didn't hurt your investigation?"

"I got all of that information by the fourth day. I was so sick of being the socialite and hearing people lie to me and pretending to enjoy myself that I considered coming down with some putrid infection just to get away. I think I gave Elizabeth d'Arden the impression that someone I know is dying."

The man laughed. He stood up, came around the desk, and embraced her. "Welcome home, Telaine."

She hugged him back. "It's good to be home, Uncle Jeffrey."

The King of Tremontane gave her one more squeeze, then released her and examined her face. "You look troubled. Overwhelmed by your talent?"

Telaine shook her head. Her uncle was one of the few people who knew she had the magical ability to hear lies when they were spoken to her. Having inherent magic might not mean death anymore, but the memory of the Ascendants who'd once dominated the kingdom with their magical powers hadn't faded. Ungoverned heaven alone knew what the citizens of Tremontane might do if they discovered their royal family was tainted by it.

"Just tired. Ready for a rest. I want to spend time with Julia, because...are the rumors true, then? About Lucas?"

Uncle Jeffrey nodded. He looked grim. "He has a mistress in the city. I find it hard to believe he would dare treat his wife—treat the heir to the Crown, for heaven's sake—with such disrespect, but then he always was a bit of a bastard. I should never have allowed the match."

"Where is he now? In hiding?"

Uncle Jeffrey let out a short laugh. "He thinks he is. He's still sworn and sealed to the North family, so I know exactly where he's gone to ground." His eyes went unfocused briefly as he used his own magic to locate Lucas. "In Lower Town, right now. Probably drinking Julia's money away."

"I don't suppose we can arrange a nice accident for him?"

He laughed mirthlessly. "Imogen wants him drawn and

quartered. I think she even has the horses picked out. No, I'm afraid it will have to be divorce and dissolution. I wish I could spare Julia all that, especially during her pregnancy, but there's nothing for it but to weather it out."

"I'll do what I can. I can't bear to think of her suffering."

Uncle Jeffrey turned away. "I'm afraid you won't be here."

Telaine's heart sank. "I've been the Princess for three months without a rest."

"I know. I have bad news from the Riverlands. Good news too, but mostly bad. I've gotten word that Harroden is smuggling to the Veriboldan rebels."

Harrison Chadwick, Count of Harroden. Marshal of the Riverlands and responsible for the border crossing where the Snow River entered Eskandel, their southern neighbor, as well as keeping the peace along the western border with Veribold. Tremontane's relations with Eskandel were cordial. They were not so friendly with Veribold. Telaine tried to remember the Count, but came up only with a sagging, aging figure and a face that had once been handsome. "I can see how that's good and bad news," Telaine said, but Uncle Jeffrey was shaking his head.

"The bad news is that an agent was killed getting that intelligence back to me," he said. "It might have been an accident, but it's possible he was exposed. We still don't know whether it was the rebels, or someone in Harroden's pay. Either way, I have to assume suspicions have been raised."

"Can you prove his involvement?"

"If the agent had documentary proof, it wasn't on him when his body was found. And I hope to heaven there wasn't any. That would definitely tip Harroden off."

"What do you want me to do?"

Uncle Jeffrey closed his eyes and raised his head as if looking for heavenly guidance. "The Chadwicks are throwing a party in three days," he said, looking at her again. "You've probably already received an invitation. I want you to see what you can find out. He's probably smuggling weapons, but I'd rather not make assumptions. Find out what the rebels' plan is. Learn whether Harroden is in league with the Veriboldan government; it's never been certain whether they're behind the rebel incursions into our territory. Get documentation and get out."

"I'm yours to command, my King." Julia would want her to stay, after so many weeks' absence. Telaine pictured her cousin's face when she told her she would be leaving again, and the knot of tension began re-forming at the base of her neck.

Uncle Jeffrey took her chin and tilted her face to meet his gaze. "Are you sure this is what you want to do?" he asked. "It was one thing when you were young and it was an adventure, but now…I can't help feeling it's beginning to wear on you. And this is far more dangerous than anything I've asked you to do before."

"It's still a challenge," she said, smiling. "How can I pass that up? As tired as I get of the Princess sometimes, it still thrills me to walk through a crowd without anyone knowing who I really am. Don't worry about me."

"You ask the impossible," he said, and released her. "Be ready to leave day after tomorrow."

She nodded and left the room, shutting the door quietly behind her. She smiled brilliantly at the King's secretary as she passed, turning his objections into a scarlet-faced mumbling. That should remind him not to object to the Princess's wishes. She tripped lightly down the North blue carpeted stairs and went at a sedate pace through the tangled corridors to the east wing, home to the royal family. Two soldiers in North blue and silver, fully armed and armored in steel plates over leather, stood flanking the wide door of three-inch-thick oak and nodded to her before opening the door and admitting her.

She took in a deep breath, inhaled the faint spicy-sweet scent that came from everywhere and nowhere at once, and proceeded down the short hallway to the great drawing room of the east wing. Light Devices cast a warm glow over the cream-colored walls and the maple wainscoting that combined with the scent of cinnamon and roses always meant home. No one was there, thank heaven. Much as she loved her cousins, the long trip and the knife-edged terror of driving like the madwoman the Princess was well known to be made Telaine want nothing more than a hot bath and a nap before dinnertime.

She briefly glanced down one of the hallways that led off the drawing room, then shook her head and turned away. She wanted to see her beloved cousin Julia, to give her comfort, but she was too much on edge to be good company. She went to her own rooms instead, which were far away from the rest of the family...why? She couldn't remember now why she'd chosen them; they'd been hers since she was eight years old and she'd never wanted to move in the fifteen years since. Privacy mattered to her, and she needed a place where she could shed her alter ego, but today it felt like isolation.

She pushed open the door to her personal sitting room and shuddered. Frilly pink cushions teetering on overstuffed pink sofas and chairs. Tables topped with pink marble, their spindly legs gilded. A mantel that might have been made of any wood, except she couldn't tell which one because it was covered with a thick layer of pink paint Telaine always had to resist the urge to pick at. Rosy damask drapes and a dusky pink carpet thicker than the breadth of her two fingers. It was a room the Princess could entertain in. Telaine hated it.

There was a stack of envelopes on the horrible pink mantel; she sorted through it until she found the invitation from the Chadwicks. She entered her bedroom, which was decidedly non-frilly and had no pink in it anywhere, and flopped face-first onto her bed. "I am *so* sorry about the drive," she said to Posy, who had just put away the last of Telaine's undergarments. "Have I ever told you how wonderful you are?"

"Yes, but you ought to say it more often," Posy said. "And it's not like I didn't know what I was in for when we made up this persona eight years ago." She sat down and stretched out her long legs. "No harm done, though I don't know as I'd say the same if you'd crashed and killed us both."

"At least I wouldn't be in a position to hear whatever it was." Telaine rolled onto her back and stared up at the ceiling, plastered and painted white. "Thank you for putting everything away. I hate to tell you you'll need to pack it all up again tomorrow."

"I thought we'd have some free time finally."

"Unfortunately, no. We're off to Harroden day after tomorrow." She tossed the envelope at Posy, who caught it and tore it open so carelessly the invitation inside ripped as well. She read the contents, then passed it back to Telaine, stretching her legs even further and putting her hands behind her head, which was how she showed displeasure. Telaine glanced at her over the card. "Sorry," she said.

"Not your fault. And stop apologizing, *your Highness*. I've been an agent for longer than you've been alive and these things come with the job."

"I'm sorry—" Telaine covered her mouth, and Posy's eyebrows went up a second before she grinned. Telaine smiled back. "I'm having trouble shedding the Princess's persona today. Finding out about this new assignment made it worse, I think."

"This'll maybe help." Posy tossed something at Telaine's head; she caught it automatically. "It's been running backwards since a day ago." Posy stretched and left the room. Telaine turned the thing over in her hand. It was her spare pocket watch, a palm-sized Device encased in a smooth silver shell, and it was indeed running backwards. Running backwards at an alarming rate, no less. Well, that was something she could fix.

She swung her legs off her bed and went to her dressing room, which was filled to bursting with the Princess's gowns and walking dresses and riding garb and court attire. Occupying the rest of the space was her vanity table, a large marble-topped oaken thing with an oval mirror five feet across its long end. It had a dozen drawers of varying sizes and was covered with pots of cosmetics and jewelry boxes. Like her choice of suites, Telaine couldn't remember why she'd ever thought it was a good idea; it hulked in its corner of the room, daring anyone to approach it. Though—possibly *that* was why she'd chosen it; no one was likely to go rooting around in its innards and discover Telaine's best-kept secret.

Telaine opened the second drawer from the bottom, which was full of odds and ends, half-used cosmetics in unflattering colors, beauty implements used once and then discarded, a few broken pieces of jewelry. She removed the entire drawer and pulled out the shallow tray with its false bottom, revealing a treasure trove of a different sort.

Neatly organized tiny tools filled racks slotted into the bottom of the drawer; small bins contained bits of metal, some glowing, all cut into strange shapes and coils. Sheets of thin metal, silver, copper, and brass, were stacked upright at the back of the drawer, and a pair of metal shears the size of nail scissors hung on a hook next to them. The public had the Princess, her uncle had his agent, but this belonged to her alone. Her family knew she was interested in Devisery, but she'd concealed from them the extent to which she'd taken her interest… why? She had so many secrets already, things she kept hidden for the sake of her agent's identity. They were like knives she had to tiptoe across. This was a tiny flame nestled close to her heart.

Telaine cracked open the shell with one hand and studied the watch's innards. She saw nothing obviously broken, so there was something wrong with the imbued motive force, the piece of metal holding the magical energy that powered all Devices. She used a small screwdriver to remove some of the mechanical parts and exposed the little coil—ah, it was silver, that explained a lot. Digging in her parts bin, she found a coil identical to the damaged one, but made of copper, then used a hook to pop the silver coil out of the watch. The whirring stopped.

Next she needed to figure out where her source had drifted to. The lines of power that intersected in her dressing room, two of the hundreds of thousands crisscrossing the world, created a strong power source at their nexus, but they kept shifting and the source moved with them. Telaine sniffed. No one could see source any more than they could see the lines of power, but there were other ways to sense it, and to Telaine source always smelled like lilac and mint. There it was, between a couple of winter coats the Princess should have gotten rid of two seasons ago.

She laid the copper coil on her palm, and the source's power spiraled up around her hand. Gently, she drew it into the coil, pulling delicately at the source as if spinning out a thread of spider's silk. After a minute, it began to glow with a pale coppery radiance. She fed it threads of source until it turned into a spiral of white light, released the source before the coil became too bright to look at, and set it on the dressing table.

Uncle Jeffrey had told her how rare she was, having both inherent magic and the ability to sense and manipulate source. Since she had no intention of becoming an Ascendant and ruling the world with her twinned abilities, she took pleasure, but not pride, from that fact.

Removing the piece had caused some of the other parts to sag together, leaving little room for the new coil. She dug out tweezers and a pair of snub-nosed pliers with tips the width and thickness of her pinky nail. Funny how the dexterity it took to manipulate the fiddly bits Devices were made of had improved her lock picking skill. Or was it the other way around? She'd been an agent longer than she'd been a Deviser.

It took her a few tries, but eventually she dropped the coil into place and heard the Devisery begin to whir gently. She reassembled the watch and snapped the case back into place. She'd have to set the time by the clock in the great hall, but it was fixed. The old silver coil she pulled into a straight, fine wire about an inch and a half long; it was too damaged to be used again. She dropped it into the false drawer, another casualty of the Princess's ongoing quest for beauty.

Telaine put the drawer and its false contents back in its place. She sat on the floor awkwardly, constrained by her narrow pink skirt, and contemplated the watch. It stared back at her, its tick louder in the silence than her breathing. Here in the privacy of her chambers she could feel sorry for herself. It had been weeks since she'd had time to herself, time to indulge in her passion for Devices. The Princess didn't care anything for them except for how they made her life easier.

She threw her head back and sighed. Pity the watch's current, incorrect time wasn't right, because she would have time to change her clothes, wipe away all traces of cosmetics, and sneak out of the palace to go into Lower Town to Laura Wright's Deviser's shop. She had a good arrangement with the woman: Mistress Wright kept the money she made from selling Telaine's inventions, and Telaine was free to study and experiment without Mistress Wright poking into her business. She even had a real Deviser's certificate, though it was under her assumed name of Lainie Bricker; Mistress Wright had no idea who she really was.

She picked up the Device and pushed the button to make it chime, an imprint of a tinkling cascade of tiny bells. She felt more at ease now, but she could still feel the presence of the Princess at the back of her mind. *At what point,* she wondered, *did I start thinking of myself as two personalities? And as tiresome as the Princess is, is she any less me than the Deviser?*

CHAPTER TWO

Telaine surveyed the Chadwicks' ballroom and suppressed a yawn. Harroden Manor was small for a Count's home, and though she knew it was unworthy of her to be critical, she couldn't help feeling the Count of Harroden was trying to compensate for something.

Five crystal chandeliers in a space that should have held only three shed their brilliant light over the polished parquet floor, which was a mosaic of intricately carved wood in a pattern no one could make out at floor level. Waist-high pedestals bore vases of pink and white flowers that filled the room with a sweet, almost cloying scent. Telaine had no idea what the flowers were called, but they were showy and overbearing and probably a mistake on Lady Harroden's part. Telaine guessed she'd intended to bring her famous garden indoors.

"I need fresh air," Julia said, hooking her arm through Telaine's and almost dragging her onto the verandah. It was cooler outside, and the distant scent of roses and honeysuckle was calming rather than nauseating. Julia pulled Telaine away from the promenading couples, down the steps, and into the garden, where she dropped heavily onto a marble bench and took a deep breath.

"Julia, you shouldn't have come," Telaine began.

"Why, because I'm pregnant? Or because of the scandal?" Her flippant tone covered a much darker emotion. Telaine's heart ached for her.

"Because you get dizzy when you stand too long, and I'm not strong enough to carry you out of here if you faint," she said.

Julia glanced her way, a faint smile touching her lips. She was widely considered the most beautiful woman in Tremontane, with her dark hair, cornflower blue eyes, and rosy complexion. That she was nearly six feet tall and had a well-rounded figure made her the perfect model of the fashion Imogen North had set for curvy women. It infuriated Telaine that Lucas could have abandoned her for any other woman, let alone the sharp-nosed creature he'd taken up with.

"It's not my fault you're short and scrawny," Julia said, teasing.

"Oh, but I'm a Princess. That makes my figure *slender* instead of scrawny, dear coz, my hair ash blonde instead of mousy, my eyes sparkling hazel, and my height petite instead of just plain short. If not for cosmetics, I'd be completely nondescript."

"Cosmetics and your dimple."

Telaine touched her cheek. "Ah, yes. I have captivated many a man with my dimple. It has far more power than I do."

Julia's smile widened, then disappeared entirely. "Oh, Lainie, how did I come to this? Pregnant and abandoned and the subject of gossip from Ravensholm to Kingsport?"

"It's sympathetic gossip. Everyone hates Lucas on your behalf."

"I can't bring myself to hate him, Lainie. I loved him so much—"

"And he taunted you about his woman and called you a broodmare. If you don't want to hate him, do you mind if I do?"

Julia laughed. "You're right. About everything." She stood and ran her hands over her stomach, which at five months' pregnancy was visibly rounded despite the high-waisted cut of her gown. "And I do feel dizzy. I should leave. Enjoy yourself, Lainie, and don't worry about me."

"Do you want help getting back to your suite?"

"I think I can manage to walk up two flights of stairs, Telaine. I told you, you don't have to worry about me." She hugged Telaine, who followed her as far as the verandah, then watched her cross the well-lit courtyard to the guest wing of Harroden Manor. At least she'd stopped trying to lie to Telaine about her situation; like her father, she knew about Telaine's talent, and for her to lie to her cousin regardless was a mark of how miserable she was. Telaine pictured Lucas's handsome, arrogant face and wished she knew how to wield a sword or shoot a gun, anything to make him feel even half the hurt he'd done her dearest friend and cousin.

"Don't tell me you're hiding from me?"

Telaine recognized that voice. She put on a smile she knew made her look vapid and turned around fast. "Michael! Of course I'm not hiding from you! Shall we dance?"

Michael Cosgrove approached her with his hand outstretched, a smile creasing his acne-pitted face. "I was under the impression it was the man's duty to ask the lady for the pleasure."

"We're too good friends to bow to stuffy old custom." Telaine linked her arm with his. "I've missed you."

"More to the point, you missed the Hardaways' summer gala," Michael said, escorting her to the center of the ballroom. Golden light from the chandelier spangled the folds of her dark green dress like drops of evening sunlight. "Though I shouldn't deny Elizabeth d'Arden's prior claim on your presence."

The violins and cellos struck up the first notes of the dance, and Telaine bowed to her partner. "It doesn't mean I don't miss my other friends," she said, taking his hand and beginning the long, sweeping promenade around the ballroom. It was a fast-moving dance, complicated, and she felt like she was flying as Michael turned her once and then let her fly away again. The pleasure of the dance and the excitement of her clandestine mission combined into a laugh she couldn't contain. It was a beautiful evening.

"I say, you are in good spirits tonight," Michael said. "Dare I hope it's my company that pleases you so?"

He was teasing her; he enjoyed dancing with her, but was attracted to men, had a fiancé even, which made him a safe companion whose romantic overtures she didn't have to fend off. "Of course," she said, winking at him as she spun past, "that and the moon and the garden and my new gown—you like it, don't you?" It was lovely, but that wasn't the point. Her lock picks brushed her thigh from inside one of the gown's many hidden pockets, and she smiled again. So many secrets.

"Of course." Michael smiled. "I wish I could dance more than once with you."

"I think Jonathan might be jealous."

"He knows us both better than that."

They bantered until the dance was over, and Telaine, laughing again, clung to Michael's hand for a moment, dizzy and over-warm. "Champagne?" he said. "Or are you about to be torn from my side by one of your many swains?"

She laughed again and swatted him lightly with her green-gloved hand. "Swains?" she exclaimed. "I have no *swains*. I have *admirers*."

"Your Highness?" Another man, much younger and taller than Michael, with golden curls and an angelic face, held a champagne flute almost in her face. "I took the liberty—that is, I thought you might be thirsty—"

Telaine gave a wry smile to Michael, who returned it with a bow. "Speak with me again later," she said in a low voice. He nodded and raised her gloved hand to his lips before backing away gracefully.

She took the champagne from the young man's hand, which gripped the glass tightly enough that she almost had to pull it away from him. "I thank you, Mister—I beg your pardon, I don't recall your name."

"We haven't been introduced, your Highness. I'm Roger Chadwick. The Count is my father." He blushed. "I apologize… perhaps I should not have been so bold…but I thought…"

"Not at all, Mister Chadwick—or should I say Lord Harroden?" She laughed a brainless titter. "I'm so silly, I don't even know your title! Isn't that foolish of me?"

"You could never be foolish, your Highness," young Chadwick said, and blushed again. "I wish you would call me Roger."

I bet you do, young one. He couldn't be more than seventeen. They were so sweet at that age. "Oh, I couldn't possibly be so informal when we've only just met! Perhaps later…" She used the arch of her delicate eyebrow, expertly plucked and shaded, to devastating effect. Chadwick went almost beet red. She sipped her champagne and enjoyed the moment. If the poor boy was going to reach for the high-hanging fruit, he had better be prepared to fall.

"I believe this is my dance, your Highness," said someone behind her, a man with an unpleasantly familiar deep voice. Edgar Hussey. Who invited *him*? She put on her most arch smile and turned to greet him. He bowed oh-so-correctly over her hand. Unlike young Chadwick, he would be hard to get away from.

"Mister Hussey! I had no idea you would be here. Do you know Mister Chadwick? Or is it Lord Harroden? I'm *so* scattered tonight."

Chadwick bowed stiffly to Hussey. "Her Highness and I were having a conversation," he said.

Hussey clapped him on the shoulder; Chadwick winced. "I imagine you were," he said. "Thank you for entertaining milady until I could claim her for this dance." He took the champagne flute from Telaine's hand and passed it off to the sputtering youth. "Your Highness?" He linked his arm with hers and led her onto the floor.

As she bobbed and swayed down the line of the country dance, she thought furiously. Hussey was one of her most persistent suitors, always trying to get her into dark corners and hinting broadly at his family's prospects. She needed a distraction. Hussey passed her going up the line as she was going down, and she smiled her most dazzling smile at him and saw him stumble a bit. Good. Having power over him meant having some control.

She swiftly glanced around the ballroom and saw Count Harroden standing near one of the long windows, talking to a few men. Now was a good time. And *there* was the distraction she needed.

The dance ended and Hussey offered her his arm again. "Would you care for a stroll on the verandah? **it's rather warm in here**," he said.

Telaine flashed her dimple and cast her eyes down, inwardly laughing at the lie that echoed, discordant, in her ears; despite all the people, the room was comfortable enough that anyone, magical talent or no, would have known Hussey was dissembling. "I believe I'd prefer a cool drink," she said, and steered him gently toward the long table where a white-gloved servitor in a dark brown jacket held a tray of drinks and a trio of elegantly gowned women stood.

"Why, Stella Murchison, how *are* you?" she trilled, putting just the right note of surprise and pleasure into her voice. A blonde woman conversing with the other ladies turned, gasped theatrically, and embraced Telaine. "Stella, I haven't seen you for simply *ages*. Do introduce me to your friends."

"Of course! My dear, this is Lady Patricia Foxton of the Emberton Foxtons, you know the family. And this is Diantha Wemberly, lately made Baroness of Marandis. Ladies, this is her Highness Telaine North Hunter."

"Charmed to meet you," Telaine said, bowing over each lady's hand in turn. "Oh, I mustn't forget—this is Edgar Hussey of the Millford Husseys. You know, Lady Arabella's nephew? He's the most divine dancer." She giggled and squeezed Hussey's arm. "Are you enjoying yourselves? I certainly am! Oh, Mister Hussey, would you mind keeping these ladies company while I freshen up? I promise to be back soon, and maybe we can have that walk on the verandah?" She raised her eyebrow coyly and made her escape before Hussey could protest.

The facilities at the Chadwick manor were on the floor below the ballroom, not convenient for guests, but perfect for Telaine's purposes. Telaine descended the well-lit stairs, the ruddy wood paler in the center as if hundreds of guests had walked away with the color, but turned left instead of right, walking casually as if she had a right to be there. With every step, she left the light behind, until she reached another staircase, this one carpeted in dark blue but worn where feet had trodden it over the years. The Chadwicks had never been a wealthy family, but they kept that secret concealed from their many guests.

Telaine went up two flights of stairs, listening for servants or lost guests wandering the premises, but she met no one. At the second landing, where a many-paned window looked out over Lady Harroden's garden, she paused and listened again, but everything remained still. The servants were either busy with the ball or taking a welcome rest from their employer's demands.

When she was certain she had this floor of the manor to herself, Telaine made her way down the hall, staying alert for the sound of anyone approaching. The Princess would likely not be challenged on roaming the manor freely, but if necessary she would claim she was going to a romantic rendezvous and use her haughtiest manner to overwhelm whoever had the temerity to stop her—a ploy she'd used more than once before. It hadn't hurt her reputation—or, rather, it hadn't hurt her cover story—to have the Princess be known as a flirt as well as a frivolous socialite.

But that ruse wouldn't be needed tonight; the hall remained silent except for her own quiet movements. In her dark green dress and gloves, she could barely see herself against the walnut paneling, with only her fairer arms and face standing out in the dimness. Her full skirt made the faintest noise as she walked, like the distant whisper of conversation. Unfortunate, but it couldn't be helped.

She counted doors, one, two, three, then gently turned the handle of the fourth door. It wasn't locked. That could mean her intelligence was wrong and the Count didn't keep anything important in here, or it could mean he was too cocky, or too stupid, to imagine anyone might steal from him. She guessed the latter.

Telaine silently pushed the door open and entered with a quiet swish of fabric. Closing the door, she removed her gloves and pulled a cubical Device out of one of the skirt's deep pockets and squeezed it. A thin beam of light illuminated the room. She set it to hover over her right shoulder and began searching.

The Count's study was far tidier than her uncle's, though to be fair there were bird's nests tidier than her uncle's study. Two cabinets with glass doors held books that were too uniform to be anything but décor. A locked tallboy proved absurdly easy to open, but held only the Count's liquor supply; she relocked it and moved on.

A door to the left was a closet holding only a few old uniform jackets and a worn out side-ball bat, its padding frayed and spilling out of its case. That left only the desk, a beautiful mahogany creation with neatly organized pens in a stand, a brass inkwell, a blotter, and a letter opener laid out across its smooth red surface.

The desk held seven drawers, only two of which were locked. She quickly went through the others, tapping them for false bottoms, feeling behind them for anything concealed at the back. Nothing. She slid her lock picks out and had the first locked drawer open in less than a minute. Posy would be so proud.

The drawer contained a stack of files, and Telaine blessed the Count's obsession with neatness; every one of them was labeled and every paper sorted within its file. Telaine skimmed the file names. It was probably too much to ask to find one with the words "Veribold Smuggling Operation" written on it in large block letters, but with luck one might hint at the Count's connection with the rebels.

None of the files in the first drawer were related to what she was looking for. She tried not to think about the possibility that there *was* no documentation, relocked the drawer, and started on the second. Her patience was rewarded almost immediately; in a folder labeled "Western Trade" she found several letters, all written in the same careless hand, listing items, quantities, and drop locations within Veribold. Two other letters confirmed that the lists referred to shipments of trade goods, including weapons, received by the Veriboldans from the Count's agent acting with the Count's approval. Perfect.

She was about to fold the letters and slip them into her gown when she heard the faintest sound of voices, and footsteps, approaching. Instinctively she put the letters back where they'd come from, locked the drawer—did the lock actually catch?—and slipped into the closet, squeezing her light off and shutting the door. Her heart pounding, she tried to calm her breath and listened. Maybe the person would pass by.

About half a minute later, she heard the study door open, and a light went on, the narrow gap at the bottom of the closet door shedding a pale gleam across Telaine's feet. "I can't be gone long," said a voice muffled by the closet door. Count Harroden.

Another male voice, one she didn't recognize, said, "You should have thought of that before you became involved."

"I'm involved against my will," said the Count. "In fact, I should call my guard and have you thrown out. You're not supposed to be here."

"You'll suffer far more than I if you do," said the second person. "You still have things you can lose. Would you like me to call the guards for you?"

Silence, then, "What is it you want, Harstow?"

Telaine held her breath. Hugh Harstow, Baron of Steepridge. She'd never met him, but she knew his unsavory reputation. Her uncle suspected him of any number of shady dealings, but didn't have enough evidence to convict him. He'd settled for exiling the man to the far northeast, pretending it was an honor for Steepridge to contribute to the defense of Tremontane against the Ruskalder. He *wasn't* supposed to be here; his "honor" might be a thinly disguised fiction, but there was nothing fictional about his restriction to his lands.

"I'm not satisfied with the shipments I've received recently," Steepridge said. "It's shoddy work, frankly, and our deal was for top of the line material, not whatever fell off the boat on the way upriver."

"I can only skim so much off the top, Harstow," said the Count. "I'm doing my best."

"Do better," Steepridge said, "or I'll have to send out a few letters. Drop a word in the right ear."

"Don't. Please. My family—"

"Oh, don't pretend it's your family you care about. That sissy boy of yours? Your fat wife? It's your own skin you want to protect, you whining, pathetic failure. You're in this because you're weak, Chadwick, and if you disappoint me, I will destroy you. Do as I say, and you've nothing to fear. Understand?"

"I'll do whatever you want." The Count sounded defeated.

"Yes. You will." Steepridge, by contrast, sounded pleased. "Do you have the latest request?"

"I keep everything in here. My security if I ever have to turn in my rebel 'friends.'" The sound of a drawer sliding open.

"What's wrong?"

"…Nothing. It's nothing. I thought—but I must be wrong. See, it's here."

Paper rustled. "Can you fill this?"

"Yes."

"I want it diverted to me. Make up some excuse. They don't have any recourse if you tell them you can't get it. I'm tired of your sloppy seconds."

"Yes, Harstow."

"Call me Baron Steepridge, Chadwick."

"Yes, Baron Steepridge."

"Very well. Now, what about the other matter?"

"It will have to come in pieces." The Count sounded as if he was afraid Steepridge might get angry, but the Baron didn't respond. "It will all be there before the snows come. You'll need to find someone to put it together."

"Don't worry about that. You get those shipments to me. More roundabout this time, too. I don't want anyone connecting us and neither do you."

"Of course."

Paper rustled again, and Telaine heard the drawer close. "Was there anything else you wanted to tell me, Chadwick?"

"No, Baron Steepridge. I'll make sure everything's in hand."

"See that you do. I'm going to leave now while the party's still going strong. You should return to your guests." The light went out, and the door closed.

Telaine waited five minutes before opening the closet door. The room was empty. She pulled out her light Device and scanned the room. No one waited silently to grab her. She went back to the desk and unlocked the drawer again. She didn't think she'd successfully relocked it before hiding; had the Count noticed?

Quickly, she dug through the file and retrieved a handful of the most damning letters, leaving enough papers that it wouldn't be immediately obvious the rest were missing. Someday, some clever Deviser would figure out how to turn those enormous photography Devices, with their glass plates more than a foot square and the need for the subject to remain perfectly still, into something small enough you could carry in one hand. Until then, she'd have to settle for collecting evidence the old-fashioned way.

With some reluctance, she put back the list dated most recently; that one he would certainly miss, if it was the one the Baron wanted diverted to him. She folded the papers and tucked them away in her skirt, then relocked the drawer, tugging on it and its mate to make sure they were secure, and put her lock picks away.

As she crept through the hallways toward the facilities, Telaine considered what she'd learned. Steepridge roaming free was a problem; the Count smuggling goods to him was another. Harroden had access to trade coming to and from both Veribold and Eskandel, and it wasn't impossible that he was using that access to conceal illegal foreign shipments, or even stealing goods that came in legally. She'd have to get her report to the dead drop immediately.

She worried, too, about that unlocked drawer. Her instincts told her Harroden had noticed and had kept silent, probably to keep the Baron from becoming angry at his lax security. The Count's fear of his blackmailer had kept her mission from going completely pear-shaped, but he knew, she was certain, that someone had been in his papers. And unless he had more than one illicit operation going, he would suspect someone was now aware he was smuggling arms and supplies to the Veriboldan rebels.

CHAPTER THREE

She put her most cheerful face on as she ascended the stairs to the ballroom, and ran into Michael, literally ran into him, making him spill a few drops of his drink. "I do beg your pardon," she said.

"You need never apologize to me, my dear," he said. "But sit down, you look a little shaken. Have some of this wine."

She hadn't concealed her agitation well enough. "It must be the heat," she said, fanning herself with her hand and realizing, as the breeze brushed her skin, she wasn't wearing her gloves. "Oh, look at how scattered I am!" she exclaimed, aware that she couldn't exactly pull them out of the hidden pocket in her skirt. "I must not have put my gloves back on after I used the facilities. How careless of me."

"**i find you charming in every circumstance**," Edgar Hussey said, appearing out of nowhere like some kind of ancient imp, bringing a dark curse with him. "I was about to send a search party for you, you were so long."

Telaine playfully slapped his wrist. "Now, Mister Hussey, you would never be so indelicate as to comment on how long a lady takes to refresh herself. I am sorry to keep you waiting—oh, I am *so* sorry, I see my partner for this dance. Will you excuse me, both of you? Mister Hussey, I positively *depend* on you to walk on the verandah with me later." She sailed off into the crowd, moving quickly so Hussey couldn't stop her, and took Roger Chadwick's arm.

Chadwick looked down at her in surprise, then an elated smile spread across his face. "Your Highness," he said.

Telaine dimpled at him and watched his fair face flush. "I know how forward I sound, but I am quite certain you meant to ask me to dance earlier," she said, drawing him toward the center of the room. "And you must know how I adore dancing."

"Yes—that is, I've heard—your Highness, of course I'm pleased—" he stammered, and Telaine smiled and swept him a low curtsey as the music began.

Roger Chadwick wasn't a good dancer, though he seemed

unaware of this. Telaine didn't care. She was too busy surveying the room, looking for his father. There, standing near the stairs. He looked better than she'd remembered, less sagging and more muscular, but his face was unhealthily bloated and his skin pasty. Possibly he was still sweating from his meeting from Steepridge. He didn't seem self-conscious or guilty, but his gaze fixed on her longer than necessary. Of course, she was dancing with his son, but she was uncomfortably aware of the papers nestled in the hidden pocket of her skirt. There was no way he could know she'd been in his study.

She extricated herself from young Roger at the end of their dance, smiling in a way that promised nothing, and made a circuit of the room. Her shoes were pinching her feet, but she put on an even brighter smile and vowed to get rid of them once she returned to Aurilien. The first part of her mission was over, leaving her feeling tired and achy as if she'd run the stairs of Harroden Manor from top to bottom ten times without stopping. But the Princess couldn't leave so soon, so neither could Telaine.

Concealing her weariness, she flirted and laughed and dimpled at everyone she knew—that was almost everyone at the ball, wasn't it? She knew all of them, and not one of them knew who she truly was. The thought was enough to make her feel more cheerful, though it did nothing to ease the needles stabbing her toes.

Stella Murchison stood near the ice sculpture, which had started the evening as a swan but now looked like a molting duck. Edgar Hussey had vanished, so Telaine sailed over to Stella and said, "I'm having such a delightful time, aren't you?"

"Your Highness, I wondered where you'd gone," Stella trilled. "Such a long time to use the facilities!"

"Stella!" Telaine said, pretending to be shocked. "So indelicate!"

"*I* think you had an assignation," Stella said. "Tell me, who was it? Not Mister Hussey, he was with us, and not Roger Chadwick, he's barely an adult. Stephen Wainwright?"

"Of course not," Telaine said. "I don't know how you can think such a thing."

"Richard Argyll? Fortunate for him he didn't inherit his father's ears. Desmond Lowery?"

"Stella!"

Stella laughed her brainless giggle. "You were gone far too long to simply have been refreshing yourself. I won't give up until you tell me who your newest swain is!"

"Can a lady not simply have a moment's peace?"

Too late Telaine realized Harroden was standing about ten feet away. Stella's high-pitched voice carried, and Harroden was looking at her with narrowed eyes. She laughed again, mirroring Stella's titter. "You've found me out," she said. "But I won't tell you who. You'll have to guess." She linked her arm with Stella's and drew her away into the crowd. Harroden suspected something, Telaine was certain of it.

She wanted to flee the room, get her information to the dead drop and get out of Ravensholm, but that would make her look more guilty. She would simply have to dance and flirt more outrageously than ever, and emphasize her reputation as a giddy socialite. Tomorrow...no, this was too important to wait for the dead drop. She would have to send word of Steepridge's involvement to her uncle via telecoder. Then perhaps a trip far from Ravensholm, far from the capital, was called for. Something to make Harroden believe she could have nothing to do with spying on him.

The telecoder office in Ravensholm, a blocky red brick building with narrow windows, had both public operators and private booths, an innovation Telaine was grateful for. She approached one of the empty booths and nodded politely at the operator. "Good morning," she said.

"Your Highness," the man said, bowing. So he recognized her. That might work in her favor.

"How much for a booth?" she said.

"Seven staves." The telecoder operator held out a hand. So, he recognized her, but was unimpressed at dealing with royalty. Not helpful.

"Expensive," Telaine said, handing over the silver coins.

"Don't think you'll miss it." He eyed Telaine's expensive summer dress and new hat with calculating assessment. Telaine resisted the urge to take him down a peg.

"Of course not," she said airily. "And here's a little extra for your trouble."

He looked suspicious. "What do you want?"

"For you to walk away and give me some privacy." Telaine put steel into her words and was gratified to see him flinch. She smiled pleasantly, and entered the booth and shut the door firmly behind her.

The telecoder was the latest model, no bigger than a shoebox, its long brass arm and base plate screwed to a block of ash stained black and polished to satiny smoothness. Telaine checked to make sure the pressure-sensitive tape was aligned properly, then entered the receiver code on the interlocking wheels at the back. It was a code that would connect this Device to one of the private telecoders at the palace, manned night and day by agents whose only job was taking messages from agents in the field. It was the most secure connection in the entire kingdom.

She sent the "clear all" signal, four distinct long taps with the key, and waited for the return signal that meant she was clear to send her message. While she waited, she took a scrap of paper, folded it to the size of a copper, and wedged it between the duplicate key and its tape. She didn't want any record of this conversation.

She'd worked out the coded message late last night, using a code known only to herself, Posy, and her uncle. Telaine was aware she was being paranoid, but the way Harroden had looked at her—that he suspected her at all, the frivolous socialite—left her inclined to paranoia.

HAVE DOCUMENTS. STEEPRIDGE CONSPIRING WITH HARRODEN. DETAILS UNKNOWN. MAY HAVE BEEN COMPROMISED. REQUEST INSTRUCTIONS.

She leaned back in her seat and flailed to catch her balance when she remembered it was a stool with no back. The telecoder began tapping out the return message.

MISSION COMPROMISED OR PERSON COMPROMISED?

She thought for a moment, then tapped out a quick response: UNSURE. GOING ON LONG TRIP AS PRECAUTION. This development meant her uncle couldn't act immediately on Harroden's involvement with the Veriboldan smugglers, despite now having documentary evidence. He wanted the Baron's head even more than he wanted Harroden's.

Telaine leaned forward and put her elbows on the table. Where should she go? A resort on the Eskandel coast, that sounded like a relaxing way to spend a few weeks. Pity she had to go as the Princess, but bathing in the warm ocean currents could make up for wearing her public persona for a few more weeks.

There went the telecoder again. Telaine took up the tape and decoded the message as it arrived. NEGATE. REASSIGNED TO STEEPRIDGE. INVESTIGATE BARON AND REPORT. FIND HOLD HE HAS ON CHADWICK AND CONFIRM ITEMS BEING SMUGGLED. DO NOT SAY THIS IS NOT THE JOB I WAS TRAINED FOR. YOU ARE ONLY OPTION AT THIS TIME AND WILL GET YOU OUT OF SIGHT. SEND DOCUMENTS BY DEAD DROP.

Telaine gripped the tape in nerveless hands. A field assignment. Never mind her uncle's instructions, this genuinely was not anything she was trained for. How was *she* supposed to learn anything about the Baron? She obviously couldn't go as the Princess. Why under heaven couldn't they send someone else? What would Julia think? She read the message over again, but its contents hadn't changed.

With a shaking hand, she tapped out PLEASE CONFIRM THAT YOU ARE NOT OUT OF YOUR ROYAL MIND. This had to be a mistake.

Almost immediately the reply came. Uncle was clearly expecting her reaction. CONFIRMED THAT YOU ARE DISRESPECTFUL GIRL. GO TO LONGBOURNE AND FIND MISTRESS WEAVER. SHE WILL

PROVIDE ROOM AND INTRODUCTION TO TOWN. YOU WILL BE HER NIECE. FIND A WAY TO ACCESS BARONS HOME. SEND REPORTS THROUGH CODED MESSAGE ELLISMERE TELECODER.

Ellismere was a city in Barony Silverfield, in the foothills of the Rockwild Ridge and Mount Ehuren. Wherever Longbourne was, it didn't even have a telecoder. Lovely. She was being sent to the back of beyond, to find a way into the home of a dangerous man, to learn what kind of crime he was committing with Count Harroden and how he was able to manipulate someone ranked higher politically than he. And she was supposed to do all this with no support other than a local woman who didn't even know her. It was one thing being the Princess. It was quite another to pretend to be…what? A peasant? A laborer? She had no idea what life was like on the frontier.

MUST TELL JULIA SOMETHING, she tapped out. Maybe this would change Uncle's mind; Julia would never believe Telaine had enough unbreakable social obligations to keep her away when Julia needed her so badly.

It took a while for the response to come, but it didn't make Telaine feel better: FAKE ILLNESS TWO DAYS DIAGNOSIS LUNG FEVER GO SOUTH TO RECUPERATE YES PEOPLE GET LUNG FEVER IN SUMMER AND HISTORY MAKES IT BELIEVABLE. STOP LOOKING FOR EXCUSES AND GET TO WORK.

She stared at the tape for a full minute, then tore the tape off and removed the folded paper from the duplicate key, spun the Device's wheels a few times to clear the private code, and tucked the tape into her reticule. History indeed. Lung fever had killed her mother and was extremely communicable; Julia wouldn't challenge her and risk exposing herself and her unborn child to the disease. The logic didn't make Telaine feel any less sick at lying to her cousin.

She got into her patiently waiting coach and handed the tape to Posy, who read it without comment as the coach rattled off down the street. "What do you think?" she asked when Posy finally lowered it to her lap.

"I don't like it. I can't go with you."

"Why not?"

"Longbourne's a small town, not much more than a village. It'll look funny if you come with a maid."

"Couldn't we be traveling companions?" Telaine pleaded. Posy had been her partner and companion for eight years. Telaine had never gone on an assignment without her.

Posy shook her head. "Think straight. To make this work, you got to look like you're going one way when you're really going somewhere else. I've got to be your double."

Telaine looked Posy up and down, skeptically. "You've got four inches on me and I weigh at least ten pounds more than you do."

"Not really a double. It'll be hard, but we can figure it out. I'll go south to Eskandel the way you planned and you'll sneak north to Barony Steepridge."

"But I don't know what I'm doing!"

"Stop whining," Posy said, and Telaine, startled, shut her mouth. "If you don't know enough after eight years to make this work, then I sure failed. You can work a crowd, you can make people talk, you can move quiet and pick locks—least I hope so, don't know when you practiced last—"

"I did all right last night!"

"There you go, then. You're smart and you figure stuff out fast. All you need is a cover and a way to get the Baron's attention, and you've got those already."

"What do you mean?"

Posy smiled wickedly. "You're too young to remember Harstow at court. He's obsessed with Devices. He was never happy that he couldn't build 'em. If a Deviser shows up on his doorstep, well, you might have to beat him off with a stick."

"And my identity?" It came to Telaine in a heartbeat. "Everyone knows who Princess Telaine North Hunter is," she breathed. "But almost no one has ever heard of Lainie Bricker."

CHAPTER FOUR

Telaine stepped off the coach and took in a deep breath of warm, fragrant air. Cranky Mister Dalton had insisted on traveling with the windows up, no matter how hot and smelly that made the interior of the coach. Now Telaine reveled in the scents of hot bread and flowers from the bakery and florist across from the coaching yard.

Ellismere was a pretty place, not what she'd expected of the frontier. For one thing, it was nearly the size of Ravensholm, though its buildings were planed lumber instead of stone and the roofs steeper and shingled with slate. Most of the buildings were half-framed and painted in lovely muted colors, not drab white. She looked down the street at the town hall, which looked like a tiny fortress except for the pansies growing in beds all along its walls. It was unexpectedly civilized. Maybe Longbourne wouldn't be as rustic as she feared.

She set down her bag outside the coaching ticket office. "Excuse me," she said to the woman behind the counter, "I'm going up to Longbourne. Can you tell me where to find the coach?"

"No coach," the woman said, smiling pleasantly in a way that blunted the sting of her curt words. "There's a wagon leaves from the hitching station every other day around noon. You're in luck, this is one of those days. But you'd better not dawdle."

"Where is it?"

The woman leaned out of the window and pointed up the street. "Go that way, then turn left at the sign of the blue owl and straight on to the end of the road. It's on the right."

"Thanks. How about the telecoder office?"

"That's on the route. You'll see the sign."

Telaine nodded and shouldered her bag, heading off the way the woman had indicated. People smiled and nodded at her as she walked. She smiled back, feeling the expression come naturally. She hadn't felt much like smiling the whole trip. She'd thought she was prepared to be a nobody, but the first night they'd stopped at an inn where no one offered her the best room in the house and she'd actually been angry about it. She'd had to remind herself, alone in her tiny room with the none-too-clean bed, that Lainie Bricker would be grateful to have a room to herself, but it didn't keep her from shedding a few self-pitying tears she was embarrassed about the next morning.

Now she breathed in the clean, fresh air and smiled more widely. She no longer hesitated when someone called her by her new name, she'd become accustomed to the coarse fare most places along the coaching route served, her boots didn't chafe as much as she'd feared, and braiding her hair every morning had become second nature. This assignment wasn't going to be so terrible.

It turned out the hitching station was an inn and stable actually called the Hitching Station. It stood three stories tall, freshly painted in pale green with white trim that reminded Telaine of the east wing dining room. Delicious aromas of roast beef wafted from the open door, but Telaine bypassed it and went around to the stable yard, scuffing up dust as she went. With luck, the wagon would still be there; she was already a day later than Uncle had promised the mysterious Mistress Weaver, and another day's delay…well, it wouldn't make much difference, but Telaine wanted to make a good impression. Punctuality would help.

The stable yard fit neatly into an L formed by the back of the inn and the stables perpendicular to it. It seemed unusually quiet to Telaine, but she was used to the bustle of the palace stables, people and carriages coming and going at all hours. An old wagon, splintered and worn, that sagged dangerously at the rear stood near the center of the yard. Beyond the wagon, a couple of enormous horses tethered to a waist-high rail fence nosed the ground, looking for something to eat. The lean woman brushing one of the animals paid no attention to Telaine as she approached.

"Excuse me," Telaine said. "I was told this is where I can get the wagon to Longbourne."

The woman turned her head away from Telaine and the horses and spat. "This is it," she said, nodding at the broken-down contraption.

"Oh. Is it...leaving soon?" It looked as if nothing could induce it to move.

The woman shrugged. "Be leaving soon's Abel gets his ass off that bar stool. Takes him a while to recover from the trip down mountain." She spat again and resumed grooming the horse.

"Oh," Telaine repeated. "Is that...will he take long?"

"No idea," the woman said.

Telaine looked into the wagon. It was half-full of boxes and bags and wrapped parcels. A satchel bearing the emblem of the Royal Mail lay on the wagon's seat where anyone could walk off with it. As she was trying to decide where to put her own bag, a couple of men came around the corner. One, a tall, middle-aged man with a blond beard and thin, elastic arms that seemed only loosely connected to his body, had his hands on the second man's shoulders, steering him around unseen obstacles.

The second man was at least forty years older than his guide and as lean as if he'd been dried in the sun for a week. He looked as if he hadn't shaved for two days, and what was left of his white hair stuck out in all directions.

"Edith, get the horses hitched, Abel's ready to go," the middle-aged man said. He glanced at Telaine and said, "Can I help you with something, miss?"

"I'm going up to Longbourne," Telaine said. "Where do I pay my fare?"

"No charge," the man said. "Longbourne pays Abel here a flat fee no matter what he hauls. You got family up mountain?"

"Going to stay with my aunt, Mistress Weaver. I'm a Deviser." She was in the habit now of adding that little piece of information every time she introduced herself. It didn't hurt to spread the word, even among people who weren't likely to tell the Baron, and it gave her a warm feeling to identify herself that way.

"Mistress Weaver, huh? Good luck with that. She's a tough lady. But you didn't hear it from me. She'd never let me forget I said it." He winked and extended his hand. "Josiah Stakely, miss."

"Lainie Bricker."

"Nice to meet you, Miss Bricker. Abel, Miss Bricker's going up with you. You want to make room on the seat?"

Abel, who'd climbed onto the wagon, squinted down at her. "You want to go up?" he said, sounding as if that were the strangest thing he'd ever heard of.

"I'm Lainie Bricker," she said. "I'm a Deviser. Going up to stay with Mistress Weaver. She's my aunt."

Abel stared at her in incomprehension. She was about to repeat herself when he said, "Come on up then," and shoved the mail bag under the seat. Telaine hauled herself onto the wagon and settled her bag on her knees. "Never heard of Agatha Weaver havin' no niece," Abel muttered, but he made a clucking noise at the horses and they turned out of the stable yard, making a wide circle. Telaine waved at Stakely and Edith, then had to grab the edge of the seat to keep from being bounced off as they drove away from Ellismere.

The road soon went from paving to hard-packed dirt the horses and wagons turned into puffs of dust. There was little to see here except long grasses, the pale line of the road, and the approaching mountains, and Telaine heard no noises beyond the wheels creaking and the horses' hooves striking the hard ground. It was eerie, like being inside an invisible dome that blocked every sensation except the warm rays of the sun that were making Telaine sweat. Abel drove in a silence that matched their surroundings. Telaine examined him covertly and wondered if he were as drunk as he'd looked. Did he even remember she was there?

She tried out a few conversational gambits in her head, but discarded them. Her life as the Princess hadn't prepared her to talk to anyone like Abel. Now that seemed like an oversight. She wasn't sure if that life had prepared her to talk to whatever kind of woman Mistress Weaver was. A tough lady, Stakely had said, and she had the feeling he'd only been partly joking. Telaine wondered what pressure her uncle had brought to bear on Mistress Weaver, whether the woman even wanted her there. This could turn out to be unpleasant—but that didn't matter, because she was in Longbourne as an agent of the Crown, not a Deviser, not as someone's niece.

After a long, silent hour, the wagon entered the pass and began its slow ascent. The road was narrow, barely more than a ridge jutting out from the side of the mountain, and Telaine edged closer to Abel, away from the steep drop-off. From her position, it looked as if the wheels were perched on the edge of the cliff, mere inches from plummeting over. Just how drunk *was* the driver? But his hands on the reins were steady, the horses unfazed by the slope, and gradually she convinced herself they weren't all about to fall to their deaths and was able to admire the view.

Evergreen trees, varieties she couldn't begin to name, surrounded the road. Where the path narrowed further, she dared look down the side of the mountain at even more trees growing on the steep slopes. Some of their trunks lay parallel to the mountainside as if someone had shaped them from clay, bending them near the roots. Scruffy yellow grass covered the slope surrounding the trees, bent and broken by the passage of animals, though Telaine had trouble imagining what animals could cling to the mountainside, some of which was nearly vertical.

"I hear water. Is there a river nearby?" she said.

"Comes from the slopes of Mount Ehuren," Abel said, rousing from his silent stupor to nod in the direction of the distant peak. "Can't see the river from here."

It was an obvious statement, but more than she'd gotten out of Abel the whole ride, so Telaine let it go and contented herself with inhaling the scent of cool water, even though it made her thirsty. Birds darted from treetop to treetop, calling to one another, and small gray squirrels scurried across the way and scampered up the dark, rough trunks.

She wasn't sure exactly how long the journey was, because she was superstitiously afraid if she took out her watch, it would leap out of her hand and fling itself over the cliff. But after about two hours, they came out of the pass and saw the valley stretched out before them, tall grass blowing in the breeze. Telaine drew in a deep breath. She'd never seen anything so beautiful as the groves of aspens stretching out into the distance, their leaves golden in the afternoon light, or the dark evergreens providing a background for them to shine against. The smell of water came to her again, and she closed her eyes and enjoyed the cool breeze brushing her skin as the wagon jounced along. At least her undesired field assignment had brought her someplace lovely.

Another hour passed before she saw signs of civilization. In the far distance, buildings clustered, becoming less densely packed as the town spread out on both sides toward the valley walls. At the limit of her vision, Telaine could barely see the road emerge from the town and wind its way farther up the valley. Her heart beat faster. Longbourne. The last five days had been nothing more than practice for this.

They didn't so much enter Longbourne as be absorbed by it, a few houses here and there becoming many houses cheek-by-jowl and then being supplanted by larger buildings Telaine supposed were businesses. Many of the buildings were single-story and made of stone, fist-sized irregular pieces mortared together. Some had upper stories of wood. Almost all had steeply-sloping roofs of dark blue slabs of slate fitted tightly together, and all had paned glass windows, if small ones.

There were plenty of people on the main road — street? Whatever it was, it was paved with gravel that crunched under the horses' feet. They stopped to stare at Telaine as Abel drove past; she smiled at each of them and was surprised to see most of them turn away. Shy, or unwelcoming to new folks? *That's not why you're here, Telaine. Lainie.*

Abel came to a stop at a crossroads where the only two major streets in the entire town met. A gazebo sat in the middle of the intersection, all carved white wood and tiled roof, with red and white petunias growing in a bed encircling it. It seemed out of place, like a — well, like a frilly socialite in a village square. She sympathized with it.

"This is it," Abel said, then hopped off. Telaine climbed down and pulled first her bag, then the mail bag from beneath the seat. She went to hand the mail bag to Abel, but he'd already trotted away. There were a few people standing near, but none of them seemed inclined to unload. Reluctantly, she left the mail bag on the seat and picked up her bag.

Here at the center of town there were any number of well-kept buildings, a general store, a dressmaker's shop, but nothing that was obviously Mistress Weaver's establishment. Down the road past the gazebo, she saw a small group of men standing beside a short rail fence. She smelled hot metal and heard a rhythmic *tap, tap, tap*. The forge. She might as well ask for directions there, since no one else seemed willing to meet her eyes.

She knew the men noticed her approach by the way they didn't look at her. *Come on, boys, I* invented *that technique.* "Good afternoon," she said politely as soon as she was close enough. "I'm looking for Mistress Weaver's establishment."

"*Establishment*? Well, ain't we lah-di-dah!" said one of the men, a tall, burly fellow in his thirties. All four laughed. So did Telaine, hoping to project a hapless innocence. Antagonism wasn't the response she'd expected.

"You're right there, I don't have any idea what to call it!" she exclaimed. "My name's Lainie Bricker. My aunt Mistress Weaver's waiting on me. Can one of you tell me where to find her?"

"Don't know as Mistress Weaver's exactly *waiting*," said another man, this one in his late forties or early fifties, with an L-shaped scar across his cheek and graying hair tucked up under a brimless knit cap. "Sounded like she wasn't waiting so much, eh, fellows?"

"Don't tell me she's given up on me already? I'm only a day late! Help me out, please?"

"Happen you're not much welcome here," said the first man. "Don't know as Mistress Weaver were much excited to see you, eh?"

"If you go now, happen you'd make it back down the mountain 'fore dark," said Scarface. He took a step toward her. "If you go now."

There was a loud hiss, and a cloud of steam blew between Telaine and her antagonists. Telaine looked over at the blacksmith, who had been silent this whole time. He was unexpectedly young, no older than herself, and not tall, but he was well-muscled and the look in his brown eyes was calm and direct.

"If you go back that way," he pointed, pushing light brown hair off his forehead with the back of his free hand, "there's a store with a needle and thread on a sign above the door. Next house south of that is Mistress Weaver's place. Happen you'll find her there, this time of day."

"Thank you," she said, trying not to sound as relieved as she felt.

The blacksmith nodded. "Welcome to Longbourne, Miss Bricker. And"—he turned back to the group of men, who seemed abashed—"happen you fellows might find something more useful to do than making wind with your mouths."

Telaine shouldered her bag and marched away. Reticence, she'd expected. Dislike, not a surprise. But outright hostility? What kind of place had her uncle sent her to? Fitting in might not be a priority, but she couldn't investigate freely if she was fighting the townspeople all the time. Did they treat all strangers this way, or was she a special case? Those men knew she was coming, so Mistress Weaver had mentioned it...but would she have outright told the townsfolk that Telaine, Lainie, wasn't welcome? Those men hadn't been lying when they'd suggested as much.

She passed the needle and thread sign and set down her bag at the next door. The building was long and wide, with a small second story perhaps half the size of the ground floor; it was larger than its neighbors on either side, but looked worn-out from not having been painted recently. She could hear a clacking sound somewhere nearby.

Telaine knocked, ignoring the stares from the people who passed her. It might have been a more aggressive knock than necessary, but she was tired and irritable and still jumpy from her encounter with those men. She wasn't used to being the focus of male aggression and it made her feel helpless, which made her angry and inclined to let the Princess come over haughty and disdainful at them. That was definitely not what she was here for.

The knob turned, and a girl opened the door, making the noise swell. She might have been eleven or twelve, but she was tall for her age. Her brown hair was covered by a kerchief and she wore a wraparound apron with long sleeves. "Happen I can help you?" she said in a fluting voice.

"I'd like to see Mistress Weaver," Telaine said, trying to speak over the sound without shouting.

"Come in," the girl said. "Are you Miss Bricker?"

"I am. Is Mistress Weaver in?"

"She is," called a voice from far inside the room.

Telaine stepped inside. The room took up most of the ground floor of the building. Brightly colored skeins of yarn hung on every wall, giving the room a festive, exotic appearance. Two spinning wheels stood near the front door, next to baskets full of wads of puffy grayish wool. Telaine had never seen wool in its natural state before, and she wished she dared pick one up to see how it felt.

One of the spinning wheels was being used by a beautiful young woman who deliberately paid no attention to Telaine. Beyond this was an enormous loom like a wooden mantis, its many limbs jerking and shifting in a peculiar rhythm, that took up nearly half the room. It clattered and thumped away without pause as the half-visible woman operating it said, in a voice pitched to carry over its noise, "I'm Mistress Weaver. I take it you're my niece?"

"I am, mi—Aunt," Telaine said, swallowing "milady" just in time.

"Sit there. I'll be with you shortly." The clattering and thumping of the loom continued, loud enough to ring in Telaine's ears. It was a wonder none of the three were deaf. Telaine sat on the stool Mistress Weaver had indicated. The young girl, hesitating between Telaine and her mistress, settled at the second spinning wheel and began to work the pedal.

Telaine watched them both spin. The girl seemed to be a true novice; how good the young woman was, Telaine didn't know, but she never seemed to stop and only paused briefly to pick up a new wad of wool and somehow splice it into the old one. Telaine observed the mechanism of the spinning wheel. *A Device could do the work of the pedal, ease the strain on the leg. I wonder if you could do anything about that pause to put the two pieces of wool together? Probably not, that looks finicky. But it would be simple to set up a Device to do the up-and-down motion, or better yet, create a wheel that runs by itself...*

"Come with me," Mistress Weaver said. The loom went silent, and so did the spinning wheels as the two girls stopped to watch. "Back to work, girls. And, Alys, I want you to go stir the dyeing pot and make sure the fire's fed up nice."

Mistress Weaver came out from behind the loom and regarded Telaine with a look that said she thought Telaine was wasting her time. She was a tall woman in her early thirties, with tightly pinned black hair, fierce blue eyes, and a stern mouth. She didn't look like someone who laughed often. The shape of her face reminded Telaine of someone, though she couldn't remember who. It would come to her eventually.

"Upstairs," she said, and Telaine followed her down a narrow hall to an even narrower stairway with no handrail and no light. Telaine tried not to walk so closely she'd trip over Mistress Weaver's skirts, but the dimness, and the cramped stairwell, made her nervous. Going downstairs in the dark could be dangerous.

The second floor wasn't more than a hallway, narrow and dim, with three doors opening off it. Mistress Weaver went to the door at the far end and opened it. "I haven't had time to spare cleaning it up," she said as Telaine goggled at the room, which had no carpet and a small window overlooking the street.

It was not a large room. It contained a bed, and a chest at the foot of the bed, and a small table with a cracked mirror over it. It also contained a hat stand, a stack of boxes labeled WINTERSMEET, a piece of garden statuary that might once have been a bear cub, a pile of fur coats covering the bed, a straw hat that was not on the hat stand, a framed landscape in oils, and a woven belt coiled on the floor like a snake. Telaine checked twice in case it actually *was* a snake. She glanced at Mistress Weaver. There was a definite look of pleasure in the woman's eyes. "You can store whatever you won't use in the room next door," she said.

"How long did it take you to haul everything in here?" Telaine asked, following a hunch. The look of pleasure was replaced with one of caution.

"**don't know what you mean**. Happen things pile up, over time. Not too good to do a little honest work, are you?"

She turned, and Telaine asked, feeling somewhat desperate, "You *do* know why I'm here, don't you?"

"Best not speak of that with little ears in the house. Later." She stumped off down the stairs.

Telaine wanted to collapse on the bed, but that would have meant moving the boxes out of the way and pushing the furs to the ground. Besides, there was no sheet on the bed, and the mattress looked dusty. Wasn't there something you did with mattresses, to clean them? She vaguely remembered hers were removed once a year, but were always back by bedtime.

She dropped her bag on the floor and decided to take a look next door. That room was even more cluttered than hers, filled with what looked like fifty years of detritus. There was barely room for what was already in it; she couldn't imagine how she'd fit in the things Mistress Weaver had stowed in hers. Telaine sighed and began shifting piles of old newspapers—not even Longbourne newspapers! *was* there a Longbourne newspaper?—to rest on a vast wooden sea chest.

When Mistress Weaver came to tell her supper was ready, Telaine had moved all the useless items into the junk room and was still able to close its door. She'd thought about dragging the mattress outside, but decided she didn't know what to do with it, so she'd settled for spreading a worn but soft blanket she'd found in the chest over it. Her belongings were stowed, with her Deviser's kit under her clothes, and her lock picks hidden under a loose floorboard beneath the bed. She'd even found the kitchen and got water to wipe down all the surfaces. It was the first cleaning she'd ever done and she was proud of it, even if her attempt to wash the filthy window hadn't done more than make a streaky mess.

Mistress Weaver surveyed the room. She ran her finger over the top of the mirror and displayed it, gray with dust. "Happen you missed a spot?" she said. Telaine gritted her teeth.

"I'd like to clean the mattress, but I don't think I can manage it," she said.

"Get it hauled downstairs, I'll show you. But supper first."

Telaine followed her back to the kitchen, where thick stoneware bowls painted red and white, matching mugs, and a couple of large spoons lay on the battered pine table. Mistress Weaver took a bowl and helped herself from a pot bubbling over the fire. "We eat stew or soup, most nights, I ain't got time for anything fancier. Don't expect me to wait on you, *milady*."

"My name is Lainie. No miladys here." Telaine scooped up a serving of thick, brown gravy with bits of…something…floating in it. It smelled like beef and, to her rumbling stomach, it also smelled divine. She set her bowl down and accepted a mug of icy cold water that sent shivers down her arms and legs. The mysterious bits were root vegetables. She took a small bite; it was too hot, so she waved her spoon until she saw Mistress Weaver looking at her with disdain. She stirred the stew, hoping the heat would dissipate. "Is it safe to talk?" she asked.

Mistress Weaver shrugged. "Depends on how worried you are. Nobody else is in the house, certain sure."

Telaine laid her spoon down. "Mistress Weaver, have I done something to offend you? I met some men over at the forge who seemed sure I wasn't welcome here."

Mistress Weaver waved her hand as if brushing away her words. "Don't much like having my ways interrupted," she said. "I do things my way and happen I ain't so good at what's new." But her mouth continued in that hard line.

"All I was told was to come to Longbourne and pretend to be your niece," Telaine continued. "What story did you give for my…visit?"

"Told 'em you'd had some trouble in the city and needed to get away for a spell." Mistress Weaver filled her mouth with stew. "You're my half-brother's daughter who's been raised by her uncle, your mother's brother. I'm told that's as near truth as can be."

"It is." Telaine's parents had died before she was eight, and she'd grown up with the North family. "Shall I call you Aunt Agatha?"

"You can start by dropping the shall's and may's, 'less you want to seem stuck up. And Aunt Weaver suits me fine."

"Yes, Aunt Weaver." She'd eaten her fill of stew and now pushed back her chair from the table. "What do I do about the mattress?"

"Right. Go fetch it."

Telaine went up the stairs and heaved the mattress off the frame. It was thin, but awkwardly bulky, and shed a fine shower of dust when she picked it up. She carried it down the stairs, every minute expecting to miss her step and go plummeting to the bottom. *At least I'd fall on something soft.* Getting it through the doorways was almost impossible; whatever part she didn't have her hands on flopped over and caught on things.

She dragged it through the kitchen and out the back door, which Aunt Weaver held open for her. That was more help than Telaine had expected from her, but with the mattress sagging in her arms, she wasn't inclined to be overly grateful. "Hold a bit," Aunt Weaver said, and opened the door of a shed at the edge of a small yard, though like no yard Telaine had ever seen before.

Instead of grass, there was packed earth; tall weeds grew along the edges of the house and the two sheds. Both sheds looked like they wanted to fall down. The larger one, the one Aunt Weaver had opened, had a steep roof matching the house, shingled in blue slate, and its coat of red paint needed touching up. The smaller shed looked more like a cupboard, narrow and unpainted, and leaned slightly to the left. Telaine shifted the mattress over her shoulder and hoped Aunt Weaver would finish her business, whatever it was, soon, because she was about to drop the thing.

A large fire was built up in the center of the yard, over which hung an enormous stainless steel pot filled with a dark liquid. Its presence in Aunt Weaver's backyard surprised Telaine. The Devices responsible for the process that made the metal were new, and the products they made were expensive. Aunt Weaver must be more prosperous than her home suggested to be able to afford such a thing.

Near the fire stood a tall pair of metal poles with crosspieces at the top that made the shape of a T, connected by three thick wires. Hanks of wool dyed a rich amber brown hung over the wires, but Aunt Weaver removed them and took them inside the shed. "Hang it up there," she said over her shoulder. Telaine heaved the mattress over the wires and looked at it, dangling limply off the ground.

Aunt Weaver returned with a contraption that had a wooden handle with a couple of thick iron wires emerging from it. The wires intertwined to make a flattened pattern about a foot wide like interlocking hearts. "You beat it," she said, thwacking the mattress by way of demonstration, then handed the thing to Telaine. She shoved a lid over the pot of brown dye, then heaved it off the fire to sit on the ground. "Hard." She turned and went back into the kitchen.

Telaine gingerly patted the mattress with the beating tool. A tiny puff of dust arose. She struck it harder and was rewarded with a larger puff. Warming to her work, she slammed the flat tool into the mattress again and again. *That* was for "Aunt" Weaver. *That* was for those awful men at the forge. *That* was for having to move all that junk out of her room. *That* was for being away from home and *that* was for having to beat dust out of her bedding before she could go to sleep even though she was weary and sore and wanted the day to end—

"I thought, happen you want a hand with that, but seems you're doing well enough," said someone behind her. It was the blacksmith, standing at the corner of the house and appraising her work with his steady gaze. Telaine's shoulder and arm ached. She loosened her grip on the handle. "I don't know if I'm doing this right," she admitted.

He approached her and held out his hand. She surrendered the tool. "Step back a bit," he said, and began whacking the mattress with a smooth rhythm in a pattern that went from top to bottom. Dust flew. No wonder Aunt Weaver had moved the freshly-dyed yarn. "Looks like this mattress hasn't seen use in years," he added.

"It's from Aunt's spare room, I think," Telaine said, and coughed before stepping back farther. "I've about got the room cleaned up."

"And I've about got this finished," he said. He gave the mattress a few more whacks and handed her the tool. "Came to see how you're settling," he said. "Those fellows have an odd sense of humor, but they're harmless."

"I'm sure they are," Telaine said, thinking, *If that's harmless, I don't want to be around for violent.*

He stepped forward and held out his hand. "Ben Garrett," he said.

She switched the tool to her left hand and took his with her right. "Lainie Bricker, but you know that already." His hand was callused but perfectly clean. She wouldn't have guessed his occupation if she hadn't seen him at the forge.

"Most likely the whole town knows it. Not much excitement around here."

"I don't know if I qualify as excitement. I'm looking for a quiet retreat."

"You're new and you're a Deviser. Never had one in Longbourne before." He paused, then said with some hesitation, "You ought be prepared for people to stare at you."

"Thanks for the warning." She tugged the mattress down and felt him supporting the far side. "Thanks, but I can manage," she said. The idea of letting a strange man haul her mattress into her bedroom made her uncomfortable. Not to mention inviting someone into a house not her own.

He helped her arrange it in a less awkward position and said, "Good night, Miss Bricker."

"Good night, Mister Garrett. And thank you again."

He nodded and went back around the corner of the house toward the street. Telaine wrangled the mattress back inside and put it on the bed frame. No dust arose when she dropped it. Now, how did one make up a bed? She'd seen sheets and blankets in the chest when she stowed away her clothes.

Tucking the sheet over the mattress proved challenging; when she tucked one corner in, another came loose. She finally managed to get the sheet in place and lay another one, and a blanket, atop it. Still no pillow. She'd have to get used to doing without.

Telaine was accustomed to watching the sun set, but up here the sun disappeared behind the mountains without fuss, leaving behind a diffused evening light. She opened her window, pushed aside the curtains, and leaned out. Although there were lights in the buildings along the street, they were so few by comparison to the bright lanterns of Aurilien that burned all night that she was able to watch the stars come out.

Here in the mountains she felt closer to the sky, close enough to reach out and pluck one of those brilliant specks of light from the black velvet it was pinned to. Her anger and frustration drained away. Yes, this was a difficult mission, and she hadn't been trained for anything like it. She didn't know how to get into the Baron's home—she barely knew what she was looking for. But it was impossible to worry about those problems when she looked at the encircling mountains that held up the sky, with Mount Ehuren's upper slopes still gilded by the setting sun. It was the most beautiful thing she'd ever seen.

"Don't go falling out," Aunt Weaver said, and Telaine had to catch herself on the window ledge. The woman carried a lamp that glowed dimly but enough to illuminate the room. "Forgot to leave this for you," she grunted, and Telaine wondered if that might be an apology— a watered-down, reluctant apology, but Telaine would take whatever was offered.

"Thank you," she said.

"Say 'thanks' instead," Aunt Weaver said. "You want to not stand out, happen you tone down your fancy language."

"It will come, I think—I mean, happen I'll make do."

Aunt Weaver sniffed. "Don't make fun."

"I wasn't—never mind. Thank y—thanks for giving me a place to stay."

"Didn't have much choice," she said, and turned to go.

"Aunt Weaver," Telaine called, and the woman stopped without turning around. "Is there anything else I can do to fit in?"

The woman still didn't turn around. "Don't know why you'd want to," she said, and went on down the hall.

Telaine closed the window and the curtains, then shut the door. Good point. Why did it matter if she fit in? What mattered was drawing the Baron's attention and getting into his house, not making friends. But she was cold inside, realizing she didn't have a single friend in this town, not even the pseudo-friends the Princess had, and that nobody but the blacksmith even acted friendly. She felt alone for the first time in her entire life.

She examined the lamp. It was not Device powered, but ran on—ouch—oil. She sucked her burned finger. *Stop making assumptions.* She experimented with a knob on the lamp's base and learned how to turn the flame higher and lower.

As she gazed at the lamp, wondering how she might convert it to a Device, the day's exertions caught up with her. She barely managed to change into her nightgown and turn off the lamp before sinking into a deep, troubled sleep.

CHAPTER FIVE

The first sunlight creeping over her windowsill woke Telaine the next morning. Her back hurt, her legs ached, her arms felt as if she'd done nothing but lift rocks for ten hours, and her feet were sore in a way that said they'd be even sorer once she tried to use them. She had no idea how poorly prepared she was for physical labor. She sat up and realized there was a part of her body that desperately needed to be relieved of its burden. Where could the facilities be?

She got out of bed and pattered down the stairs in her bare feet, hoping not to be seen, but unable to wait long enough to dress. The great room downstairs with the loom. A tiny formal drawing room, full to bursting with a couple of uncomfortable chairs and a table with chipped legs. The kitchen, dominated by the black iron stove. A store room filled with bolts of woven cloth. No toilet. There had to be a toilet somewhere. Every home needed one. You couldn't—or could you? She'd seen a chamber pot under her bed, but it was old and dusty and looked antique. That left…

…oh, no. Surely not. Longbourne couldn't look so prosperous without having basic amenities, right? She went out the back door, crossed the yard to the second shed, and opened the door. It swung open and revealed a wooden bench with a hole cut into it. Apparently Longbourne *could* be that prosperous without basic amenities. Or maybe it was Aunt Weaver's peculiarity. Either possibility was irrelevant.

She shut the door, hiked up her nightgown, and made use of the… facilities. It crossed her mind that this might be a huge joke, that somewhere nearby was an actual toilet and this was a relic, but the smell was too ripe to be antique. She hurried to finish her business, washed her hands at the kitchen sink, and ran back upstairs to her room.

Telaine sat on her bed and thought through her plan. Part one involved making the Baron aware of her presence. Step one of part one was, unfortunately, making herself known to the good people of Longbourne. Remembering her reception the day before, she cringed. But she didn't see any other option short of setting up shop as a Deviser, and she had a feeling that would be seen as arrogance by those same good people.

She picked up her shirt and trousers from where she'd dropped them the night before. She would have to care for her own clothes now, too. There was so much she took for granted, like laundry service, and her maid bringing her breakfast and making her bed, and even having her day scheduled for her. The most she'd ever done along those lines was find time to sneak away to Mistress Wright's workshop. Having the whole day free was, contrary to sense, stifling.

Thanks to her exertions, her shirt was too dirty to wear again, but her trousers were fine and she did have one other shirt. She'd have to humble herself and ask Aunt Weaver what to do about laundry, and put up with that disdainful look that said quite clearly what she thought of uppity wealthy girls not knowing how to do for themselves. Telaine was starting to appreciate the Princess's life a lot more than she'd imagined.

She dragged her hair into a braid. That, at least, she'd practiced, and she didn't think she'd look too much like a city girl trying to fit in in the country. *Not that it matters,* she reminded herself. *Don't let all this get to you. Remember why you're here.*

Downstairs, Aunt Weaver was finishing off her meal of scrambled eggs and bread toasted on one side. Of course she wouldn't have a toasting Device. "Morning," she said with her mouth full.

"Morning," Telaine replied. "What's for breakfast?"

"Whatever you feel like making for yourself," the woman replied, putting emphasis on the last two words. "I've got no time to wait on you."

"Oh," said Telaine, completely taken aback. She hadn't expected to be waited on, but cook her own food? She had no idea how to begin.

"Eggs and milk in the cool room," Aunt Weaver said. "Bread in the bread box. No meat today. Guess you never had to do for yourself in the kitchen?"

"No," Telaine said, then in a firmer voice, "but I suppose I'll learn."

Aunt Weaver gave her a measured look. "You will at that," she said. "Supper's at six. You're on your own for dinner." She relented somewhat and added, "Happen you'll find a meal at the tavern around noon."

"Thank you. I mean, thanks, Aunt Weaver," Telaine said, her spirits rising. But when the woman had left the kitchen, she became depressed again. Cook her own meal. As far as Princess Telaine was concerned, eggs came out of the chicken already boiled. Lainie Bricker, on the other hand, was competent enough to figure it out herself.

She looked around the room. The fireplace had a small fire lit in it and the ubiquitous stew pot hung from a spit over the flames. There were cupboards on either side of the boxy iron stove. One contained the cleaning supplies she'd made use of the previous day; the other held heavy jars filled with flour, sugar, salt, some kind of grainy meal, and other basic kitchen supplies.

The cold room was behind a narrow door and it was indeed chilly. So either Aunt Weaver wasn't totally opposed to Devices, or there was some natural feature that kept the room cold. Among other things, the cold room contained a basket of eggs and a covered pitcher of milk. She wondered where they'd come from. She left them alone for the moment and continued exploring.

Other cupboards yielded pots, pans, plates and cups, flatware (neither silver nor stainless steel but finely carved wood), and other kitchen tools. There was also a big porcelain sink next to a wooden counter with a rack Telaine guessed might be for drying dishes. A towel hung over the side of the sink. Telaine turned the tap and fresh cold water poured out. There was only one spigot, and it had only one handle—no hot water. This combined with her toilet experience made her wonder, horrified, how she was ever going to get a bath. She turned the water off.

Now, food. Boiling an egg shouldn't be too difficult; it would be edible even if she boiled it too long. She hoped. The stove had three doors, two small, one much larger; Telaine opened that one and discovered it was an oven, warm but not overly hot. She couldn't figure out how to open the smaller doors, but they, too, were warm to the touch. She held her hand palm-down over the stove top and felt heat radiating off it, but not enough to burn.

She didn't know how to boil water.

She had no idea how to light a fire.

She didn't even know what fueled the stove.

At home, she knew, the ovens and stoves were all Devices that turned on and off with a flick of the finger. Telaine stared at the stove, insanely hoping it might ignite simply from the power of her increasingly distressed mind. She could ask Aunt Weaver—no. She would *not* ask Aunt Weaver. Tonight, maybe, but she wasn't about to go out there in front of those two girls and reveal she couldn't even light a fire in the stove. *That* story would get around town quickly.

She cut two slices of thick, nutty bread and poured herself a cup of fresh milk. She would kill for coffee right about now. She would settle for bread and milk. Just like a five-year-old.

Having eaten her fill, Telaine went back upstairs and hid in her room. She pretended she was inventing a plan, but she knew she didn't want to face those townspeople with their unwillingness to meet her eyes or their all too willingness to insult her. She dug in her chest and pulled out her roll of tools. Should she take them with her? Reluctantly, she put them away. Today was about meeting people. She checked her hair and clothing in the mirror, gave her reflection a stern look, and left the room.

Aunt Weaver and her two apprentices were hard at work. "You want me to do anything for you, Aunt?" she called out over the noise of the loom.

"Could use a bottle of honey over at the store," she replied. "Ask for a figgin."

Telaine caught the young apprentices exchanging laughing glances. "I'll do that, Aunt. Be back later." If there was such a thing as a figgin of honey, she'd eat the straw hat that had been on her floor.

Having closed the door behind her, she stood on the stoop, closed her eyes, and prayed for endurance. How many days would this take? Five? Five would be nice. Ten would be bearable. Any longer than that, and she might not survive to go home.

Stop whining, Telaine. This is no different from moving through a ballroom looking for signs that two supposed strangers are conspiring. You've been playing a role your whole adult life. This is just a new one. She opened her eyes and strode in the direction of the poor, out-of-place gazebo.

She passed a lot of people on her way, nodded cheerily to every one regardless of how they looked at her. Most looked away when she greeted them. *So much for the friendly small-town welcome.* She stayed off the street to avoid the horse-drawn wagons that went in both directions, northbound ones carrying crates of varying sizes, southbound ones laden with lumber or stone. There were quite a few of the latter. No wonder Longbourne was prosperous.

She paid attention to the layout of the main street. Longbourne didn't seem to care about separating businesses from homes, though most of the buildings lining the main street appeared to be stores and the side streets seemed mostly houses. Aunt Weaver's lack of a sign was an anomaly; most of the businesses sported boards declaring in word or image what could be sold, traded, bought or borrowed.

A large number of the businesses were related to weaving or sewing. Telaine wondered if Aunt Weaver's name was a coincidence or a conscious declaration of her trade. From what little she knew of the woman, it wasn't impossible she'd invented weaving and named the whole trade after herself.

She saw the general store, but passed it by, deciding to explore the town without hauling around a non-figgin of honey. Was there a laundry? She didn't see a sign. If she got up the courage, maybe she'd ask someone. Or—horrors, might she have to wash her own clothes? She was willing to try almost anything, but her instincts told her she would make a terrible mess of that experiment.

She stopped to examine the gazebo, wondering what Longbourne used it for. Maybe it was just some kind of civic decoration. The town hall faced the gazebo on the southwest corner of the crossroads; it had a peaked cupola and two stories' worth of gleaming windows. The shorter building across the street east of it had a sign that said POST OFFICE above the door; Telaine hoped the mail bag had found its way there eventually.

The building on the corner north of the town hall was a school, which surprised Telaine, then she was ashamed of her surprise. Of course people who lived on the frontiers had schools. There was no reason they shouldn't. She remembered Aunt Weaver's younger apprentice and wondered why she wasn't in school. Telaine herself had been tutored and knew almost nothing of actual schools, but she thought there were rules about what age you had to be before you left. She shook her head. She was letting this town get to her. *Still, what would it hurt to find things out, while you're waiting on the Baron's notice?*

The fourth building, standing next to the forge, looked empty, not exactly abandoned but not in use either. It was built entirely of wood rather than the stone and oak of its neighbors, and its dark brown stain was weathered as if it hadn't been cared for in years. Large-paned windows lined both stories, lighting it clearly despite the thin clouds blocking the sun. Telaine gazed up at it, wondering what it might have been used for once.

"You thinking of buying it?" said a drawling voice. Telaine identified it as belonging to Scarface. She put on a cheery smile and turned to face him. *No fear.*

"Why, are you selling?" she asked, and heard with relief a chuckle from Scarface's cronies. "No, of course not, I was just wondering what it was for," she added quickly, in case Scarface got angry at being the object of ridicule. What were all these men doing in town in the middle of the day, instead of at work?

"Not for anything, not now," said one of the others. He had a barrel chest and skinny legs. "Been empty these seven years. Used to be a weaving factory, 'fore the local weavers drove it out."

"Happen you don't need to bother your pretty face about it,"

Scarface interrupted.

Yesterday he'd scared her. Today, she got angry. "You never said your name," she said.

"That's right," he said, leaning toward her. His breath smelled of whatever meat he'd had for breakfast.

"He's Irv Tanner," said another man with black hair and rosy cheeks. A fourth man, the tall burly one who'd spoken to her yesterday, shoved him a bit. "Well, he is."

"Mister Tanner, do you really think I'm pretty?" Telaine said, dimpling at him. Scarface Tanner looked confused. "Thanks for making me feel welcome. It's so sweet of you. It's hard, being a stranger here, and I'm glad to know you." She stuck out her hand and reflexively he took it. She shook it hard, trying not to think about how much bigger his hand was than hers.

"I was so hurt when you told me I might need to leave town when I'd only just arrived, I thought maybe you didn't think so highly of me. But now I see you were hiding your true feelings!" She put on a shy, downcast look. "I'm flattered, Mister Tanner, I really am, but I'm afraid I can't return your regard for me, since I won't be staying long and I'd hate to build your hopes up like that. But I'm sure we can be friends."

Tanner looked bewildered now, and afraid. "See, I told you she couldn't be nothing like herself said," the black-haired man said in a loud whisper. He stepped forward. "Ed Decker, miss, and these here is Mikey Kent—" the tall burly man—"and Hal Johnson—" barrel chest. "Good to know you."

"Good to know you," she replied, retrieving her hand from Tanner's massive grip and shaking Decker's. "Now I'll know your names to say 'hey' next time." Kent and Johnson showed no interest in shaking her hand, so she waved at them and added, "Goodbye for now, fellows," and continued past the gazebo. She could feel them watching her go and suppressed the urge to put a shimmy in her walk. That wasn't the sort of interaction she had in mind.

As she passed the forge, Garrett glanced up from his work, then looked down without comment, but she saw him smile, the faintest curve of his lips but unmistakably a smile.

So, "herself" had said things about her, had she? And unflattering ones, it seemed. For someone who was supposed to be her ally, Aunt Weaver was turning out to be something closer to an enemy. What could she do about it? Not much, as yet. She'd have to watch herself around her "aunt."

A sign ahead bore the picture of a mug of beer, much faded by time and weather, but Telaine would have recognized the tavern anyway. It had a porch broad enough for a crowd of friends to gather, windows that were single sheets of glass five feet square, and a door flung open to welcome all comers. Telaine thought about passing it—it was still mid-morning, after all—but then decided if anyone in this town was likely to be friendly, it would be the tavern owner. It was practically part of the job description.

When her eyes adjusted to the dimness, she saw a large room crowded with tables and chairs cut from what Telaine guessed was local timber. The style was unfamiliar, a streamlined, minimalist approach to furniture that suited the uncluttered look of the taproom. The bar took up one corner an L-shaped curve of much-notched oak that matched the furniture, clean and brightly polished. A broad, short woman stood behind it, wiping glasses with deft gestures. She looked up, assessed Telaine with one long glance, then bent her head to her work again. "We're not open till past noon," she said.

"I thought I'd drop by and ask you about dinner," Telaine said. "My aunt told me I could get a good meal here, come dinnertime."

"Your aunt not feeding you?"

"She's busy. I've hardly seen her, she's so much behind the loom."

"Nothing wrong with that."

"No, she's a hard worker. It's impressive." Would the barkeep consider that a big word? The woman's terse answers were making Telaine nervous.

The woman was silent for a moment. She put down one glass and picked up another. "I serve plain fare starting at one o'clock. Happen you're not used to it, fancy city ways and such."

"I like plain food," Telaine said, her temper rising. "I like Longbourne. I wouldn't have come here if I didn't."

The woman looked at her, this time with her full attention. "Heard you had to come, because of getting free of your trouble," she said.

"Well, I could have gone anywhere, but I wanted to come here," Telaine improvised. The woman had gone from terse to uncertain. "I wanted someplace different."

"You from the capital?"

"Yes."

"Happen you won't get any more different from there as here." She went back to polishing the glass. "You're not what I expected," she added.

"You know who I am, but my name's Lainie Bricker, just in case," Telaine said.

"Maida Handly," the woman said. "I'd shake hands but mine is full, as you can see."

"No problem, Mistress Handly."

"It's Miss Handly," she said, but without rancor.

"Miss Handly. I'll see you around one o'clock, and thanks."

Telaine left the tavern and stood for a while on its porch, breathing in the fresh air and thinking. Aunt Weaver had given a negative impression of her, and the people of Longbourne were unfriendly when they weren't being downright antagonistic.

This was all too strange for her to ignore, even if it wasn't her primary goal, and it made her angry. Nobody was better than Telaine North Hunter, in any guise, at making people do what she wanted, and by heaven she was going to make these people like her. It would be something to occupy herself while she was trying to make contact with the Baron. That reminded her she'd forgotten to make sure everyone knew she was a Deviser. The dinnertime crowd at the bar would be a good time to start.

The dinnertime crowd didn't exactly freeze in their tracks when Telaine entered the tavern, but there was a decided hush as she walked to the bar. The place was only about half full, not what she'd expected, but she guessed the men and women who worked at the quarry and the sawmill wouldn't walk back into town every day for their dinner. These must be local shop owners and employees.

Miss Handly met her at the bar and said, before Telaine could speak, "There's mutton and there's bean soup. Mutton's better."

"I'll have that, and some of whatever beer you have on tap," she said. Was it her imagination, or had someone sucked in a breath? "Can I sit over here?"

"Sit where you like," Miss Handly said with a shrug. Telaine pulled out a chair at an empty table in the middle of a cluster of other diners. None of them tried to meet her eyes. Telaine sat back and waited for her food. And an opening.

It came almost immediately in the form of a young woman, maybe sixteen or seventeen, who unluckily caught Telaine's eye. Before she could look away, Telaine said cheerfully, "I'm Lainie Bricker. I'm new in town. You probably know my aunt, Mistress Weaver? What's your name?"

Bowled over by the torrent of words, the young woman said, "Glenda…Brewster."

"Good to know you, Miss Brewster. Where do you work?"

"I'm—"

"She works in my store," said the older woman seated with her. Her face was narrow, her tone was icy. Telaine ignored it.

"Really? Which store?"

"I'm the dressmaker."

"Oh! I've seen your shop. It's beautiful! And I love the dresses you have displayed." Telaine wasn't exaggerating much. They weren't outstanding, but she'd been surprised at how fashionable the clothing was. Even so, she would have said the same even if the clothing had looked like it was made for cats. Ugly cats. *Vanity. No better way to reach a woman's heart.*

"You do?" The woman was startled. "But you're from the city!"

"I don't see what that has to do with whether your clothes are nice or not. You have excellent taste." Telaine kept her tone confiding and faintly impressed, though she could tell it wouldn't take much to change this woman's attitude.

A faltering smile spread over the woman's face, though the furrow to her brow said she was still expecting trickery. "Why...thank you," she said, and added, "My name is Mistress Adderly."

The other diners watched this interchange in silent fascination. "It's good to know you, Mistress Adderly. I wish I didn't spend so much time in these old rags," Telaine said, gesturing down at herself. "My work is too hard on dresses."

"What work's that?" Now Mistress Adderly had forgotten her coldness in favor of curiosity.

Ah, I love a straight line. "Didn't Aunt tell you all? I'm a Deviser. Mostly repairs, but sometimes I build things."

"A Deviser!" Mistress Adderly's eyes gleamed. A man at a nearby table kicked the leg of her chair. She ignored him. "Miss Bricker, happen you can help me? My sewing Device's been going off, these few weeks. It skips stitches and stops in the middle of a seam. Been using the old manual one, but it's tiresome and I'd love the other fixed."

"Why, I'd be happy to take a look at it, Mistress Adderly," Telaine said. She was having trouble ignoring the reactions of the rest of the diners, who were distressed that the seamstress might have anything to do with her. "May—can I come by later this afternoon? If I can't fix it happen I could at least tell you if it's fixable at all." *Did I use "happen" in a sentence? Correctly?*

"That would be most good of you, Miss." Mistress Adderly kicked the chair of the man next to her, but missed and hit his leg. He swallowed a yelp.

Miss Handly swooped down at that moment with Telaine's food: a mutton chop, the inevitable root vegetables, and a mug of beer. Fortunately, she'd included a knife to go with the fork. Telaine was all in favor of blending in, but she didn't think her reputation would be enhanced by having mutton grease all down her front.

She took a long drink of her beer, which tasted better than any she'd had before—maybe that was the added spice of playing a new role—and applied herself to her food, ignoring the whispered conversations that sprung up around her. If she was any judge of character, they were all about her.

CHAPTER SIX

The highly waxed floor of the dressmaker's back room made it easy for Telaine to slide beneath the sewing Device, though the place was crowded enough with bolts of fabric that there wasn't a lot of room for sliding. "It'll be easy to fix, Mistress Adderly," she said. She held the motive force, a long, flexible strip of brass, by one end and let it dangle. "This just needs to be imbued. The skipping and stopping is because it's giving off pulses of source."

"That sounds most magical," said Mistress Adderly with a weak laugh.

"Well, it *is* magical, but it's not too hard to fix." Telaine inhaled shallowly. No nearby source, unfortunately. "I have to take this with me to find a place where I can imbue it, but I'll be back right soon."

They've got me talking like them, she thought as she walked down the street, sniffing discreetly. *But how lucky to find someone who needs my services so quickly. And I've managed to turn one person's attitude around.* The real question was how quickly this news would reach the Baron. He was unmarried and unlikely to have any contact with a dressmaker. Still, it was better than nothing. And Devisery was something she loved.

She picked up a scent near the gazebo and followed it to the rear of the forge. She was peripherally aware of Garrett watching her as she went around the building and up a slight rise to find a strong source nestled at the base of a pine tree. She sat down next to it, held the length of brass between her thumb and index finger, and pulled a long thin strand from the source and wound it around the strip as if winding thread onto a spool. The metal piece began to glow emerald green, then paled to a white-green blaze.

"What are you doing?" asked Garrett. He stood a few feet from her, his eyes fixed on the glowing metal.

"Re-imbuing this for Mistress Adderly's sewing Device."

Garrett shook his head. "Heard you were a Deviser, but didn't hardly credit it until now. Never in all my life seen something like that."

Telaine stood, dangling the glowing metal between her fingers and thumb. "It amazes me too, and I've been doing it for seven years. You want to hold it?"

Garrett stepped back. "It doesn't hurt?"

"I'm holding it, right? Go ahead."

Garrett took the fully imbued metal from her hand, fumbled and nearly dropped it. "Sorry," he said, sounding nervous.

"You can't hurt it. See, it doesn't even feel like anything special."

"How does it work?" He held the brass strip by his fingertips, mesmerized by the green glow.

Telaine wound another thin strand around her fingers and tangled it into a cat's cradle of source. "You know how there are a lot of lines of power running through Tremontane? They don't just bind our families together. Where they cross, they make a bulge Devisers can sense. The thicker the line, the larger and more potent the bulge. This one must be at the crossing of two bigger than average lines to be this powerful." She shook the threads off her fingers and let the source reabsorb them.

"What does it look like?"

"I don't know. Nobody can see source any more than we can see the lines of power. I know how to find it because I can smell it. To me it's sweet, like lilac and mint. And I can feel it in my hands when I start to draw on it, like pulling fibers from a puff of wool." It was a comparison she'd never thought to make before watching Aunt Weaver's apprentices spin their fluffy gray wads into thread.

"Must be amazing, being a Deviser."

"I love how I feel when I'm working with source. But it's also humbling, touching the power that binds us all together." She held out her hand and received the imbued brass from him. "Now I put this back and tighten up the fittings, and Mistress Adderly gets her favorite Device back."

Garrett shook his head. "Never in all my days. Not that there've been all that many of them," he said with a smile. It flashed across his face so quickly she almost missed it. Another person who didn't smile all that often, though in his case it didn't seem to be because of a permanently sour nature.

"I hope you don't mind if I come back here sometimes," Telaine said. "That's a good strong source."

"Certain sure. I've thick curtains," he said, with that flash of a smile.

"You live here?" Telaine asked, looking up at the two-story building.

"Close to the forge," he said. He wiped his hands on his leather apron. "Be seeing you."

"You too."

She waved and went back to Mistress Adderly's store, where she had the Device running in half an hour. Mistress Adderly clapped her hands together and beamed at Telaine.

"Miss Bricker, I'm most grateful for your help." She gave Telaine a few coins and clasped her hand. "Happen you're not what they say you are."

"I—thanks for that, Mistress Adderly," Telaine said, bewildered. Not what they say? She wished she dared ask what it was people were saying about her. That she was an upstart city girl? That she'd pushed her way into Mistress Weaver's life without permission? That she was a troublemaker? She packed up her tools and went back to Aunt Weaver's, musing on how strange this town was.

She decided she'd had enough interacting with the natives for one day and was going to do something for herself. Halfway up the stairs she cursed, remembering the laundry. She fetched the shirt, trotted back down and cursed again, remembering the honey. "Aunt Weaver," she said over the noise of the loom, "is there someone I can get to wash my shirt, or should I do it myself?" *Please say there's a laundress in town.*

"Mistress Richardson takes in laundry," the woman replied. "Hers is the house next to the forge, on the north side."

"Thank you. I'm off to get that honey now." Though it probably wouldn't be a figgin. She made sure she had her money with her and set off for the laundress's house.

Mistress Richardson's home was bigger than Aunt Weaver's, with a second story that extended the full width of the house. Telaine rapped on the door frame and called out, "Hello?"

A small child—Telaine wasn't good with ages younger than her twelve-year-old cousin Jessamy, but she guessed four or five—came to the door. "Ma's busy," she said. She had a cloth doll which she dragged by one arm.

"I'm here to see if she'll do some laundry for me," Telaine said.

The girl looked at her without comprehension. "Ma!" she called out. That lovely lilt again, "mawr."

A woman with red hair and a careworn expression came to the door. "Yes?" she said in a neutral tone.

"My aunt said you do washing?" Telaine asked politely.

"Yes?"

"Um...I have this shirt...it..." Telaine stumbled to a halt. It was like talking to an unfriendly red-headed wall.

"Your name on it?"

"My name? No. Should it be?"

The woman curled her lip. "If you want to see it again. Wash all goes in together."

Telaine defaulted to helplessness. "I'm sorry if I seem foolish, but how do I mark it?"

"Sew it in," the woman said.

Telaine's heart sank. She'd always been terrible at needlepoint. The woman seemed to sense her despair, and her unfriendliness faded slightly. "I can do it for you," she said. She took the shirt from Telaine's hands. "Your name Bricker?"

"Lainie Bricker."

"Bricker's good enough. I'll have it for you tomorrow."

"Thanks so much. I'm grateful to you."

The woman held out her hand. "Rather have coin than grateful." Telaine took out a few coins, held them out to Mistress Richardson, uncertain of how much to pay. The woman took one and tucked it away in a belt purse, then went back into the house without a farewell. Telaine pocketed the rest of her coins. If the laundress could clean her shirt so Telaine didn't have to, she was welcome to whatever payment she wanted.

At the general store, Telaine decided she was tired of making friends, and simply approached the shopkeeper with "Mistress Weaver needs some honey."

The man nodded and said, "What size?"

Figgin, my eye. "What sizes are there? I don't remember what she said, but I'll know it when I hear it."

"There's double-dram, pint, figgin, bottle, and jug."

Telaine blinked at him. "Figgin, then," she said.

"One minute," the man said, and disappeared into the back room. Telaine leaned against the counter of knotty pine and kicked her heel against the counter. She'd never seen any store that carried such a wide variety of goods—copper-bottomed pots and pans, bins of spices, a barrel full of nails with a silvery steel scoop standing upright in it, a child's rocking horse with a mane of real horsehair. Dust floated through the air, visible when it passed through the light coming through the windows. The place smelled of flour and cinnamon.

"You're Agatha Weaver's niece, aren't you?" A woman dressed in a cotton gown printed with blue roses approached from the far side of the store. "How're you settling in?" The woman's smile looked pleasant enough, but her eyes had a nasty gleam to them.

"Lainie Bricker," Telaine said, offering her hand. The woman ignored it.

"Agatha ain't said much about you," she said. "You had some... trouble in the city?"

Telaine wished again she dared ask what kind of trouble Aunt Weaver had invented for her. Or maybe she'd been circumspect and kept her explanation vague enough that anything Telaine said wouldn't contradict her. "I thought Longbourne would be a good place to visit."

"It's a nice town. Guess you wouldn't know that yet." The woman scratched the side of her nose. "Staying long?"

"I'm not sure. As long as I need to, I guess, Mistress…"

"Rose Garrity," the woman said. "Agatha treating you okay?"

"Um…yes?" Mistress Garrity was angling for something, but Telaine had no idea what it was. "She's been…very welcoming," she lied.

"Of course she has," Mistress Garrity said. "Could've been a lot less understanding about your…trouble."

"I guess," Telaine said. Mistress Garrity smiled unpleasantly, as if she'd scored one off Telaine. It was the strangest of all the strange interactions she'd had in Longbourne so far.

The shopkeeper returned with a round container about the size of her doubled fists. "Afternoon, Rose," he said. "Six coppers, miss." Telaine handed over her money, nodded politely to Mistress Garrity, and left the store. So. One more person who believed…what? Something bad, anyway. Maybe she should have just asked. No, she hadn't liked the look in the woman's eye, as if she were waiting for Telaine to make a fool of herself, and Telaine had enough trouble without looking like a fool.

She managed to suppress a laugh at her paranoia over the figgin until after she was halfway up the street. *It was smart to be cautious, though,* she told herself, nodding at the people she passed and smiling. So Aunt Weaver wasn't totally trying to humiliate her. Yet she'd definitely said something that had everyone in town suspicious of her. Should she confront the woman, or pretend she had no problems? So far, her pride was winning; she'd not give Aunt Weaver the satisfaction. But it was past time for her to start investigating what "trouble" she was supposed to be escaping.

Telaine passed through the weaving room with no comment and set the figgin on the kitchen table, then went up to her room. Time for something just for her. She spread a spare handkerchief on the dressing table and disassembled the oil lamp, spilling a few drops of oil despite her care. It was a simple object that would be less than simple to alter, but the result should be worth the work.

She had just fitted the lamp glass to the altered base and was contemplating the unnecessary oil when Aunt Weaver said, "Supper's ready." She turned away without waiting for a response. Telaine followed her to the kitchen. This time the meal was bean soup, bland but filling. They ate in silence. When Aunt Weaver took her bowl to the sink, she said, "Fiddling with my lamp, are you?"

"It'll save you the cost of oil," Telaine said, sensing a chance to cut her irritated "aunt's" objections off at the root.

"Don't have much use for Devices here," the woman grumbled, after a tiny pause. "Nobody to maintain 'em, and you won't be here long."

"I can put it back the way it was before I go." Telaine hadn't realized she had professional pride until it was challenged.

"No matter," Aunt Weaver said. She rinsed her bowl and, after another pause, held her hand out for Telaine's. Telaine surrendered it, feeling surprise at the woman's willingness to do any chore for her. Which reminded her of something else.

"I need to ask a favor," she said. "I—don't know how to use the stove."

Aunt Weaver gave her a look of disbelief married to disdain. "Don't know anyone can't use a wood-burning stove," she said.

"Aunt Weaver, there are a lot of things I don't know how to do," Telaine said wearily. "Can you at least give me credit for wanting to learn?"

Aunt Weaver gave her a long, hard look. "Happen I might," she said. She opened the small drawer below the top of the stove, revealing a narrow, deep cavity dusted with ash. "Start a fire in here," she said. "You know how to start a fire?"

"No."

Aunt Weaver sighed. "Balled-up newspaper first," she said, "then twigs. Matches are here. Wait for it to start burning strong, then put in the wood." She opened a box beside the stove and took out a couple of short, stubby chunks of wood. "That's about it. Can blow air through here—" she worked a bellows that was a miniature version of the one

Garrett had in his forge—"to make it hotter. Pot goes on the top."

"Thank you," Telaine said, though she wasn't sure she'd be able to start a fire quite so easily as Aunt Weaver had. Still, it was a start.

"Thank me once you've made it work," Aunt Weaver said gruffly. "You going out tonight?" she added, seeing Telaine head for the back door.

"I'm going to the tavern to meet more people," she said.

"Don't see why you need to. You won't be staying long."

"I'm hoping one of these people will get word back to the Baron. Trust me, I don't want to be part of this town any longer than I have to. They obviously don't want me here." She paused, leaving a gap in the conversation for Aunt Weaver to fill, but the woman shrugged and turned away.

The sun had almost set, leaving the town hazy in the twilight, but lanterns along the main road guided Telaine toward her destination. She couldn't tell if they were actual lamps or Devices; there were districts in Aurilien where the light Devices were made to imitate flames. Based on Aunt Weaver's attitude and what Abel had said, she guessed the former.

Most of the businesses along the main street were dark, but lights burned in the house attached to the forge, in Mistress Richardson's laundry, and in a few other places. Music drifted toward her on the slight breeze from the direction of the tavern. A pianoforte was going strong and some beautifully melodic singing accompanied it.

She slowed as she neared the building, whose windows all blazed with light. This could be an enormous mistake, if everyone there decided to be antagonistic. However, if she wanted to draw the Baron's attention without actually walking up and knocking on his door—a move that would likely make him more suspicious of her than not— she needed to make more contacts. She firmed up her chin and her resolve and stepped through the open door.

The noise lessened when she entered, but didn't die off entirely. The pianoforte player, his back to the door, kept on playing. Telaine smiled and nodded at the few faces she recognized, saving an extra-friendly grin for Irv Tanner—he blushed, and she was satisfied at discomfiting him—and went to sit at the bar. An unfamiliar young barman got her a beer. She was starting to like the unsophisticated beverage. Wouldn't it shock, for example, the d'Ardens if she asked for beer at their next supper party?

She surveyed the crowd covertly, amused that so many others were watching her without bothering to make a secret of it. There were a lot of unfamiliar faces, probably those quarrymen and sawmill workers who'd been absent at dinnertime. They were, in general, large and heavy men with deep voices who kept to themselves and paid her no attention beyond a couple of curious glances.

"Hey there, you're new in town," said a young man. She looked up and blinked; there were two of him. She hadn't had all *that* much to drink. As she took a second look, she realized although they looked similar, with red hair and pale blue eyes, one had a long face and the other was broader across the shoulders.

"Welcome to Longbourne. I'm Trey Richardson and this is my brother Liam." The young man thrust out a hand. There was nothing at all angry or disdainful in his expression. On the contrary, he had a light in his eyes she hadn't seen for days. It warmed her. She shook his hand, and that of his brother, and introduced herself.

"Oh, we all know who you are. Been waiting for you to show up for days," broad-shouldered Liam said.

"Didn't think you'd be so very pretty," said a third young man. "Jack Taylor, miss, at your service." He was extremely handsome, blond and dark-eyed and tall, with a smile that could compete with the most accomplished flirts of her acquaintance. After a moment, Telaine identified him as the pianoforte player.

"I was enjoying your music," she said.

"We're a musical lot here in Longbourne," he said with a wink. "Happen you're here for a wedding, you'll hear a real concert."

"Hope you won't leave for a while," said Liam Richardson. "Never sad to see a new girl in town." He leaned on the bar, a little too close, but Telaine had too much practice diverting overly-attentive young men to worry about it. She smiled at him flirtatiously.

"Jacky, you said you'd play for me." Aunt Weaver's apprentice Alys inserted herself beneath Taylor's arm. She gave Telaine a hateful look. Oops. The new girl in town was stealing away all the young men. Telaine smiled back at her politely.

"I'd love to hear you sing," she said. "Shouldn't you take to your stool, Mister Taylor?"

"Jack," he said. "If you promise to come over and listen." He held out his hand; his arm dropped away from Alys's shoulders. Telaine knew she shouldn't interfere with their relationship, wouldn't have done so even if she were the person she claimed to be—Taylor was too consciously handsome to be interesting to her—but after the day she'd had, it was nice to be appreciated. And it was fun to annoy Alys, who was clearly under the impression that beauty was all it took to attract a man.

Telaine could feel eyes on her, unfriendly eyes, calculating eyes, appraising eyes, but she chose to ignore them and settled herself against the pianoforte, arms crossed on its tall top. "Play 'Late in Spring,'" Alys instructed.

She gave Telaine one more glare as Taylor played a few introductory bars, then opened her mouth and sailed into the song with an extraordinary soprano voice. It startled Telaine enough that she couldn't conceal her astonished reaction. Unpolished her performance might be, but Telaine had heard professionals who didn't have half the range this country girl had. It seemed Alys had more than just her looks going for her.

The room went quiet out of respect for her singing, and burst into applause when she finished and curtsied, her color high. She darted a glance Telaine's way, triumphant, and her smile widened when she saw Telaine's expression. "Didn't think we had anything worth hearing, out here?" she said.

"You're good enough to sing in the city," Telaine said, taking a stab at flattery.

A murmur went up. Alys said, "I don't need you putting on airs at me. Not everything's about the city, you know."

She'd overplayed her hand. Pride trumped vanity every time. "I'm sorry. I only meant to say how much I liked your song. I don't have anything else to compare it to."

"We're proud of our town," said Liam Richardson. "Happen you should remember that."

"I'm sorry," she said again. *Lovely work with the crowd there, Princess.*

"Come on, Jack, forget the city girl and play something we can sing along to," said a voice. Telaine, now feeling deeply discouraged, smiled and nodded at random and made her way to the door.

It opened when she was only a few steps away, and five men entered. Their shabby uniforms of green and brown looked nothing like what Telaine was used to from watching the Army drill on the parade grounds outside the palace. Those uniforms were clean, neatly mended, with fully buttoned jackets and crisp uniform caps. These men's uniforms looked as if they'd been slept in for several days, some of them bore food stains, and their scuffed boots might have been through weeks or months of hard marching without being polished. Telaine stepped aside, and one of them leered at her as they went to the bar.

"Whiskey all around," said one. The room had gone silent. Taylor, who had started playing another song, trailed off and turned around. One of the quarrymen standing near Telaine closed his meaty hands into fists. The soldiers acted as if they didn't notice the tension, but even so they walked lightly, preparing to defend themselves against whatever attack might come.

The barkeep laid out five whiskeys and stepped away, nervous, but unable to take his eyes off the men. *Yes, let's add alcohol to this volatile mixture,* Telaine thought, and wondered what she'd stepped into.

Maida Handly came out of the back room. "Thought I told you fellows not to come in here again, after last time," she said. Her voice was even more unwelcoming than it had been that morning. She held a glass stein as if she were thinking about using it as a weapon.

"That warn't us," said the soldier who'd ordered the drinks. "You wouldn't keep us thirsty 'cause some other fellows tore up the place?"

"You all look the same to me. Happen you better leave before trouble strikes."

"Now, Miss Handly, we're not looking for trouble, so if it strikes, it won't be my boys who cause it," said another man from the doorway. He was more handsome than Taylor, tall and broad-shouldered, dressed in a high-collared black jacket and tan trousers, with boots polished well enough to see reflections in them. He wore his long, dark hair gathered at the nape of his neck, drawing attention to the elegant bones of his face and the dark curve of his brows.

He surveyed the room, and unlike the soldiers he was genuinely unconcerned about the tension. His eyes passed over Telaine once, then flicked back to rest on her face. He smiled, and a chill went through her. "I don't believe I've had the pleasure," he said.

Telaine felt like a small animal who'd stepped into the path of a fox. "I'm Lainie Bricker," she said, and thrust out her hand. "I'm staying with my Aunt Weaver. I'm a Deviser."

She'd had so much practice saying it that it came out of her mouth automatically, without engaging her brain. By the time she realized she didn't want this man touching her, it was too late. The elegant stranger took her hand and, instead of shaking it, brought it to his lips and kissed it as formally as any prince. "Morgan," he said. "I'm *very* pleased to make your acquaintance."

"You're a soldier?" Eight years of relentless training in the niceties of conversation came to her rescue. *Get him to talk about himself. It's every man's favorite subject.*

Morgan chuckled. "No, **just a watchful eye when the fort allows its soldiers a few hours of free time.** Miss Handly, I see we're not welcome here. We'll be on our way. I hope, though, that this little episode shows our men can be...civilized." He bowed over her hand again, released it, then gestured the soldiers toward the door. The same soldier leered at Telaine as before, but half-heartedly, as if by rote.

She stared after them even after they shut the door on themselves and the cool late summer night, then shook her head to break free of the spell Morgan had cast. "Who was that?" she asked in a faint voice.

"Archie Morgan," said Miss Handly. She still sounded tense. "The Baron's right-hand bully boy."

Someone who looks like that is named Archie? He ought to be called Dirk or Sylvester or Raphael.

"Don't let his smooth ways fool you," said Taylor, animosity forgotten. "He'd be a stone killer if the mood struck him right."

"That's never been proved, Jacky," said Alys. She had a starry-eyed look in her eyes. "Happen some men could learn something about treating a lady right from him."

Taylor pulled Alys closer. "I don't want you having aught to do with him," he said, and Alys transferred her starry-eyed look to him. It dimmed when he released her and said, "Nor should you, Miss Bricker. Would hate for anything to happen to you."

"Thanks, Mister Taylor," Telaine said. "And thanks for the drink, Miss Handly. It's bed for me."

"So early? No, stay a while," said Liam Richardson, and his brother added, "You wouldn't leave us alone with just Jack for company, would you?" They seemed to have forgotten she'd been an uppity city girl minutes before.

Telaine smiled and dimpled at them, and was rewarded to see them blush. *I do love having that power.* "I suppose I could stay for a few more drinks," she said, and settled at a table and spent the next hour having her three admirers pay her some welcome attention.

Nearby, Alys fumed, but Telaine had no intention of making these men actually fall in love with her. Her novelty would pass in time, and Alys would go back to being the acclaimed town beauty and songstress. She *was* beautiful; she just didn't know how to use it. Pity she would never be willing to take lessons from Lainie Bricker.

CHAPTER SEVEN

Telaine woke the next morning to dull, cloudy skies. She felt dull herself, foggy and desperately in need of coffee. Nothing went right, starting with breakfast. It turned out knowing how to light the stove didn't mean knowing how to boil water, and while she was failing at that, her toast in the archaic toasting fork burned. She had to settle for bread and milk the way she had the day before, but even that was disgusting because the milk had gone off, something she only discovered after taking a big drink.

Aunt Weaver was already at the loom when she was ready to leave. "Good morning," Telaine said. It wasn't really, but maybe if she pretended hard enough, the day would improve. Aunt Weaver only grunted in reply. Telaine caught Alys's eye as she withdrew from the great room; Alys gave her a glare that could have melted wax. Telaine decided against answering in kind and left the house.

As before, no one met her eyes as she walked down the street, trying to decide what to do first. If only Taylor and the Richardsons were around...but they probably worked at the sawmill or the quarry, and she wouldn't see them again until nightfall. Garrett might have had a pleasant word for her, but the forge was empty when she passed it. She tried not to feel downhearted. After all, making friends wasn't important. The job was.

She decided to wait a few hours before approaching Mistress Richardson. She told herself it was a desire to explore the town and not cowardice that motivated her. After wandering the side streets for a while, she knocked at Mistress Richardson's door and waited for the red-haired woman to emerge. She looked at Telaine with even more sourness than before. "Yes?" she said.

"Please don't take this as nagging...it's only that I forgot to ask you when my laundry would be done, yesterday." The woman, who was shorter and older than Telaine, intimidated her more than Irv Tanner's looming menace.

"Had a problem with that." She went back inside and returned with a wad of cloth she shoved into Telaine's hands. "Got caught in the mangle. Sorry." She handed over a coin. "No charge."

Telaine held up what had once been her shirt. One of the sleeves hung by only a few threads, and there was a jagged tear down the back. "Oh," she said faintly.

"It happens sometimes," said Mistress Richardson, and shut the door.

Telaine stared at the shirt. She knew nothing about laundry, but she was certain Mistress Richardson had ruined the shirt on purpose. Fury built inside her. What under heaven had she ever done to the woman? Wait. Richardson. Trey and Liam Richardson. Of course. Mistress Richardson was afraid her boys would be led astray by the… the…whatever she believed Telaine was.

Telaine turned around and strode back to Aunt Weaver's place, stomped up the stairs and threw the shredded shirt into a corner with as much force as she could. It fluttered down unsatisfactorily and landed without a sound. She wanted to kick something. This was without doubt the worst idea her uncle had ever had. Better to send in a troop of Army regulars to break into the Baron's manor, tear his home apart, drag the man into the street and force him to reveal his secrets. They could convict him of smuggling just as well that way. And she could go home.

She kicked the shirt again and got no more satisfaction out of it than before. Of course they couldn't convict him that way, or she wouldn't be in Longbourne. Why did the Baron even care about smuggling goods when he already had fortune enough to buy anything he liked?

She rubbed her temples and willed the incipient headache away. She shouldn't make assumptions. He might not be smuggling things for his personal use; possibly he was going to sell them on the black market in some other province to increase his personal fortune. She should probably find out what his personal fortune was. Maybe he *couldn't* afford things, and he *did* need to smuggle in luxury items. *Stop making assumptions just because you're frustrated, Lainie.*

Her stomach chose that moment to announce that it was hungry. She sat on her bed and tried to calm herself. *These people are not the job. That Morgan fellow – you told him you were a Deviser. He'll tell the Baron. Just a few more days and you can leave this awful place.* But at that moment, she was going to eat.

The tavern was as full as it had been the day before. Again, Miss Handly offered her mutton or soup, and Telaine took mutton. While she waited, she smiled at Glenda Brewster, who was there alone, and nodded politely at the other customers, but didn't try to engage any of them in conversation. There was no more need to make nice with the natives. The thought of it made her head begin to throb again. Maybe she ought to invite herself to the Baron's home, after all.

"Miss Handly? Do you have any whiskey? I feel the need for something stronger today," she said. Miss Handly raised her eyebrows, but brought her a little glass of amber liquid. Telaine took a sip and let it roll down her throat. It was nothing like what she was used to, harsh and with a strange flavor, but it was alcoholic and it set a much-needed fire burning in her belly.

"Miss Bricker?" Glenda said. "Should you...."

"Could you say that again, Miss Brewster? I didn't hear you."

Glenda cleared her throat. She looked even more anxious than usual. "Should you...I mean, I've heard...isn't alcohol bad for your baby?"

Telaine inhaled sharply and sucked in a few remaining drops of whiskey. She coughed and choked so hard she thought her eyes might pop out of her head. "My *what*?" she exclaimed when she could speak again.

Glenda looked terrified. "I'm not pregnant," Telaine said. She looked around the room. People studied their tables, their laps, as if nothing could be more interesting. Everything started to fall into place.

"I'm not pregnant!" she shouted. She slammed her fists on the table and stood, feeling her fury come back with a vengeance. "You all thought I was pregnant and unbonded, didn't you? That I was trying to get out of my responsibility to provide my child a family bond? I cannot *believe* this." She took a deep breath, her voice shaking. "That's why you've all been so rude and nasty. You felt entitled to treat me like dirt because you thought I was flouting the law!"

She glared around the room, catching the eyes of every one of her captivated listeners, who looked away in shame. "Well, let me tell you something, *good people*. Where I come from, we aren't happy about children born outside a family bond, but *we* don't think there's anything shameful about it. And if I *were* pregnant without being sworn and sealed to a husband, I wouldn't need to run away, because I'd have any number of people to support me, starting with my family."

She took another breath. "And if I'd known what you people were like, I sure as hell wouldn't have come *here*." Telaine pounded her fists down on the table again and stormed out of the tavern, slamming the door behind her.

Now she knew what Aunt Weaver had told everyone. "Got into trouble" indeed. She probably hadn't even come out and said her niece was an unmarried mother-to-be, she'd just let everyone assume it. Telaine was done being polite to the woman. She was going to tear her apart.

She saw Mistress Richardson on her stoop and veered over to meet her. "Let's get this straight," Telaine said. "I have no interest in your sons. I would have no interest in your sons even if I *were* trolling for a father for my illegitimate child. That's what you thought, isn't it? How dare you take it on yourself to judge me? You are a nasty-minded, mean-spirited woman, and next time you should have the decency to say what your problem is instead of taking it out on my clothes."

She left the woman gaping, her face as red as her hair, and stomped away in the direction of the forge. Stomping was nearly as satisfying as kicking.

Garrett was in the forge, laying out tools. "I am *not pregnant*," she snarled at him as she passed.

"Never thought you were," he said, meeting her furious eyes with that calm look.

That brought her to a halt. "Really? How did you manage to be practically the only person in town who didn't?"

Garrett cleaned off his hands with a stained rag. "You act like someone with nothing to hide," he said.

Her face must have been a wild scene of contradictory feelings, because he chuckled and added, "And I noticed your aunt never said you were pregnant. All the rest was rumor. Thought I shouldn't jump to conclusions."

Her anger drained away, leaving her with the empty, clean feeling that comes after a good rage. "Thanks for that," she said.

Garrett nodded. "Happen you'd take a look at something for me?" he asked. He gestured to her to enter the forge. She did, curious, and followed him through the forge to the back door of his house.

His home was small but tidy and smelled of pine and, more faintly, the hot metal of the forge. The kitchen and the—well, it wasn't a drawing room exactly, but she didn't know what else to call it—were a single room, with a fireplace in the center surrounded by a half-circle hearth made of small stones and two closed doors on either side of it. At the far side of the room she could see a steeply rising staircase.

The wooden floor, planed smooth, was covered by an Eskandelic woven rug dyed blue and green that was a long way from home. There was a sofa covered in green cloth matching the shades in the rug and a cushioned rocking chair in the drawing room, and a table and chair in what would have been the center of the kitchen if it was a separate room. The table was scratched and worn, but in a homey way that suggested many people over the years had eaten at it. Garrett's iron stove was larger than Aunt Weaver's and his sink was smaller. The sink—

Telaine drew in an awed breath. Fitted to the tap was an antique Device of brass and silver, with a brass handle at the top and an engraved spout where the water emerged. She ran her fingers over the curve of the Device; it was slightly rough with pitting. "It's got to be almost a hundred years old," she said.

"Happen it's as old as the house," Garrett said. "Was here when I moved in, certain sure, but that was only four years ago, and it's much older."

"You didn't grow up here?" Telaine said.

"I was born in Overton, apprenticed there, and then Longbourne needed a smith. If it helps, took most of a year for folks to get used to me." He gave a half-smile and a shrug. Telaine laughed.

"I don't know if I'll be here all that long, but that's a comfort," she said. "I'm guessing you need this fixed."

Garrett turned the handle to the right. Water poured out of the tap. "Supposed to get hotter the further to the right you turn it," he said, "but now it's nothing but cold."

Telaine dabbled her fingers in the flow, then wiped them on her trouser leg. The water was icy. "They don't make them like this anymore," she said. "I might not be able to fix it. And I'm afraid I don't have the materials to build a new one."

"You can't make it worse," he said. "Besides which I hear from Mistress Adderly you brought her Device back from the dead, so happen you'll do all right."

"Thanks for having faith in me," she said, and he fixed her with another one of those direct, calm looks that made her wonder what went on inside this quiet man's head.

"I'm outside if you need anything," he said, and shut the door behind him. Telaine turned off the water and examined the ancient Device.

"You deserve to work again," she told it. Then she put a hand to her forehead and said, "Which will not happen if I don't have tools. Big ones. Good thing I brought a few." That would mean going past Aunt Weaver without killing her. Telaine found her rage had subsided somewhat. Her "aunt" ought to thank Garrett for preventing her untimely death.

She retrieved her tools and her bag of spare parts without so much as a look at Aunt Weaver, a task made easier by the loom that hid almost all of her from view. The weight of the adjustable spanner in her hand calmed her somewhat; Telaine rarely needed the large tools, preferred working in miniature, but she liked its solidity and how it contrasted with the rest of her Deviser's kit. Even so, she ignored the people she passed on the way back from Aunt Weaver's. Making friends was no longer a priority, and she'd probably lost any chance at doing so with that outburst in the tavern, so smiling and nodding was pointless and would make her angrier when they snubbed her. *Time to focus on the job.*

She had to have Garrett remove the elbow joint, which had frozen sometime in the last hundred years, but aside from that disassembling the Device was easy. *They might not make them like this anymore, but maybe they should,* she thought as she looked at the Device's innards spread out neatly on the table.

She sat down and began reconnecting the pieces, two at a time, discovering the function of each and looking for what had broken. There were, to her eye, too many iron pieces; iron had finally been phased out by silver only twenty-five years before, after some clever Deviser realized the iron was causing other pieces to fail sooner than expected. If an iron piece needed replacing, that could become expensive.

When the door opened, Telaine said, without looking up, "Can you cast something other than iron?"

Garrett didn't say anything, so she looked up and saw him staring at his table, covered with bits of Device, with some dismay. His expression was so comical she had to laugh. "Don't worry, I know how to put it all back together," she said.

"You'd think I'd have heard the explosion," he said. He leaned against the sink and added, "It's suppertime."

"Oh!" Telaine gasped. "And here's a mess all over your table."

He waved his hand. "I eat at the sink, most nights. But...you *can* fix it?"

She nodded. "But there's bad news." She picked up two pieces and fitted them together. "I found the broken piece and I had a replacement for it, so that's all right. But this—" she picked up a toothy spoked gear half the size of her palm—"this is iron, which is making the Device run less smoothly—you've probably got to swing the handle all the way to the right to get really hot water, and that shouldn't happen—and, worse, it's got a crack. So it needs to be recast, but in order to make the Device work its best, it should be cast in silver. And that would be a *lot* of silver." She bounced the gear in her hand.

"What would you recommend?"

She bounced the gear again. "If you don't mind the way it's working now, iron. If you can afford it, silver, and it will run another hundred years."

Garrett thought about it. "It'll have to be iron," he said. He sounded as if he were afraid of hurting her feelings by not wanting the best Device she could produce.

"That would be my suggestion. You're lucky," she added, "you can make the part yourself. Anyone else, this might not be worth the effort."

"Lucky to have you around, too," he said with a smile. She was starting to look forward to those rare smiles.

"I should probably put this back together," she said.

"Won't you have to take it apart to get at the gear?"

"I can leave that out. You won't be able to use your tap, but it's not good to leave all these little pieces lying around. When can you make the cast?"

"Tomorrow. Can you come back then?"

"Certainly."

"How much do I owe you?"

"Mister Garrett," Telaine said, "for a chance to work on a Device like this, I ought to be paying *you*." He opened his mouth to protest, and she named a price. "But it's still a real pleasure."

He went through the door beyond the fireplace and returned with a couple of coins. "Happen you're undercharging me?"

"Not at all. I have to live, too. I don't want to be a burden on my aunt." Thanks to Mistress Wright handling the financial side of their uneven partnership, she had no idea how much her Deviser work was worth. She probably *was* undercharging Garrett, but she liked him and he was…if he wasn't a friend yet, he was at least the only friendly person in this town who wasn't making flirtatious advances. And she didn't need the work to survive. Not by a long way.

"You want to eat with me? Nothing fancy, but I did keep you past suppertime." He looked down at his hands.

"I should probably join Aunt Weaver."

Garrett glanced up and met her eyes. "Happen that's not a good idea."

"Why not?"

"Not sure you aren't still ready to tear her apart."

So he'd been paying attention. "I…think I've calmed down. But we're going to have a conversation."

"So long as it's not the kind of conversation ends with someone getting stabbed." Garrett didn't look convinced.

Telaine began fitting pieces together, holding a couple of metal pieces in place around the imaginary broken gear. "I don't know how to use a knife. But I wouldn't stab her even if I could." She'd had the basic self-defense instruction Aunt Imogen insisted all her children learn, but nothing more, reasoning it was out of character for the Princess. Fighting her way out of a tight situation would blow her cover to heaven and back. *I could always scratch her eyes out.*

Garrett held the door for her when she'd finished. She felt him watching her as she walked down the dark street, her head high. She didn't feel angry. She felt righteous. And she was going to have it out with her strangely antagonistic landlady.

There was one light on downstairs, and Telaine found Aunt Weaver in the drawing room, putting skeins of yarn and knitting needles into a cloth bag. She didn't look up when Telaine came in. "There's supper in the cold room," she said. "I'm off to knitting circle."

"You know, up until noon today I would have been grateful you'd saved me something," Telaine said. She sat down on the uncomfortable chair opposite her "aunt;" its horsehair-stuffed cushion had molded into the shape of some long-ago sitter's rear end. "But now I'm grateful the rumor you started about me being pregnant didn't also have me fleeing from the murder of a houseful of unbonded orphans."

Aunt Weaver looked up, startled. "I never said you were pregnant."

"You said something that let everyone think that!"

"I—" Aunt Weaver's lips thinned in an angry scowl. "That wasn't how I meant it. Happen I could've been less...ambiguous. Young Jeffrey said give you an excuse, but I didn't want to get too creative in case our stories were at odds. So I told folks you'd had some trouble you needed to get away from. I can see how that could be misinterpreted." She looked away, and said, "Sorry about that."

"I can't believe you didn't know what they were saying."

"Been busy since I got word you were coming. Haven't got out much these last few days. But I bet I know who's responsible, and Rose Garrity's going to get an earful next I see her." She thrust another skein into the bag, forcefully. "She needs to be reminded not to trifle with me."

"It's not only that. You haven't been even a little friendly since I arrived." Telaine rubbed the bridge of her nose. Her head was beginning to ache. "Mistress Weaver, did I do something to you? Something you feel you need to get back at me for? Or are you resentful that I'm here at all? Because if that's the case, you ought to take it out on my uncle. The way I'm feeling now, I'd even help. But stop finding ways to make my life a misery."

Aunt Weaver set the bag on the other chair and gave Telaine an angry glare that once again gave her the feeling she'd seen this woman somewhere else. Right. Julia had the same expression on the rare occasions she was angry. "You're right, I don't want you here," she said, "fooling these people into thinking you're something you're not. They're good people and they don't deserve it."

"Good people who think it's all right to shame someone for having an illegitimate child? They assumed the worst of me!"

"That sort of thing means more in a small town than in a place as big as Aurilien. Men and women who don't provide a bond for their children can set off bad feelings that last for years, and there's nowhere to get away to. Don't go judging 'less you plan on making a home here."

"But I'm *not* staying! I'll do what I came here for and then I'll be gone. And they'll all remember me as your odd niece who couldn't cook or do her own laundry and wasn't actually pregnant."

"Really? Then why'd you care so much about them thinking you were pregnant?"

Telaine's mouth opened. "I—" she began. Aunt Weaver was right. She'd taken it personally, as if it mattered what these people thought. Because it had. "I don't know why," she said.

"Don't know much about your real life," said Aunt Weaver, picking up the bag and shouldering the long strap. "Your uncle said you were good at reading people, making 'em react the way you want. Happen that's not something you can give up doing. Happen you see these folks the way you do the ones you manipulate back home."

Telaine leaned back in the chair, whose hard cushion dug into her spine. It had been easy to play on Taylor and the Richardsons' interest in her; it would be just as easy to turn them into her doting swains whether she cared for them or not. She'd flattered Mistress Adderly by stroking the woman's ego without caring that she was being insincere; mostly, she realized in shame, to prove to herself she could. The only person she'd had any genuine interaction with was Garrett, if you didn't count the way she'd ripped into Mistress Richardson. It seemed she hadn't left the Princess behind in Aurilien after all.

"You're right. I do it without thinking," she admitted. "The people of Longbourne aren't friends. They're pieces I'm using to do my job. And the truth is, I don't need to treat them that way to do what I'm here for. I don't mean them any harm, but if I were planning to live here, I'd be abusing their trust."

"And since you're not staying, you ought leave 'em be."

Telaine put her elbows on her knees and her face in her hands, and groaned. "Aunt Weaver," she said, her voice muffled, "if I swear I won't manipulate these people anymore, will you stop putting obstacles in my way? Starting with showing me how I'm supposed to bathe?"

Aunt Weaver nodded once. "But you're not going to like the bathing," she said.

CHAPTER EIGHT

She *hated* the bathing. Telaine stood naked in a large metal tub in the darkened kitchen, calf-deep in lukewarm water, and scrubbed herself more quickly than she'd imagined possible. Washing her hair in the sink was worse; the water was cold, her waist-length hair took forever to dry, and she resolved to be out of Longbourne before winter, because she imagined hair-washing didn't even happen then.

But once she was clean, she felt so much better. It was late when she finally crawled into bed. She slept, and had pleasant dreams of places far from this awful town where no one liked her.

Breakfast was a surprise. When she came downstairs, Aunt Weaver was in the process of frying flat cakes on a griddle set on the top of the stove. She lifted one off with the spatula and deposited it on a plate she handed to Telaine. "They're good with honey," she said. Telaine poured a dollop on and tasted it. It was delicious.

"I thought you'd made up 'figgin,'" she confessed without thinking.

"Does sound like a made-up thing," Aunt Weaver agreed. "Did you ask for one?"

"No, I asked him to name all the sizes."

Aunt Weaver grunted. It might have been a kind of low-grade laugh. "You're not stupid," she said.

"Thanks for the compliment," Telaine said. She gobbled her flat cake and had another one, then cleared her plate and washed it under the tap. She was starting to figure out how washing dishes worked. "I worked on a Device for Mister Garrett," she said. "It heats water as it comes out of the tap."

"Boiling water over the fire's always been good enough for me."

"But I think I could get the materials — wouldn't it be nice —"

"I got my own ways of doing things, thank you."

Telaine gave up. "I'm going back over there now. I'll be back for supper."

"Have a good day," said Aunt Weaver.

Telaine stopped. "You know," she said with an arched brow, "that was almost pleasant. I might get the idea that you approve of me."

Aunt Weaver grunted again. Telaine smiled and left the kitchen through the back door.

She came around to the front of the house and jumped, startled, because Morgan stood by the front door, leaning against the wall as lazy as a cat. "Miss Bricker," he said without looking at her. "I wonder if you might be interested in a commission."

Her heart began to beat faster. "What might that be, Mister Morgan?"

"Baron Steepridge has a Device he needs repaired. I told him of your presence in our little community and he was so pleased you could help him."

Not so much a request as a command, then. She didn't care. Finally, she could start work. "I'd be happy to work for the Baron. When would he like me to begin?"

"How does 'now' sound?"

"I'd...certainly. Let me fetch my tools." She ran back upstairs, checked the roll and bundled up the larger tools, and hid her lock picks in her boot. She probably wouldn't get a chance to use them today, but taking them along was a good habit. She once again felt full of fizzy excitement. Time to begin.

Today it seemed everyone she passed looked at her. Or maybe they were looking at Morgan, who was as elegant as before in a cream-colored silk shirt, full-sleeved, with a tightly laced black vest and black trousers of heavy twilled cotton. His boots still shone like mirrors, quite a feat considering how much rock dust came off the road. He wore a knife in a sheath dangling from his belt; it bounced off his leg as he strode.

It was like having an extra shadow, him towering over her as they walked side by side down the street. Were they going to walk all the way to the Baron's manor? Morgan's footwear certainly wouldn't survive that trip unscathed. And she had trouble picturing him doing anything so plebeian as walking any farther than the length of the town.

They approached the forge, and Telaine remembered where she'd been going before Morgan accosted her. "Excuse me one moment, Mister Morgan," she said, and went to the forge rail, smiling reflexively at Tanner and his cronies, whose conversation stopped when she neared. As far as she could tell, lounging around the forge was their only employment.

Garrett turned away from tending the forge fire and flashed one of those quick smiles, but then he looked beyond her to Morgan, and his face went still. "Mister Garrett, I'm going to the manor, but I'll be back this afternoon to finish that repair. If the gear is ready."

He looked away from Morgan and back at her. "Be careful," he said quietly, and went back to his work.

Morgan smiled when she returned to his side. Unlike Garrett's elusive smile that flashed and vanished, Morgan's smile was like a cat's—pointed, wide, and rarely reaching his eyes. "Don't tell me you have an admirer?" he drawled.

"A job," she replied. Even without Garrett's warning and that of her actual admirers two nights ago, she would have found Morgan alarming. On the surface, his regard of her was the kind of appreciation the Princess was familiar with and could manipulate with ease, but Telaine had a feeling his interest went beyond simple admiration into a darker emotion that made her uneasy. She would think carefully before trying to captivate or manipulate him. He might see through her plan, and weave a far more cunning trap for her.

"How nice that you're making a place for yourself here," he said, with an emphasis on "nice." His drawling upper-class voice made everything he said sound as if it were invested with a double meaning, as if he were having a joke at everyone else's expense. That was a mystery; what was someone who sounded as if he belonged in a palace drawing room doing in the back of beyond?

"I don't plan on staying long," she said. She was about to add more, but caution held her tongue. If he was as dangerous as she suspected, it would be a bad idea to give him any more information about herself than necessary. *But what exactly am I afraid he might do? Am I being paranoid? Good.*

Morgan led her to the tavern, where a beautiful bay horse was tethered to the porch rail. "Can you ride?" he asked, mounting, and reached down a hand to help her mount. Telaine almost refused right there; getting on a horse controlled by this man made her nervous. She steeled herself, took his hand, and let him pull her up behind him. The horse went from standing still to a trot in a heartbeat, and Telaine had to throw her arms around Morgan's waist to keep from falling. She heard him chuckle, and she flushed, moving around until she didn't have to grip him so tightly. It was a good horse, a tall gelding with an excellent gait, and Morgan rode well.

"**i would have brought a mount for you,** but I didn't know if you were a rider," he said without turning his head.

"I do ride fairly well," Telaine said. The lying echo confirmed her instinct that he'd wanted to make her uncomfortable. That she'd known what he intended left her unsettled. She was good at reading people, but this went beyond simple observation; it was as if they had some kind of connection, and it was a far from lovely feeling. She took a slow breath, then another, and thought *This isn't the job. Don't let him rattle you.*

Morgan rode beyond Longbourne and up a wandering path to the end of the valley. It was a beautiful, sunny late summer day, and Telaine enjoyed the ride despite the company. At least Morgan had stopped speaking. The dark pines began to close in around them as the valley narrowed, but it was peaceful rather than oppressive, as if the trees were reaching out to shelter them, though why the trees didn't shrink from Morgan's presence was a mystery.

After about ten minutes of their silent ride, Telaine could see the dark blot that was the fort in the distance, with another, smaller blot off to the right. Another ten minutes brought them in full view of both the Baron's manor and the fort, which straddled a narrow cut in the mountains like a lion crouched over its prey. Morgan turned off the main road before they reached the fort and down a smaller road that turned into a graveled drive running in front of the manor.

The manor, in contrast to its peaceful surroundings, huddled in on itself, shrinking from the pines that surrounded it on three sides. It was small for a noble's house, but still bigger than any five buildings in Longbourne combined; four stories tall, it had the now-familiar stone foundation and wooden upper stories, with large glass windows gleaming in the morning sun. The foundation stones were light-colored granite, larger and more regular than the ones Longbourne residents used, but the wooden upper stories had been painted a dour brown which, with the black leading of the windows, gave the place a haunted look. Telaine could not imagine living there, however opulent it was on the inside.

A long flight of stairs led up to the second story, to a double door framed in heavily carved square timbers. The abstract curlicues and triangles of the carvings were no older than the manor itself—Telaine judged it to have been built some fifty years earlier—but resembled those of the long-ago era when Tremontanans still worshipped gods instead of ungoverned heaven.

Morgan pulled up his horse at the foot of the stairs, dismounted, and helped Telaine down before she could protest that she could dismount very well on her own, thanks. She followed him up the stairs, where two footmen dressed in what could only be the Baron's livery stood at...you couldn't call it "at attention," could you, when they slouched and seemed not to notice the visitors? Morgan opened the door himself and bowed Telaine in.

Her guess about the opulence of the interior turned out to be inadequate. The Baron of Steepridge might have gone into exile, but he had taken his wealth with him and turned it into mahogany paneling, fine art, tiled flooring, and furniture that would not have looked out of place in the palace. Sweeping staircases curved up both sides of the entry hall, meeting in a gallery on the floor above; doors of mahogany and glass on the entry level led further into the house. It was exquisite without being tasteless, and Telaine's amazed appreciation for the place apparently showed, because Morgan said, in his lazy drawl, "Impressive, isn't it? Even to a city girl?"

"I don't exactly move in these circles," Telaine said. *Not at the moment, anyway.*

"We will have to change that," said a voice Telaine recognized. She looked up to the gallery and saw, for the first time, Hugh Harstow, Baron of Steepridge. She had pictured him as a lean, hawk-nosed man with narrow eyes. She was completely wrong.

From this angle, she couldn't tell how tall he was, but he had a bit of a paunch and unusually red lips. He wore a dove gray morning coat and trousers with a white shirtfront and a beautifully tied cravat pinned with a ruby the size of her thumbnail, exactly as if he expected to call on the King in half an hour.

He came down the stairs slowly, allowing her to absorb his magnificence, and to do him credit, he was magnificent, despite his physical shortcomings. When he stood before her, she saw he was several inches taller than her and, when he inclined his head to her, that his brown hair was thinning on top.

"Miss Bricker, thank you for coming," he said, extending his hand. Telaine reached out to shake his hand, but he grasped hers and lifted it to his red lips, just as Morgan had done. She forced herself not to jerk her hand away; his lips were wet and surprisingly cold. "Has Morgan explained my little problem to you?"

"Only that you need a repair done." Steepridge released her hand and she refrained from wiping it on her leg.

"I hope you'll find it an interesting challenge. Please, follow me."

The Baron led the way through one of the glass-paned doors into a room brightly lit by half a dozen windows looking out over the approach to the manor. Chairs and couches upholstered in golden brown velvet made a half-circle around a glossy pianoforte, sheets of music spread out on it as if waiting for a performer. To the left was the huddled shape of a harp swathed in sheets, almost blocking a glass-fronted cabinet containing bound books of music. Their footsteps were swallowed up by the thick carpet, making the room feel dull, as if any sound, even the most beautiful, would simply fly into the walls and fall disregarded to the floor.

In one corner a large birdcage made of ornate wires of many different metals hung from a hook in the low ceiling. The Baron opened a wire door in its side and reached in. He pulled out a dead bird and showed it to Telaine. "Remarkable craftsmanship, don't you think?"

Telaine overcame her revulsion to look closer, and was stunned. The Baron held a large bird-shaped Device whose black feathers were iridescent in the indirect light. Its head was made of gold and its lidless eyes were round, cabochon sapphires.

"Take it," the Baron said, offering it to her, and she accepted the thing with wonder. It was heavier than it looked—the body under the feathers might be as gold as the head—and warm from more than the Baron's body heat.

"It's astonishing," she said with real feeling. The Baron smiled, his red lips glistening.

"It's two Devices, actually," he said. "The cage accepts wax discs imprinted with music—or, rather, with grooves and depressions it translates into music—and the bird produces the sound. It's supposed to move its body as well, to look as realistic as Devisery can achieve. Unfortunately, it's stopped responding altogether."

"Are you sure the cage is still working? Milord?" She almost forgot to add the honorific, and mentally shook herself. Time to be impressed with the collection after she'd achieved her goal.

"That's an excellent question. Of course, it would be hard to know without the bird, yes? But I believe it's still functioning."

"Then if you would have someone bring me a table, milord, I can begin the repairs."

The Baron looked surprised she would address him so directly, if respectfully. "Morgan, see to it," he said. "I don't suppose you'd let me watch?" he asked Telaine, and she thought he looked wistful.

"I—to be honest, milord, I think your attention would make me nervous," she said, with a laugh she hoped struck the right note of discomfort and awkwardness. The Baron nodded, disappointed, and said, "Please ask any of the servants to fetch me when you're finished. How long will it take?"

Telaine said, "I won't be able to tell until I've taken it apart, because I've never seen anything like it. But I hope it will only be a few hours."

The Baron nodded again and left the room, passing a servant carrying a folding table she set up without looking at Telaine. Then the servant was gone, and Telaine was alone. She thought briefly of sneaking away to explore the manor after they all left the room, but it was a bad idea. Too many people knew why she was here, and being caught where she shouldn't be would probably mean never being allowed inside again, which would make her job infinitely harder. She'd have to work quickly and skillfully to make a good impression so the Baron would give her a return invitation.

The hardest part was opening it up; it was so well made the seams were virtually invisible. Finally, with a tiny *pop*, the head came off and the body fell into two pieces joined by a concealed hinge. Telaine was disappointed to find that the Device was of the most basic design, once you got past the ornate exterior, and had to remind herself again that speed was important, that having a challenge would work against her in this case.

The repair was simple, none of the pieces were broken, just misaligned, even the motive force was fully imbued...*oh,* that *would have given me an excellent opportunity to wander around,* she thought after she'd put the whole thing back together. She'd have to remember it for next time.

She had to work out how to fit the Device back into its cage, but once that was done, it began to move like a real bird. She poked around to figure out how the cage worked. A casket on a nearby stand contained the wax discs the Baron had mentioned; more investigation turned up a slot where the discs could be inserted. She slid one in, shut the lid, and the bird rewarded her by breaking into the first notes of "Let Me Sit Beside You." Apparently the Baron was fond of music-hall tunes.

"Lovely," said Morgan, clapping a slow rhythm. "And so is the music."

Telaine allowed herself to blush, which was no doubt what he wanted. "Just doing the job I'm paid for," she said.

"Oh, yes, you'll want paying. I suppose it's too much to ask you to do it for King and country." He approached her too closely, forcing her to step back as he unlatched the lid and removed the disc.

"I have to eat, Mister Morgan."

"Speaking of which, will you dine with us? It's nearly noon."

The time had passed without her noticing. Four hours. "Me? Is the Baron in the habit of dining with his hired help?"

"Only the Devisers, who you must admit are not ordinary craftsmen. Or women." He inclined his head, but kept his intense eyes on her. His attention was beginning to overwhelm her to the point that it lost all meaning. Did he realize he was overplaying his hand? No, that peculiar, uncomfortable extra sense told her sleek Archie Morgan *meant* to seem not in control. But to what end? *Leave the analysis for later. Stay focused.*

She plucked at her trouser legs. "I'd feel uncomfortable, dressed like this."

"Nonsense." He ran his finger down a crease in her sleeve. "It's like a uniform, isn't it? And uniforms are acceptable everywhere."

"If you're sure his lordship won't mind, then I accept," she said, quashing the nervousness that had sprung up again as he touched her. This would be an excellent opportunity to get to know her target, if she could keep from giving too much of her game away.

CHAPTER NINE

If Telaine hadn't been used to the palace, which had at least five dining halls twice the size of the Baron's, she might have been impressed. The oak-paneled room—the Baron was fond of wood paneling, wasn't he?—was two stories tall with a plaster ceiling crossed by dark, intricately carved beams. A balcony that was probably accessed from the gallery at the top of the entry staircase ran along three sides of the room, perfect for a string quartet to provide music for dining or for dancing. Telaine guessed the room doubled as a reception hall, or would if the Baron had anyone to receive.

Extravagant floor-to-ceiling glass panes gave a view of the pine forest that pressed close against the manor. It was a depressing view, and Telaine reflected that if the manor had been oriented differently, most of the rooms could have looked out over the beautiful valley toward Longbourne.

She put on a properly overawed expression and went to greet the Baron, who stood looking out the window. He turned to face her and Morgan as they entered.

"Were you successful, my dear?" the Baron asked.

"Yes, milord. I'd be happy to demonstrate my work after the meal. That is—I don't expect any special treatment, and it's an honor to be asked to dine with you."

The Baron waved this away. "Not at all. I have a great respect for Devisers. It was my ambition to become one in my youth, but I'm afraid I lacked the necessary dexterity and sufficient ability to sense source. Please, have a seat." He, the Baron, actually held a chair for the lowly craftswoman. If Telaine didn't know better, she would have believed this man to be a genuine, kind egalitarian. She might even have believed it if she'd only heard about his abusive personality secondhand. Having heard how viciously he'd threatened Harroden, she wasn't fooled at all.

The Baron seated her on his right hand, and Morgan took the chair on his left. Servants in formal livery brought beef in gravy, green vegetables, soft rolls, and a selection of wines from which the Baron chose a favorite. Telaine fumbled her silverware, tried to serve herself from the platter of fresh chard instead of waiting for the servant, and made a point of watching the Baron closely and mimicking his actions. She decided against appearing to have a poor head for alcohol, choosing to save that ploy for a possible future event.

"Miss Bricker, please tell me about yourself. How did you come to be a Deviser?" asked the Baron, his red lips moving unpleasantly as he chewed.

Telaine said, "It's not an interesting story. I was apprenticed several years ago, worked my way up, got my Deviser's certificate and went out on the road."

"You didn't choose to set up shop for yourself?"

"I found I enjoyed the challenges of traveling more. In the city, in a shop, the work is generally the same—clocks, lights, guns, the occasional bauble. On the road, you never know what you might encounter."

"If I may ask, what is the most exotic thing you've had to repair?"

Telaine wiped her lips with her napkin. "Besides your bird?" she laughed. "I think I would have to say—" not Garrett's tap Device; she was reluctant to draw their attention to him in any way—"a sword cane where the sheath was meant to sprout blades when it was released. It was a challenge because the locking Device had failed and every time I tried to adjust the blades, the thing would pop off and try to impale me."

She chuckled, and the Baron joined her in her laugh; Morgan remained silent, his elbow propped on the table—such bad manners!— and his chin resting on his palm. When she glanced his way, he smiled that feline smile.

"But you never create new Devices? I would think that would be far more exciting."

"I have, yes, and I find great pleasure in working out the details of a new Device. But that's a disadvantage to traveling that a shopkeeper doesn't have. People are more likely to commission a Device from an established shop than from a traveling Deviser."

"I see you're finished," said the Baron. He patted his lips, which did nothing to reduce their wet appearance. "Would you care to accompany me? There's something I'd like to show you."

Telaine rose and followed him, paying close attention to the manor's layout. The dining room was at the center of the house, with wings extending to either side. The Baron led her out of the dining room and up the right-hand stairs to the gallery, then down the hallway on the right, which was lined with doors. The Baron passed all of them until he came to the far end of the hall, where he opened a door on the left and gestured for her to enter.

Telaine gasped. The room wasn't remarkable in its size or décor, which matched the wood paneling the Baron preferred. It did not have an exceptional view, facing the trees at the rear of the house which were visible through smallish windows. What it did have were Devices on every conceivable surface, shelves, pedestals, and lecterns. Some were under glass. All were unique. Telaine surveyed the room and saw no duplicates anywhere.

"Extraordinary, isn't it?" the Baron said in a smug tone. "The work of a lifetime. Some I commissioned, some I purchased, some I—dare I say it?—stole. No, my dear, don't look at me that way. I mean only that I found some of these under such circumstances that acquiring them felt like I was getting away with something, you understand? An overlooked box at an estate sale, a watch buried in dust at the back of some old shop. I am very proud of my collection."

He went to a lectern and lifted the cover of the book that lay there; it began speaking in a tiny voice. "It reads to you. Clever, no? It's over two hundred years old and one of only four ever made, since the Device that powers it requires a human to speak the words into the Device, and again for a second copy, and so on. The Eskandelics who Devised them believed that was simply too much work to be cost-effective. Unusually pragmatic for Eskandelics, they were."

"May I...?" Telaine asked. For the moment, she'd forgotten her mission, though not the dark presence of Morgan in the doorway, blocking her exit.

"Please," said the Baron. Telaine wandered the room, admiring, exclaiming, and, with a glance for permission, touching. A "flea circus" swung into motion at the tap of a fingernail. Binoculars automatically adjusted to her vision. A glass case at the far end of the room contained an assortment of projectile Devices, including one that looked like a prototype for the currently popular weapon used by Tremontane's military.

"You have a most wonderful collection, milord," she said.

"Thank you. I may need your services again. Some of these Devices are in disrepair."

"It would be a pleasure, milord."

The Baron nodded and extended his hand. "Morgan will return you to Longbourne, and I may be in contact with you soon."

"Oh, milord," Telaine said, alarm rising again, "I don't want to put you to any trouble. I'm able to walk back."

"No trouble at all. Morgan does what I tell him." Morgan nodded, but Telaine caught a glimpse of his eyes, and they said that Morgan did not at all like being told what to do.

On the ride back, Telaine once again clinging to Morgan's waist, her purse fatter by several coins, she said, "I'm surprised milord Baron chose to live all the way out here. He's so sophisticated."

"the baron loves it here. he loves the wilderness."

I already know the Baron hates it here, thank you, Morgan. "Is he in charge of the fort?"

"Captain Clarke has command of the fort, though the Baron is ultimately responsible for its upkeep. **the baron is proud to assist in the kingdom's defense.**"

"Those soldiers the other night frightened me." This was somewhat true. "Are all the soldiers like them?"

"Fighting men have to be tough. **you have nothing to fear from them.**"

Telaine gritted her teeth as Morgan took a curve too fast, causing her to cling more tightly. "That's…what I thought."

Morgan again, unnecessarily, helped her dismount in front of the tavern. "Thank you for the ride, but I'd like to go under my own power next time," she said. "It's a lovely walk and I could do with the exercise."

"As you wish…my dear," he said, leaping back into the saddle and smiling at her in a way that raised goose pimples all down her arms, not pleasant ones. He lashed the horse into a gallop that sprayed gravel around her ankles. She watched him go, thinking *He probably knows I'm watching him, but not for the reasons he imagines.* He wanted to make her uncomfortable. He was succeeding.

When he was safely out of sight, she shuddered and decided to go into the tavern. She needed a drink, and she didn't care what the other patrons thought of her. If anyone should be ashamed of that outburst of hers, *they* should be. She wasn't.

Miss Handly was at the bar, polishing glasses. When she saw Telaine, she smiled. A big smile. No question about it. "Miss Bricker!" she called out. "What can I get for you?"

Telaine looked around. It was past dinnertime, so the crowd had thinned out, but the few patrons there met her eyes without flinching. A few of them smiled or raised their glasses in welcome. "Excuse me?" she said to the barkeep.

"I said, what can I get for you? Beer? Something to eat?"

"Beer," Telaine said, mystified. Miss Handly filled a large mug from the tap until it nearly foamed over and slid it across the bar. Telaine took a longer drink than she'd planned and successfully kept from choking to death on the pale golden liquid. "Miss Handly?" she asked when she was able to speak. "Is there something I should know about?" She waved the hand not holding the glass to encompass the entire tap room.

Miss Handly's smile vanished. "Happen we weren't all that kind to you," she said, her voice low. "You got people thinking and, well, they're ashamed and trying to make it up to you. So, that one's on the house."

"You mean, all I had to do to make you all like me was yell and stomp around?"

"Saying the right words." Miss Handly's voice lowered more. "We all thought you were here because you didn't want to make things right with your baby's father, see?"

"Why would anyone do that? An entailed adoption isn't so hard. And I might have been fleeing an abusive relationship. You all jumped to some nasty conclusions."

Miss Handly reddened. "You know how rumors are. Someone says the wrong thing, and it spreads and gets worse from there. We shouldn't have listened to the rumors, and even if we did, we shouldn't've taken it on ourselves to judge you like that. So take it in the spirit it's offered, and let bygones be bygones, understand?"

"Don't hang on to my grievances, you mean?"

"If grievances means being entitled to be mad 'cause you got slandered, then yes."

Telaine drained her glass and set it down on the bar with a tap. "That is some good advice that I plan to take, Miss Handly."

Miss Handly took the glass and rinsed it, polished it up again. "You're going to keep coming in here, suppose you should call me Maida. My regulars all do."

A grin tugged at the corners of Telaine's mouth. "Then you should call me Lainie so I'll feel welcome." She held out her hand. Maida took it, and smiled. "I ate up at the manor, so—what's wrong?"

Maida had gone pale. "Nobody goes to the manor doesn't have to," she said. "Servants all live in. What were you doing there?"

"Just repairing a Device. Maida, everyone's been telling me the Baron is dangerous. Why?"

"Nobody knows for certain sure, but there's always been talk. People gone missing, or livestock stolen, and himself not being over quick to find the truth. Like yesterday evening—Nev Sheldon left his parents' house to go to his grandmother's and never arrived, but it was his village went looking for him, not the Baron's men. You watch yourself if you go back there."

"I will. Thanks for the warning." She wondered how many other people would feel the need to warn her. On the one hand, it was nice to know they cared, but on the other, she'd like to have a few more details beyond rumor—which, as Maida had said, she shouldn't listen to. People gone missing, huh? No wonder going up to the manor was such a big deal. And they were worried about the Baron, not just Morgan, who was certainly the more obvious menace.

Garrett had just plunged something hot into the quenching barrel when she approached the forge. He glanced up the road behind her, frowning, then relaxed when he saw she was alone. "I have not been eaten by the Baron," Telaine said when he opened his mouth. "I have not been poisoned by the Baron's food. I have been paid by the Baron and I may have repeat employment by him."

"Not something to laugh about," Garrett said, frowning. "Baron's not best loved around here. And that Morgan is the kind of fellow enjoys torturing animals. You might not be safe with him."

He'd come right up to the rail, and Telaine came forward and laid her hand on his arm. "Thanks for being so concerned. I mean it. And I'm going to take everything you say about them seriously. But I also have to work." His muscular forearm tensed under her fingers, and she released him. "I won't do anything foolish," she added.

"Happen just going up there is foolish," he said. "Heard about your song and dance in the tavern yesterday," he added, turning back to his work.

"My—oh. You mean my temper tantrum." She leaned against the rail and watched him pull a length of metal out of the fire and flatten one end with a short-handled hammer. "It was unexpectedly effective."

"Funny how shame can make people think harder on a thing." *Plink, plink, plink.*

"I didn't mean to make anyone feel ashamed. Well, no. I suppose I did. But I wasn't trying to manipulate anyone."

"I know." Garrett pushed the metal back into the coals. "That gear's done, if you want to take a look at it."

Telaine came around the rail and picked up the gear, where it lay on a table with other bits of metal, mostly scrap. "Do you have a rasp? A file?"

Garrett pointed at the back wall. "Take your pick."

Telaine chose one, leaned against the table, and began shaving the rough edges down. "It's a good match." The sound of the hammer began again. It was a soothing sound, and the scrape of the rasp fell into rhythm with it.

"What's it like?" Garrett asked.

"Fine. I'm taking off the burrs."

"I mean the Baron's manor."

She lowered the rasp. "Fancy. Dark. Big." She'd been about to say "not too big" but remembered in time that Lainie Bricker's scale of comparison wasn't like the Princess's. "It was depressing, all that space with just him and Morgan rattling around inside."

"Don't expect me to feel sorry for him."

Telaine laughed. "You shouldn't. He's got his Devices to keep him warm at night. I mean, not literally. Though he might have a Device to keep him warm at night, too."

"They make those?"

"Sure. Goes inside a mattress, or between mattresses."

A pause. "Can't imagine having more than one mattress on a bed."

"Most beds don't." How she missed her bed, with its two fluffy mattresses and four pillows and as many blankets as she wanted. And someone to make it up for her in the morning. Better not to think about it too much, and be disappointed by the reality that awaited her in Aunt Weaver's spare room.

"I wonder if you could work it into a blanket instead," she continued. *Plink, plink, plink. Scrape, scrape, scrape.* "Be a nice way to keep warm during the winter." She blew iron filings off the gear and held it up to the light. "I'm going to put this in now," she said, taking the rasp with her.

Telaine only needed the spanner for this stage of the repair. The gear slotted into its place and meshed perfectly with its brothers. She screwed the case down tight, made a few last twists with the spanner, and gingerly moved the handle a fraction to the right. Water trickled out.

She continued to turn the handle, slowly, feeling for misalignments inside the Device, but it turned smoothly all the way. She ran her hand under the fixture; the water was hot, but not enough to burn. With the right parts, that far-right setting would produce boiling water, which was dangerous and probably another reason they didn't make them like this anymore. Using the iron gear had been the best choice.

"It works," Garrett said from the doorway. She smiled and worked the handle back and forth quickly, still feeling for any problems. He took the handle from her and moved it back and forth himself, ran his fingers under the hot water at the extreme right setting. "Nice to know I don't have to shave with cold water anymore," he said.

"If you were shaving with *that* cold water, I'm impressed. That had to have come all the way from a frozen mountain spring."

He flashed a smile, then ducked his head, looking at the Device. "Thanks again," he said. He seemed to be looking for something else to say, but finally just nodded. "Thanks."

"Any time you need one of these antiques fixed, you know where I live," she said, and went out through the forge and back to Aunt Weaver's home. On that short journey, no fewer than twelve people waved, ten smiled, and five called out her name in greeting. She returned all their gestures in kind. She was determined to take Maida's advice and behave as if the last three days hadn't happened. As far as she was concerned, she'd be happy for that to be true.

The smell of chicken soup met Telaine halfway to the back door. In the kitchen, Aunt Weaver stood over the pot, fishing out and shredding pieces of chicken meat. "Supper's ready in a few minutes," she said.

"Thanks." Telaine sat at the table and stretched out her legs. "I've been meaning to talk to you about my keep. The Baron paid me and —"

"Not takin' money from you. You're my guest."

"But you're feeding me, and —"

"This ain't a debate."

"Is Uncle paying you at all?"

"It's an exchange of favors. Don't worry about it."

Telaine gave up. "Did you have a good day?"

"Can't complain."

"Everyone's decided to be nice to me now. I never realized how effective a shouting tantrum could be."

Aunt Weaver shrugged. "They're good people."

And you inadvertently tricked them into giving me a cold welcome. "Do you have plans tonight?"

"knitting circle."

Telaine raised an eyebrow at the echo. "I thought that was last night."

Aunt Weaver gave her a sharp glance that Telaine once again felt she ought to recognize. **"sometimes it's two nights in a row."**

"Oh? That must be...nice." So where was Aunt Weaver going, really?

Aunt Weaver ladled up a bowl of soup and handed it to Telaine. "You any closer to finishing this job of yours?"

"Getting into the manor was the first step. So it's a qualified 'yes.'"

"Good." She sat down opposite Telaine with her own bowl. "Sooner you finish, the better."

That hurt, though it was Telaine's thought as well. "I'm sorry to be such a burden," she said stiffly.

There was the sharp-eyed glance again. "Thought you was in a hurry," Aunt Weaver said. "Happen you're not so much a burden as I thought."

"Well...thanks." Telaine ate the rest of her supper in silence, then washed her bowl and set it in the drying rack. "I don't suppose I could come to knitting circle?" she said off-handedly.

"don't think you'd feel welcome," Aunt Weaver said, clearing away her own bowl. "And I thought I told you not to meddle in these folks' lives. No sense you making a place for yourself here when you ain't stayin'."

"That makes sense." So, Aunt Weaver was going somewhere she definitely didn't want Telaine tagging along. From a woman who didn't shy from airing her opinions, this counted as strange.

Telaine nodded and said, "Good night, then," and went up the stairs into her room, leaving the door open a crack. She heard Aunt Weaver ascend the stairs and go into her own room, then the house was silent. Telaine waited. This wasn't as boring as the time she'd sat concealed in a cupboard, waiting to eavesdrop on a meeting between two women that turned out to be nothing more than a romantic tryst, but it was close.

The sun set, the room grew dark, and Aunt Weaver's door opened again. Telaine waited until she heard the familiar slam of the back door, then hurried downstairs to follow. It was probably nothing, but she was tired of being at a disadvantage when it came to her occasionally hostile landlady.

Aunt Weaver was wrapped in a black cloak, which was a mistake; pure black stood out at night in a way dark gray or green didn't. But then she probably didn't expect to be followed, judging by how she strode down the streets of Longbourne and into the forest. Telaine kept a good distance, though she had to shorten it when they entered the forest, which closed in around her with unsettling rapidity.

The bright moonlight filtering through the branches guided her steps, and the smell of pine and the soft rolling feel of needles under her feet brought back memories she hadn't thought of in years. *Let your feet find the way,* her father said in memory, *trust them when your eyes let you down.* How young had she been? Five? And she'd walked right up to a doe and laid her small hand on its warm flank, saw it look at her with liquid brown eyes and then dart away, quick as summer lightning. How different her life would have been if her father had lived.

Telaine came to the edge of the forest and stopped before walking out onto the downs. Aunt Weaver was already a good way across the field. Telaine knew only two things about Barony Steepridge: it was completely isolated during the winter, and it was famous for the quality of its wool. This had to be one of the sheep farms. The fields were wide open, with nowhere to hide, and even Aunt Weaver, as preoccupied as she was, might turn around and see her. She'd have to return to the house.

Grumbling to herself, she retraced her steps with only slight hesitations. It seemed she hadn't forgotten her father's training entirely.

Back in her room, she undressed, then lay atop the blanket on the thin mattress. Whatever Aunt Weaver was concealing was none of her business, but Telaine North Hunter hadn't lasted eight years as an agent by keeping her nose out of other people's affairs. Now that she'd made it past the Baron's door, she'd probably finish her assignment quickly, but if not, discovering Aunt Weaver's secret would make for an interesting way to pass the time.

CHAPTER TEN

The Baron didn't call on her again for a week. During that week, Telaine went slowly crazy with impatience. She ran dozens of plans for investigating the manor through her mind until they kept her awake at night.

Plans for when it was empty. Plans for when the Baron and Morgan were there. Plans for when one or the other was there, which involved subsidiary plans for avoiding Morgan; she was certain he would hover around her like a wasp at a picnic.

Excuses to get into as many rooms as possible—searching for a source still seemed her most likely one, though getting into the Baron's study might only require him having a Device in it that needed repair.

Or could she hint around that she might create a new Device for him? What unusual Devices had she seen in people's studies? Was the study even the place to find the evidence she needed? Should she try to get into the fort? If the shipment Harroden had diverted to Steepridge contained weapons, mightn't they be stored there?

She considered breaking into the manor one night, sneaking around when everyone had gone to bed, and decided that was a bad idea. She didn't know enough about its layout to be efficient in her searching, and if the Baron caught her, that would mean the end of her snooping around, possibly permanently. Some nights she paced the room, trying to tame her thoughts, or went down to the tavern in the hope that alcohol might solve her problem. It never did.

She passed the time in between pacing and worrying in getting to know the people of Longbourne. At first she kept her distance, not wanting to fall back into the habit of thinking of them as pieces in her game with the Baron. But as the days passed, and she began to fear she wouldn't be leaving for weeks (she refused to consider it might be months) she realized it would look strange for Mistress Weaver's niece to appear standoffish.

Now that the initial misunderstanding was past, Telaine found the people of Longbourne to be friendly and outgoing. Fuller, the general store owner, always threw in a little extra when she picked up things for Aunt Weaver; Telaine and Josephine Adderly were on a first-name basis; and of course Garrett always had a nod and sometimes a flash of a smile for her.

Even Mistress Richardson had come around. After her first rush of anger had faded, Telaine developed an agonizing guilt over the horrible things she'd said to the woman. She couldn't decide if she should make the first apology—but *she* was the one more wronged—or wait for Mistress Richardson to take the first step—but was it too self-righteous to demand the offender speak first?

The decision was taken out of her hands when Mistress Richardson showed up at Aunt Weaver's back door—this was another thing Telaine learned; real visits were conducted via the back door—with a package and asked to speak to Telaine privately. In the yard, Mistress Richardson handed her the package and said, "I did something I'm not proud of. I'd like to make it up to you."

Inside the package was a shirt, a much nicer shirt than the one the laundress had ruined. Telaine felt a rush of guilt all over again. She said, "I said some things I'm not proud of. I hope you'll accept my apology. I'd like us to be friends." It was perhaps too city-girl-uppity, but it sounded right.

Mistress Richardson looked at her, her eyes narrowed, but in thought, not anger. Her red hair was gathered loosely at the back of her head and little wisps escaped in all directions. She was still a pretty woman, despite the hardships of her work and of raising what Telaine now knew to be a brood of seven children without the help of a husband. "I worry too much about my boys," she said, and Telaine interpreted this as acceptance of her apology.

"I can understand that," Telaine said. "My aunt—my other aunt, not Aunt Weaver—has six children, plus me, and she's always worrying about her two oldest boys."

"Your aunt raised you?"

"Since I was a little older than your Hope. I'd like to say I never gave her any trouble, but I'm sure she worried some about me too."

A faint smile touched Mistress Richardson's lips. "The way you talk to strangers, I don't doubt it," she said.

Telaine's eyes went wide, then she laughed. "Oh, Mistress Richardson, you do have a sense of humor!"

Mistress Richardson laughed, too, and stuck out her hand. "Eleanor."

"Lainie." They shook hands, grinning at one another in relief.

But all the time Lainie was making friends, Telaine couldn't stop thinking about what the real job was, and went back to making plans, over and over again until she once again paced her room or went out for a drink.

When the Baron's summons finally arrived, it came, thankfully, not via Morgan but by way of a servant. The Baron had an 'interesting project' and would Miss Bricker care to join him to discuss it? Telaine packed her tools into a knapsack and headed out for the manor.

She felt Garrett's eyes on her as she passed the forge, and chose not to look at him. There was no way to explain why she had to go to the manor, why she couldn't avoid the Baron. She couldn't explain why she wasn't in danger from him—or why it didn't matter if she was. It surprised her to find she valued Garrett's good opinion. Maybe that made them friends after all.

She had a pleasant forty minutes' walk to the manor, walking along the verge in the soft, untrimmed grass that had about as much resemblance to the manicured lawns of the palace as Irv Tanner did to Morgan. A bird flew overhead, calling to its mate, who responded with the same song. A breeze came up and ruffled the pine needles, bringing her the scent of pine and, surprisingly, lilac and mint. She'd have to follow up on that source sometime. She hoisted her pack higher.

The slouching attendants had been replaced by ones with more starch. One of them opened the door for her and closed it behind her. The entry was empty, the Baron nowhere to be seen. Quietly, hoping not to be heard, she called out, "Is anyone there?" No response.

She opened the dining room door and peered inside. Still no one. This wasn't the best opportunity, but it was worth taking advantage of. She started off down the right-hand hallway, the one on the southeast side of the manor, bypassing the music room and pausing to try each subsequent door.

The first held a billiard table and a few other gaming accoutrements. The door opposite was some sort of hunting trophy room, heads of wolves and deer and moose adorning the walls. It didn't seem to be a study. But the next room was. An oversized desk and leather-upholstered chair faced the doorway, bookshelves lined the walls, and a side table held a decanter of brandy and some fat-bottomed snifters.

"Miss Bricker," said the Baron. She gasped and jumped.

"I'm so relieved to see you!" she said, turning to face him with a guileless smile. "I'd started to worry I was the only one here. It's so quiet."

"You should have waited in the foyer," he said, and took her elbow to steer her back to the gallery. His grip was hard and painful.

"Oh!" She put on a remorseful expression. "You won't send me away, will you? I feel so silly, like I was snooping in your house."

"Because you *were* snooping in my house," the Baron said in a low, vicious voice. "You are here because I summoned you." The grip grew tighter, and she heard herself whimper like an injured dog. "I will not tolerate intrusions." He ground his fingers against the bone.

Telaine gritted her teeth and managed not to whimper again. "I didn't mean to," she said in a pleading voice. "I won't do it again."

"I believe you won't," the Baron said, yanking her along. He pushed open a door—Telaine hadn't been paying much attention to where they were going, except it was on the third floor—and said, pleasantly, "Come in, let me show you something."

He released her elbow. In the space of two breaths he'd gone from vicious to cordial, once more the country gentleman who'd met her on her last visit. The rapidity with which he'd changed his demeanor made her uneasy. His smooth urbanity of their previous encounter had made her forget the truth, that he was cruel and manipulative and cared only for getting his way. She was certain he was more dangerous than Morgan, who was at least predictable in his attentions, and she needed not to forget that.

The room was the Baron's bedchamber. She would have expected, from the man who had so coldly threatened Harroden, severe furnishings, a thin mattress, a few oil paintings in somber tones. She did not expect the lush, exotic chamber she found herself in. The walls were heavily upholstered, to the point of looking puffy, in jacquard silk in blue and pale yellow stripes. The ladder that stood beside the bed wasn't for show, it was essential for anyone trying to climb in or out of it.

Piled atop the frame were several mattresses, a number of quilts in colors matching the walls, and a dozen pillows of varying shapes. Sleeping in the bed would feel like drowning in a flock of sheep, though probably sheep didn't smell of roses as this room did. The tall bedposts supported a canopy of trailing net that draped and puddled on the floor at each of the bed's corners, decorative rather than functional, since it was unlikely the Baron had an insect problem he'd need to shield his bed against.

Tables matching the bed's height supported lamp Devices, both currently unlit because sunlight streamed in through long windows on either side of the bed. Smaller doors faced one another across the room, barely visible in the upholstery. The floor was entirely carpeted with a rug so plush the pile nearly covered the tops of Telaine's boots.

"Miss Bricker, I seem to have a problem with my bed," the Baron said. Telaine looked at Morgan, who wasn't smirking any more than usual, so it wasn't innuendo. The Baron knelt beside the bedframe and dragged the corner of something from between the top two mattresses. It was a heating Device of the type she'd described to Garrett. "I turned it off for the summer, but it started running again of its own volition. Could you perhaps take a look?"

Telaine knelt beside him, stripping off her knapsack. "This is a complex Device," she said. "But I've seen this sort of problem before.

Milord, the top mattress will have to come off."

The Baron looked at Morgan, who sighed and left the room. It was a sigh that came dangerously close to insubordination, but when Telaine glanced at the Baron, he didn't seem bothered by it. She might understand Morgan, but she didn't understand his relationship with the Baron. He obeyed orders, but he didn't act like the Baron's subordinate in any other way; they didn't act like friends, either. *Finish the job,* she told herself, *and it won't matter.*

Morgan returned with a couple of tall, healthy-looking young men dressed in the Baron's livery who moved the mattress, bedding and all, to one side. The Device thus revealed was a flexible mat made of flat strips and wires of metal woven irregularly together. It had crumpled on one side, and Telaine straightened it to lie flat. "That's half the problem right there," she said. "The other half is the complicated part. If you wouldn't mind stepping back, milord?"

The problem was obvious once the mattress was removed. Telaine reached across to the center of the Device and unkinked a couple of wires. She took a tiny pair of flat-nosed pliers from her kit and ran them over the crooked wires, crimping them straight so they didn't touch any of the others near them.

She had to stop occasionally and blow on her fingers, heated to an uncomfortable degree by the still-running Device. Once the wires were as straight as she could make them, she closed her eyes and ran her fingertips along the mesh, feeling for other defects. It still wasn't cooling off, so something else had to be wrong—and there it was, a redundant strip of copper the width of her thumb that had started to twist into a helix.

She took out another tool, this one a miniature set of tin snips, and cut the copper piece at both ends. She wiggled it out, crimped the cut ends tight along the rigid brass frame, and the heat immediately drained from the thing. "Let me test that it's working properly," she said, and knelt, feeling along the twisted wire cord covered with white cotton down to the switch.

It was nearly beneath the bed; she ducked her head under the frame and froze for a moment, stunned, then repulsed, then amused by what she saw. She captured the switch and stood swiftly, acting as though nothing were wrong.

She handed the switch to the Baron and placed her palm flat against the Device. "Some Devisers put extra strips of copper into these things," she explained. "They're supposed to be a redundant heat control system, but I've found they mostly just cause trouble. Do you mind if I keep this, milord?" She picked up the copper strip. The Baron waved his hand, giving permission.

The Device was cool to the touch. "Milord, if you wouldn't mind switching it on now?" The Baron tapped the switch, and the mesh began to heat again, reaching an uncomfortable level in minutes. Under the mattress, that uncomfortable heat would translate into a nice warmth.

"It's working fine now, milord," she said, and the Baron tapped the switch again.

"My thanks again," he said. "You are truly remarkable."

Telaine made herself blush and ducked her head. "Not to contradict milord, but I'm only average. But I thank you for the compliment." Was it he who used the...contraption...under the bed? Or Morgan? Their relationship was even stranger than she'd imagined.

"Pay the Deviser, Morgan," the Baron said. Morgan dipped into a belt pouch, but instead of holding out coins for Telaine to take, he gripped her wrist with one hand, turned her hand over, and with a little pressure caused her fingers to extend. He laid the coins in her open hand with what was almost a caress.

She controlled a shudder and kept her eyes downcast, hoping she looked demure and not repulsed. Much as she was reluctant to try to manipulate the man, it might be useful to let him believe his bizarre "courtship," or whatever he thought he was doing, was successful. Though after her discovery, she *really* wondered at his sexual preferences.

The Baron escorted her down the stairs, chatting pleasantly as she tried hard not to picture him bound, spread-eagled, with the iron manacles she'd seen under his bed. If that's how he liked his...ew, those red lips glistening, *stop thinking about it before you go blind.* It was none of her business what he did in private. Surely he wouldn't trust a servant to pleasure him, but Morgan? She hadn't gotten the sense that the darkly handsome man was oriented that way, especially since he was paying so much attention to her. Maybe she couldn't read him as well as she'd thought. She managed to say her obsequious goodbyes and get all the way down the drive to the main road before laughing.

CHAPTER ELEVEN

Summer turned to autumn. Across the valley, the few deciduous trees turned the hills butter yellow, fire red, dotting the evergreens like bits of colored paper strewn across a giant's lawn. To the south, geese honked their distant cries as they arrowed across the brilliant blue sky.

Telaine was drawn into the excitement surrounding the upcoming marriage of Trey Richardson and Blythe Bradford, to be celebrated with something called a shivaree. Sarah Anderson, Aunt Weaver's younger apprentice, explained this was a party and dance and concert all in one. It was all anyone in Longbourne wanted to talk about, but to Telaine it was simply a distraction from the task she felt was failing at.

She made the trip down mountain to Ellismere every three weeks, reporting on the progress she wasn't making. She still hadn't gotten into the Baron's study; she still hadn't explored the fort. On her second visit to Ellismere, she received an immediate response to her message reminding her that her time was short, that the mountain passes would be snowed in shortly before Wintersmeet and she would be unable to communicate anything she *did* find. There wasn't a rebuke hidden in the hidden message, but Telaine felt it all the same.

She was called up to the manor at least twice a week, and her one great pleasure was being able to work on the Baron's curio collection, despite her impatience at not being able to explore. But eight weeks after arriving in Longbourne, she got her chance.

The Baron welcomed her at the door, as was his custom after that second visit, but he was distracted. "Morgan and I are needed at the fort," he said. "Some ridiculous supply problem. You can manage on your own, Miss Bricker?"

"Of course, milord," she said, bowing. She had to work hard to conceal her excitement beneath an expression of pleased disinterest. Morgan joined the Baron on the doorstep, his head lifted as if sniffing something on the cool breeze. Early autumn in the mountains was still warm, but the crisp smell of the air told Telaine winter was coming.

Morgan turned to look at Telaine with his pointed smile. His eyes were disturbingly intent on her. He'd come to fetch her a few times, always without a spare mount, always maneuvering her to clutch him tightly, and despite her initial suspicions about him and the Baron, Telaine was now certain he had a sexual interest in her.

She met his eyes with innocent unconcern. His obsession might be countered for a while by her pretense at not understanding what he wanted, drawing out whatever game he was playing, but at some point Telaine was going to have to do something drastic. She wished she knew what.

A groom led two horses around to the front door. One was Morgan's and the other was an indifferent gray mare, not a bad horse, but suffering by comparison to Morgan's elegant bay. The Baron mounted and gave her a wave of dismissal, his attention already on the fort. Morgan fixed her with a long, intimate stare before following.

Telaine went inside, allowing the servants to close the front door behind her. She looked around. No other servants near. She decided to lay the foundation for her snooping rather than go straight for the study, and went up the stairs into the curio room. Her job today was to repair the self-focusing binoculars, although she had no idea what the Baron used them for. Watching non-existent birds in trees far too close to require long-distance vision, perhaps?

She cradled the exquisite Device, brass wrapped in leather with finely-ground glass lenses, then left the room and, ostentatiously sniffing, went back down the hall. She encountered no one; she kept on playing her part anyway. *Always assume you have an audience.*

She made a show of going into each room in the southeast hall, admiring the billiards table, wrinkling her nose at the trophy heads. Still no one. Where were all the servants, anyway? She almost never saw the same servants twice. It must be hard, working for the Baron.

The study door was locked. Telaine glanced both ways, tucked the binoculars under her arm, took her lock picks out of her boot, and worked at the lock until it clicked. It took far too long. She was falling out of practice.

The study was as she'd seen it before: desk, chair, bookshelves, drinks table. None of the drawers in the desk were locked, a bad sign. She went through all of them quickly but thoroughly. No correspondence from Harroden, no records of mysterious shipments. She closed the last drawer, looked around the room, and thought.

The room had been locked. The Baron had things in here he didn't want disturbed. Things he didn't want out in the open, even if the open was a desk drawer. Telaine checked the bookshelves, ponderous things of oak with gilded finials that looked like they could kill a man if they fell on him, though that would mean getting them to move at all. They were thoroughly dusted, so she wouldn't find any suspiciously clean books marking a hiding spot.

She surveyed the shelves, hoping she wouldn't have to check every single book in the room. Grandmama Alison the Royal Librarian would have been able to cast her expert eye on the collection and tell exactly how many there were. Telaine had to settle for "a lot."

There. Something had caught her attention, something so subtle her conscious brain hadn't noticed it. She scanned back over the shelves. A hair, a short, fine brown hair, lay lengthwise across two books as if it had been overlooked by the maid in her vigorous dusting.

Telaine grinned. *My dear Baron, if you're going to employ this old trick, you shouldn't let your maids be so thorough.* She gently laid the hair well to one side and lifted out one of the books, checking first to make sure it *had* been thoroughly dusted. Leaving her finger marks behind would be bad.

Inside the front cover lay a handful of folded letters. Telaine removed them one by one and scanned their contents. Ah, the letters from Harroden. Naturally there would only be one half of the conversation here. They were sorted in chronological order, oldest first.

The first was noncommittal, free of details, just some general hand-wringing about having to do favors for the Baron. The second was more interesting. Harroden had developed a spine and—so that's *what hold the Baron has on him.* Harroden was a seqata addict. That explained why he'd been so quick to suspect her at the ball and probably why he was working with the Veriboldan rebels, since the plant grew abundantly in Veribold. It altered the body at the cost of the mind—built muscle, improved heart and lung function, but made the user paranoid and manic by turns, eventually to the point of total psychosis.

Harroden claimed in this letter that he didn't care if Steepridge revealed his "little problem." He must have been in the irrational stage of the drug to say anything like that; seqata addiction could ruin his social standing and get him stuck in a forced rehabilitation hospital. That was part of her assignment fulfilled. Telaine moved on.

The third letter. Harroden repented of his earlier outburst and fawned over the Baron, promising anything he wanted if he'd only keep his secret. Telaine thought briefly of young Roger Chadwick, whose father was going to ruin both their lives. Harroden, the idiot, laid out all the details of his industrial connections and royal appointments and how he could abuse them for Steepridge's sake.

Telaine was disgusted at the man's belly-up toadying. She wished she dared steal these letters, but her word swearing to their existence and contents would have to do. The word of an agent of the Crown was supposed to be equal to evidence in court, but she'd never seen it tried. With luck, her uncle's soldiers would be able to retrieve these when they finally arrested the Baron.

The fourth letter referred in a more general way to "shipments" the way the letters she'd found in Harroden's study had, but the fifth letter referred to a shipment that was "the fourth part" of something bigger. The letter was written in response to a probably infuriated letter of the Baron's, because Harroden came across as even more spineless and toadying than in the other letters. It seemed the shipment had been damaged in transit and Harroden promised not only to replace it, but to increase the rate of the other shipments.

Still no mention of what those other shipments were. The one Harroden and the Baron had discussed had involved weapons, but Harroden had fingers and a couple of toes in so many pies it would be foolish to assume that was all Harroden was shipping him, especially since Harroden had access to so many other, more valuable trade goods.

Telaine put the letters back exactly as she'd found them, replaced the book and the hair, then stared a moment at the heavy desk. Something didn't seem right about this. She needed to find out what the Baron was receiving from Harroden, which would tell her whether he was smuggling goods for his own use or reselling them elsewhere. Barony Highton adjoined Steepridge to the west and was as cut off from the plains as Steepridge during the winter; there'd be a good market for trade goods there. Silverfield, where her Aunt Catherine was Baroness, was also a possibility, though less likely, given that winter would cut that trade route off for almost six months. The chances of the Baron bringing in supplies to help provision Thorsten Keep out of the goodness of his heart were vanishingly small. At any rate, she'd learned enough to know she should look elsewhere for further information.

She checked to make sure she hadn't left any traces of her presence, such as her own hairs, then left and crouched to relock the door, far too slowly. She needed more practice.

She'd just made the lock click back into place when someone said, "What are you doing there?" She concealed the lock picks in her sleeve and turned slowly, not a trace of guilt anywhere on her.

She waved the binoculars at the maid who had addressed her. "Looking for a source to imbue this," she said. "I think I smell one in there, but it's locked. I don't suppose you have a key?"

"Milord's got the keys," the woman, a plump lady in her thirties, said. "You best not poke around there. That's himself's study and he don't like it over much when we do."

"Oh. Well, that's all right, I'll find another one. Happen he'll let me use it when he's back." Telaine smiled and saluted the woman, who shrugged and proceeded down the hall toward the front doors. Wait. The woman had been between Telaine and the near end of the hall, but Telaine knew she hadn't passed her, and the only other door at this end of the hall was directly behind her.

Telaine approached the end of the hall and looked at the paneling, which looked like all the rest of the manor walls, but on inspection proved to be cheap pine stained and distressed to look expensive. Behind it lay steep, narrow stairs going up and down. Servants' stairs. Now that she was paying attention, she could smell something cooking. She decided to investigate the ground floor.

The narrow, uncarpeted stairs led down to a hallway that turned sharply to the right. The smell of food was stronger now, boiled vegetables and roasted pork and chicken broth mixed with spices. The air hummed with movement and the murmur of pots boiling.

Telaine poked her head around the corner and saw two giant ranges, each twice the size of Aunt Weaver's stove, fire glowing behind their grates. Slabs of six-inch-thick oak, scarred with cuts and burns, lined the walls between them, and another took up the center of the vast room, bristling with blocks of knives and a rack of carving forks. Women in dark dresses and brown aprons hurried between counter and pot, fireplace and stove. One small girl stood on a stepstool in front of a sink big enough for her to sit in, scrubbing a china platter.

"What are you doing here?" said an elderly woman with a loud voice who was standing at the central counter. She came toward Telaine, wiping her hands on her apron. "This place is off limits."

"I'm sorry to intrude, but I was following a source for this," Telaine lied, holding up the binoculars.

The woman eyed them with suspicion. "Don't know what that means."

"I'm a Deviser. I'm fixing the Baron's Devices. This one needs...it's a kind of energy Devices run on. I can smell the source down here."

"Surprised you can smell anything but roast chicken," the woman said, her face still filled with suspicion.

"I'm sorry to have bothered you." Telaine turned to go.

"You from Ellismere?" the woman asked.

"I'm living in Longbourne with my Aunt Weaver."

The woman's face cleared. "Our Alys is apprenticed to Mistress Weaver. You're her niece?" She gestured to Telaine to enter the kitchen.

"Come in and have a seat. Haven't seen our Alys in weeks. Don't get much time off."

Her smile made her wrinkled cheeks more deeply lined, the creases at the corners of her eyes giving her a merry look. "I'm Mistress Wilson. Alys is my daughter's youngest. Pretty as they come." Telaine agreed, keeping her opinions on Alys's character to herself.

"Here, have a taste of this," Mistress Wilson said, holding a spoon to Telaine's lips.

Telaine tasted and said, "That's delicious."

"That's supper, that is," Mistress Wilson said with satisfaction. "Say what you like about himself, but he sets a good table."

"Mistress Wilson, what *is* it they say about Baron Steepridge? I've been working for him, on and off, for several weeks now, and no one will say why he's disliked." Telaine helped herself to an apple.

Mistress Wilson's eyes went guarded. "Not my place to speak against the Baron," she said. "He's got his ways and they ain't Longbourne ways. Happen people don't warm to them as aren't the same."

Telaine was certain that although the woman wasn't lying, she wasn't giving Telaine the whole truth. Well, time enough to press Mistress Wilson on future visits. She was an interesting, pleasant lady, and she was a fabulous cook. *And she'd be a good asset to cultivate*, she thought, an agent's thought, and was surprised to find it had been her *second* thought.

"Don't let that boil over!" shouted Mistress Wilson, turning her attention to a hapless assistant at the fireplace. Telaine, munching her apple, casually exited the kitchen and proceeded in the direction opposite the stairs. The next doorway revealed a table laid with a white cloth and four benches drawn up around it. Servants' dining hall.

Opposite the dining hall were a number of closed doors; she peeked into a few and found storerooms for spices and baking needs, the housekeeper's offices, and a short stairway leading down to the wine cellar. Nothing interesting.

She turned another corner and found a short hallway with three doors, one straight ahead and two to her left. The two to the left, broader and squarer than normal, were locked with reasonably good locks Telaine was sure she wouldn't be able to pick without being noticed by a servant. The door at the end of the hall swung open easily, revealing bright midday light and a view down the valley. Telaine noted how wide the doors and the hall were. *Easily able to accommodate large, mysterious shipments.*

She scrutinized the locks again, then regretfully turned away. Whatever was in those rooms would have to wait until some time when all the servants were busy elsewhere.

She went back around to the stairs and up to the third floor. Time to get back to work before the Baron returned. Telaine hadn't caught a whiff of mint and lilac anywhere; how inconvenient. At some point her need for a source would be real. The binoculars were a simple repair, just a new spring, but they were beautiful and she couldn't help taking them apart further to see how they worked.

She was tightening down a minute screw when the door opened and someone entered without speaking. *Morgan.* She was as certain of it as if he'd announced his presence. He made no movement to approach her, so she chose to ignore him. Then he took a step, and another, and her heart began beating faster with anxious anticipation— should she continue to pretend unawareness, or greet him with that innocent, ignorant expression she'd cultivated just for him?

She moved on to another screw, waiting for him to speak, her nerves making her hands shake enough that holding the tiny screwdriver was difficult. Then he stopped, very near to her, and his hand caressed her spine, from the base of her neck to above her hips. She jumped; several tiny pieces fell to the floor. "Mister Morgan!" she exclaimed, squatting to retrieve the pieces. "Please don't take such liberties."

"But you're so attractive when you're intent on your work," he said quietly. He took a step back, but was still far too close for Telaine's peace of mind. She laid the pieces back on the pedestal where she was working, and turned to look at him. Now her hands were shaking too much to hold a tool at all. She clasped her hands and kept her voice steady.

"Mister Morgan, I'm here to work for the Baron. That's all. I would rather you not stand so close to me while I'm working."

"Does that mean you'd welcome my...closeness...at other times?" The pointed smile was back. It still didn't reach his eyes. She tried a demure smile.

"I don't have time for any sort of closeness now," she said. "Though I'm honored by your interest. Please don't be offended by my refusal."

The smile widened. "On the contrary. I find it...refreshing."

The Baron entered the room. "Morgan, are you disturbing my Deviser?" Telaine, her hands no longer shaking, had to clench one of them on that "my." "My dear, are you finished?" Funny how the Baron's "my dear" never had any tenderness in it. Funny, and a relief.

"One more moment, milord. I'm afraid Mister Morgan startled me and I dropped the last few pieces." Telaine twisted another screw, then held the binoculars out to the Baron. "Would you test them, milord?"

The Baron turned toward the window. "Perfect," he said. He laid them back on their pedestal. "Can I tempt you to join us for dinner?"

She put on a sad but firm expression. "I'm afraid I have another job back in town to return to. Maybe another time?"

The Baron lifted her hand to his red lips. "Certainly." The air of distraction he'd worn earlier was gone. What kind of problem would the fort have had for him to deal with? Getting inside the fort would have to be her next priority. Those shipments had to be somewhere.

CHAPTER TWELVE

She hadn't been lying about having a job in Longbourne. She stopped at the tavern for dinner, then knocked on Mistress Richardson's — Eleanor's — door. The little girl, Hope, answered, flinging herself around Telaine's knees.

"You're *late*," she accused. "I been waiting all day."

"Hope, I told you not to annoy Miss Bricker," said Eleanor. Her hands and face were red from washing, and she pushed a strand of her hair out of her eyes. "She's been watching all day for you. I couldn't stop her," she said in a quiet voice.

"I much prefer her embraces to the one I had earlier," Telaine said, then bit her tongue. Eleanor straightened and gave Telaine a worried look. "The Baron?" she asked.

"Nothing I couldn't handle," Telaine said. "Hope, why don't you show me the problem?"

Hope took her by the hand and dragged her through the large front room in which Eleanor did laundry and up a short flight of stairs that practically qualified as a ladder. She led Telaine to the room she shared with her mother, went to her trundle bed, and held up her rag doll. "She doesn't talk," she announced, then gave the doll a two-armed hug that would have crushed a real baby.

"Is she supposed to?"

Hope nodded. "She used to talk when Marie had her. Then she stopped."

"Can I hold her?" Hope nodded and handed the doll over. Telaine felt it all over and found, in the head, a hard yet still pliant knot. "I'm afraid this is going to take some work," she said. "And your ma will have to help because I can't sew."

Hope screwed up her face. "How come you can't sew if you're big?"

"Because I make Devices instead," Telaine lied. The truth was she'd always been awkward with a needle, despite everything master seamstress Imogen North could do. The discovery that she had a talent for Devisery had been a relief from the fear that she was fumble-fingered, period.

"Let's go downstairs," she continued, and Hope again put her small hand in hers. The gesture gave her a rush of pleasure at being trusted by this small girl, who reminded her so much of Jessamy when he'd been this age. He'd been mad after Devices even then, and that passion had never gone away. How relieved she'd been when he turned out to have the magical ability to match the passion.

Telaine went to the broad, age-worn kitchen table that had fed generations of Richardsons and pulled a handkerchief out of her sleeve, which she spread across its scarred top. "Do you want to watch? Only I have to cut your doll open. You might not like that."

Hope looked at her with the disdain only small children can muster. "She's not *alive*," she said.

Telaine raised her eyebrows. "Well then, stay and watch," she said with amusement. She laid open her roll of tools and took out her tin snips. They'd do as scissors. She cut the stitches along the seam at the back of the doll's head and removed the padding and the little Device. It was a knot of wires the size of a walnut, its round shape distorted, but Telaine thought that was on purpose.

She poked at the threads of wire, moving them to get a look at the interior. "Hah," she said, finding a hinge. It only looked like it was a ball of wire. She found a catch, depressed it with a flattened rod the size of a penny nail, and it popped open.

"This is easy to fix. You can come with me, I think you'll like this," she said. She carried the opened Device outside and around the back of the forge, feeling Garrett's eyes on her. It was a much nicer feeling than Morgan's attentions, but she still didn't want to meet his gaze, knowing he'd again have something to say about her safety with Morgan.

She crouched near the source, which had drifted only a bit, said "Watch this" to Hope, held the Device like a cracked nut in the center of the source, and pulled at the source to make a loose end.

Hope's eyes and mouth went round as the tiny ball of silver inside the Device began to glow a pale purple. It soon became bright enough to cast an ethereal glow over both their faces. Telaine clicked the latch shut when she judged the motive force had been imbued enough. Hope looked disappointed. "It has to be closed if you want your doll to talk," Telaine reminded her, and the girl's face cleared.

Back inside, Telaine repacked the Device in the cloth head, then said, "Now she has to be sewn together. Your ma can do that when she's got a minute."

"I have one now," Eleanor said. She had a needle and thread ready and re-stitched the seam in no time.

"I wish I could do that," Telaine sighed.

"Not hard to learn," Eleanor said. She handed the doll to Hope.

"Hard to do, though, for me. You have no idea how hard my aunt tried to make a needlewoman of me. Do you know how to make her work?" she said to Hope.

Hope shook her head. Telaine took the doll, gently, held it to her face, and said, "I love my baby."

A tinny voice said, "*I love my mommy!*"

Hope snatched the doll and ran away, up the stairs. "Say thanks to Miss Bricker, Hope!"

"Thanks," came a muffled voice, far above. The two women chuckled.

"How much do I owe you for that?" Eleanor asked.

Telaine shook her head. "I don't charge children. They remind me of my cousin, and I never made him pay. Well, not in the traditional sense."

"There's a story there, I wager."

Telaine grinned. Could she tell stories of her royal family? It wasn't like she had to name names or say anything pompous like "When my cousin Prince Jessamy, seventh in line for the throne..."

"My youngest cousin—you remember I went to live with my aunt and uncle when I was young? Well, he was born several years after that, so he thinks of me as his sister. Anyway, my youngest cousin always wanted to be a Deviser, ever since he was younger than Hope. And one day, when he was five or six, he stole my tools and wrecked them. Some of them are delicate and easy to break. I caught him banging away at this toy train he had, shouting 'Device! Device! Device!' I gather he wanted to make it move by itself." Eleanor laughed.

"Anyway, when I found out, I was furious. Devisers' kits are expensive. So I went into his room one day when he was out playing, and I fixed a dozen toy soldiers to march on their own, but light-sensitive, so they'd move only when it got dark. So he'd hear something moving around, but when my aunt came in, they'd stop.

"It was a horrible trick to play on a five-year-old, but I was sixteen and at the time I thought it was funny. Then the next day I explained what I'd done and told him if he ever took my things again, I'd find something else of his to ruin. Then I took the soldiers apart and showed him how the Device worked. He's been responsible ever since."

"That's both cruel and funny," Eleanor said, laughing again. "But I can see how it'd leave you feeling like you owed him something."

"So I pay it back to other children."

"Well, I have something I *will* pay you for, if you can do it."

"What's that?"

Eleanor furrowed her brow. "I don't quite know, but happen you can work it out if I tell you what I figure on. See, Trey's wedding, they're having the shivaree down by the lake. It's where the spring festival is held, there's a maypole and such. But this being nearly autumn, and them not wanting to wait until spring—"

She pulled a worried, annoyed face, and Telaine nodded agreement, because it was common knowledge that Trey and Blythe hadn't exactly waited for their wedding vows to consummate their union. "I wanted to do something to make it pretty. It's getting brown out there. And I was thinking, what about tiny lights floating in the air? But happen that's not possible."

Telaine leaned back on the bench. "Floating…maybe not. They'd try to fall down. But…lights on strings? They could maybe run between the maypole and nearby trees. It would be like a tent made of light."

Eleanor's face was lit up itself. "That sounds near perfect, Lainie. Could you do it?"

"I'd need to see the place, and I'd need a whole lot of string or twine. And components to build the Device. But, yes, happen I can."

Eleanor went to the door. "Ben? You got a minute?" Telaine heard his muffled reply. "Lainie needs to look at the maypole, something she's doing for the wedding. Can you show her, or are you busy?"

"In a few minutes," Garrett said.

"Thanks so much," Eleanor said, and turned back to Telaine. "I can get you all the string you need," she said. "And anything else."

"It'll be so pretty."

Garrett was a comfortable companion through the forest to the maypole, telling her things about the lake, the typical autumn weather, and what a shivaree was like. "Lots of dancing," he said, "lots of food. The bride and groom make speeches."

"Most of the weddings I've been to, the bride and groom's friends do the talking."

"Here, they talk about the families they're leaving behind and the family they're joining. If it's not a direct adoption, they might say something about the new family they're making."

"It sounds nice."

Garrett smiled. "Depends on how drunk they are."

The forest opened up on a clearing that might have been natural once, but had been widened by axe and saw until it was nearly forty feet across and roughly circular with the maypole at its center. Telaine walked around the maypole, looking up at its height and the trees circling the cleared area.

"I think I can thread wires back and forth from the pole to the trees," she said. "And maybe weave some in and out of the long wires to keep it rigid."

"Good thing you know what you're doing. I can't exactly picture it."

She looked back over her shoulder at him, standing at the edge of the clearing. "Think how surprised you'll be to see it."

"I'm always surprised at the things you come up with." He looked up at the sky again, and said, "Best hurry back. There's a storm coming."

When they were within sight of Longbourne, he said, "You having problems with that friend of the Baron's?"

"It's nothing I can't handle."

Garrett shook his head. "Morgan's a mean fellow. Might turn into something you can't handle."

"I don't think the Baron would let that happen."

He grimaced. "Baron's not much better than his pet."

"Even so, I try not to be alone with Morgan."

"You're alone with him every time he takes you up on his horse."

"He cares more about his horse than he does about me, I think."

Garrett sighed. "Don't think you're taking this seriously."

"I am. I promise I know what I'm doing, and I'm being careful."

He shook his head again, but said nothing more until he bade her goodbye at Aunt Weaver's back door.

"Thanks," she said, and went back to her room. Little sparks of light. Raw motive force would work—no, not for each one, it would be blinding. Imbued pieces lighting others. That would be easier. But how to make them stay on the string?

She pulled out the box of parts she'd scavenged, some from the Baron's Devices, others she'd brought with her, a few pieces from the forge Garrett had let her have, some coils of wire. A few of them were imbued already. She sat on the floor and began to experiment.

Telaine rocked and bounced on the wagon seat beside Abel Roberts. It had only been a week since she'd last ridden down the mountain with him, but he'd already forgotten her name, her face, and the fact that she lived with Mistress Weaver.

They again rode in silence, Telaine gazing in wonder at the changing colors on the mountain above and below them. She occupied herself with mentally coding messages to send to her uncle, reviewing the parts list she needed to fill in Ellismere, and thinking about how she'd make her tent of lights work.

That reminded her of her conversation with Garrett the day before. He interested her. She was sure there was more going on inside his head than he let on, as quiet as he was. And she liked his directness and his smile, the way it warmed his eyes and never failed to make her smile in return. Passing the forge was starting to be one of the highlights of her day. But he was more worried about her than he needed to be. Morgan was dangerous, but so far she was in control. She remembered Morgan's wide, pointed, mirthless smile, and refused to let herself consider the possibility she was wrong.

They pulled into the Hitching Station before noon, Telaine having rousted Abel at sunrise. Josiah Stakely came out to meet them and a pleased look came over his face when he saw Telaine.

"Miss Bricker! Back so soon?"

"Hello, Mister Stakely." She hopped down from the wagon seat and beckoned him closer. "Could you do something for me?" she whispered. "Make sure Abel doesn't leave without me. I'm not sure how long this will take."

Stakely winked at her. "I'm sure I can find some way to keep him occupied."

"Don't let him get too drunk," Telaine said. "I don't want him driving off the cliff."

"Abel Roberts can drive that wagon full to the eyeballs with beer," said Stakely, "but I'll keep him as sober as I dare."

Telaine thanked him and set off through the streets of Ellismere. She didn't remember it being this noisy and busy—then she realized she was comparing it to Longbourne's peaceful quiet. How quickly she'd become acclimatized to her...home? Not a home. Her posting? That sounded better.

The trend in individual telecoder booths hadn't reached this far east, but the telecoder office looked the same as all the other ones she'd ever used: dingy white walls, low-hanging Devices that shed insufficient light, and a long row of iron grilles painted white, behind which sat the operators, who generally looked bored.

She waited in line, then laid down her forms and the fee. "Waiting for a reply," she said.

The operator took her money and the forms without comment. This message wasn't going to the ultra-secure Device in the palace — there was no way Telaine would give that setting to a public telecoder operator — but to an ordinary, almost as secure Device that would nevertheless turn around her response in less than an hour.

As any operator would give her a funny look if she turned over a form filled with random numbers and letters, she'd had to break her message into three telecodes, which made her feel terribly insecure. Her greatest security was, of course, that no one was watching Lainie Bricker, but it didn't stop her worrying that someone might be suspicious about the stilted language her coded messages used.

Rather than wait at the office for her replies, she walked the short distance to Crafters' Way, which earned its name by having every conceivable kind of craftsman, smith, and builder you could imagine packed into a single long street. She came out half an hour later with several hundred feet of fat copper wire, a bag of brass eyelets, and the tiniest torsion screwdriver imaginable. She didn't need the last, but how often was she going to get to town? She deserved a reward after almost nine weeks of hardship, not to mention the outhouse.

Her return messages were waiting for her at the telecoder offices. She decoded them in a quiet corner, pretending to be reading the newspaper, in case one required a reply. The first was simply an acknowledgement of the information about Harroden's addiction. The second was a list of the items Harroden had groveled to the Baron about that he could easily smuggle or embezzle to the Baron, so she'd know what to look for.

The third, in plain text, read simply: STAY SAFE ALL MY LOVE UNCLE. She folded the messages and put them into her trouser pocket. This was more direction than she'd had before, but still left her with the problem of how to get into the fort and the locked store rooms. It was time to work out a more direct approach.

Abel hadn't rolled out of the tap room when she returned. Edith looked at her over the horses' heads, spat, then turned back to brushing them down. To Telaine's eye, they'd already been brushed thoroughly, but then Edith was a horse lover. Telaine poked her head into the tap room and caught Stakely's eye. He snatched the tankard away from Abel, whose head was bowed as if in sleep, nudged the man and said, "Abel, it's time to head back up the mountain. Abel, wake up!"

Abel raised his head, looked around, then slid off his stool. He seemed surprised to see Telaine at the door. "You going up the mountain?"

"I came down with you, remember?"

Abel shook his head. "Hop on up, then."

On the way back up the mountain, Telaine contemplated how different this journey was from her first. Then, she'd been facing a total unknown; now, she knew she'd greet twenty people on her way into town, trade nods with Garrett, spend the afternoon working on the new Device, have supper with Aunt Weaver, and settle into a bed that no longer felt lumpy and hard. She was actually looking forward to it all.

AUTUMN

CHAPTER THIRTEEN

Telaine sat in her bedroom, clad only in an underskirt and brassiere, and fingered the soft cotton fabric of her dress. It was a dark green that reminded her of the gown she'd worn the night this whole thing had been set in motion, but much plainer, with a skirt that flared out when she spun and a bodice that fitted snugly but wasn't too tight. The neckline covered her collarbone and was higher than any dress she'd worn since she was a child. The buttons were in the front, so she wouldn't need to ask Aunt Weaver for help. She couldn't think why she was so reluctant to put it on. *Because the Princess is a bitch*, she told herself, *and these people don't deserve to meet her.*

She'd never thought of her alter ego in that way before, because everything she'd done and said as the Princess had been in the service of the Crown, and it hadn't mattered what kind of woman she was. But the idea of setting the Princess loose in Longbourne...she'd promised Aunt Weaver not to manipulate the townspeople, but this went beyond that promise into a desire not to hurt any of these people, because they were her friends in a way the Princess's "friends" were not.

Telaine slid the dress over her shoulders and buttoned the bodice. It flattered her slim figure and—she took an experimental twirl—it would be fun to dance in, if anyone asked her.

She freed her hair from its braid and brushed its mousy-brown waves over her shoulders to fall nearly to her waist. Josephine had assured her it was appropriate for young unmarried women to wear their hair loose, but she still felt...could you call it naked, not doing your hair up? She brushed it again, unnecessarily, and wished she had some jewelry to wear, a gold chain, anything.

She looked at herself in the mirror and her heart lightened. There was her everyday face, unaccented by cosmetics, her hair hanging loose like a girl's. The Princess was nowhere in sight.

Aunt Weaver had already left when Telaine came downstairs, so she walked alone through the town's back streets to the forest. She followed the trail left by men and women and skipping children to the clearing where the maypole stood. Though the crowd was gathering beyond it, Telaine stopped to admire her tent of lights. Strands of glowing specks wove from the maypole to the branches and between those long ribs, shedding a warm glow over the clearing and the tables laden with food for the shivaree. She was proud of her Device, but not on her own behalf; the look on Eleanor's face when she saw it had been a greater reward than if she'd sold the thing to the Baron for a hundred guilders. One of the strands was sagging, but there was nothing she could do about it now. It still looked perfect.

She pushed through the crowd to join Aunt Weaver, who wore a dress of dark red wool and an expression less severe than usual. "You look nice," she told Telaine in a voice that said she shouldn't expect any more praise than that.

"So do you," Telaine said, not exaggerating. The dark red of the dress and the black of her hair set off Aunt Weaver's youthful skin. Telaine again had the strangest feeling she'd seen her before. Someone she'd seen at a distance, perhaps? The Princess had a hundred "friends," enough that Telaine might find dozens of people who resembled them. Maida looked like Elizabeth d'Arden, for heaven's sake.

Past the crowd, Blythe Bradford's father stood at the far side of the clearing. The townspeople had left a space, big enough for Eleanor and her children, minus Trey, to stand in a semicircle behind Mister Bradford. Next to them was a thin, dark woman Telaine didn't know, who had to be Blythe's mother. She and Eleanor were talking; from the stiff way Eleanor stood, Telaine guessed she wasn't all that fond of Mistress Bradford, and Mistress Bradford responded to Eleanor's conversation so tersely it looked as if the feeling was mutual. Unfortunate, if the two families had to meet often socially.

More townspeople were joining the crowd, chatting quietly, calling out to corral or silence children, but no one spoke to Telaine, and she shifted her weight, uncomfortable for the first time in many weeks. She felt like an invisible observer dropped into Longbourne, a witness and not a participant. She began to say something to Aunt

Weaver, thinking if she spoke, she might feel less disconnected, but Aunt Weaver was talking to one of her many knitting circle friends. Telaine felt awkward breaking into the conversation when she had no idea what she wanted to say.

A pure, beautiful note rang out over the clearing. It seemed to come from everywhere at once, rich and full as if they were in a concert hall and not outdoors. It was so beautiful Telaine didn't at first realize that voices around her were harmonizing with it, building to a chord that made her feel as if she were inside a symphony. Then she wondered, nervously, if she should join in. She was a terrible singer and would ruin the effect, but suppose this was something expected, something part of the marriage ceremony?

Just as she'd determined she should at least try, the high note ended, and the rest of the chord tapered off, not discordantly but deliberately beautiful. Silence pressed down, broken only by a cough and the wail of a baby, cut short. Then the crowd moved, rippling, dividing in half as if an earth mover were plowing a furrow through the clearing, pushing people to both sides. Telaine ended up separated from Aunt Weaver, standing by herself in a knot of people she didn't know well, and tried not to feel abandoned.

A murmur went up at the far end of the crowd, and soon Telaine saw Trey and Blythe, pacing hand in hand down the aisle formed by the divided crowd, their eyes fixed on Mister Bradford. Trey wore a gray vest and trousers and a shirt as white as his mother's efforts could make it. Blythe's dress was a pale green wool that was a perfect replica of Elizabeth d'Arden's fashion-setting gown. *Nice work, Josephine.* Blythe wore a circlet of autumn leaves in her dark hair and was radiant. Trey looked happy and a bit stunned.

They stood before Mister Bradford, still clasping hands. "We're here to celebrate the joining of these two young people," he announced, "and the joining of Trey Richardson to the Bradford line. Does anyone dispute?" Silence. Mr. Bradford extended his hand to grasp Trey's right wrist, and Trey followed suit. "Trey Richardson, do you of your own free will give up all claim to the Richardson name, to take the name of

Bradford to yourself and your children?"

"I do," said Trey.

Tears were running down Eleanor's face. Telaine felt a pang of sympathy for her. With the Bradfords having only one child, it made sense for Trey to adopt into their family, but it still couldn't be easy for her to feel like she was losing her son as he gave up the family bond he'd been born with.

"Join hands," Mister Bradford said, and Blythe took Trey's right hand in her left. Telaine hadn't realized Trey was left-handed. "Blythe Bradford," Mister Bradford said, and stopped. When he spoke again, his voice sounded rough with tears. "Blythe Bradford, do you take Trey Bradford as your husband, father of your children and strong left hand for all your days?"

"Yes," Blythe said. If she had been radiant before, now she out-glowed every one of the lights above her head.

"Trey Bradford, do you take Blythe Bradford as your wife, mother of your children and strong right hand for all your days?"

"Yes," said Trey, sounding certain and strong.

"Then exchange rings, and your heart's oaths."

Blythe took Trey's right hand and slid a ring that glinted, starlike, onto his middle finger. "Trey, I swear to be the strength to your weakness, now and for the rest of my life."

Trey took Blythe's left hand and said, "I'm yours, Blythe, strength to your weakness to the end of my days." He slid a ring down her middle finger, then held her hand. Gold and silver shone.

"Do you gathered here witness these vows?" called Mister Bradford.

"YES!" roared the crowd. Telaine, caught off guard, remained silent. *It's not as if I'm one of them,* she thought, and was surprised at how painful the thought was.

"Then as patriarch of the Bradford line, I declare this marriage sworn and sealed!"

The crowd cheered and shouted again, even more loudly, and Blythe and Trey both closed their eyes as the marriage bond took effect.

Then Trey swept his wife off her feet and kissed her; she put her arms around his neck and returned his kiss.

Telaine met Aunt Weaver's eyes across that divide. Alone in the crowd aside from Telaine, she was silent. There was some question in her eyes Telaine couldn't read, let alone answer. Then Aunt Weaver came toward her. "Now there's congratulations, and food, and song and dance," she said, raising her voice enough to be heard above the crowd. "You might say a word to the bride and groom, if you can make it through."

Telaine let herself be buffeted by the crowd rather than force her way through, and eventually it carried her past the bride and groom with barely enough time to congratulate them. The crowd spat her out near the circle of fairy lights, which was surrounded by folding chairs and trestle tables, some of them nearly bowing under the weight of the food they bore.

She sat down in a chair, feeling lonely and out of place. She couldn't speak to Eleanor, who was caught up in the whirl of congratulations, didn't want to talk to Aunt Weaver, and none of her other friends were visible. She got up and helped herself to a tiny cake. With her luck, eating food now would break some sort of shivaree taboo. She ate it anyway.

"What are you doing!" Maida Handly exclaimed. "You can't eat now!" Telaine, chagrined, her mouth full of cake, tried to excuse herself, but Maida burst into laughter. "Just having a bit of fun with you," she said. "The look on your face...!" Telaine glared at her and swallowed. "Looked like you were feeling a bit lost. Never been to a shivaree before, eh?"

"Our weddings, we have receptions." Telaine wiped away crumbs. "This looks like more fun."

Some men and women were gathering near a review stand made of boards stacked on trestles three steps high, and Telaine saw musicians tuning up to one side. She recognized violins and cellos, familiar to her from years of string quartet music, but there were other instruments she'd never seen before, and she'd never seen an orchestra, however small, include pipes and drums. Even some of the familiar instruments had strange shapes, as if they'd come from a foreign land.

"Singing first," said Maida. "Then dancing. Then happen there's a bit more singing."

"Does everyone sing, like at the beginning of the ceremony? That was incredible."

"That was nothing. Just tuning. No, tonight it's only a few, but during the winter...you make sure you come to the tavern, that's all I'm saying. We can shake the timbers if we try." Maida hopped up and drew them both a beer. "You dance?"

"Probably not the same dances you do."

"Not too hard. Happen you'll like it."

Telaine sipped her beer. It was darker than she was used to and she found she liked it better than the pale stuff. "Happen I will," she said. She scooted her chair closer to the table so Jack Taylor could make his way past it and sit next to her.

"Want to take a turn at singing?" he said, but the twinkle in his eye told her he wasn't serious. "I play the fiddle as well as the pianoforte."

Telaine shuddered. "You wouldn't want to hear me sing."

"Everyone sings, come winter," Maida said. "Even if they're bad at it."

"I don't know if I'll still be here come winter," Telaine said, and another stab of loneliness went through her.

Maida and Jack looked at each other, then back at Telaine. "We forgot," Maida said, and then there was an awkward silence, because Telaine couldn't think of anything to say to that. They'd expected her to still be here, but why? She was an outsider, however many friends she'd made; she belonged to the palace and that glittering world, to the life of an agent of the Crown. She'd finish her assignment, and return to that life, and they'd eventually forget her.

She looked away toward the review stand so she wouldn't have to see whatever it was Jack and Maida were thinking. Garrett had taken a place there, with Ed Decker and four other men she didn't know.

Maida cleared her throat. "You'll never have heard the like of this before," she said.

The six men were talking among themselves. Garrett looked up and scanned the crowd. His eye caught hers for a moment, then passed on before she could acknowledge him. He said something to the other men, who nodded, then the six stood up straight.

Garrett's eyes met hers again. He looked as if he were asking her a question, though she had no idea what, or how he expected her to respond. It was as if all her friends had conspired to confuse her tonight. Telaine smiled at him, but without real feeling; she was already working out a plan for sneaking away. Too bad breaking into the fort was even more insane than breaking into the manor.

Garrett opened his mouth, and that same pure tone that had silenced the crowd rang out, joined by other notes as the five other men harmonized with him, the lowest note being more of a rumble than a sound. Then they broke into song. The six-part harmony captivated her, so intricate and compelling that she didn't at first register the words they were singing:

> Come, my girl, and walk with me,
> On some old hidden way,
> We'll laugh, and fight, and merry be,
> And talk, just talk, all day.

Garrett's eyes never left hers. *It's for me,* she thought wildly, *he's singing it for me, why is he singing to me?* She glanced around the clearing, looked back at Garrett, closed her mouth, which had fallen open in shock, and wrapped her fingers around the handle of her tankard, gripping it hard. The smooth wood was warm, an anchor preventing her from falling out of her seat in pure astonishment.

> Come, my girl, and dance with me,
> Out in the pale moonlight,
> We'll sway, and swing, and merry be,

And dance, just dance, all night.

She felt as if every light above her head was pointed at her. Surely somebody else had noticed? But no, they were all watching the singers. Garrett was the only one looking at her, and his eyes…she blushed at the intimacy of his gaze. She ought to look away. She couldn't bear to look away.

> *Come, my girl, and love with me,*
> *I pledge you all my days,*
> *We'll talk, and dance, and married be,*
> *And love, just love, always.*

The men ended on another intricate chord, and the audience cheered and clapped. Dazedly, Telaine clapped with them, barely knowing what she was doing.

Garrett held her gaze for a few seconds after the music ended, and once again she couldn't understand the question in his eyes. Then he looked away, toward the other singers, and said something that made them laugh. *He wouldn't…they're not laughing at* me, *are they? Would he do that?* But they didn't seem to notice her at all. Some of the men stepped down, a few women stepped up. Garrett remained on the stand. She'd never heard a voice as extraordinary as his before.

And he'd been singing to *her*.

CHAPTER FOURTEEN

Telaine looked away from the singers and prayed her face didn't reveal her confusion to Maida and Jack. "Told you it was amazing," Maida said. Telaine nodded. Who knew what might come out of her mouth if she spoke?

"I think I need another beer," Jack said. He didn't notice Telaine's agitation.

"Me too. How about you, Lainie?" Maida said. Telaine shook her head. She buried her face in her tankard after they left, wishing she had a place where she could think. The noise around her was overwhelming.

The singers began again, this time with female voices soaring above Garrett's tenor. She didn't dare look at him for fear she'd catch him watching her again, singing to her again. This new song was an innocuous one about the seasons of the year, but suppose it had a double meaning? She drank again, deeply. Maybe the beer would wash away her confusion. Or, possibly, make her drunk enough that this evening would start to make sense.

So. *Think straight, Lainie.* He'd been singing to her, no question, addressing the words of the song to her as surely as if he'd stood in front of her and spoken them. Maybe he just meant to be friendly; maybe he'd seen how lost she felt and wanted to make her feel part of the celebration.

Telaine rubbed her eyes. *Or, you idiot, he could have meant it exactly the way it sounds, as a courting song.* But...Garrett? Her quiet, half-smiling friend who had never given her any indication he was interested in her other than as a stranger who needed help?

Unless...unless he had. If you replaced *quiet* with *shy* and stepped back a few paces, he'd done practically nothing but try to court her from the day they'd met. Stepping in to rescue her from Irv Tanner's gang. Coming to see how she was settling in. Those flashing smiles. His unrelenting concern about her safety with Morgan. He'd even asked her to share a meal with him, for heaven's sake. He'd done everything except come right out and tell her how he felt. So how could he suddenly gain the courage to be direct—indirectly direct, if that made sense—tonight? *Because he knows where he is when he's singing*, she thought. *And that's an incredibly romantic way to court a girl.*

Maida returned with a plate of food. "You should get some of this chicken," she said, tearing into a leg. "It's going fast."

Telaine obediently got up and went to the food tables, which were, fortunately for her peace of mind, far away from the singers. She hovered over the chicken legs, but decided on a slab of ham instead. Her mind taunted her, *You don't want him to see you all greasy with chicken.* She wanted to smack that inner voice down. She filled her plate automatically, even though her appetite was gone, then returned to sit with Maida.

She'd had plenty of admirers in Longbourne, but hadn't thought to include Garrett in the group, hadn't even considered trying to attract him, because…why? Because he was a friend, if a more formal one than Maida and Liam; she still called him Mister Garrett, for heaven's sake. But now she was having trouble thinking of him as only a friend.

How did she feel, really? If he was only a friend, why did the memory of his song make her pulse race and her cheeks flame? Why did she look forward to seeing him; why did his fleeting smiles make her so happy? *He's never been only a friend*, she thought. *You just weren't paying attention.*

"No chicken? Too bad," said Maida.

"Too bad," Telaine said, grateful not to be alone with her racing thoughts.

Liam Richardson dropped onto a chair beside her. "Dancing starts soon, and I want to dance first with you," he told Telaine.

"Liam, I don't know these dances," Telaine said.

"Not that hard," Maida repeated.

"Don't worry. Got a lot of men lined up to dance with you, make sure you feel welcome," Liam said, winking. "'Cept Irv Tanner. Went all green when I asked him. Don't know what you done to him, but I like the effect. He ain't nearly as bullying since you came to town."

Telaine heard Garrett's magnificent voice rise above the noise of the crowd, and shivered. "You cold?" Liam asked. She shook her head.

"Happen somebody walked over your grave," Maida said.

"Hush that! No talk of death at a wedding, thanks," Liam said.

The singing stopped, and the crowd applauded. Telaine joined in, once again with no idea of what she was applauding. "Now there's dancing. Don't go anywhere, Lainie, I'm coming right back."

Maida winked at her. "There's a man could make some lucky girl a good husband."

"You looking to marry?" Telaine teased, trying to regain her calm. Maida laughed. The sound of the band tuning up again drifted over the crowd. Movement became more orderly as men and women sought each other out. Telaine couldn't stop herself looking for Garrett. There he was, holding a beer and talking to some of the other singers. He was more animated than she'd ever seen him. Probably because she'd only ever seen him when he was trying, and failing, to talk to her.

"All right, Lainie, I asked 'em to start with an easy one," Liam said, taking her hands and pulling her up from the chair. "It's four steps, one, two, three, four. Then you change them a bit." He demonstrated. "Now you try."

Telaine took his offered hand and took a few tentative steps, *one, two,* and on *three* she accidentally hooked her foot around his ankle and nearly knocked them both over. "You sure you know how to dance?" Liam said.

"You go to a ball in the city and we'll see how well you do," she retorted.

"I'm teasing, Lainie. Let's try it again."

It can't be as hard as the Capering Widow, and that nearly crippled me once. She paid attention to the beat, and after a few repeats of the steps, Liam said, "Let's try it out there," and led her to where couples hopped about to the rhythm of the dance.

She tried to keep up with Liam and pretended she didn't feel horribly exposed. She'd never danced in public without the Princess's mask to hide behind. "*Relax*, Lainie," Liam said, grinning at her, and his comical expression made her laugh.

She tried a variation on the steps, and Liam matched her, his smile widening. He was right; it was easy. And fun. No one was watching her perform, no one was judging her dress or her hair, and for the first time in her life she could dance just for herself. She threw back her head and laughed, and Liam laughed with her.

When they finished, both of them out of breath, Liam said, "Not so hard, right?"

"No," Telaine said, "but—"

"Dance with me, Lainie?" said Ed Decker, emerging from the crowd with his hand outstretched. Startled, Telaine took it, and he drew her back into the dance with no time to say yes.

For an hour, two hours, she was never without a partner. Friends from the tavern and men she barely knew presented themselves one after another, and she learned new dances, and laughed at her mistakes, and danced again.

Finally, her feet sore, she cried mercy and went to draw herself another mug of the delicious dark brew before sitting down at an empty table. Men and women flew past, their bright colors like a moving tapestry, or like oils swirled together by an unseen artist. The empty, lonely feeling had vanished. How fortunate she hadn't given in to her impulse to leave. She hadn't had this much fun in years. Or ever.

"Will you dance with me?"

Surprised, Telaine turned to face Garrett, who'd come up quietly behind her. Her heart, which had slowed from the rapid pace of the dance, began beating harder again. She made herself look at him, afraid of what she might see, but met only his usual calm gaze. It threw her into more confusion than if he'd once again had that intimate, questioning look in his eyes.

"The next dance hasn't started yet," she pointed out. It was inane, but better than asking *Why did you sing to me?* She was afraid of what he might say if she did.

"I know," Garrett said, pulling out a chair to sit next to her. "I thought, seeing as how you were so popular, happen I should ask before someone else swooped down on you."

The image of a predatory bird winging down and carrying her off made her smile. "I guess that's true," she said. "I didn't know—" She paused. "I didn't know how many friends I had."

"More than you know," he said, and the way he said it made her blush, as if he'd said something far more intimate. "There, that's the next dance. Do you know it?"

"I don't," Telaine said. Then, daring, she stretched out her hand. "Teach me?"

He smiled at that, a familiar smile that made her cheeks go hot. Taking her hand in his callused one, he led her away from the tables and demonstrated. Telaine was conscious for the first time of not wearing gloves, how his hands held hers gently but firmly, not letting her fall when she nearly tripped because she could barely hear his instructions over the sound of her pulse roaring in her ears. "I think we're ready," he finally said.

They stepped into an opening made by the other dancers, and now Telaine did stumble, and strong hands kept her from falling. "Steady on," Garrett said, and guided her until she regained her poise.

He was an excellent dancer, leading her without making her feel dragged through the rapid pace of the dance. When she finally reminded herself *don't look at your feet, your Highness, give your partner your attention,* which was what her first dance instructor had told her constantly when she was thirteen, she could look at him without embarrassment. His eyes never left her face, though he didn't smile, just gazed at her with that direct, calm look she'd thought she was so familiar with. It was as if she'd never seen him before.

The music came to an end, but Garrett didn't release her. She didn't want him to, didn't want to let go of his hands that clasped hers, firm and gentle. She took a step toward him, wishing she could think of something to say that would let this moment go on.

"Lainie! Teach us one of your dances!"

Telaine half-turned, still holding Garrett's hands, toward Blythe

Bradford. "One of my what?"

"A dance from the city! I want my wedding to be on the front edge of fashion!"

Telaine looked at Garrett. Did she dare...? No one but she would know what it meant that they danced twice in a row, but was that kind of declaration what she wanted?

"Will you dance with me again?" she said, all in a rush, and Garrett smiled and nodded. She let go of his hands and ran to where the musicians waited. "Will you play something not very fast, in 3/4 time?"

"Sure," the bass player said. "Happen it'll set a new trend."

"Happen it might," Telaine said, and ran back to where Garrett stood. He hadn't moved at all. "Put your hand on my waist—right— and take my hand with your other one. It's a steady one-two-three beat," she said in a louder voice. "Just follow me and pretend you know what you're doing. It's not hard," she added with a wink, and Garrett laughed, a rich, warm sound that thrilled through her.

The music started, and Telaine began counting *one*-two-three, *one*-two-three, and saw other couples imitating them. "Now," she said, and handed off the lead to Garrett, who swept her across the clearing as if he'd been doing it his whole life.

Telaine had chosen the dance because it was the simplest one she knew. She hadn't considered it was also the most intimate. Garrett pulled her closer to him until she could feel his breath on her face; it smelled pleasantly of what he'd been eating, ham and cake and beer, which combined with the fresh scent of his soap made her feel dizzy.

She couldn't stop looking at his face, at the sweep of his brow and his dark brown eyes and his strong chin. *He's so handsome*, she thought, and wondered that she'd never realized it before. He never took his eyes off her, though he didn't smile, only slid his arm around her waist in a way that made her shiver with delight.

When the dance ended—far too soon; she should have specified a *long* song—he once again didn't release her. Telaine stood in the circle of his arm, breathless, waiting for him to speak. Then he let her go, and bowed to her, just a bob of the head. "Miss Bricker," he said, and walked away without another word.

Telaine stared after him, dumbfounded. What was *that?*

"Lainie, dance with me," a man said, and she mumbled something he probably took for assent. She was grateful that this was one of the men who didn't feel talking was necessary during a dance, because she couldn't have maintained a conversation after that.

Garrett had sung to her, he'd danced twice with her — granted, he probably didn't know that by high society's rules, dancing twice in a row with the same person was a declaration of intent to court, but it was still one more dance than anyone else had got from her — he'd been so close to her, and then he'd just walked away? What was he thinking? Maybe she'd been wrong about his feelings, or maybe he'd changed his mind, but in any case that hollow, empty feeling was back, and she didn't think dancing, or beer, would do anything to fill it.

She danced, and drank, pretending to enjoy herself, until the crowd dissipated, then she walked home, alone even in the middle of the crowd. Halfway to Aunt Weaver's house, she remembered the tent of lights and cursed. She could leave it up until tomorrow, but she knew she would only find excuses to delay if she didn't take it down immediately, and it *was* a magnificent Device that didn't deserve to be left out in the cold all night.

Telaine turned around and went back to the clearing, where men were taking down tables and hauling wooden folding chairs to wherever they were stored. Wearily, she began tugging at the strands. She'd set it up so a gentle pull would bring down a string of lights, but there were a lot of strings, and as she wound them back onto their spool, she thought of her narrow, thin mattress with longing for the first time since she'd arrived.

She wound some more, tugged harder to get one strand to come down, wound again. The chair-carrying and table-toting men had vanished, leaving her alone in the clearing with only the light of the moon and the glow of the long strands to guide her hands. It was late, and the night was cold, and she wished she'd left it until the next day after all.

"Happen you could use a hand with that," Garrett said. She squeaked and dropped the spool, where it rolled to fetch up against his feet. "Sorry. Thought you heard me coming."

"I was thinking of something else. You could start pulling down those strands while I wind. Thanks." Her voice sounded as shaky as her hands, which had begun to tremble.

"No problem." Strands of still-glowing lights fell down in curlicues around her. Telaine wound and wound and wished she hadn't drunk so much, because maybe then she'd be able to think straight. He'd left, and then he'd come back—did he mean to confuse her? If so, it was working. Her head ached with confusion and beer.

"That's the last of it," Garrett said, handing her the loose end. She wrapped the string a few more times around the spool, then tucked away the loose end, banishing a vision of the whole thing unwinding and having to wind it all up again, over and over.

Garrett held out his hand, and she gazed at it dully. He wasn't asking her to dance, was he? "I'll carry it for you," he said after a long moment, and Telaine, coming to herself, handed it to him.

"What happens to it now?" he said as they walked back through the forest, side by side.

"Tomorrow I'll remove all the motive forces and store everything in Aunt Weaver's spare room." He was almost as close as he'd been during their dances, close enough that she could smell the clean scent of his soap again.

"Sounds complicated."

"Just tedious." Why had he come back? Was he interested in her, or not?

"I'd help if I could." The back of his hand brushed hers. Then, tentatively, his finger stroked the back of her hand just before his hand slid around hers, holding her again with that firm but gentle touch.

All the nerves in her hand went off at once, burning a path up her arm and lighting up her brain. It was the oldest gambit of all, one a hundred men had tried on her, and she'd always teasingly but firmly rebuffed them. *That was the Princess,* she thought, *that's not me,* and she squeezed his hand lightly and felt him squeeze back.

They walked like that, hand in hand, through the woods until they reached the outskirts of Longbourne, and Telaine, unable to bear it any longer, said, "I don't understand."

He let out a low chuckle. "Wasted a lot of effort tonight if that's so."

"I mean—I didn't even know you were interested in me." He was a shadowy figure beside her and a warm, electric hand in hers.

"Never knew what to say. And you always had so many other men after you, like moths courting a lantern."

She blushed. How to explain she'd only flirted with them to protect her alter ego? "They weren't—it didn't mean anything. Just having fun. There's no one else."

She heard him let out a deep breath. "I didn't know how to compete with them on their ground. So I decided to compete on mine."

"It worked." *Not that you had any competition. How blind have I been?*

She turned her head to look at him and saw him smile, not a fleeting one, but a wide, brilliant smile that struck her to the heart. She'd never have guessed he had that in him.

They reached Aunt Weaver's yard, and Telaine held out her hand for the spool, wishing the night didn't have to end. Who knew if this could even last past sunrise, whatever it was? But Garrett set the spool down on the ground behind him and said, "Just one thing. I'd like to kiss you, Miss Bricker, if you don't mind."

It was the sweetest thing anyone had ever said to her. She nodded, afraid to speak.

Garrett stepped close and brushed his lips against hers. It was almost too light to feel, tender and sweeter than honey, and she felt as if she'd never truly been kissed before, as if all her flirtations had been nothing more than preparation for this moment. He moved as if to step away from her, and she made a noise of protest, put her arms around his neck, and kissed him back.

He was only startled for a second, then his arms were around her waist and he pulled her close, kissing her with an intensity that set her body burning with her desire for more. His hand slid up her back and under her hair to caress the soft skin at the nape of her neck, his gentleness a stark contrast to his kiss. She leaned into him and let everything else slip away, the chill of the night, the distant cries of an owl, the weeds growing at the edge of Aunt Weaver's shed. There was nothing but the two of them holding each other close and kissing as if nothing else in the world mattered.

When they finally separated, Garrett—Ben—brushed a strand of hair away from her face, touching her cheek. "You are so beautiful," he whispered, as if her beauty might fly away if he spoke too loudly. "Miss Bricker—"

Telaine laughed. "After that, I think you're allowed to call me Lainie."

There was that wide, brilliant smile again. "Lainie," he said, making her shiver at how his magnificent voice caressed her name. "Lainie, will you walk out with me tomorrow?"

She didn't know what that meant, but at the moment she would have promised him anything. "Yes."

"Until tomorrow, then," he said, and kissed her again, slow and tender, like a promise. Then he walked away, looking back only once before rounding the corner of Aunt Weaver's house and disappearing from sight.

Telaine let out a slow, deep breath, and bent to pick up the spool. She was going to take the memory of those kisses to bed with her. She touched her lips, and smiled. How beautiful, and how unexpected. She strolled toward the back door. What a tomorrow it would be.

When she opened the door, Aunt Weaver sat at the table in the darkness, waiting for her.

CHAPTER FIFTEEN

"What was that," Aunt Weaver said. It was not a question. She sat at the kitchen table with her arms crossed and her face at its most forbidding.

"That was private," Telaine said, feeling defensive of her kisses and the young man who'd given them to her.

"Wasn't talking about the canoodling, though that's a question too," Aunt Weaver said. "You told me you'd stop interfering with the people of this town. You forget who you are?"

Her words had the effect of an icy dip in the lake. Telaine dropped the spool on the floor and sagged into a chair. She had completely forgotten who she was. For the last several hours, she'd been nothing more than a girl named Lainie Bricker who'd danced and laughed and started to fall in love for the first time. Yes, falling in love. All things Telaine North Hunter had no business doing in Longbourne.

"I forgot," she said in a hollow voice. "I forgot everything."

"You got no business fooling around with that young man when you can't give him what he wants," said Aunt Weaver. "Not fair to him. He's a good man who never done anything to you 'cept have no common sense where women is concerned."

"I didn't lead him on."

"Not sayin' you did."

"I was caught off guard. Did you hear him sing to me?"

"I did."

"I didn't know how I felt about him. I swear it."

"Not sayin' you did."

Telaine knocked her forehead gently against the table. "How could I have let this happen?"

"Happen you played a part got too real," said Aunt Weaver. "You never let yourself be too much like the Princess?"

Telaine shook her head. "I hate the Princess," she said, and stopped. It was a revelation. The Princess was vain, and shallow, and

151

treated people like things, and she'd always known this about her alter ego, but until that moment Telaine hadn't realized she hated having anything to do with her.

"I like Lainie Bricker," she went on. "I like the life she has. Maybe—maybe on some level, I want her life. I know if I had to choose a role to play I'd pick Lainie over the Princess in a heartbeat."

Aunt Weaver shook her head. "You're not seeing it clear. Lainie isn't a role. Lainie is *you*."

Telaine, caught in the middle of a protest, went silent. Lainie *was* her. She'd been thinking of her as a separate person, but now she realized that, unlike the Princess, she hadn't ever had to tell herself how Lainie Bricker would behave. She hadn't seen the people around her as part of the game, to be manipulated toward her goal, practically since her arrival. She had been...herself, the self that hid behind the Princess's cosmetics and clothing and laughed at everyone who couldn't see through the disguise. Lainie Bricker was just another name for Telaine North Hunter.

But it was cold comfort. She might be Lainie Bricker in spirit, but she was still a Princess of Tremontane and an agent of the Crown, neither of which she could reveal to the people she was growing to love. She was lying to them even as she showed them her true self.

"What am I going to do?" she groaned, laying her face on the table again. Her head ached from all the beer, all the revelations.

"Finish the job fast. Start detaching yourself from Longbourne. Remind yourself every day what your real name is." Aunt Weaver paused for a long moment. "Break with that young man."

Telaine felt sick. The memory of Ben's kisses turned sour in her mind. Tears rose in her eyes. "I don't even know how to begin," she said, which was a lie. She knew all too well how to break a man's heart. The Princess had certainly done it often enough.

"Tell him it was the beer. Certain sure you put away enough of it." Aunt Weaver stood, and Telaine looked up at her. At this angle, her nose was a sharper, straighter line, her expression more imperious— and Telaine knew exactly where she'd seen her before.

She was older, of course, but even so Telaine couldn't imagine how she hadn't recognized the woman before. Well, of course she wouldn't have; why look for someone who was dead? No, it was impossible. She looked again. Not impossible, then, just mindboggling. The surprise drove the tears from her eyes.

"Try to sleep," Aunt Weaver said. She hesitated, then laid her hand on Telaine's head. The unexpected kindness made the tears rise again.

She sat at the table, sightless, until she couldn't hear Aunt Weaver moving around anymore. Then she picked up the spool and went upstairs. She tossed it into the store room, heard it knock something over that rattled, and went into her bedroom, closing the door as if it weighed as much as the oak tree it was hewn from.

She turned on the lamp, sat down on her bed and began unbuttoning her dress, but got only halfway before her hand fell to her lap. She looked at herself in the mirror. Astonishing how she still looked the same as she had only a few hours before. Astonishing how much the woman in the mirror had done and learned in that short time.

Telaine finished unbuttoning her dress and pulled it off, then hung it up on its nail. She needed to get rid of it. She'd never be able to forget any of this if it hung there mocking her all the time.

She got into her nightgown, turned off the lamp, and slid between the sheets. Aunt Weaver's face appeared behind her eyelids. It wasn't possible. She'd have to ask Uncle. He had to know, sending Telaine to her was far too big a coincidence if he didn't, but surely it wasn't possible. It would make Aunt Weaver a bigger hypocrite than her.

She opened her eyes and stared into the blackness. She couldn't let Ben court her with this false identity between them. It wouldn't matter that she only lied about her name and family, that everything else about her was genuine. It would still be a lie. But Lainie—*Telaine* could never bring herself to hurt him. So the Princess would have to.

A careless laugh, a mocking smile—"Oh, I was so drunk last night I can barely remember what we did!"—and the usual drill of studied ignorance of his presence, of refusing to meet his eyes. Oh, yes, the Princess was *very* good at what she did, which was keep any man at a distance no matter how it hurt him. Telaine rolled over and sobbed into her mattress. The Princess would do the breaking, but Telaine would have to watch Ben's face as he realized the Lainie he cared for didn't care for him. Her first love affair, and she had to kill it.

She drifted into a restless sleep, waking once to see the shape of the dress on the wall and sit up, heart racing, thinking it was Morgan in her room. She woke again before dawn to empty her bladder, then finally, as dawn made its way through her curtains, she slept for real.

She woke at nearly noon, head aching more from the restless night than from the beer, with a bad taste in her mouth (*that* was probably the beer) and a sense that everything was wrong with the world. When she came more fully awake, she remembered that was true.

She punched the mattress in anger at what she had to do, anger at the Baron for bringing her to this place, anger at herself for being so weak. Then she rolled out of bed and began, wearily, to dress in her everyday clothes. She avoided looking at the dress hanging like a green blot on the wall.

Removing the glowing strips of copper turned out to be an all-afternoon job. She unwound the string, laying it out in the yard, prying off each folded strip as she came to it, and some of them were fastened tightly. It was every bit as tedious as she'd imagined. *Next time, I'll do it differently,* she thought, then remembered there wouldn't be a next time and had to stop working for a minute while she controlled her bitter tears.

Then she wound the long, long string of wire and brass rings back on the spool, gritting her teeth at the memory that she'd had help with this the night before. He was working at the forge in blissful ignorance of what she was going to do to him. She swept the bits of copper into a cloth bag and wrapped it to the spool with the end of the string of lights.

It was after four o'clock when she finished. She was hungry, but going to the tavern meant passing the forge, and she wasn't ready to face Ben yet. She went down to the kitchen and dug up some leftover pork pie, which she ate standing over the sink. If she'd been in a better mood, she'd have been amused at the image of the Princess eating with her hands out of a pie tin. Right now she didn't want to think of the Princess at all.

She rinsed her mouth and hands and the empty pie tin, scrubbed it, and set it in the drying rack. She checked her watch. 4:35. When did people "walk out" together? What did it even mean? Were they going to parade down the main street for everyone to see? The pie threatened to reappear, and Telaine clenched her back teeth together hard to keep it down. She had to figure out a way to keep Ben from looking like a fool, going out proudly happy and coming back like a kicked puppy.

She went back up to her room and lay down on the bed. She would make a clean break and that would be that. He'd never know he should be thankful to her. Then she'd start pressing the Baron hard. If she could get him away from Morgan, she could manipulate him into taking her to the fort. Something about the new guns—they'd have the new guns, right? Suppose she said there was a flaw in some of the batches and she'd offer to check them over? It could be something she'd heard, some rumor floating around Ellismere. He'd probably believe that. Find out what Harroden was shipping, find out why, go down the mountain and never come back.

"Suppertime," said Aunt Weaver from the doorway.

Telaine swung her legs over and sat up. "What does 'walking out' mean?" she asked.

"Means declaring you're courtin', in public," Aunt Weaver said. "Bein' seen together, and so forth. If that young man has gotten to that point so quickly..." She shook her head compassionately. "Best do it quickly. Give him plenty of time to get over it."

Telaine pushed past her without a word. She ate in silence and then sat in silence, waiting in the sitting room on the uncomfortable chair. The rug curled up at one corner, revealing that its mat backing had been nibbled by mice. Aunt Weaver had tactfully retreated upstairs. It was so quiet she could hear her own heartbeat. That traitorous organ insisted on pumping blood through her body against all reason.

She heard a knock at the kitchen door. She closed her eyes, took a deep breath, and let a smile spread across her face. Let the Princess have her day. Telaine retreated deep inside. She didn't want to watch this.

She opened the door for Ben. He looked good. He'd cleaned up and was wearing, not his nicest clothes, but surely his second best. He smiled at her, and she nearly lost her resolve. "Hey there," she said.

He offered her his hand. "Could we walk by the lake?" she asked.

He looked puzzled, but nodded. "Something I'd like to show you there, anyway," he said. She linked her fingers with his and pretended not to feel the electric tingle that ran through her hand.

They walked through the woods to the maypole and then beyond. Telaine hadn't been down to the lake before, having been too busy for sightseeing. It was wide and reflected the blue of the evening sky, lined with rushes that at this season were the dry yellow of straw. A breeze blew them so they bowed as if in homage to that vast blue eye. Far at the other side, a pair of ducks left behind by the migration huddled their heads into their feathers against the breeze. On this side of the lake, the grass ended several feet from the lakeside, and ripples lapped at the rocky shore. Telaine stopped to admire the shadowed lake, the beauty of blue sky, green pines, and yellow rushes making her heart hurt more.

"Come over here," Ben said, tugging gently at her hand. He led her to a giant oak rising some sixty feet in the air, a few dead leaves clinging to its branches, its trunk wider than she could put her arms around. On the side facing the lake she could see the oak was dead, or if not dead, probably should be, because something had carved an enormous gouge at its base. It was deep and tall enough for two people to sit close inside.

"Found it when I first came to Longbourne," he said. He released her hand, squatted, and turned to sit. "That was a hard first year, not knowing anyone, so I'd come out here and watch the ducks, or the water. Nobody comes here but me. And you, now." He reached out his hand. "Sit with me?"

Telaine turned her back on him and looked out over the lake. *Try "oh, it's too dirty, can we go back now?" Or, the less ambiguous "I'm sorry but I've led you on." Or you could punch him in the face. You've never done it before, so this would be a perfect time to learn. Throw what he's shared with you back at him. He'd thank you if he knew the truth.*

"Lainie?" he said. She turned to face him, opened her mouth, closed it again. He was puzzled again but not unhappy, not yet. She looked at him. *This is a man I could love,* she told herself. *I can lie to him about my name, but there is no way I'm going to lie to him about something that truly matters.*

She sat next to him, letting him put his arm around her shoulder and taking his hand in hers. "I think it's a perfect place," she said, and turned her face up to kiss him.

They were gone for about an hour, talking quietly and kissing now and then. Ben, the perfect gentleman, never tried to do more than kiss her, although Telaine, feeling wanton, would have let him get away with a little more. He returned her to the back door before sunset, kissed her again, and walked away around the corner. She liked watching him go. She liked watching him come back. She was at peace with herself and the world.

Aunt Weaver again waited for her at the kitchen table. She arched an inquiring eyebrow at her "niece." Telaine had no idea if she'd seen that last kiss, or that they'd come back holding hands. She drew in a deep breath.

"I know I can't tell him my name or what I really am," she said. "Maybe that's a lie. But it would be a worse lie to tell him I don't feel what I feel. I can't lie to him about the things that matter. And I want this, Aunt Weaver, I want to be selfish and have something for myself just once in my life, and he is what I want. So I'll figure out the rest when the time comes. And I'm not sorry." *And if you are who I think you are, you'd better not say anything about my decision.*

Aunt Weaver looked her up and down. She nodded. "Hold on to

that, when it all comes crashing down," was all she said, and Telaine was too surprised at not being criticized to ask what she meant until the woman was already up the stairs.

Emotionally overwhelmed by the events of the day, Telaine went up to her room and tidied up. Then, although it was early, she undressed, got into bed, and let herself be wrapped in memories of callused hands and wonderfully soft lips.

CHAPTER SIXTEEN

She smiled at Ben as she passed the forge the next morning and got a real smile in return. "Lainie," he called to her when she'd almost walked past. She turned around. "You're going to the manor," he said. The direct, searching look was back.

"I'm going to be careful," she assured him.

"Can't help thinking you're making a mistake, with Morgan there," he said.

"I can take care of myself."

He frowned. "Nothing you could do if he decided to carry you off somewhere."

"I'm not going to let myself be alone with him to give him the chance."

"Wish you'd let me do something about it." He took her hand in his, rubbed his thumb across the back of it, and looked dismayed when he left a smear of coal dust. She laughed and gripped his hand tight when he would have removed it. "I ought'n't touch you when I'm all over dirt," he said. He sounded ashamed. It warmed her heart.

"You listen to me, Ben Garrett," she said in mock sternness. "I would rather have your work-dirty hand in mine than the lily-white hands of any shopkeeper or…or anyone else whose work leaves them with lily-white hands."

She dimpled at him, for the first time in her life using her nicest feature to reassure a man instead of captivate him. His eyes lit up, and without seeming to care that they were practically in the middle of the town square, he leaned across the rail and kissed her, lightly. "If it worries you, I carry a handkerchief," she added, taking it out and wiping the smudge away.

"Don't think you've made me forget about Morgan," he warned, but he was smiling.

"I know. I really think, as long as I'm not alone with him, I'm safe." She remembered the way Morgan had run his hand down her

159

spine and suppressed a shudder. Ben gave her a resigned look, but the smile was still on his lips as she walked away.

She waved at Hope, playing in the yard next to the forge, and smiled sweetly at Eleanor, whose wide eyes and slack mouth told Telaine she'd witnessed Ben's kiss. She bought a fresh roll from the bakery across from the Richardsons' and stopped to see Maida about returning for dinner before setting off down the road. It was a beautiful day, and everything was right with the world.

After just over a mile she saw a horse and rider approaching her. Her heart sank. Morgan. And after she'd assured Ben she wasn't going to be alone with him. Suddenly it wasn't such a beautiful day anymore.

She kept walking, choosing to ignore him until he drew up his horse a few feet from her and forced her to stop. "Miss Bricker. And without me coming to fetch you," he said, smiling his feline smile. "How very...eager...of you."

Telaine dipped her head in a bow. "I shouldn't have been so forward, but I heard something I thought the Baron ought know."

"The Baron? Not someone else?" Morgan chuckled. "**i'm crushed**."

"I'm sorry, Mister Morgan, but I told you I wish you wouldn't take such liberties. I can't think about such things right now."

He slid off his horse and approached her, reaching out to tip her chin so she would meet his eyes. "Can't, or won't?" he mused. "Miss Bricker, I find you utterly fascinating. **you don't have anything to fear from me.** I can wait you out." The pointed smile widened, never touching his eyes, and he slid the backs of his fingers down her throat to caress her shoulder.

She looked at his hand, then back at his face with her widest, most innocent gaze. "I'm flattered you find me so interesting," she said, projecting that same innocence with her voice.

He ran his eyes over her body while she pretended not to understand what his attention meant, then tossed her behind the saddle, mounted, and pulled his usual trick of kicking his horse into a gallop so she'd throw herself against his back to stay upright. Her gorge rose to think of him enjoying her body pressed against his.

It was all part of his game. He loved the chase, loved tracking down his prey and putting them at his mercy. He would wait for her to show awareness of what his attentions meant, then fear, then submission, which he would interpret as love. But she could only go on acting the naïf for so long before he realized it was a game. She had no idea how he would react at that point.

She did, however, have a good idea what he would do if he found out about Ben. Morgan already thought of her as his rightful prey, and if he thought Telaine's affections were engaged elsewhere, he would eliminate his "rival" in a way that would punish Telaine for spurning him. She could never, ever suggest to Ben that Morgan's attentions were becoming persistent. He would think he had to go after Morgan, and Morgan would kill him without thinking twice.

To her surprise, Morgan passed the turnoff for the manor and continued along the road to the fort, which was exactly where Telaine wanted to go. It amused her that her carefully planned ploy wasn't necessary after all. Then she became worried. Why would the Baron need her there?

The fort was as dour and grim as the manor, as if everything the Baron touched turned to lead. The fortress outer wall was made of upright timbers, each a foot around and sharpened like spikes at the top, and extended in both directions for hundreds of feet. It was a lot of timber all in one place, and Telaine had to remind herself the trees had been sacrificed for the kingdom she loved. They served Tremontane just as she did, which was an unsettling thought. She hadn't been called on to give up her life, thank heaven, and she wasn't sure what she would do if she was.

A gate made of squared-off logs sat in what Telaine guessed was the center of the wall. It was open and flanked by two of those grubby soldiers Telaine had seen on her first night in town. Morgan passed through the gate without acknowledging them. They looked up at her where she sat behind Morgan with a complete lack of interest, as if she were a bundle of cloth Morgan had for some reason decided to haul around with him. It was unsettling and comforting at the same time; she didn't know how much leering she could endure without shouting at someone.

The space beyond the gate was long and narrow, almost an alley between the fort's two walls. Though the fort stretched out for hundreds of feet in both directions, it was no more than seventy or eighty feet from the outer wall to the inner one.

Stone buildings, these made of much larger blocks than those used in Longbourne, stood against the outer and inner walls, some of them short with slate roofs, others tall and round with pointed tops. They looked like giant versions of the type of buildings a child might construct, down to the impractical cones perched atop the towers.

Directly ahead of the gate, flush against the high, crenellated inner wall, stood a stone keep only two stories tall. It looked even more like a child's plaything, complete with soldiers striding casually along the top of the wall with their weapons swinging loosely by their sides. The inner wall also extended out of sight in both directions, curving as if holding the pass cradled in its grasp. Telaine guessed both walls ended where the mountains began. Thorsten Keep looked like it was meant to plug this gap in the Rockwild Range.

Morgan dismounted and held out his hands to catch her; she endured his hands on her waist and managed to look innocently grateful instead of disgusted. She could feel his attention on her as she turned away.

"It's not what I expected," she said honestly. Only a few of the soldiers seemed to be properly turned out, clean and careful of their weapons. She saw no women among them, which was unusual. Maybe women were better at getting out of postings as bad as this one. Everywhere she looked seemed dirty, depressing, or oppressive.

Morgan bowed her toward the keep, where another unkempt soldier stood; he opened the door for them as if it were an imposition on his busy staring-into-the-air schedule. The door opened on a short hallway with a low, curved ceiling of stone that looked and smelled like a tunnel deep inside a mountain, wet and loamy. The passage led to a square room, two stories tall, that looked as if it had simply been hollowed out of the granite blocks the keep was made of; it was perfectly cubical, with a flight of stairs with no handrail rising along one of the walls to an open balcony on the second story.

The floor was covered with a mildew-stained Veriboldan carpet with a yellow and red pattern, and the whiffs of sourness that sprang up wherever Telaine stepped warred with the stink of old smoke from the sconces high on the wall. They burned steadily, but were inadequate to light a room this size; an iron chandelier full of ancient candles hung from the ceiling, unlit, as if the keep's deficiencies would be worse if they were clearly visible. Soldiers in untidy green and brown uniforms stood at inattention here and there throughout the room.

A table like a discus, with its edges rounded off with wear, and several chairs with threadbare padding occupied the center of the room. The Baron stood at this table, talking to a man who wore a captain's insignia. He was one of the few who looked like he wasn't playing soldier; his uniform was clean, and his boots were polished and his blond hair cut military-short the way her cousin Jeffy's had been the last time she saw him. Neither man paid any attention to Morgan and Telaine as they approached.

"I still say it's unnecessary, milord," said the captain. He was in his late forties and had a scar that extended beneath his hair, along his hairline, and terminated above his left ear. "We've plenty of them already. We should send these back and have them repaired professionally."

The Baron said, "I prefer to think of it as having a precautionary surplus. And I already have a professional." He looked up at Telaine and gestured in her direction. "Miss Bricker, Captain Edmund Clarke. I've been explaining to him that you're the solution to our problem."

Captain Clarke bowed. "No offense to your capabilities, Miss Bricker, but the military does things a certain way, and bringing in a civilian, ah, technician isn't one of them."

"Good morning, milord, captain," Telaine said. "Could you

explain what it is you're disagreeing about?"

"Miss Bricker, how much do you know about the situation along the border here?" the Baron asked.

"Very little, I'm afraid," she lied. "I know this fort holds Thorsten Pass against a Ruskalder attack. That's about it."

"Very good, Miss Bricker. If such an attack were to come, Thorsten Keep would be the only line of defense. As such, it must remained stocked as if for a siege at all times. We receive shipments of food, clothing, arms, et cetera, all year round. The problem now is that we've received a shipment of weapons that were damaged in transit. Devices.

"We've already received a replacement, but Captain Clarke and I disagree on what to do with the damaged shipment. Captain Clarke —" he nodded politely to the other man — "thinks we should return it to the central armory. I believe *you* —" he nodded politely to her — "might be able to repair them. This would allow us to maintain a surplus and save the military on the time and effort needed to process the weapons."

Telaine wanted to laugh at how her made-up rumor had turned out to be true. But...shipments coming from the government *and* from Harroden? Telaine made a mental note to inquire about how this fort was supplied, and how often. She blushed and cast her eyes down. "I'm so honored, milord, that you think I'm capable," she said. "But the captain might be right. I'd have to see the weapons before I could promise anything."

"Milord, I insist we not allow this young woman to see classified government ordnance!" said Captain Clarke.

"Miss Bricker has already demonstrated remarkable good sense and discretion," the Baron said. Telaine wondered if he knew she knew about the little secret under his bed. "And the design of these weapons is not so different from the civilian model."

He drew out a chair and sat down as if enthroning himself. "Suppose we make a compromise? Bring *one* of the weapons here for Miss Bricker to examine. If she agrees she can repair it, we allow her access accompanied by a soldier at all times. If she can't, then she hasn't seen inside your defenses and we send the shipment back."

Captain Clarke looked as if he wanted to argue, but couldn't. "That's...acceptable, milord," he said. He snapped his fingers at a soldier, who sauntered over. "Bring me one of the weapons from the damaged shipment. And move quickly!"

The soldier stepped up his pace until he reached the passage, at which point he reverted to sauntering. Telaine felt sympathy for Captain Clarke. What kind of captain was forced to make compromises with a civilian ally, even one technically his superior?

They waited in silence for the man to return. Telaine let herself openly gawk at the room, though in truth she found it boring; the stair was the only route to the upper story, there were no extra rooms on the bottom floor, and only one way out. It might as well have been the inside of that hypothetical child's block castle.

The Baron idly picked at his nails with his belt knife. Captain Clarke stood at parade rest, not meeting anyone's eyes. Morgan watched her like a lion stalking a water hole, seeing what prey came calling. She ignored him and reminded herself she had him under control. *For the moment*, she thought, and refused to allow herself to fear.

The soldier returned, holding a long-barreled gun Device which he handed to the Baron. *Not to Captain Clarke. And the captain doesn't protest. Interesting.* The Baron handed the gun, butt end first, to her.

She turned it over in her hands, awkwardly due to its length. The casing was mostly polished wood; that was an innovation, making it lighter than current civilian issue weapons but still heavy. How familiar should she seem with gun Devices? Her cousin Mark was mad for guns, and she'd heard him talk about them so often that she could name most of the parts of this gun and guess at how it went together despite never having seen it before. Best to err on the side of ignorance; it was working for her so far.

"Captain Clarke, can you explain how this works?" she asked. "I understand you pull the trigger—"

"*Squeeze* the trigger," the captain said. He sounded smug, as if he'd been proven right about something.

"Squeeze the trigger, thank you captain, and the motive force propels the bullet from the barrel and rotates the next bullet into place. But I'm unfamiliar with this piece, and I'm sorry if I'm being stupid, but I don't see the bullets or the motive force. And I'd rather not see if the barrel is rifled until I'm sure I won't be pointing a loaded gun at my head." There was no chamber that she could see, just a wide slot at the top in front of the hammer. That smug tone had stung her into showing off.

The captain looked more surprised and less smug. "It's rifled, yes," he said, "but the firing assembly is different. It's a compromise between the old black powder rifles and the new six-guns. The old models had the motive force embedded in the gun, imbued enough to fire six bullets. Then you'd have to reload the gun and wait for someone to re-imbue it. With the new model, the bullets come in a cartridge wheel with the motive force installed in the wheel. Snap the—"

He looked fully at the gun for the first time. "Stentson, why are there no bullets in this weapon? Bring me a box at once!" Stentson ambled off again. Telaine wondered why Clarke put up with such flagrant disrespect. She knew little of the military, but surely that man ought to be disciplined.

"At any rate," Clarke continued, "the wheel goes in at the top, you lock it in place with a push of your finger, and cock the hammer. When you squeeze the trigger, the hammer brings the firing assembly into contact with the motive force. You take your six shots, cocking the hammer each time—that unfortunately slows the rate of fire, but I'm told there's no helping that—and eject the wheel with this button, here. Then you slap another cartridge in and you're set to fire again."

Clarke had apparently forgotten Telaine was a civilian in his enthusiasm for the new weapon. Telaine was impressed herself, and she'd never owned or fired a gun in her life. She looked it over, examining it for obvious defects and for any evidence of how to open it up.

"How do you know the gun is failing and not the bullets?" she asked.

"The bullets work fine in the guns from the other shipments."

"I'd probably need to see it shoot before I could draw any conclusions." She had to remind herself she was here for espionage, not Devisery, but this was too much of a challenge not to be exciting.

Stentson returned and offered a box to the Baron, but Clarke intercepted it. The Baron didn't seem offended. Clarke opened the box and removed what looked like a six-pointed snowflake of silver holding brass and copper bullets at each tip. Clarke pushed it into the gun with a click, then looked around for a target. On the far wall was a wooden shield, a decoration left over from some long-ago commander of Thorsten Keep; Clarke pointed the gun at it and fired.

It was less than spectacular. Something snapped, and the bullet flew a few feet out of the gun and bounced off the mildewed carpet. Clarke lowered the gun and turned to look at Telaine. "Well?" he said.

"May I try?" she asked. When he furrowed his brow at her, she added, "I won't have any better luck than you, captain, but sometimes if I feel a Device malfunction, it gives me an idea of what's wrong." She already knew what was wrong. She just wanted to feel what it was like to shoot it.

Clarke held it out to her, and she took it in both hands, braced herself, and pointed it at the shield. She heard Morgan, whose attention she could still feel on her, suck in a breath. *So you find this arousing, do you? Wonderful. And I thought I'd done well at cooling your ardor today.* She pulled—squeezed—the trigger, felt the motive force miss its striking surface, and heard the bullet scrape down the barrel and fall to the floor.

She lowered the weapon. "I think I know what's wrong, but I'd like to take this one apart to make sure," she said. "May I use the table, milord?"

The Baron waved to indicate she should take a seat. "I'm going to watch," he announced. "Morgan, go find something else to do. I believe my Deviser finds your presence unsettling." Telaine kept her attention on the gun, but she felt Morgan smoldering with anger before he turned and left the keep. Someday Morgan might decide he no longer cared about whatever hold the Baron had over him, and then... it didn't bear thinking about.

She focused her attention on laying out a handkerchief and her tools. The handkerchief had a black smudge on one corner that eased her heart. Ben was waiting for her to come back. Morgan's attentions meant nothing beside that.

The hardest part was cracking the case. That was common. People wanted to see the outside of a Device, not its whirling, clicking innards, and they certainly didn't want their Devices coming apart unexpectedly.

"Oh. I could use one of the rifles that works, please," she said absently, not noticing she had addressed the Baron until he'd risen from his chair and spoken to a soldier. The gun appeared like magic on the table beside her. She took that one apart, too.

"Care to take a look at this, milord?" she said, and the Baron edged his chair closer to hers. Strange how she didn't feel the menace from him that she did from Morgan, despite her conviction that he was the more dangerous man.

She used a slim rod to point to the affected pieces. "The broken one has a misaligned firing assembly. The motive force propels the bullet and then moves the next one to the firing chamber, here, you see? In the working gun, this piece, and this, line up properly. But I think you can see how in the broken gun, this piece is in the wrong place. I loosen the screw, rotate the piece just so, tighten the screw, and the gun works fine. It's a simple repair."

She looked at the Baron. He looked ecstatic, as if experiencing physical bliss. "Miss Bricker, you are a marvel," he said. He was so close she was afraid he might kiss her in the throes of whatever passion he was feeling, but he sat back and stared at the disassembled weapons.

"Prove that it works," he instructed her, his voice icy. That rapid shift in his mood — *that's why he's more dangerous than Morgan. Don't forget it, Telaine.* She quickly reassembled the guns and handed him the previously broken one.

He snapped the cartridge wheel into the Device, pointed it at the shield, and fired without taking careful aim. The bullet pinged off the stone wall and flew off into the shadows. Telaine sat frozen, aware there was no reason that bullet shouldn't have come back to hit her. The glamour of the weapons vanished.

Captain Clarke picked up the one weapon and held out his hand for the other. He examined both. "Excellent work," he said absently. He thumbed the eject button and caught the wheel in his hand. "Milord, if you will allow one of my men to accompany the young lady, I will allow her to repair the defective shipment."

Telaine bowed to the Baron. First step complete. She'd still have to find out what Harroden's shipments were, but she'd made it through the door.

CHAPTER SEVENTEEN

Morgan was gone when they emerged from the dank keep. The Baron didn't seem perturbed by his absence, mounting as if he didn't expect to wait for him.

"Captain, see that your men know Miss Bricker will be coming daily," he said, not bothering to ask Telaine if she was willing to work on this every day or, for that matter, if she would officially take the job. Did this mean she was working for the government? Could the fort afford to pay her? Fortunately, she didn't need their money, but it ruffled her professional pride.

She followed him out the gate, but he made no move to take her up on his horse. Apparently she was walking home.

"I beg your pardon, milord," she said, not having to try hard to act nervous, "but tomorrow is my day to go to Ellismere and send word to my family. Is it—will you mind terribly—can I be allowed to start the day after?"

The Baron gave her a hard-eyed stare and her nervousness became more real. "Do as you like," he said curtly. He kicked his horse in the sides harder than was necessary and the animal broke into a ground-eating stride.

"Miss Bricker," said the captain, nodding to her politely. "When you arrive, please come immediately to the keep and I will assign one of my men to assist you." Had she heard the slightest emphasis on "my"? She wondered at Stentson's deference to the Baron over his commanding officer. She would bet those professional-looking soldiers were the men who actually obeyed when Clarke gave an order. It disturbed her that the slovenly ones outnumbered the professionals by so much.

Telaine walked back to the town, expecting Morgan to swoop down on her at any moment. He didn't appear. It was dinnertime, so she went into the tavern and shared a table with Josephine Adderly, who was glowing with the success of Blythe Bradford's wedding dress.

"Everyone wants one like it!" she exclaimed. "Lainie, I can't thank you enough for providing me with the pattern."

"It was hardly a pattern, just a set of drawings," Telaine protested. "I still can't believe you were able to recreate the dress from a picture."

"Well, I can't believe you built those lights, they were so beautiful," Josephine said. "So romantic." Her eyes went merry, and she added, "*Very* romantic for some, I hear."

"What do you mean?"

"Don't be silly. Everyone knows you're walking out with Ben Garrett," Josephine said in a low voice, as if despite her words it was a great secret. "Oh, Lainie, I'm so happy for you! I know more than a handful of girls who are so jealous of you. That voice..." She sighed and closed her eyes. "Is it true he carried you home from the shivaree, draped in those lights?"

"No!" Telaine exclaimed, laughing. "Really, Josephine, it's only been a day, and we haven't even gone out in public. How do these rumors get started?"

"I don't know. But I do know Mister Garrett was mooning about all day yesterday with the silliest smile on his face. Nobody makes that sort of face 'less they're courting. And tale is he sang to you right in front of everyone and nobody noticed."

"If nobody noticed, how does anyone know?"

"Well, *somebody* noticed. And *I* saw you were awfully close during the dance, *and* you danced twice with him in a row, and I know what that means. I read the social news from the city."

Telaine covered her burning face with her hands. "Do I have no secrets left?" *Let's hope I do.*

"Maybe," said Josephine, with a satisfied smile. "Is he a good kisser?"

"Josephine!" Telaine exclaimed. Josephine laughed like she'd made the funniest joke of all time.

She finished her meal and strolled off down the street toward home, feeling cheerful. She'd always enjoyed passing by the forge; now she knew why. Ben had his back to her, working some yellow-hot metal, when she approached, but before she could reach the forge rail Eleanor came out of nowhere, grabbed her arm and dragged her into the laundry.

"You and Ben," she said, and wrapped her arms around Telaine. "I'm so happy for you both!"

"We're just walking out, Eleanor," Telaine said, feeling her cheeks heat again.

"You obviously don't understand what that means," said Eleanor, releasing her. "Oh, my dear, he's like a different man."

"I don't understand."

"He's been my neighbor for four years, always quiet, mostly keeps to himself," Eleanor said. "Took a while for folks to get to know him, but then there was Wintersmeet that first year, and he sang for us... well, you know how he can sing, of course you do, and it made him well-liked, gave him a way to fit in, but he still didn't talk much. Friendly, but shut off. Everyone knows what he's like, they don't mind his ways.

"But all yesterday, he was saying hey to anyone who passed by, smiling and talking like he usually only does when he's been singing. He went to the tavern for supper. Don't think he's been in there since last Wintersmeet, and that was for the chorals. You've changed him, dear. And in just one day. It's amazing, it truly is."

And I was going to destroy all that. Thank heaven I came to my senses. "That's...quite a burden to bear," she said.

Eleanor steered her to sit at the broad table. "I didn't mean to lay that on you. Happen I exaggerated." She patted Telaine's hand. "Lainie, walking out together doesn't mean a promise. It's how you get to know each other, what you're like together. But a man like Ben, when he gives his heart, he gives it all at once. Remember that, will you?"

"Happen you should give him a talk about not expecting too much of a girl," Telaine said, and laughed. "No, don't, I wasn't serious," she added when Eleanor firmed her chin in the way she did when she was planning on giving someone a good stiff lecture. "But you have to admit it's fearsome to have that much power over a man." The Princess would have loved to be in her position, to know she could make Ben dance to her tune. Telaine didn't have any idea what to do with it.

"Fearsome and beautiful," Eleanor said. "My Robert was like that. Loved like a bonfire burning."

Robert had died only three years before. "I wish I could have known him."

Eleanor nodded. "I miss him still," she said, dry-eyed and resigned. "But I have his children. And the way Trey and Blythe are going, I might have his grandchildren soon."

"They are rather like rabbits, aren't they?" Telaine said, and Eleanor laughed and nodded.

Ben still had his back to her when Telaine left the laundry. She stood at the rail, watching him, ignoring the murmured conversation a couple of old men were having nearby in which they alternated between staring at her and staring at Ben.

He wore a sleeveless shirt with a leather apron tied over it, and the muscles of his arms and his back slid and stretched as he worked the bellows. His head was bowed over his work, his light brown hair sweaty around his neck. How had she passed him every day for nine weeks and never realized how good he looked? And she'd made him happy. She leaned on the stone pillar at the corner of the forge rail and waited for him to notice her.

It took him a few minutes to turn around. He twitched, surprised someone was there, then smiled that new, wonderful smile when he realized it was her. *I've made him happy, but he's made me happy too*, she thought. "I hope I'm not a distraction," she said.

He plunged whatever he'd been working on into the quenching barrel. "Never that," he said, then the corners of his mouth twitched up in amusement. "Not an unwelcome one, certain sure."

"I wanted you to know I'm back, safe and sound, and I've got a new job that will keep me away from Morgan for a while. I thought you'd feel better knowing that."

"Much better." He took the metal from the barrel, but stood there holding it. "Watching you ride off with him all those times, and how he made you hold him so close...never hated anyone so much in my life."

Anger made him sound nothing like himself, and Telaine clasped his arm.

"I need you to promise me something, Ben," she said. "You have to promise you won't go picking a fight with Morgan. I don't care what he does. If he kills you, I—I don't want him to kill you. Please."

"Happen I'll kill him instead," Ben said, clenching his fist and making the tendons rise up on his arm.

"I'll stay away from him, and you'll leave him alone, and Morgan won't be part of our lives. Promise me."

Ben cast his cool, steady gaze on her, unsmiling. "**promise**," he said, and Telaine jerked. He had never lied to her before. She thought he never would. She had no way to challenge him on it.

"Thanks," she said instead, and released him. All that was left to her was to ensure that whatever Morgan did to her, Ben would never find out.

He gave her a half smile. "Walk out with me tonight? In public this time?" He sounded amused.

"How can I refuse such an invitation?" she said, and dimpled at him. She loved the way it made him catch his breath and look at her lips as though kissing them was the only thing on his mind.

They spoke a little longer, low-voiced words that were no one's business but theirs, before Telaine went back to Aunt Weaver's to clean up and encode the day's intelligence to be sent out the next day. Soon, very soon, she'd finish her work, and then...then anything was possible.

That evening, "walking out," to Ben Garrett, meant going down to the tavern. They walked together down the main street, hand in hand, in silence. People passed them, eyeing their clasped hands, then giving Telaine knowing looks and smiles that had her wishing she was invisible. It was so much easier being the focus of attention when you wore a mask.

She clutched Ben more tightly until he exclaimed, in mock pain, "I'm going to need that hand later."

"I feel like everyone's staring at us," she said.

"Everyone's staring at *me*," he said. "Not you."

"How can you be so sure?"

"I know how they think. They're thinking," he dropped his voice to a near-whisper, "'How did that homely fellow end up with such a mysterious, beautiful woman?'"

Telaine blushed. She'd blushed more in the last two days than in the whole rest of her life. "You are the least homely man I've ever seen," she said. "And I'm hardly mysterious or beautiful."

He put his free arm around her waist and picked her up, making her first gasp, then laugh with delight as he spun around with her once before setting her back down. "You are beautiful," he said in a low voice, "and I'll tell you a truth, every unmarried man in Longbourne wishes you were walking out with him tonight."

"Guess that makes you the lucky one," Telaine said, trying not to blush again.

"It does," Ben said. The serious look was back, the one that always made her heart beat faster, and without remembering that they were standing in the middle of Longbourne, she kissed him lightly and was rewarded with his brilliant smile. Somebody hooted at them from the other side of the street, and Ben waved absently in the man's direction.

"Don't know how I earned that," he said, and led her on down the street.

"By being who you are," Telaine said. "And because you think I'm beautiful." She laid her head on his shoulder briefly. "You know so much, what are they going to do when we walk into the tavern?"

He tilted his head back to look at the sky as if reading the future there. "They're going to say, hey there, haven't seen you in a while, you buying the next round of drinks?"

"They are not," Telaine said, laughing.

"I've no idea what they'll say. Probably tease us a lot. Everyone teases the new couples. Then they get used to us, and then next time we'll be the ones teasing."

Ben held the door to the tavern open for her. It was too noisy inside, at first, for anyone to notice them. One of the quarrymen was playing the pianoforte with more energy than accuracy, while his comrades belted out a well-known song about a young man and his walking staff. It was a song that relied heavily on innuendo and double meanings, and the quarrymen found it hilarious.

Ben saw her seated—he was the perfect gentleman, far more well-mannered than several noblemen Telaine knew—and went to fetch them beer. Telaine watched the pianoforte player and tapped her toe along to the rhythm.

"Sitting alone, sweetheart?" said a man dressed in the woven white shirt and suspenders favored by the loggers. He sat across from her and leered. He was such a stereotype Telaine had to pinch her lips shut to keep from laughing at him.

"Actually, I'm waiting for someone—"

"And here I am, darlin', the one you've waited your whole life for." He tilted back in the chair until it rocked on only two legs.

The Princess took over. "If I'd known you were him, I'd have waited a while longer."

The man looked confused. She added, "You know, your mother warned me about you. She said you were like to put yourself where you're not wanted. Happen you could go back to your friends now."

"That's some good sense there," said Ben, holding a mug in each hand. He set the mugs down on the table and stood next to her with his arms folded over his chest, looking down at the man with cheery good humor. Telaine had to cover her mouth; he'd taken a pose that clearly outlined the hard flat muscles of his chest, the long muscles of his arms.

Unfortunately, the man went from confused to belligerent. "You ought leave the lady alone," he told Ben. He was drunker than she'd first thought. He swayed as he stood, several inches taller than Ben and more heavily muscled. Telaine looked around, wondering what to do. Maida and her barman weren't in sight. The man's friends had taken notice of the confrontation and looked like they were thinking about joining it.

Ben shook his head. "Women make everything complicated, don't they?" he said. He had a resigned, mournful look on his face. Telaine, outraged, opened her mouth to speak, and a foot pressed hers into the floor. "Tell you what, friend, let's ask the lady which of us she favors, let her make the hard choice."

The man's face cleared. "Let her make the hard choice," he repeated. He turned to Telaine. "Which is it?"

Timidly, Telaine pointed at Ben. He sighed and threw his arms up. "Guess that's that," he said. "You're a lucky man, friend. You might've had to take her home." The foot was removed from hers. "Now I'm stuck with her, and you're a free man." He took the chair away from the man and sat with his chin in his hands, looking despondent.

The man looked from Ben to Telaine and back to Ben. His face cleared. "Lucky me," he declared, and went back to join his friends.

"Drunks can be fun," Ben said. He took a long pull from his mug. "Thanks for not stepping in there."

"I was going to," she said, "but somebody kept my mouth shut by way of my foot."

Ben laughed. "Doesn't have to come to a fight if you think fast."

Telaine drank her beer. That had been unexpected. Clever. She gave him a narrow-eyed look. "Didn't know you had so much cunning in you."

"Lots of things you don't know about me yet." He smiled, his eyes warm. "Looking forward to you learning them."

Telaine took another long drink. "I'm looking forward to that too."

"Lainie!" Liam Richardson's exuberant voice rang out. "And… who's this, fellows? The recluse of Longbourne? Lainie, what did you do to get this fellow out after seven? We not good enough for you, Ben?"

Ben waved his mug at them and grinned. "Don't take this the wrong way, fellows, but you're not nearly pretty enough."

An "oooooh" went up among the crowd. Liam clutched at his chest. "This what you left me for, Lainie? Hope he's worth it."

"Oh," she breathed, taking Ben's hand, "he is." A roar of laughter went up around her, and several people started talking at once, but she no longer minded being teased.

Maida came up and set down two more mugs. "You people are having an awful lot of fun," she said. "Lainie, you sly fox, and here's me never seeing what was going on right in front of my face."

"That's all right, neither did I," she said, and got another roar of laughter. It seemed her friends would laugh at anything tonight. Liam sat down next to her and pulled Isabel Colton onto his lap. She squealed and laughed. Jack Taylor, solo tonight, took a nearby table and waved for a drink. Her other friends—how had she gained so many friends in so short a time?—gathered in, laughing, talking, drinking, teasing Telaine and Ben.

Somebody proposed Jack take over at the pianoforte. Isabel disposed her legs across Liam's lap and leaned over to Telaine.

"You been out of Longbourne today, Lainie?" she asked.

"I was up at the fort," Telaine replied.

Isabel looked disappointed. "Thought maybe you'd heard more about this news out of Granger," she said.

"What news is that?"

"You haven't heard? Little girl—maybe not so little, eleven or twelve—went missing this morning. They've been searching around the crevasse, but haven't found her. Not likely to find her now dark's come."

Telaine shuddered. "That's terrible. Are they sure she fell in the crevasse?"

Isabel shrugged. "Only place she could've disappeared so fast, so completely."

"Stop talking about other people's troubles," Liam said. "I'll buy you a beer."

Isabel giggled, her good humor restored. She bounced up and led Liam to the bar.

"That makes four," Ben said.

"Four what?"

"Four kids missing," he said. "Since I moved here, anyway. All about that age, all from villages in the valley. A couple from Longbourne, even. They think maybe they drowned or fell down the crevasse—that's probably why they're looking up there even if she disappeared from someplace else." He finished his second beer and wiped his mouth. "Let's go someplace quieter."

"Someplace darker?" Telaine suggested.

"Someplace warm."

"Someplace you can admire my dimple?"

He took her hand again. "You know that means I have to be right up close to you?"

She sighed. "I suppose I can live with that."

An hour later, she walked through Aunt Weaver's back door into the dark kitchen and stopped to lean against the wall, smiling. All those years of being courted by the nobles and gentry of Tremontane, and a country blacksmith was the one to sweep her off her feet. He was gentle, and passionate—not a combination she'd ever thought to find in a man—and his kisses made her head whirl, and... She smiled again, closing her eyes in happy reminiscence. And she'd almost thrown all of that away.

She went up the stairs cautiously, not wanting to light a lamp and disturb Aunt Weaver. Though it was strange, her going to bed so early; on nights when she didn't have knitting circle, she usually sat up knitting in the uncomfortable drawing room.

"I'm home, Aunt," she said, knocking on her bedroom door. There was no answer, but the door jigged and then swung open as if it hadn't been latched securely. No one called out sharply from within to shut the door and leave her business alone, so Telaine pushed it open further. The room was identical in size to Telaine's, had the same furnishings, though Aunt Weaver's mirror wasn't cracked, and it was empty.

Telaine contemplated the bed, which hadn't been slept in, then went into the room and felt the base of the oil lamp beside it. Cold. There was a chest like Telaine's at the foot of the bed, not locked, and

Telaine took a quick look inside and found nothing but clothes. It was a boring room. She pulled the door shut behind her and, after a moment's thought, pushed the latch open enough that the door was closed but not latched. Just in case.

She went downstairs again and confirmed that the heavy black cloak was missing. So Aunt Weaver was out on another one of her mysterious errands. Telaine hadn't caught her at it since the first time, but she didn't spend a lot of time monitoring the woman's actions. After her discovery of two nights before, she'd started wondering if she should.

She intended to confront Uncle about it via telecoder the next day, when she went into Ellismere, though she wasn't sure what she would say. If he didn't know, should she give away Aunt Weaver's secret? What if Telaine was wrong? In any case, she didn't want to go on wondering.

Grinning to herself, she took a seat at the kitchen table and waited in the dark kitchen. Serve Aunt Weaver right for accosting Telaine this way the night of the shivaree. The night Ben had kissed her for the first time. He was wonderful. She sat there, remembering their times together, anticipating the next day when they'd add to those memories, feeling again his kisses on her lips and cheek and throat, so beautiful.

She wasn't sure how much time had passed when the door creaked open, then slammed hard. Aunt Weaver cursed. "That's a tricky door," Telaine said.

There was a silent pause in which neither of them moved. "What are you doing?" Aunt Weaver demanded.

"Just waiting up for you. Wanted to make sure you got in all right."

"That's a kindness." It was sarcastic enough that Telaine might have cringed if she weren't so full of amused righteousness.

"Where've you been?"

"None of your business."

"Probably. But I'm curious about why you feel the need to sneak around."

She could see the outline of Aunt Weaver, unmoving in the darkness. "Do you tell me what you get up to when you're at the Baron's manor?" Aunt Weaver said.

"No."

"Then I ain't sharing my business with you." Aunt Weaver strode past, going into the front room to remove her cloak. "Stay out of this."

"What 'this'? Look, it's clearly important to you—"

"It's Longbourne business. You're leaving eventually." Aunt Weaver went to the foot of the stairs, then paused. "You've got enough to do without taking on more. Leave this to me."

She was up the stairs before Telaine could come up with a response. Something was going on in Longbourne, or possibly in all of Steepridge, and she— She shook her head and ascended the stairs to her own room. Aunt Weaver was right; she would leave, and she shouldn't interfere any more than she already had. It just felt…wrong. And she wasn't sure why.

CHAPTER EIGHTEEN

Telaine handed over money and the telecoder form and thought about what to do while she was waiting for the reply. Pity there wasn't a Device that let you talk to someone directly, no waiting for the message to be turned around, no worry that the wrong someone might read your message or its reply. She went out into the street and decided to explore. Outside the Ellismere town hall she bought a newspaper and took it to the park across the street to read.

The front page story was about the Crown Princess's divorce. Telaine's breath caught. Poor Julia. She read the story and gradually went from sad to furious. The journalist who'd written the story was clearly sympathetic to Julia, but that hadn't stopped the woman from humiliating her by including an interview with the "other woman" who'd told everyone she was carrying Lucas's child.

At least the family wouldn't have to deal with the nightmare of an entailed adoption, paying Lucas's mistress's upkeep and that of her bastard child. Knowing Lucas, it wasn't impossible he'd try to force the Norths to adopt the baby into the royal house. Thank heaven Julia was out of it. The divorce would be finalized at the end of the week.

Telaine folded the paper, unable to read any more. She should have been there for her cousin. Going through the dissolution of her marriage bond, enduring the gossip, all while heavily pregnant...Julia had needed Telaine's support, and she hadn't been there to give it.

Maybe it was time to think about giving up espionage. It certainly made her life harder. It had kept her from being at her cousin's side when she needed her. If she hadn't been an agent of the Crown, she could have told Ben her true identity two days ago. But now, telling anyone she was Telaine North Hunter would mean coming up with a reason why Telaine North Hunter was slumming it in Longbourne. That would mean lying to Ben again, because of rule number one: never, under any circumstances, no matter how much you love or trust the person, tell anyone you are an agent. You had more lives than your own in your hands, as an agent.

But…being an agent gave her a rush like she'd never known. Giving it up — what would she be willing to give it up for? Her family, certainly. Ben? Maybe. Who knew where their relationship might go? Until Longbourne, she'd never considered life as something other than a spy. Now she found such consideration surprisingly easy.

She imagined being the Deviser she was passing herself off as, pictured having a workshop somewhere and…her imagination failed her. What else did she want that she didn't already have? She didn't know the answer, but felt in her bones that whatever the answer was, it would surprise her.

She walked slowly back to the telecoder office and received two encoded reply sheets. She was so familiar with the code now she could read it almost as easily as if it were plain text. One told her the fort received new shipments of arms once a year, the old, outdated weapons were returned to the central depot, and the most recent shipment had been made three months ago and the outdated weapons received two weeks later. The second told her, again, to find out what contraband Harroden was shipping to Steepridge and report. She rolled her eyes. As if she needed to be reminded.

Telaine did some calculating in her head. The fort would now have three weapons shipments: one from the government, a damaged one from Harroden, and a replacement one from Harroden. She was willing to bet Captain Clarke had no idea how often weapons were supposed to come in. No wonder the Baron was so loath to send back the damaged weapons; they couldn't go back to a depot they'd never come from, and the more often shipments went back and forth from Harroden, the more likely someone would notice.

But she'd seen far more crates and boxes than could be accounted for by the weapons shipments. It was those boxes whose contents she'd have to discover. She put the papers in her pocket to destroy later.

She hadn't been able to figure out a way to ask Uncle about Aunt Weaver, even in code. She'd have to confront the woman personally. If she was wrong, no harm done. If she was right…she'd have so many other questions.

She rode back with Abel in what was now customary silence. Tomorrow she'd work on the weapons. Tonight she'd speak to Aunt Weaver; she didn't want to wait any longer to learn the truth. With luck, this evening she'd spend time with Ben. Just thinking about him made her heart feel light. How had she gotten to be twenty-three without ever feeling this way? *How did you expect a secret agent to have any kind of personal relationship when you couldn't tell anyone the truth? Having Ben in your life is a miracle.*

They got back to Longbourne late; the telecoder office had been slower than usual, and Stakely had almost had to sit on Abel to make sure he waited for her. The forge fire had been extinguished for the night, and lights burned in the windows of Ben's house. She thought about knocking on his door, but she was tired and hungry and now that she was here, she found she couldn't wait to confront Aunt Weaver.

Her aunt was in the sitting room, knitting. "Supper's in the cold room," she called when the door squeaked open. Telaine found a few pieces of chicken, which she devoured along with a glass of cold milk. She washed her face and hands and went to sit on the uncomfortable horse-hair cushion across from Aunt Weaver. "How was your day?" she asked politely.

"Can't complain." *Click, click.*

"How about your evening? Going well?"

"Well enough. Your young man came by. Told him you weren't back yet. He said to say he'd see you tomorrow."

So we won't be interrupted. "My cousin Julia is getting divorced."

"That's too bad."

"Not for her. He's sort of a bastard. In the pejorative sense."

"What did I tell you about using fancy uppity words?"

"I wouldn't with anyone but you. Do you want to know why?"

"I got nothing better to do." *Click, click.*

Telaine leaned back, thought better of it, sat upright. "It's an interesting story. Well, it might not interest you, but I like it. I didn't grow up in the palace. I mean, I did, but not from infancy. I didn't live there until I was eight. I was so young, I'd lost my father, and I had trouble adjusting to life there. Did a lot of running around, hiding from tutors and governesses. I got to know the place the way most people don't. You know what my favorite place was, all that first year?"

"Couldn't begin to guess."

"It was this long, long hall filled with portraits of the Kings and Queens of Tremontane." The clicking stopped for a moment, then continued as if there had been no interruption. "I didn't know that's what it was. There were name plates, of course, but I couldn't read back then. I just knew there were all these faces, staring down at me, and I had this idea they were related to me, but mostly I liked to make up stories about them. I got to know those faces well."

She paused. Aunt Weaver said nothing, but Telaine could tell she was listening intently.

"A few years later I went back. I'd almost forgotten how much I'd loved the place as a child. Now I could read the name plates and put faces to the names I learned about from my history tutor. King Edmund Valant. King Domitius. Queen Willow North—I felt sorry for her, that seemed like such a frivolous name. And then my own relatives. King Anthony North, my grandpapa. Queen Zara North, my great-aunt, the one who was killed."

Silence.

"She was always my favorite. The painter really captured her likeness, or at least that's what my grandmama said. She had this way of looking at you that said, 'You had better not be wasting my time.' And blue eyes just like Julia's. Cornflower blue, soft as a kitten, but make her angry and it's like being cut by glass. I've never forgotten Queen Zara's face."

Silence.

Telaine took a deep breath. "So what I want to know, Aunt Weaver, is what that face is doing in Longbourne, looking only a few years older than it does in that portrait, when everyone knows Zara North is dead and would be well over seventy if she were still alive?"

Aunt Weaver laid her knitting in her lap. "You asking questions, or making accusations?" she said.

"Questions. I want to know what happened to you. I want to know why you look younger than my Aunt Imogen when you're actually older than my grandmama. I want to know what brought you to Longbourne."

"Suppose I tell you that's none of your business?"

"Then I guess I'd have to go on wondering. But you know what I think, Aunt Zara? I think you want to tell someone. I know I'm chafing at not being able to tell anyone the truth and I've only been doing this for two months. It's been almost fifty *years* for you." Telaine leaned forward. "I only know a little of what it's like to live with a secret like this, and I wish…" She trailed off, uncertain how to finish that sentence.

Zara North sighed deeply. "You comfortable in that chair?" she asked.

"No."

"Good. This isn't a comfortable story, and despite what you might think, I'm only telling you because you figured it out. You could have gone on ignorant forever as far as I'm concerned. But your uncle gave me his secret in return for mine, so you might as well make four who know why Zara North had to get herself killed."

Telaine became aware that she was holding her breath and let it out slowly. The intensity of Zara's expression made her afraid that she'd stumbled into a story she'd rather not know.

"It's not so bad now," Zara said, "but back then having inherent magic could mean death. Would definitely mean being ostracized or attacked. Even today people are still afraid of magic they can't see right in front of 'em. Devices are all very well because they can be controlled by anyone, turned off. You can't turn off a person who can see through walls…well, you can, but it's permanent.

"Some things, healing and the like, that was accepted because it was stupid not to let someone save your life 'cause they did it with magic. But mostly people who had those kinds of magic kept quiet about it. If they could. And I couldn't, because I could heal myself.

"Didn't know it for years, just figured I was extra healthy, never got sick. Then I broke a leg, going over a fence, and two days after it was set I was back on my feet. I gave out that the palace healer did it, but by then I knew the truth."

"I don't see why that would be a problem. You said even back then healers were accepted."

"If you can heal other people, sure. But you're not thinking it through. Amazes me how you've gotten this far without thinking things through. My body heals itself all the way down past the bone and blood into whatever makes up our bodies. It heals the damage of aging. I was getting older, but not so's anyone could tell. If I didn't live forever, I was certain sure going to live a very long time."

"A monarchy that goes on forever," Telaine said. "A Queen whose rule lasts over a century."

"Or more," Zara agreed. "Even if there hadn't been a prejudice against the inherently magical, even if people didn't care that it had infected the royal family, which they would've, mine was a power that could bring down a country. Stability is good, but too much longevity is moribund."

"What did you tell me about not using fancy uppity words?"

"Don't apply to me. I know when to use 'em right. You want to know the rest or not?"

"I'll be quiet."

"So I had to get out. Didn't relish the idea of killing myself, not to mention that seemed impossible, so I staged an assassination. Got killed, went as far away as I could so's people wouldn't know my face, cut my hair off and learned to say 'happen' and 'certain sure.' Left Zara North in the dust and became Agatha Weaver."

"When did the Mistress come in?"

"Hank Hobson was a good, plain spoken man, and I loved him dearly. I never did tell him who I was. No point, because I was never going back to being Zara, so don't give me that look like I'm a hypocrite. *You* plan to go back to the palace when this is all over." She jabbed Telaine in the breastbone with a sharp finger.

"But you weren't going to age and he was. That wasn't exactly fair to him."

"I ain't saying I chose right every time. But I wanted him enough to tell myself I'd find a solution. Happen that sounds familiar to you."

Telaine nodded. "What happened to him?"

"Died in a mining accident almost thirty years ago. I didn't much feel like remarrying. Moved to different towns, moved on after five or ten years in each. Been in Longbourne for seven now."

Telaine remembered something. "Wait—you said *four* people knew your secret. You, me, Uncle, and…who?"

"Your grandmama." Zara picked up her knitting again. "She helped me make my escape. Happen she'll tell you the story someday, about her and me and your grandpapa. Ain't my story to tell, that one."

"But now I *really* don't understand why you didn't help me! We're both in the same situation. I could have used advice from someone who knows what it's like to live a double life."

"We are *not* in the same situation," Zara said grimly. "I told you already you ain't giving up your real life. I ain't living a double life because this is the only one I have. And…happen I was put out by your uncle makin' me take you in and watch you make a place for yourself among my friends when you didn't care anything for them. *Shouldn't* care anything for them. But I suppose I can't say, anymore, we don't have anything in common."

Telaine leaned back again. This time she didn't care that the back of the chair was uncomfortable. "I suppose I should go on thinking of you as Aunt Weaver," she said.

"Good idea. Nobody'd believe the truth," Aunt Weaver said.

"I wonder Uncle didn't reckon on me figuring out who you are."

Aunt Weaver shrugged. "It was a chance we both had to take. Said I was the only choice and he had to take what he could get. Never have understood that young man. He put a lot of effort into tracking me down."

Telaine laughed. "It must have been a stunner when his inherent magic finally grew powerful enough to sense a North living all the way out here." Then she stopped. "I don't understand how you could still be a North if you changed your name to Weaver and then were sworn to your husband."

"Changing the name don't eliminate the family bond. I'm still a North where it counts. Happen I couldn't bring myself to give that up, those few seconds of connection with my family at the solstices. If I'd known young Jeffrey and his freak gift was going to come along, happen I'd have done something about it."

"I remember now. I could feel someone extra, every solstice. But Uncle said it was a distant relative. I can't believe I believed that."

"Easier than the truth." Aunt Weaver bundled up her knitting. "I'm for bed," she said, "'less you have any more impertinences for me."

"Just one," Telaine said. "What are you knitting?"

Aunt Weaver laughed. "Baby blanket," she said. "Don't yet know whose. Those young Bradfords, like enough. Couple of weasels wouldn't go at it any less than they do."

She stood and fixed her grandniece with those sharp blue eyes. "Think careful about what you're doing," she said. "I ain't going to tell you again, I told you enough already. Way you're going, someone might get hurt, and if you're honorable, you'll let it be you."

Telaine watched her leave in stunned silence. What *was* she doing? She liked the people of Longbourne, liked Ben a lot, loved how he made her feel, but she'd be able to leave it behind, yes? *I'm not going to worry about that now,* she thought. *Plenty of time to worry about it when it's time to leave.*

CHAPTER NINETEEN

The next morning, she presented herself at the fort's gate and was waved through with no more interest than if she'd been one of the carts. Despite Captain Clarke's instructions and the heavy black clouds threatening rain, she took a wandering path through the fort, trying to get a better sense of its layout.

The short, square buildings with slightly inclined slate roofs lined the inner wall of the fort, three on each side of the keep, under the jutting wall-walk where the soldiers sauntered. On either side of these buildings were smaller versions of the main gate, closed and barred. That struck her as a potential security hazard; they looked like exactly the kind of weak spot a Ruskalder attack might focus on. It seemed Thorsten Keep hadn't been designed entirely for defense, after all.

The taller, round buildings with the conical roofs stood against the outer wall. Unlike the square buildings, the round ones had large double doors, wide enough, she judged, for an oxcart to back into for unloading. So, the square buildings were probably barracks, and the round buildings were for storage. There were a lot of the round buildings. If what she was looking for was in one of them, it might take her a long time to ferret it out. She tried not to let the idea make her despondent.

Thunder rumbled in the distance. A cold drop landed on her forehead and she made a dash for the keep. As with their counterparts at the gate, the soldiers posted at the door ignored her. She entered the central chamber and went directly to Captain Clarke, seated at the table going over paperwork that clearly had him worried. "Miss Bricker," he said when he looked up. "If you'll wait, I'll bring you a...guide." She guessed he'd been about to say *keeper* instead.

She wandered around the room, pretending to be interested in the wall decorations left behind by generations of soldiers with no taste, until Clarke returned with a clean-shaven, neatly dressed young man who couldn't have been older than seventeen. "Lieutenant Hardy,"

Clarke said, "please assist Miss Bricker in her work."

Lieutenant Hardy made a motion as if to salute her, but controlled it. Telaine saw Clarke's mouth twitch. So the man had a soft side after all. "Thanks for sparing him, captain," she said. In her wanderings, only three of the approximately fifteen soldiers she'd seen were the clean-dressed ones she'd identified as actually Clarke's men. If she was right, Clarke couldn't spare even this one.

Lieutenant Hardy escorted Telaine through the sprinkling rain to one of the storage towers and unlocked it with a giant, ancient key that had some rust on the shaft. Inside, filling the space, were several dozen long crates. "Are those all full of defective guns?" Telaine asked in a faint voice.

Lieutenant Hardy nodded. "Happen you've got your work cut out for you," he said without rancor. He lifted the lid from one of the boxes, which had had its nails pulled for easy removal. Telaine looked inside. The guns were packed in straw, and as she reached down to the bottom of the crate, she guessed there were about ten guns in it. She counted crates. Four hundred guns. "This is a lot of weapons for one fort, isn't it?" she asked.

Hardy said, "Supposed to be one for every soldier plus a hundred more as spares."

Telaine dragged an unopened crate away from the rest—they were heavy, and Hardy had to help her—and began to disassemble the first weapon. "I didn't think you had so many soldiers here," she said.

"We're temporarily understaffed. Had a problem with the paperwork for some transfers. We're expecting a bunch of new troops in a few weeks." He pulled up a crate and sat down. "Doesn't matter to me. I'm transferring out after the snows end."

"Are you happy about that?" Telaine said. She already knew the answer.

"Damn—I mean, very happy, begging your pardon, miss. Been here nearly a year and I'm ready to get back to civilization. Someplace that ain't cold and wet eight months out of twelve. You hear that?" The rain was coming down fiercely now and Telaine could hear it hitting the ground like hail, pounding the roof above her head. "It's full autumn now and it rains so much we got moss growing on anything sits still long enough. Then the snows close down the passes for four, five months or more. A man can go out of his mind cooped up here that long."

"But if the passes are closed, you don't have to be as worried about attacks, right?"

"We don't worry about attacks at all. Never seen the Ruskalder put so much as a nose hair past the edge of Thorsten Pass." Hardy leaned back against the wall, apparently not remembering how he'd railed against the wet moments before, because dampness had begun to spread across the stones of the tower. "All these weapons shipments, they're a waste of time if you ask me. New weapons every year when we haven't even fired the old ones."

"They probably send the old ones to other forts," Telaine said. She snapped the case back into place and set it well to one side. It took three times as long to disassemble and reassemble a weapon as it did to make the repair, and with all the guns being identical, she didn't want to open one and find she'd already fixed it.

"Probably," said Hardy. He realized his back was wet and cursed, then apologized.

"So are all these towers full of weapons?" Telaine asked.

Hardy laughed. "Not hardly. Food, dry rations, clothing and blankets, armor and helmets. Stuff to take us through the winter. The storage towers are bursting at the seams these days, just before the passes close."

"That makes sense." The young man had to be wrong. Based on the letters she'd found, Harroden was sending far too many shipments up the mountain to fit into the locked storeroom at the manor, however big it was. Some of those shipments were undoubtedly in the fort's towers. Though if she was right about Hardy's loyalties, his ignorance made sense; Captain Clarke would disapprove strenuously of his fort being used to store the Baron's black market goods.

So the captain believed these were all legitimate shipments; what did he think of the ones that went out again, to be sold in Highton or possibly Silverfield? Not only wasn't she finding answers, she kept finding new questions.

Telaine closed up another gun. Eight left in this crate. Thirty-nine crates to go. If she'd actually cared about this job, she'd have curled up and died inside to think of the tedium. She cast about for another innocuous but telling question. "The Baron seems deeply involved in the fort's affairs," she said.

It was the wrong question. Hardy went stiff. "Not my place to comment on my superior officer, not that he is," he said.

"I'm sorry I brought it up," she said. "Only the other day he and Captain Clarke were talking, and it sounded like—"

"Not my place to comment," Hardy said. "Don't poke your nose in the Baron's affairs, is my advice."

"I'll keep that in mind," Telaine said, and repaired five more guns in silence. She already knew Clarke didn't have the control over his soldiers and his fort that he ought to have, and that he and the Baron didn't agree on things. But Hardy made it sound as if the Baron's involvement was more serious than the superficially civil conversation she'd heard the other day suggested. Was he afraid to talk about it for his own sake, or for his captain's? Either way, she needed to regain his trust. It was possible she could get him to open up over time.

"Do you know where you'll be stationed next, Lieutenant?" she asked, and guided him into a conversation about postings he'd had and the ones he liked best, and did he have a girlfriend, and how did his family feel about his joining the military. The tension between them dissipated, and Telaine relaxed, feeling Lieutenant Hardy might turn out to be a valuable asset after all.

By the time she finished the first crate, it was dinnertime and Telaine was ravenous. She discovered, almost too late, that no provision had been made for her meal. She trekked back down the valley, telling herself she'd get Maida to make her up a box dinner next time; it was too far to walk back and forth.

She devoured her food and raced back up to the fort, and

managed to finish another two crates as darkness fell. She'd never walked alone down the valley after dark, and even though the rain had stopped, it was still cold and she wasn't wearing a cloak or even a jacket. When she realized someone else was on the road, approaching her, she had to control her panic. *Morgan. He wouldn't be on foot, but who else could it be?*

"I'd started to worry about where you were," said Ben. "Knew you weren't dressed warm enough, and then it got dark." He put a coat, and then his arm, around her shoulders. "You *are* cold," he said, touching her cheek. His hand felt like a brand, it was so hot. "Let's get you warmed up."

She leaned into his embrace, too tired to think. "It's been a long day," she said. "I think I need some warmer clothes. Didn't reckon I'd be in Longbourne this long."

"Can't say I'm sorry you're still here," he replied. He steered her down the road and into the tavern, where he asked Maida for some whiskey. Telaine sat at a table and laid her head down on her folded arms. "Sit up and drink this," Ben said, sliding his hand under her cheek and lifting her head. She drank, sputtered, and the world came back into focus.

Maida slid a plate of roasted chicken breast and boiled carrots in front of her, handed her a fork and knife. Telaine thought she could eat the plate as well, she was that hungry. She ate in silence, feeling Ben's amused eyes on her. "Don't know what you think is so funny," she mumbled through a mouthful of carrots.

"Never seen anyone go at their food quite so determined," he said with a chuckle.

"I've been taking apart guns and putting them back together all day. I'm starving." She cut off some chicken and took an enormous bite.

"Guns?"

She nodded. "Damaged shipment. Baron wants me to fix 'em rather than waste time sending 'em back."

"Don't you think that's the sort of thing their captain would decide?"

It was exactly what she'd been thinking, but she couldn't tell him she was spying on the Baron to find things like that out. "I suppose," she said, "but the captain and the Baron sound like they have an arrangement."

"You want more to eat, Lainie?" Maida said, setting down a mug of beer. "Here's something to wash it down with."

Telaine took a long drink. She was full, warm, and happy. She looked up at Maida, who seemed concerned. And Ben had worried enough to come looking for her. The whiskey welled up into tears she had to choke down. "You are both being so nice to me," she said. "Thank you."

"What are friends for?" Maida said with a shrug, and went back to the bar. Ben took Telaine's free left hand, removed the fork from her right and grasped that hand too.

"I think you should know," he said in a low voice, his eyes never leaving hers, "that I will always come after you."

There went the tears again. One whiskey and half a beer shouldn't be enough to leave her a weepy drunk, right? "I promise not to make you do it too often," she said.

He smiled at her, that wonderful, brilliant smile. "Don't know if it's good or bad that I made you cry."

"They're good tears," she said. She knew she had the sappiest grin on her face, but she didn't care.

He squeezed her hands. "Wish we had someplace private to go," he said. "Getting too cold outside for the lake."

"You have a house," she pointed out.

He smiled again, but shook his head. "Too hard for me to remain a gentleman, there," he said.

He was worried about being a gentleman. He'd come looking for her in the dark. He'd held the door for her and stood up to a giant for her. He was almost too good to be true.

"Lainie? Are you all right?" Ben's smile fell away. "You just had the strangest expression. Did I—should I not have suggested that..."

He took a drink of her beer. "I don't want you to think I want anything from you we shouldn't do—"

She reclaimed her hand and laid it across his cheek. "I know," she said. "But I love that you find me desirable. I trust you, Ben."

He turned his face enough to kiss her hand. "I want to be worthy of your trust."

Almost too good to be true.

"Lainie, are you all right? You've still got that strange look."

"Better than all right," she said. "Will you walk me home?"

"Why are those crates out in the open, lieutenant?"

Hardy glanced across the yard. "Too big to fit into storage, likely."

"Do you know what's in them?"

His lips thinned. "Baron's private stuff. Too big for the manor, too."

She'd have to tread carefully. "Well, I hope whatever's in them is waterproof. Didn't know it'd be so rainy today."

Hardy unbent when he realized she wasn't going to press him about their contents. "They've been coming up the mountain all summer, every couple of weeks. Got the Baron's name on 'em but they always come straight here."

"I've been to the manor. You're right, they wouldn't fit through any of the doors." She put together one last gun and stretched. "I think I'm getting faster. Don't tell anyone, but this is really boring work." Hardy, whose job of watching her was even more boring, grinned at her. "I'll see you tomorrow, lieutenant. Maybe I can teach you how to take these apart, make the work go faster."

"I don't know, Miss Bricker, I'm all thumbs on both my hands."

"Don't be surprised if you're better than you think."

She returned the next morning and went straight to what she now thought of as her tower, but Lieutenant Hardy wasn't there to meet her. She leaned against the door and waited for five minutes before becoming impatient. If Captain Clarke weren't so fixated on regulations, she wouldn't need to wait on Hardy to do her job. She caught herself. Repairing guns was not her job. Finding the contraband was.

She wandered through the keep, acting as if she had a right to be there, and every time she passed near one of the towers, she surreptitiously tugged on the iron ring of its door handle. But the doors never budged. She reached the end of the row and turned around, still sauntering. Ahead, she saw Captain Clarke entering the fort and heading straight for the stone keep. He was walking like he wanted to tear into someone. Telaine moved faster. The captain would know what had happened to Hardy.

She passed the soldiers, who ignored her as usual, and slipped inside. Two people were arguing loudly—Captain Clarke and the Baron. She grabbed the door and eased it silently shut, though it was unlikely they could hear it over the sound of their shouting.

"Hardy's transfer wasn't due for another six months!"

"Were you going to stand in the way of a good soldier's good fortune?"

"It's that good fortune I question. Hardy was one of my best men. Why did you sign off on his transfer? That's my responsibility!"

"What are you alleging, captain?"

"Only what I've suspected all this time. You want control of this post and you're willing to transfer away men loyal to me to get that control."

"Careful what you say, captain. You're accusing me of disloyalty. I only want what's best for this command."

"*I* decide what's best for this command, milord. You're the civilian government representative who's to provide support."

"Unless the military commander is unfit for the role."

"Are you saying I'm unfit?"

"Take a look around, captain." The Baron's voice was the vicious snarl she'd heard him use against Harroden. "The men are slovenly and disrespectful. They don't drill and they don't maintain their weapons. If you were the commander you say you are, you'd have this place running like a Device. Tell me, at whose door should I lay this monstrous abrogation of responsibility? Do you think *anyone* will believe you are not an incompetent clown when I bring these matters to the attention of General Riesland?"

There was a pause. "Milord, I will resign my commission as soon as a replacement can be found."

"Don't be ridiculous, man. You were a sharp commander when you came here three years ago. I believe you can be such again." The voice had gone from vicious to silky smooth. "And I see no reason why we shouldn't work together to bring the fort back into shape."

Another pause, then Clarke said, wearily, "What do you want me to do?"

"Why don't you start with regular drills? Let me handle the supply side of things, the non-military side. You'll have your hands full with the men."

"What about Hardy? I don't want to see any more good men transferred out of here. I depended on him to keep order with the enlisted men."

"Don't worry, captain. I promise you won't need to worry about it anymore."

That sounded like her cue to make her presence known. Telaine opened the door a crack and closed it as noisily as she could, strode out of the passageway and stopped as if surprised to see them there. "I beg your pardon, milord, captain," she said. "I couldn't find Lieutenant Hardy so I came here looking for him."

"Lieutenant Hardy received an early transfer," Captain Clarke said, trying and failing to conceal his anger. "I'll find you another guide."

"Now, surely that's not necessary," the Baron said with a smile. It revolted Telaine that he could act so friendly after being so vicious to the captain. "Miss Bricker has more than demonstrated her loyalty, and I see no reason she shouldn't be allowed to work unsupervised. Don't you agree, captain?" His voice remained pleasant, but Telaine could see the look he gave Clarke, and it had knives in it.

"Very well," Clarke said woodenly. He handed her the huge iron key. "Get on with your work, Miss Bricker."

"And I will get on with mine," said the Baron. "I believe these supply manifests need organizing. Yes, Miss Bricker, I realize it's not exactly a task befitting nobility," he said, misinterpreting her appalled look, "but it's just another way I can serve my kingdom."

He was pouring it on too thick, Telaine thought as she started in on the morning's crate. In fact, he seemed entirely too cheerful. Only a few days before he'd been annoyed with her for delaying her work to go to Ellismere, then she hadn't seen him or Morgan since. And now here he was doing a menial task with every appearance of enjoyment. Something had changed. He hadn't gone down the mountain, someone would have noticed, but what—

"You're not cold, are you, Miss Bricker? Because I'm sure I could find a way to take care of that," said Morgan, startling her.

"It is chilly in here, thanks, Mister Morgan," she said, trying to sound innocently naïve, though his sudden appearance made her hands tremble.

Morgan slid around the crates and stood behind her. She focused on reassembling the gun in her hands and pretended not to notice him. "Let's see if I can…warm you up."

His hands went around her waist and pulled her close to his body, then he ran his palm over her stomach and up toward her breasts. She could feel every ridge of the muscles of his abdomen and, horribly, the hard rounded contours of what lay below his abdomen. She squealed and spun around with the reassembled gun in her hand, "accidentally" pressing it to his throat.

Morgan froze. Before he could remember that the gun wasn't loaded, Telaine slid sideways out of his grasp and lowered the weapon. "Mister Morgan, I'm sorry, but I know I've asked you to stop that," she said, trying not to let her fear show. "It's so hard for me to work when you do that."

Morgan rearranged his face into its usual slow, lazy smile. "I see I should take you more seriously, Miss Bricker," he said.

Telaine backed out of the storage room, and he followed her. "I'll have to catch you some other time when you're less…preoccupied with work." He stopped as he passed her, ran his finger down the side of her face, and raised an eyebrow coyly. "Certainly a time when your hands are less full."

Telaine watched him walk away, her heart beating painfully fast. That had been close. Morgan could have done anything he wanted to her in there. As indifferent as the soldiers were, she couldn't count on them to rescue her if she screamed.

She repacked the crate, not caring that she hadn't finished her work for the day. She could still feel his hand, stroking her body. Her hands were shaking too much to crack open the gun casings, let alone hold the tiny tools. She was done.

She walked slowly back to Longbourne, trying to dispel the memory of Morgan's…body…pressed against her. She wrapped her new jacket around her against the chilly wind. It was overcast again, and a few flurries of snow blew about her face. When the first light snows fell, Telaine had panicked, but Eleanor had told her the big storms were a ways off and not to worry about it. It would be a late winter in the mountains.

She should see about getting some more warm clothes, if Longbourne got as snowy as everyone said. Definitely one of those wool cloaks, some heavier trousers and thick socks, maybe a hat and scarf. Josephine had some nice cloaks displayed this week, and there was a tailor who might accept trade in kind for the rest. Should she learn to knit? No, she'd probably make as much a mess of it as she did with needlework—

She stopped in the middle of the road and looked up at the sky, feeling pinpoints of cold melt on her face. Here she was within days of completing her mission and she was planning a winter in Longbourne. A winter at home.

The knowledge had crept up on her slowly, a thought at a time, until Longbourne had gone from being foreign, to familiar, to comfortable, to beloved. *Home*, she thought again, and it warmed her as much as Ben's smile. She hoped her mission would be complete before the snows fell, but she wouldn't feel sorry if it wasn't. *This isn't your home,* her annoying inner voice told her, *home is ballrooms and salons full of glittering people and flirting in carriages,* but she ignored it and set off down the road again. That was the Princess's home. This was hers.

She stopped in at Josephine's shop and came out the proud owner of a thick, voluminous wool cloak in pearly gray, with a deep hood and a silk lining. It was like wearing a self-heating blanket. Suppose you could make such a Device? No one had ever cased a Device in anything but metal or wood, but she didn't think it was impossible. She'd have to look into that more seriously. She might have all winter to do it.

CHAPTER TWENTY

It was hard to make herself go back to the fort the next day, fearing that Morgan might get her alone again, hating the tedium of the work and the oppressiveness of the fort. She took her time over breakfast, dawdled talking to Ben and to Eleanor, chatted with Maida when she picked up her dinner, and made her walk up the road into more of a stroll. The storm clouds still threatened, but the wind had died down and she felt less chilly than the day before.

She closed her fingers around the iron key that weighed her pocket down and remembered why she was actually going to the fort. Today she would try to investigate the other storage towers. Somewhere, there had to be whatever contraband Harroden had sent. It was almost funny that the Baron was responsible for giving her the freedom to engineer his downfall.

The fort looked different that morning; she realized, as she approached, there were no guards at the gate, and the gate itself stood open. Her first thought was *The Ruskalder have invaded*, then she laughed at herself. She would definitely have noticed if Ruskalder warriors were loose in Barony Steepridge. Still, she slowed her steps and listened. Everything seemed too quiet, even for Thorsten Keep, which usually sounded like a sullen bear grumbling its way toward hibernation.

When she entered the fort, she saw a few soldiers milling around, not nearly as many as usual and none of them spruce and well-kempt. They were all moving faster than usual, which still meant a gait barely faster than a walk, but none of them paid any more attention to her than before.

She walked to the keep without being stopped by any of the soldiers, though the two men standing beside the door did glance at her briefly and dismiss her as not a threat. She entered, feeling unease prickle the back of her neck. " — deal with that at once," she heard the Baron say. "Everything can advance."

"Yes, milord," said another man, whose voice was husky, as if he spent a lot of time coughing.

Telaine eased the door most of the way shut, or tried to; it slipped from her fingertips and shut loudly enough to make both men stop speaking. She cursed, silently, then hurried forward before the Baron could suspect her of eavesdropping. She regretted that lost opportunity.

The Baron stood near the table next to one of the slovenly soldiers, who was standing as much at attention as she'd ever seen any of them do. He had untidy, too-long blond hair and had removed the stiff collar of his uniform. That was one point on which she was in sympathy with the man; Jeffy had complained often of how the high collar dug into his chin, and how he wished the service would do away with it.

The Baron didn't seem upset by her interruption. "You should go home today, Miss Bricker," he said. "There's been a terrible accident and the fort is rather unsettled at the moment. I'm afraid Captain Clarke is dead."

Telaine gasped. She'd rather liked the man, from what little she'd known of him. "What happened, milord?"

"He fell off the wall during the midnight watch and broke his neck. Some of the soldiers say he looked drunk. I wouldn't have thought it of Clarke, myself."

Telaine thought the chances of Clarke being drunk on duty were about the same as her voluntarily submitting to Morgan's embraces. She regarded the Baron more closely. His voice sounded unhappy and distressed, but his face was impassive, as if he were reporting on the tragedy from a great distance. "I'm so sorry to hear it, milord," she said. "If it's not impertinent for me to ask, who will replace him?"

The Baron gestured at the soldier. "This is Lieutenant—I should say, Captain Jackson. He was Clarke's second and has sadly received a promotion under tragic circumstances." Jackson nodded at Telaine. He didn't look as if he thought her worthy of his attention.

"As I say, it's perhaps better if you continue your work tomorrow," the Baron said. The gesture he made in her direction made it clear this was an order rather than a request. Telaine left quickly.

On her way back to Longbourne, she thought about the Baron's face when he'd spoken of Clarke. She remembered what he'd said to the captain only the day before…something about not having to worry about transferring away good men anymore? That phrase struck her as sinister now. She had no doubt the Baron was capable of killing someone who was in his way. Had Clarke become too much of a hindrance to the Baron's plans, whatever they were?

And now "everything can advance," the Baron had said. If he hadn't specifically instructed her to leave, and in the new captain's hearing, she'd have turned around that minute and taken advantage of the disorder to snoop in the storage towers. As it was, disobeying a man who'd arranged a fatal accident for someone didn't seem like a good survival strategy.

The fort was still disorganized when Telaine returned the next day. Clarke might not have been able to control the men, but he'd kept some level of order. This new captain either was less competent (almost certainly true) or less interested (also probably true), but either way, she again felt invisible as she entered the gate, despite the men standing on guard there.

She decided to do some work and get a feel for the activity in the fort before trying to get into the storage towers. By now she could disassemble the guns without looking and could almost make the repairs the same way. She worked, and observed, and thought. There were no regular patterns to the soldiers' movement, no marching drills or patrols. That would be a problem.

On the other hand, the soldiers who passed close to her work space either glanced at her with a total lack of interest, or didn't look at her at all. After Morgan's sexually aggressive behavior, their disinterest was welcome. And it might mean they wouldn't pay much attention to where she went.

She finished three weapons and decided to test the waters. She strolled out of the storage tower and ambled down the long row of towers to the right of the outer gate. She kept her eyes focused on the ground, or the walls, and carefully did not meet the eyes of any soldier who passed her. Continued lack of interest. There were only five towers on this side of the fort; beyond these the log wall continued until it met, as she'd guessed, the mountainside.

She walked all the way to the end, turned around, and came back. This time, when she reached the end tower, she stopped and tried her key in the lock, making an informed guess about the laziness of Thorsten Keep's designer. It turned stiffly. Heaven must be on her side.

She opened the door and went inside, deliberately not looking around. This was where instinct worked against you. It was always tempting to see if you were observed when you were going someplace you shouldn't. But that kind of movement drew attention to you the way boldness, and the air of being somewhere you were allowed to be, did not.

The crates inside, like the ones in her tower, had had their nails removed so their lids came off easily. The word BLANKETS was stenciled on every box. She removed the lid of one and found, to her surprise, that it actually was full of blankets. She felt down inside it, moved a couple of crates and searched inside those as well. All were entirely full of scratchy, gray wool blankets. She replaced everything and left the tower, relocking it.

Well. That was unexpected. So some of the shipments were legitimate goods. She hoped she wouldn't have to search every tower to find the contraband she was looking for.

She went back and worked on a few more guns. Establishing a pattern was also key. Staying still and waiting for a break in activity only made you more obvious when you did start to move. She went back and forth between her legitimate work and her sneaking, but still found nothing illicit.

One tower had crates of mail shirts, oiled and wrapped individually, standard military issue if somewhat outdated. The Ruskalder didn't use projectile weapons, so maybe on the frontier the shirts were still useful. Rations, clothing, more rations, more guns, boxes and boxes of bullet wheels, one tower holding perishable items — this one was in frequent use, so she had to observe it from a distance and hope what she wanted wasn't there.

She packed up a crate of newly repaired weapons and took a moment to rearrange everything, working weapons here, broken weapons there. The task left her sweaty despite the chill in the air, and she removed her coat and draped it on the stack of finished work. Only a few more towers to investigate, and she hadn't found anything more incriminating than a couple of bottles of good brandy mixed in with the rations, mislabeled, probably on purpose.

She pushed strands of hair out of her face and took a minute to re-braid her hair. Then she continued her exploring. It was getting dark. This might have to be the last one.

This tower again held boxes supposedly containing blankets. Telaine frowned as, once again, she found nothing but blankets. Could the secret shipments be so mundane? She put everything back the way it was supposed to be.

"I don't think you're supposed to be in here, Miss Bricker."

She spun around. Morgan. Her heart raced as if it alone could propel her out of the tower, out of danger, but he had her trapped against a pile of crates, his tall, broad-shouldered body filling the doorway. His face was in shadow, but she could see the dark arch of his brows outlined on his pale face. Acting innocent wasn't going to help her this time. She tried it anyway.

"You caught me," she said with a wry smile, holding up the iron key. "I found out this opens all the towers, and I couldn't resist taking a peek."

"Somehow I think milord Baron won't accept that as an excuse." He took a step toward her. She felt that feline smile tugging the corners of his mouth. "I wonder what he'll do if I tell him where I found his pet Deviser?"

Telaine couldn't think of anything to say. She hadn't spent eight years charming the noblemen of Tremontane without knowing how to tell when charm simply wouldn't work. This was one of those times.

And begging Morgan for anything would be suicidal. She took a step back and her foot bumped the nearest crate.

"Don't worry, I won't tell him. A secret you and I can share." Another step closer. She couldn't go any farther back. "But you know, don't you, that it's a secret with a price."

"What price?" She managed to keep her voice steady.

Now that he was no longer backlit by the watery evening light from the doorway, she could see his face clearly, his pointed, cruel smile, and it terrified her. "A kiss," he said. "Only a kiss."

Remember the game he likes to play. First awareness, then fear, then submission. And then he has you. It was past time for pretending not to understand; he needed to see her fear. That wouldn't be hard. She had started to shake from his nearness. "One kiss?" she asked, letting her voice tremble. She gripped the edge of the crate she was backed up against to keep her hands from shaking as well.

He stepped close, only inches separating them. **"one kiss."**

Before she could register the lie in his voice, before she could scramble away, his hand was behind her head and his lips were fastened on hers, hard and hungry. She whimpered, unable to control herself, and he put his other arm around her waist and pulled her close enough to feel every inch of his body pressed against hers.

Terrified, she pushed ineffectually at his shoulders. He released her, grabbed her hands and pulled them down to her sides. "Fighting back entitles me to another kiss," he whispered.

He pushed her back against the crates, making her cry out as an edge cut into the base of her spine, then took both her wrists in one hand and slid his free hand up her waist, her torso, up until his hand covered her breast. She struggled like a panicked animal in a cage as he kissed her forehead gently, in a parody of tenderness, then squeezed her breast and chuckled as she cried out again.

"Don't fight me," he murmured in her ear. "We both know this is what you want." His hand moved from her breast to the front of her trousers, and now she fought with every ounce of strength she had. Everything she'd ever learned about fighting, every technique of self-defense, went out of her head in her panic. She tried to kick Morgan or knee him or anything that would get her away from him, but he leaned against her, pinioning her lower body while his hand worked at the buttons of her trousers.

"No—" she screamed, but his mouth was on hers again, hard and pitiless, and mindlessly she struck out the only way left to her, sinking her teeth into his lower lip and biting until blood flowed.

He jerked away, released her hands and struck her hard across the face, making her bite the inside of her cheek. The taste of his blood mingled with the taste of her own. Morgan stepped backward, pressing the back of his hand to his bleeding mouth. He was breathing heavily, but his face had returned to his usual mocking expression.

"Afraid, but still a fighter," he said. "You're not ready, after all." He bowed to her. "I look forward to our next encounter." He backed out of the tower, bowed again, and vanished.

Telaine shook so hard she couldn't control herself. *It's the cold, just the cold,* she told herself. A wonder her inner voice never echoed with the lies it told her. She touched her cheek; it was sore and hot and puffy. It took her several tries to refasten the buttons he'd—she remembered the feel of his hands tugging at them and had to sit down to keep from passing out, her hand clutching the front of her trousers together.

Then she wrapped her arms around herself, rubbing her breast as if she could rub out the memory of his touch, and waited for the shaking to subside enough that she could return to her tower and retrieve her coat. Her heart wouldn't stop pounding. She saw Morgan in every shadow. Wrapped in her coat, she hurried down the mountain in the gathering dusk.

She couldn't keep herself from reliving memories, Morgan's hands, his lips on hers, until she was shaking again from more than the cold. She clenched her fists and made herself think about what she'd discovered. Storage rooms full of exactly what they were supposed to be full of. A fort full of slovenly troops—no, that was wrong, a fort barely staffed by slovenly troops. Captain Clarke killed because he was in the Baron's way *hard lips, hands pulling her too close —*

The whole time she'd been in Longbourne, she'd never seen a single soldier come through town on his way to the fort. Mistake with paperwork or not, they were sending soldiers away and not replacing them *a hand, squeezing her —*

Why did they need so many supplies if the fort wasn't even half full? Hardy's information told her the fort was supposed to have three hundred men, but based on what she'd seen there was barely a fifth that many stationed there. That was ridiculous. They had enough weapons and supplies stored to outfit an army.

An army.

Telaine stopped, her heart now pounding for a different reason. Enough to outfit an army that wasn't there. At a fort sitting across the only pass from Ruskald through the mountains, a back way into the kingdom.

He's not a smuggler. He's a traitor. He's going to let the Ruskalder in, arm them, and set them loose on Tremontane.

CHAPTER TWENTY-ONE

Telaine began to run, tripped in the growing darkness, then slowed as reason asserted itself. She couldn't get the message through until tomorrow at the earliest, when Abel Roberts drove into Ellismere. She shouldn't get herself killed tripping over things in the dark before then, because she was the only person aside from the Baron and Jackson and probably Morgan (*don't think about him!*) who knew what the Baron planned.

She walked quickly down the road to Longbourne, lost in thought. The snows would be here soon. The Baron couldn't implement his plan before then, because the Ruskalder army would be stuck in the valley until the main pass cleared in spring. That gave her an advantage.

She didn't know how long it took Thorsten Pass to clear, but if she got the message to her uncle in time, he could have the army ready to march up the mountain and make the fort defensible before the Ruskalder came. Thorsten Pass had a northern exposure, and the main pass faced south; the army would have plenty of time.

She wished she could fly down the mountain to Ellismere, break into the telecoder office and send her message right now, today, this instant. Waiting until daybreak was torture. Riding in silence with Abel would be torture.

"Lainie! There you are!" Jack Taylor called out, startling her. She'd been so preoccupied she hadn't realized she'd entered Longbourne and walked all the way down the main street to the tavern. "You've got to need a drink, long day of work like you've had. Come on in."

"I don't know, Jack," she began. Socializing after what she'd learned, after what Morgan had done to her, seemed impossible. She wanted to crawl into her warm bed and hide.

"Oh, come on, Lainie, you can't be *that* tired, nice quiet job like that. Ben's going to sing for us." Jack had his hand on her elbow now, and she nearly yanked it away, but remembered in time that he was her friend and not going to shove her up against *a stack of crates —*

"Just one drink, Jack, it's been a long day," she said, and followed him into the tavern. Noise and light greeted her, and laughter, and she put on a smile and hid her confusion and misery away where she could take them out and indulge them later, in the privacy of her room. Ben, leaning against the pianoforte, smiled when he saw her and came to greet her.

"You're late," he said, and raised his hand to her cheek. "And you've got something on your face."

Too late, she remembered Morgan hitting her. She put her hand up to cover her cheek and Ben's hand brushed against hers. He looked puzzled, then took her hand away and looked at the bruise. "What happened?" he said.

"Nothing." It sounded false even to her.

"It can't have been nothing. Did you fall?"

"I—" She was so tired. "Yes. I fell."

Ben looked at the bruise again, then into her eyes. She looked away, feeling guilty and stupid. What kind of agent couldn't come up with a good lie?

He touched her face again, gently, then his hand went still. "Morgan," he said in a low, rough voice. "I'll kill him." He strode to his chair and picked up the coat he'd slung over it.

His movement brought her out of her stupor. "No, *no*, stop, please, don't do it!" she cried, grabbing his arm.

"What's the problem?" Jack asked.

Ben ignored him. "I warned you," he told her. "You knew he was dangerous. You thought you could keep out of his way. I warned you he was more than you could handle."

"Ben, let the rest of us in on this," Liam said.

Telaine shook her head, pleading with her eyes. She couldn't let him leave. Her imagination supplied her with a dozen scenarios in which Ben confronted Morgan, all of which ended with him dead, most of which ended with Morgan flinging his body at her like some sick trophy. She shook her head again. If she could show Ben how much this mattered to her, maybe he would let it go.

Ben looked from Telaine to Liam. "Morgan's been harassing her," he said, his voice flat. "Today he went too far."

Liam looked at Telaine in puzzlement. "Why didn't you say something?" he asked. "We could've found a way to keep him away from you." There was nodded and verbal agreement from the crowd.

"Lainie, let go," Ben said.

"No. You promised you wouldn't go after him. You *promised* me."

"Happen I lied. Not going to let him get away with this."

"He's going to kill you. I couldn't bear it if he did."

"You think I—we—could bear it if he did anything to you?"

Telaine looked around the room at her friends. Every face was filled with concern for her. Tears threatened to spill over her cheeks. *No one in Aurilien would care if the Princess dropped dead,* she thought irrelevantly, and then she really was crying.

Ben stopped trying to reach the door and removed her hands from his arm. "Morgan needs to know you've got people ready to defend you. Needs to stop thinking you're helpless. You know he won't stop unless someone makes him."

"I'm not helpless. I can handle it," Telaine said, trying to sound assertive through her tears. "Stay out of this, Ben. I don't need your help."

The room went quiet. Ben took a step back, as if she'd slapped him, then he went expressionless in a way that frightened her more than his fury had. "Happen you don't," he said. He slung his coat around himself and pushed through the crowd to the door. The sound of it closing behind him was barely audible in the silent room.

Telaine stared at the door. *What did I say?* She looked around. No one met her eyes; the floor and the ceiling and the furnishings were apparently far more interesting. "I didn't mean," she began, took a deep breath, and said, "I just wanted to keep him out of this."

"Why?" asked Maida from behind the bar.

"Because I don't want him to get hurt," she said.

"Looks like you did a fine job of doing that yourself," her friend retorted.

"But I didn't mean..." Her hands were shaking again, and she took hold of a chair to steady herself. *I don't need your help.* Those sounded like words you couldn't take back.

Liam cleared his throat, drawing her attention. "Lainie, we all know you like to do for yourself," he said, "but nobody can do *everything* for herself. And when you tell the man who loves you that you don't need him, well..." He shrugged.

Telaine's mouth dropped open, and she was grateful she was already hanging on to the chair, because without it she would have fallen over in shock. "Loves me?" she said in a tiny voice.

Everyone started speaking at once, their words jumbling together in the confusion, a few voices cutting across the noise.

"Never seen any man so swept off his feet by a woman," said Liam. "Never in all my days."

"Don't know how you didn't know. Everyone else did," said Isabel.

"He looks at you like you're water in the desert," said Maida. "You can't have missed that. Or I guess you can."

Telaine was dazed, as if all the noise was happening somewhere far away and she could hear only echoes. "I didn't know," she said. She let go of the chair and found she could stand unsupported. "What do I do?"

The noise diminished. "Ben's a proud man, Lainie," said Jack. "You—he won't get past that in a hurry. Might want to give him time."

Ben's face rose up in memory, still and expressionless and without a trace of the love she hadn't realized was in his eyes every time he looked at her. It tore at her heart, and she closed her lips on the keening cry that tried to escape them. "No," she said, "I think I need to go," and pushed through the crowd and into the cold, dark night.

She stopped outside the tavern, not knowing where to go. If Ben had decided to go after Morgan anyway, she would never find him in the dark. She looked south and saw a light go on in the house by the forge.

Relief filling her, she ran, tripping and catching herself and running again, until she reached Ben's back door. She waited for her breathing to slow, then knocked. It was a perfectly ordinary, polite sound that had nothing of her tumultuous feelings in it, and she almost wanted to laugh at how absurd it sounded. She waited. Nothing happened.

Telaine knocked again. *He can't hear me*, she thought, but that was ridiculous, his house wasn't that big, and even if he had retreated upstairs he would be able to hear the knock. But there was still no answer. Her breath was coming more rapidly again, steaming in the cold night air, and she tried to calm herself. This was ridiculous. If they could just talk to each other—!

She pounded hard on the door with her fist. The light went out, leaving the house in darkness. It was like a punch to the stomach. So he didn't love her anymore. Didn't love her, just as she realized how much she loved him.

She'd assumed their relationship was—not casual, of course, they cared about each other, but she'd thought it hadn't gone any further than that. It was obvious, now, that he loved her, and she hadn't seen it because—why? Because she was too stupid to know her own heart, or to recognize love when it was handed to her. He'd told her he would always come after her. He'd showed her how he felt in a million little ways, every single day. And Eleanor had even warned her he was the kind of man who gave his whole heart. She just hadn't been paying attention. As usual.

Telaine leaned her head against the door. A proud man, Jack had called him. She'd humiliated him, and in public. He wouldn't get over that in a hurry. He might not get over it at all. It had been an emotional day, but even the shock of figuring out the Baron's plan and the terror of Morgan's assault couldn't top the misery she felt right now.

She was cold, and her heart ached, and she wished there were some kind of inherent magic that would let you wind back time, make different choices. That moment in the tavern was playing out in an endless loop in her head, *I don't need your help* and then Ben's white, emotionless face, until she wanted to run away screaming—but, then, where could she run to get away from herself? She wished she could blame the Princess for destroying everything, but no, this was entirely the fault of that idiot Telaine North Hunter.

Light bloomed, streamed through the window, and she straightened in time to avoid falling through Ben's back door as he opened it. The house was two steps up from the forge floor, so Telaine had to look up at him where he stood. He didn't look angry, or upset, just cast that level, unsmiling gaze on her and said nothing.

She gaped at him, said, "Ben," then realized she didn't have a plan for what she would say to him when she found him. She groped about for words, feeling a rising panic, and started babbling.

"I'm not good at letting other people help me. I wanted to protect you and I forgot you might want to protect me because I'm not used to being protected, and I think that means we should try to protect each other. I know it's stupid, but I didn't know you love me, and maybe that's the wrong thing to say because you might think I don't love you, because if I did I would have known how you felt. But I do love you. I just didn't know until it was too late."

The words rattled off into the distance, leaving her feeling empty and uncertain as to what she'd said. He looked at her with no change in his expression. "Happen we should have this conversation inside," he said, and held the door open for her.

She waited until he sat on the sofa, his elbows on his knees and his hands clasped together, to take the rocking chair opposite. Having said her piece at the door, she didn't know what else to say, or do. Ben's jaw was clenched, and he looked as if he might never speak again, which meant it was probably still her turn to talk. She opened her mouth, then closed it, afraid she might start babbling again. She wanted so badly to ease the pain she'd caused him.

"I don't know how it is I understand Morgan so well," she said, deciding on total honesty and openness. She probably should have told him this long before. "I look at him and I know what he's thinking, or what he's going to do next. It's frightening and it makes me sick to my stomach. But that's how I know what will happen if you meet him. He will know what you mean to me and he will kill you to torture me. So I lied when I said I was trying to protect you. I was trying to protect myself."

Ben looked up when she began speaking and kept his eyes on her the whole time. She couldn't read his expression. He was going to make her work to get a reaction. It was nice to know he had some flaws, and that stubbornness was one of them. *Maybe he and Aunt Weaver should hold a stubbornness contest,* she thought wildly, and had to choke back a semi-hysterical laugh.

Her hands were shaking again from the emotions she was trying to keep in check. She took a calming breath that was almost completely ineffective and said, "After you left, everyone told me I was stupid because I didn't know you loved me. I *was* stupid. You were never anything but clear about it, and I just didn't understand. I didn't understand even when a lot of other people hinted about it to me. I think it's because I got to be twenty-three without knowing what love was like, or even what it felt like to be attracted to someone. I was too busy with my work to let anyone get that close, I think. But it's no excuse for how oblivious I was. I'm sorry."

Ben shifted his weight, but said nothing. Telaine clenched her hands together. "I don't know what else I need to say," she said. She thought back and listed everything aloud. "I'm sorry I said I didn't need you because that was both cruel and a lie. I'm sorry I said it in public, which made things worse. I'm sorry I didn't listen to you about Morgan—you have no idea how sorry I am about that. I'm sorry I didn't know you were in love with me. And I'm sorry I hurt you."

Ben leaned back on the couch and spread his hands on his knees. His expression was still inscrutable. "What do you think I should do with all that?" he asked.

Telaine looked at the floor. He didn't sound as if her apology mattered to him. She ought to leave, go back to her room and start coding the message about the imminent invasion, forget she'd ever loved Ben Garrett. "I don't know," she said. "I would like you to forgive me, if you can. I love you. I want more than anything for you to love me again." She sounded so pathetic. How had she gotten herself into this? Falling in love with a country blacksmith she couldn't even tell her real name to?

Silence. "You weren't kidding about being stupid about love," Ben said. "You couldn't hurt me like that if I didn't love you. And love's not something you turn on and off like that tap."

She looked up at him, startled. Ben sighed. He leaned forward and put his elbows on his knees again.

"I won't say I've got a right to defend you just because we're walking out together, because that's like I own you," he said, "but you can't expect me to watch you in trouble and not do everything in my power to fix it. That's part of what love is. Lainie, I want you to need me. I want to know you look at me and see someone you can call on anytime, for anything. I don't want you treating me like a mewling babe can't take care of himself, much less anyone else. Because I don't treat you that way at all."

She nodded. Her chest was tight with tears she refused to shed. It was so easy to manipulate a man with tears.

Ben looked off in the direction of the kitchen, shaking his head, and a smile touched his lips. "Should've known you'd follow me right away. Other girls, happen they would've given up, let things fester, but Lainie Bricker can't leave things alone. I stood there behind the door, listening to you knock, and I turned out the light because I wanted to hang on to my anger a while longer. And you didn't go anywhere. So I thought, do I need my anger more than I need her?"

That, and his smile, broke something loose inside her, and then she was crying and covering her face with her hands, thinking crazily that sparing him the sight of her tears might be less manipulative, and heard him kneel on the floor at her feet.

"Sweetheart, you don't have to hide from me," he said, peeling her fingers away from her face, and that made her cry even harder. Everything she'd endured that day turned into tears that poured out of her like an endless river, and she threw her arms around his neck and sobbed into his shoulder, him stroking her hair and murmuring calming words.

"I do need you," she said when her flood of tears had abated. "There's something I need to tell you. I can't bear it alone. But I want to sit down together, because you're not going to like what I have to say."

He took her hand and sat next to her on the sofa, and in a trembling voice, with many pauses, she told him what Morgan had done to her. Telling him comforted her, made the fear more distant, though she could tell as she spoke that Ben was having trouble not leaping up and flying off into the night to find and murder Morgan. When she finished, he put his arms around her, drew her to sit close against his chest, and said, "I wish I'd been there."

"So do I."

"You going to listen to me now when I warn you about him?"

"That's not funny."

"Sorry. I meant, how are we going to keep you safe from him?"

"I've been wondering if I could appeal to the Baron. He already knows Morgan makes me uncomfortable, and I think he may value me more than he does Morgan."

"Baron's as dangerous in a less obvious way. Don't think you ought put yourself in his hands."

"I know." She sighed. "I'm not going back to the fort tomorrow. I'm going to Ellismere in the morning."

"Safe as anywhere. Wish I could come along, though." He gave her a squeeze.

"I'll come right back. I promise."

She craned her head to look at him and smile, and her heart beat faster when he gave her his brilliant smile in return. The smile turned mischievous. "Now," he said, turning her in his arms to face him, "I heard somewhere you're in love with me."

"You know how rumors are," she said. "Never can tell which to believe."

He pulled a face. "That's a shame," he said, "because I was planning to kiss you if you were."

Telaine put her arms around his neck. "I think that's an excellent plan."

He smiled again, then kissed her, trailing his fingers along her cheek and threading them through her hair. "I think I should do that again," he murmured, and she replied by sliding her hands around the back of his neck and kissing him until they both had to come up for air. He smelled so good, crisp and clean like the hot metal of the forge.

His lips met hers again, passionately, and the feel of them swept away the memory of Morgan's terrible kiss and filled her with longing for more. *He doesn't know who I am,* she thought, but it was distant and tiny and she could barely hear it over the sound of her heart beating.

Ben put his arms around her and pulled her to him, his kisses growing more urgent, his hands stroking her back and sliding under her shirt to caress her skin. She kissed him harder, willing him to touch her more. She wanted him so badly her whole body felt like it was on fire. *This is what love feels like,* she thought, but it was so much more, it was walking hand in hand down the street, laughing over a shared joke, that brilliant smile of his that told her he loved her, body and soul.

No. Loves who he thinks you are.

That inner voice was getting harder to ignore. His hands moved further up her back, brushing the strap of her brassiere, and for a moment she saw a future in which they lay naked together on his bed, sharing that ultimate expression of love. *He'll have to know the truth eventually, and how will he feel when he realizes he's slept with a woman who doesn't exist?*

She pulled away from him, gently, not wanting to hurt his feelings. "We can't do this," she said. "We have to stop."

Ben blinked at her. Then he closed his eyes and let out a deep breath. "I told you I couldn't be a gentleman in here."

"I don't know if you noticed, but I wasn't exactly being gentlemanly either."

He let go of her, but took her hand and kissed it. "I love you, Lainie. And I want to do this right."

"So do I." She was so close to being done. Go down the mountain in the morning, send her message, then…anything was possible. "At least we're not Trey and Blythe, going at it like weasels." Telaine drew her knees up to her chest and sat with her back against the arm of the sofa. She so badly wanted to tell him all her secrets, not to lie to him about anything. Not lying. There *was* something she could tell him, something more dangerous than the simpler truth of being a princess and a spy. Maybe giving him that secret would make her feel less guilty about the ones she had to keep.

"Ben," she said, "what do you think about inherent magic?"

He raised his eyebrows. "That supposed to fit into this conversation?"

"I want to tell you something." She described her ability, clasping her hands tight to stop their trembling, and watched his face grow still. "I haven't exactly put my life in your hands, telling you this," she said, "but it's still a dangerous secret. I trust you more than anyone. I hope I'm not wrong."

Ben said, "I've never lied to you."

"Only once. When you promised not to go after Morgan."

"That. Yes. And you knew I was lying and didn't say anything."

"How could I?"

"True. You couldn't." He moved to sit closer to her. "Must be an uncomfortable thing, hearing the lies people tell."

"Sometimes. Mostly it's refreshing to know people don't lie to me often. And it can be a warning. Morgan lies to me all the time."

"Morgan," he breathed, clenching his fist. She laid her hand on his.

"Let it go for now," she said. "We'll find a solution."

"Together. Not you trying to do it all yourself."

"I promise. No lies."

He laid his free hand on her cheek. "Thanks for trusting me with that."

She smiled, feeling peace fill her. "Will you walk me home?"

"Seems like a gentlemanly thing to do."

They parted at Aunt Weaver's door with a single kiss. Considering what they'd been doing only minutes before, Telaine thought, it was more than enough.

Telaine woke with the feeling she'd overslept. The light had a strange quality to it. *Abel,* she thought, *I've missed him,* and she leaped out of bed and dressed as quickly as she could, deciding to forgo breakfast rather than miss this opportunity.

She threw open the back door and was stunned at what she saw. Snow blanketed the yard, piled high on the roofs of the sheds, weighed down the pine tree that grew behind the outhouse. It was at least six inches deep across the yard and drifted more than a foot high against the sheds. Snow lay across her toes where it had dropped off the open door. It was more snow than she'd seen in one place, ever. More snow than fell all winter long in Aurilien.

She closed the door and went back upstairs, threw open her window and ducked away from a pile of snow that dropped off the window frame past her head. An uninterrupted carpet of snow had unfurled the entire length and breadth of the main street. A gap in the lowering clouds above let through a beam that turned a patch of the carpet to diamonds.

There were no paths, no indication that Abel had left yet. She might still make it. She dashed back downstairs and into the weaving room, where Aunt Weaver worked the loom alone. "Do you think Abel's left for Ellismere yet?" she demanded.

Aunt Weaver gave her a look that said Telaine was demented. "Abel's not going anywhere," she said. "First big storm of the year. The pass is closed until spring."

WINTER

CHAPTER TWENTY-TWO

Trapped in Longbourne for the winter. Telaine paced her room, cursing herself for not being faster. If she'd found out the Baron's plan a week ago, she would have been down the mountain before the snow fell and her uncle could prepare to defend against the invaders. Now he and the army would have to scramble to catch up, and suppose Thorsten Pass cleared before the main pass did?

She flung herself on her bed and beat the mattress with her fists. She couldn't stop thinking about what an army of Ruskalder would do to defenseless Longbourne.

"Don't see why you're so upset," Aunt Weaver said from the doorway. "Seems like you get your wish."

Telaine rolled over. "What wish?"

"An excuse to stay here longer," Aunt Weaver said. "Not hard to see what you was thinking."

"I have a job to do, Aunt Weaver," Telaine said. She almost told her about the invasion, but stopped herself before the words poured out. It wasn't fair to burden her with the knowledge when she wasn't an agent herself, however good a confidante she'd turned out to be. "I can't afford to be stuck here all winter. Doesn't *anyone* go down the mountain? Skis, or snowshoes?"

"Passes are worse than the valley," Aunt Weaver said. "You could try it, but you'd walk right over the edge and they'd find your bones at the bottom of the mountain come spring. Might as well enjoy your... bad luck." She turned and left Telaine staring after her, feeling guilty all over again as if her secret wish to spend the winter in Longbourne had caused this calamity.

She looked out her window again. A few people were in the street now, shoveling out pathways in front of their doors. The snow was deep enough that the paths looked like sunken ditches; the roads were clearly impassable. She wondered how many of those wagons she'd seen coming up and down the pass all summer were trapped here for the duration, too.

She tromped downstairs and began making breakfast. Aunt Weaver was right; there was nothing she could do about it, and she wouldn't make the winter pass more quickly by punishing herself for getting what she wanted.

After breakfast she took a turn with the shovel, awkwardly carving out a path that joined up with Verity Hansen's tailor shop next door. Michael, Verity's young apprentice, helped her dig the last few paces.

"You'll love it here in the winter, Miss Bricker," he said, wiping his streaming red nose with his gloved hand. "The quarry and the sawmill shut down, so everybody's got their family home and ready to play. The kids get into these ditches and have snowball fights after school, and sometimes the grownups join in too. Last year I saw Mister Fuller dunk Scottie Albright in the snow headfirst when Scottie hit him in the face with a snowball!"

"That doesn't sound like much fun for Scottie."

"Mister Fuller gave him a piece of licorice after. It was all in fun."

Telaine planted the shovel in the snow and leaned on it. "I've never made a snowball in my life."

"Happen you'll learn quickly. You'll want to be able to fight back."

It took Telaine a few days to learn to relax and enjoy herself. It helped that so many of her friends were on holiday thanks to the quarry and mill shutting down. Though they all seemed to have seasonal jobs in Longbourne, they also had plenty of time for fun down at the tavern, and Telaine could usually find good company there.

Eleanor, whose job didn't let up because of the season, always had time to chat over the laundry tubs, and Ben...what a difference being in love made. Now he made time in the middle of the day to go walking with her, hand in hand through the snow, trying to drown one another by knocking loads of snow off the trees and kissing under the dark-needled branches.

Telaine's only worry was Morgan. She stayed in Longbourne for a week, defying the Baron's instructions about mending the weapons, panic gripping her throat whenever she thought about going back to the fort. But although soldiers still came to the tavern occasionally, Morgan never appeared.

Eventually Telaine mastered her fear, strapped on a pair of snowshoes and staggered and fumbled her way to the fort. After a few off-handed inquiries, she learned Morgan hadn't been there all week. She repaired a few weapons and made her escape. He was probably holed up in the manor with the Baron, she thought. She hoped he was too preoccupied to think of her.

But the Baron summoned her to the manor nine days after the pass closed for a minor repair to his music box Device, and Morgan wasn't there either. She didn't quite dare to ask the Baron about him, but she was beginning to suspect Morgan wasn't in the valley at all. If the Baron had sent him down Thorsten Pass on some errand to the Ruskalder, he would have been trapped by the storm as thoroughly as she was. She had a moment's worry about what part Morgan's absence might play in the Baron's scheme, what could be so important that the Baron had sent him down Thorsten Pass after full dark, but it was buried under her profound relief that he couldn't assault her again.

She used the snow as an excuse not to go to the fort often; the knowledge that she was repairing guns the Ruskalder intended to turn on Tremontane made her wish she'd lied about the possibility that they could be fixed. Would the Ruskalder even consent to use them? She'd heard their aversion to using projectile weapons was a religious one and a longstanding tradition. The Baron must be confident about convincing them otherwise to stockpile so many of the Devices. Even so, putting any weapons into their hands made her angry.

Winter in Longbourne was so different from winter in Aurilien, where she would have gone to parties and concerts every night and paid visits every day. Few people in Longbourne had Devices and even fewer needed them repaired, and she had no other hobbies, so between that and her decreased employment at the fort, she was frequently bored.

She wandered around the house so much Aunt Weaver finally said, "If you've got nothing else to do, happen you should think about your Wintersmeet gifts. Never too early to worry about those."

The Longbourne tradition of exchanging gifts personally made by the giver made Telaine uncomfortable. She only had one talent—well, only one she could share—and how was she supposed to make gifts with the few materials she had left? She had little but her sack of spare parts, and she couldn't exactly go to people's homes asking for things they might want turned into Devices. Holidays were so challenging. She thought of the Wintersmeet ball held at the palace, everyone dressed in white and silver, dancing away the last and longest night of the year, and felt little sorrow at missing it.

On one of their midday walks, Ben said, "Watch this." He pointed at a burl on a nearby tree, whipped his arm around, and suddenly the burl had sprung a small knife. Ben waded over to get it.

"I had no idea you could do that," Telaine said.

"Only do it in winter. Keeps me warm and my eye sharp." He threw the knife again. "Wish I'd brought more of 'em."

"Will you teach me?"

"You planning to go hunting?"

"Just the trees. It's such a graceful thing."

Ben retrieved the knife again and handed it to her. "Stand like this...and then hold the knife like this. Then it's a quick overarm movement, *so*."

The knife flew a few feet and disappeared into the snow. They looked at each other. "I see a flaw in this plan," Telaine said. She dug around until she found the knife.

"Happen we can find a less snowy place," Ben said. "Figured out your plan was to get my arms around you, anyway."

"I didn't think I needed a plan for that. Weasel. No, don't!"

The lesson continued after Telaine shook the snow out of her shirt.

The laundry was so comfortable in winter, warm and muggy and perfect for sitting and chatting. Too bad Eleanor had more than sitting and chatting on her mind. "I think this is a bad idea," Telaine said. She waved her knitting needles. "I told you I'm no good at sewing."

"This is knitting, not sewing, and if you can turn wire and eyelets into a tent of lights, happen you can learn to turn a skein of yarn into a scarf," Eleanor said. She rearranged Telaine's grip on the needles. "Now, you remember the difference between knit and purl? This is knit one, purl one—"

The door flew open. "Baron's riding into town," Ben said. "Alone."

Telaine leaped to her feet, dropped her needles and several stitches, and followed Ben out the door. The Baron approached on his indifferent gray, glancing around with no sign of interest in his surroundings. A weight lifted from her shoulders. If the Baron himself was here, it meant his usual errand runner was not in the valley. Suddenly the long months of winter seemed like a Wintersmeet gift.

"Miss Bricker," the Baron called out while he was still several feet away. Telaine made her bow. "Excellent. My dear, I have a challenge for you. Would you mind accompanying me to the manor?" He did not make it sound like an invitation.

"Of course, milord," Telaine said, bobbing another little bow. "Give me a moment to fetch my tools."

She sped through the ditches to Aunt Weaver's house. He hadn't chastised her for not having finished the work at the fort, so maybe he didn't know about it. Or maybe he was waiting to get her alone before unleashing his fury on her. Either way, she didn't have much choice; if she refused to go with him, it was impossible to say how he might react, and he might decide to take out his anger on an innocent person.

When she returned, clutching her roll of tools, the Baron took her up behind him and trotted away without mentioning the fort, or the guns, or Morgan. Telaine looked back over her shoulder at Ben, who stood in the road with his fists clenched. He'd probably follow her if she didn't return by nightfall. She didn't know whether to be grateful for that, or afraid.

The Baron was silent the whole way to the manor, and continued silent after they were safely inside out of the cold. He escorted her down one of the hallways. "I assume you can repair a clock?" he said.

"Certainly, milord."

"I don't like how the one in the library is running. And I dislike the sound."

"The…sound, milord?"

"The sound it makes when it strikes the hour. It's tinny. I want a more full-bodied sound."

"I'm not sure the sound is created by a Device, milord, but I'll do my best."

"And your best is always excellent."

He led her to the library, which she had not yet seen. It about the same size as the Baron's study, with bookshelves much more delicate than those in the study lining the walls. The books looked as if they were actually read as opposed to being décor, which gave the room a homey feeling the study lacked. Some comfortable reading chairs sat near a fireplace in which a lively yellow fire burned steadily, with Devices hanging low to illuminate pages better than the fire would. Ladders on rails, elegant constructions of ash and gilt, gave access to the upper shelves.

A round clock almost three feet in diameter hung crookedly on one wall, well above the shelves nearest it. Thick glass distorted the numbers on its face and made the hands, which looked like they might weigh a pound each, seem bent enough to scratch the glass. Telaine looked at it in dismay.

"What's the matter, young lady?"

"It's…rather high, milord."

"You can reach it by way of the ladders, **or so i'm told.**" Telaine looked at him narrowly. Personal knowledge of how the ladders worked seemed an unlikely thing to lie about.

He showed her a Device that slid up and down one handrail of each ladder so she could take it with her as she ascended. "This controls the ladder's lateral movement, but each ladder has its own guiderail, so its area of movement is limited. I believe that ladder travels beneath the clock." Telaine climbed the ladder, sliding the Device with her, and pushed buttons until she was centered under the clock. It was still a foot out of her reach.

"Climb to the top step," the Baron suggested. Was he trying to kill her? She steadied herself, reached up, and gently lifted the clock from the wall. The ladder swayed, and she froze, heart pounding, until it steadied. Then she carefully descended, releasing a breath she hadn't known she'd held when her feet touched the solid floor.

"I suppose I can do this on the floor, if I move the chairs, milord," she said. The Baron himself dragged the chairs to either side of the fireplace and sat down in one of them. Apparently this was to be a repair with an audience.

She turned the clock onto its face and took it apart. Fine-tuning the Device took a while, because there were no obvious problems and she had to search carefully before deciding there was nothing wrong with it, whatever the Baron said. She settled for making a show of repairing it, then turned to the problem of the bell.

It did sound tinny, she thought, lifting the clapper and letting it strike, but…what was this? Someone had wedged a penny between the two bells. When she removed it, and tried the clapper again, it rang out sweetly. She palmed the penny and said nothing about it. If the Baron had sunk to sabotaging his Devices to get her out here, he was even more bored than she was. With Morgan gone, the only person he could socialize with was his pet Deviser.

"Does that sound better, milord?" she said, trying not to sound sarcastic.

The Baron smiled. "Much better."

She reassembled the clock, then hesitated. "I think it might be wise for milord's servants to replace the clock. They'd know better than me how to hang it right."

The Baron nodded. "Wise indeed, Miss Bricker. Will you join me for dinner?"

Telaine wanted nothing less than to eat with this man, but she said, "Thank you for the invitation, milord." It was hard to reconcile this genial man with the murderer of Captain Clarke. No doubt he would continue to call on her, and she would bet his summons would always coincide with dinner. But she had no choice but to accept, if she wanted to avoid drawing his anger.

A traitor and a murderer, and vicious too, she reminded herself, following him to the dining room. The consequences of disappointing him didn't bear thinking on.

"You want to do *what?*" Josephine said. She held an underskirt in both hands and clutched it to her bosom as if it were all that stood between her and indecency.

"I don't think it's all that shocking," said Telaine. "I want to see if a Device can be made using some other case than metal or wood."

"It sounds so odd. Like...like asking a cow to produce butter."

"Hardly that unnatural. Please, Josephine, help me think of something. What would be useful for fabric to do?"

Josephine lowered the underskirt and cast her eyes around the store. "Color changing fabric...no, even I know that's impractical. Self-buttoning shirt? Pointless. Heated—oh, Lainie, I have it!" She thrust the skirt at Telaine and disappeared into the back room. Telaine draped it over her arm and waited. Josephine emerged with a bundle of gray wool so pale it looked dingy white. She shook it out.

"Long underwear," she said. It was a woolen bodysuit, with buttons at the neck and a buttoned flap near the groin. "It's perfect."

"Perfect for what?"

"A self-heating Device."

"Isn't long underwear supposed to keep you warm by itself?"

"This is the usual kind. It's heavy and bulky and it itches. But suppose you could make it out of a thinner, softer fabric and turn it into a Device whose heat you could control?"

Telaine's eyebrows rose. "Josephine, that's perfect," she said. "Can you make up a suit for me in the lighter cloth? And give me a large swatch of the fabric?"

It took Josephine only a minute to pull a bolt of light cotton from her stores and cut a foot-wide piece for Telaine. Swatch tucked away in her trouser pocket, Telaine walked back to the forge. It was a clear, sunny day, and she pushed back the hood of her cloak and breathed in the cold air. The cloak wasn't as practical as her coat, but it was warmer and it made her feel mysterious, like a wise woman out of a fairy tale. Would she dispense blessings, or curses? On a day like this one, it was definitely blessings.

"I need a lot of thin wire," she told Ben, entering the forge but staying well out of his work path.

"What kind of wire?" he said, not looking up from what he was doing.

"Copper."

"What about the wire from the tent of lights at the Bradfords' shivaree?"

"It's too thick. I need something a lot finer."

"I'm not experienced with copper, but happen I can handle that."

"Good. Can you do it soon?"

Ben shrugged. "I can draw wire as fine as you like, but unless you have copper ingots lying around, I can't help you."

Telaine slumped. "If I'd gotten into Ellismere one last time, I'd have all the supplies I need."

Ben glanced her way. "Is it important?"

"Could be a major invention. Not important on the level of, say, feeding Longbourne for the winter, but important to me."

"There's a copper weathervane in the basement of the town hall. You might be able to buy it from the town. Fell off the roof a couple years back and they never put it back up. You'll see why when you look at it."

When she got into the town hall basement, Telaine did see why. It was the ugliest thing she'd ever seen designed to grace the top of a building. In this case, "grace" wasn't nearly as good a word as "defile." A sort of gargoyle thing rested at the center of the spire, surrounded by letters representing the cardinal directions. A spire emerged from the base that made it look like the gargoyle had been impaled, an effect not lessened by the gargoyle's expression of extreme pain.

"You want it?" asked Katrin Black, Longbourne's mayor and

postmistress and holder of at least six other public offices. "I could pay you to take it away."

"I can afford to buy it," Telaine said with a laugh, "but I hope we can agree on a good price. And by 'good' I mean 'cheap'."

"If you can fix the lights in the schoolhouse, that'll make us even." They shook on the deal.

The weathervane produced a lot more copper than Telaine had anticipated. She asked Ben to save half in ingot form and to turn the rest into wire. The final diameter of the wire disappointed her, as she'd wanted something finer, but Ben didn't have the right drawing plate and she had to admit, while not ideal, it would still work.

A few days later, she returned to Josephine with her finished product. They both looked at it critically where it swung on a hanger in Josephine's work room.

"It's ugly," Josephine said. "I didn't think it would be ugly." The white cotton suit hung like someone's empty skin. Copper glinted at wrists, neck, and ankles, and wove in and out of the fabric from top to bottom like red-gold snakes.

"It's supposed to go under your clothes, not be visible," Telaine reminded her. "But you're right, it *is* ugly." She began taking off her clothes. "Let's see if it works."

She put the suit on over her underclothes, buttoned the neck and sleeves, and turned a disc at her waist. "Not working yet. This fabric really is thin."

"It's what you asked for."

"I know. That wasn't criticism." A trickle of warmth spread out from near her navel. "I think it's working." More heat, this time from her wrists and ankles, and a ruby warmth circled her neck. "It's definitely working!" She clasped Josephine's hands and both women jumped up and down in excitement.

"Oops," Telaine said. Her ankle had gone cold. She bent to twist one of the wires, restoring heat. "I think I might not have secured this properly."

"I think the control knob ought to be at the neck," Josephine said.

"Too many ways for it to get damaged or turned off at the waist."

"That will make the heat spread unevenly, but I agree." An impish smile touched Telaine's lips. "Do you have a back door?"

She stood behind Josephine's shop in a snowdrift, clad only in her long underwear and a pair of castoff boots too large for her, and felt as warm as if it were a spring day. "We're going to be famous!" she shouted, and Josephine laughed. "Famous — oh!" A snowball struck her shoulder. "You little brat!" Another snowball caught her in the chest, and she waded through the drifts back to the store.

"Certain sure you gave those children a show," Josephine remarked.

"Better them than someone who'd care about how ugly it is."

"Some of that's my fault. I'll make the next one prettier."

"And I'll make it more effective." They grinned at each other.

Thunk. "That was much better. You hit the tree."

"With the handle."

"Better than last time, when you nearly knocked that squirrel unconscious. Poor critter, never did you any harm."

Thunk. "Should I be happy I hit the same tree twice in a row, or disappointed that it was still with the handle?"

"The hilt."

"Don't take that tone with me. I've got three more knives here."

"I beg your pardon, milord, but I don't see what's wrong with the Device. It seems to be working perfectly."

"I believe if you take a look there, you'll see the problem."

"…Indeed, milord, you're right. You've developed an instinct for these things."

"I consider you my inspiration, my dear."

"I can't tell you how happy that makes me, milord."

"Do you think the lace is necessary, Josephine?"

"Happen not. And it limits the appeal. But the buttons are

effective, yes?"

"I like the buttons. Would you like to try it this time?"

"Do I have to run around in the yard like you did?"

"Happen it's not a real test unless you do."

Thwack. "That's three times in a row! Point first, same tree, same...well, same general area. I think it's these new knives you made for me."

"Starting to worry you might pass me up."

"I'll take that as a compliment and a challenge."

"I'm so sorry, milord, I don't know how I could have been so sloppy. I'm ashamed that I didn't actually fix the firelighter the first time. I just don't understand it."

"Don't be so discouraged, Miss Bricker. Everyone makes mistakes. Now, it seems when I click this part of the Device, it sparks but does not ignite. Is that your assessment as well?"

"Why, yes, milord. Once again you've seen to the heart of the problem. If I make this adjustment *here*...and that should do it!"

"**i simply don't know how you do it**, time after time."

"Honestly, milord? Neither do I."

"Now *that* is an attractive piece of underwear. Amazing how much difference the new color makes."

"Yes, the copper is striking against the charcoal gray. I believe it's your turn to test it, Lainie."

"True. Let's see—oof—I still say it needs more buttons in front. All the way down to the waist. There. This one is snugger, too."

"Is that good or bad?"

"Good, I think. See, I can still stretch. Would you look out the back door and see if those hoodlums are watching?

"No one's there."

"Oh, it's so warm. That was fast. All right, hold the door for me— here I go!"

CHAPTER TWENTY-THREE

Telaine woke, stretched, and rolled onto her back to stare at the ceiling. Every morning for a month, she'd run over the telecoder message she'd composed for when the pass was clear. It had been warmer for a week, and the snow was melting, but when she'd expressed her hopefulness Aunt Weaver had warned her this mild thaw wasn't enough to melt the snow in the pass before the next storm struck.

Telaine had seen two storms come through, one barely more than a flurry, the other a beast with howling winds that beat new snow into the hardpack of the old. She couldn't begin to imagine what the pass to Ellismere looked like. And Thorsten Pass had to be even worse. It was hard to worry about an invasion in the face of all this snow.

She rolled out of her warm nest and dressed hurriedly. Her new bodysuit was a marvel. She hadn't had to turn it on yet, thanks to the warmer weather, but it bothered her hardly at all under her other layers of clothing. In her woolen sweater, thick trousers, snow boots, and jacket, she felt like a true native of Longbourne.

She took her time eating breakfast; she had nowhere in particular to be today, and planned to spend the morning chatting with Eleanor before going to the tavern to see who was available for some fun. But when she came around the corner of Aunt Weaver's house, she found a soldier about to knock at the door. He made a careless attempt at a salute when he saw her. "Baron wants you up at the fort," he said.

"What for?" she asked.

The soldier shrugged. "As if himself would tell me summat like that."

"Suppose I'm busy."

"Not sure you want to say no to himself, don't know what mood he's in."

The Baron wanted her at the fort. Was he lethally upset about the guns? No, if the Baron wanted her dead he'd have done it one of the many, many times she'd been to the manor recently. "Give me a moment."

He shrugged again. "Take all the moments you want. I'm not waiting for you. You know the way." He slogged off up the street. Telaine ran upstairs to fetch her tools and her snowshoes, then went to the forge.

"The Baron wants me at the fort," she told Ben, who immediately removed his leather gloves to take her hand.

"You're going?" he asked.

"I don't see how I can say no. Morgan was dangerous just by being Morgan. The Baron gets dangerous when he doesn't get his way."

"I don't like it."

"Neither do I. That's why I'm telling you. If I'm not back by dark, come find me."

"I'll always come after you." He kissed her, fixed her with that level gaze, and added, "Don't make it necessary."

The road from Longbourne to the fort had not been broken by more than the soldier's footprints. At the turnoff to the manor she saw those steps joined by a horse's tracks. She tromped in her snowshoes over the combined tracks until she reached the fort's gate. Drifts of snow piled high in the corners inside, where the soldiers had swept it rather than shoveling it out of the fort. She resolutely didn't look at the storage tower second from the left.

She went toward the keep only to see the Baron standing near the fort's inner wall, next to the mysterious crates she'd asked Lieutenant Hardy about weeks before. The Baron was having a conversation with Captain Jackson, but broke it off when he saw her. "My dear Deviser! Thank you for coming. I believe I have a commission for you unlike any you've seen before. Captain Jackson, if you wouldn't mind?"

Jackson picked up a pry bar and levered the lid off the nearest crate. It was approximately six feet long and three feet deep, and if it had been narrower it would have looked uncomfortably like a coffin. It was filled with straw the Baron brushed away with a gloved hand.

Steel and brass gleamed. Telaine, intrigued despite her wariness, leaned forward. "I...don't believe I know what this is, milord," she said.

"And well you should not! It's part of a larger Device. *All* of this is part of a single Device." He put his hand on Telaine's shoulder in a comradely gesture; she managed not to flinch.

"I have long been disturbed at how shut off Steepridge is during the winter. Most disturbing is how long it takes for the passes to be free from snow. It can be a month or more after the last snow before it's possible to go down the mountain. I think, as Baron of Steepridge, it's my duty to make my people's lives easier. Hence...this." He made a sweeping gesture with his free hand. "Miss Bricker, I have acquired an earth mover. And I require you to assemble it."

Telaine didn't hide her shock. Earth mover was a misnomer; the huge Devices could plow through anything, rock, earth, snow, ice, their efficiency only affected by the material they moved and the motive forces powering the Device. An earth mover was one of the biggest Devices created to date, the most powerful, and the most complex, requiring dozens of motive forces and hundreds of gears and coils all working in precise unity. She'd never seen one before and had no idea how it was constructed.

She considered telling the Baron it was impossible, that she didn't have the skill, that it would take a team of Devisers to assemble it, all of which might or might not be true. But she knew in her heart that the Baron had built her reputation so high in his own mind that to refuse would mean leaving this fort in no condition her friends would recognize.

She said, "Milord, I...I hardly know what to say. This is generous of you indeed. The villages will be so happy."

"Oh, but Miss Bricker, it is *you* and your Deviser's skill upon which their happiness depends."

"It's an unlooked for honor, milord. I would never have gotten this chance anywhere else." She was sincere about that. For a Deviser, this was a truly extraordinary opportunity.

"We wait only on your instructions as to your needs."

She thought rapidly. "I'll need a sheltered area built. It will take so much longer if I have to have your men dig it out after every storm. I'll need to make sure it will fit through the gate after it's assembled. It would be so terrible if I put it together and we couldn't take it out of the fort! And I will need specialized tools. My tiny ones simply won't work. The smith in Longbourne can make them for me." How else could she delay them? "And it will take me a few days to familiarize myself with the Device. I've never seen one before."

"I'm putting Captain Jackson at your disposal," the Baron said. Jackson looked uninterested in the conversation, the Device, and Telaine herself, but he nodded at the Baron. "He will direct his men to do whatever you ask."

"Then…Captain Jackson, if your men could build me a sheltered area from *here* to *here*, canvas should do as long as the roof is sloped to let the snow slide off…and perhaps the sides could be portable? Milord, I won't be able to begin work until that's complete, so if you don't mind, I'll go back to Longbourne and have a word with the smith."

Trudging through the snow on the way back, she alternated between cursing herself for a fool and frantically trying to come up with a solution to this new problem. The Baron wanted to clear the pass, all right, but it was Thorsten Pass he cared about.

A month for the main pass to clear? If the Baron had his own earth mover, he'd have Thorsten Pass cleared mere days after the last snow came. The Ruskalder would pour down into unsuspecting Longbourne and put it to the torch, and then drive the earth mover all the way down the mountain and into Tremontane proper with no warning to anyone. The success or failure of that plan rested on Telaine's ability to delay, deceive, and sabotage without bringing the Baron's attention, and vicious cruelty, down on her head.

"Never realized how many tools a Deviser needs," Ben said, spreading out the pages of sketches two days later. Telaine nodded, wishing she'd thought of a way to get him to measure some of the dimensions of the new tools incorrectly. The best she'd been able to do was to ask him to work slowly, which would keep her away from the fort longer.

"Do you have everything you need?" she said.

"Think so. It shouldn't take more than a couple of days—I mean, it's going to take most of a week," Ben said with a grin and a wink. "All these fiddly little things that don't look like any tools I've ever seen."

Telaine kissed his cheek. "Then I'm going to work on my Wintersmeet gifts. I'll be back later, if you want to have supper with me?"

"Can't imagine anything I'd like more. What are you giving me for Wintersmeet?"

"What makes you think I'm giving you anything? Oh—" Ben had seized her around the waist and kissed her until she was breathless. "Oh," she repeated, "I guess I'd better think of something."

"You should, because I've already made yours," Ben said.

She kissed him once more, then went back to Aunt Weaver's. But once she was in her room, she found she couldn't concentrate on her Wintersmeet gifts. Instead she fretted over ways to delay the earth mover construction.

She almost didn't have to pretend; the Device was genuinely complex, and bulky, and the courtyard of the fort an inconvenient place to assemble it. It had taken the slovenly and uninterested soldiers most of two days just to clear a space that would allow her to lay out all seven pieces at once. There was a storm coming that Eleanor said was one of the big ones. That would be another two or three days wasted. And Wintersmeet was fast approaching, which would give her another three days, at least, when the Baron couldn't possibly expect her to work, if only because the soldiers insisted on time off as well. Every day counted.

The problem was, she could only work so slowly before the Baron, who had watched her work so often, realized what she was doing. Delay wouldn't be enough. She'd have to sabotage it instead. That was more dangerous; the Baron would believe almost anything she told him about how long the project would take, but he would be unlikely to believe continual failure. Even if he didn't suspect sabotage, he might fly into a rage at her for the Device's breaking down.

She hoped once she started assembling the pieces, a strategy would suggest itself. Or…could she tell him it had been damaged in transit? It was plausible—but he'd probably expect her to repair the damage anyway. As a last resort, she could simply refuse to work on it. She wondered if she was willing to let the Baron hurt or kill her as the price of keeping the Ruskalder out of Tremontane.

She went to the fort every day while Ben was working on the tools, interfering in the building of the shelter as much as she dared without infuriating the soldiers. Bad enough they were lazy; she didn't need them antagonistic as well. But it gave the Baron the illusion she was accomplishing something, or would have if he'd been there. She'd expected him to hover, had come up with excuses that would get him out of her way, but he hadn't been to the fort since he'd showed her the earth mover. That made her uneasy. Why had he waited nearly a month after the pass closed to call her in for this?

Finally, the tools were finished, the skies were clear, and she couldn't delay any longer. She packed her new tools into a large canvas bag procured from Mister Fuller and trudged up the valley. The novelty of the snow had worn off, particularly now that most of it had melted and what remained was slushy and soaked through her boots to her thick wool socks.

The day was overcast, though Aunt Weaver had assured her no snow would fall before tomorrow morning. Being trapped at the fort for two or three days was one of Telaine's nightmares, even if the soldiers seemed disinclined to attack her.

Within her canvas shelter, she looked at the seven large pieces, laid out in roughly the places they would occupy in the finished product. A steel plow, two shining silvery wings swooping back from a sharp nose, ten feet across at its widest point and about eight feet tall. Two assemblies of small wheels constrained by tracks of iron, segmented for smooth propulsion by the wheels over any terrain the earth mover might encounter. Two complicated cylindrical sections like giant steel barrels, seven feet in diameter, containing more than four-fifths of the unimbued Devices and gears that propelled the thing. A smaller cylinder containing a pile of spheres, unimbued motive forces, which the earth mover would burn through almost as rapidly as it tore through earth. And, most innovative of all, a bulbous capsule with a hatch on the top that, if Telaine could manage it, would hold the Device's own source for re-imbuing the motive forces as they were drained. In its assembled state, the earth mover would look much like a snub-nosed wasp, or a mosquito with a stubby silver proboscis.

Harroden might at least have included assembly instructions, she thought irritably. She heaved the smaller pieces back into the boxes, rolled the cylinders to each side, and examined the nose by walking around it. Four soldiers had tried to lift it out of its crate without success before Telaine suggested taking the crate apart around it. She'd worked out that one function of the motive force was to lift the nose just enough off the ground that it wouldn't drag and flip the whole Device end over end.

She knelt down behind it and reached inside, feeling around for the copper wires that would connect it to the next section. They were as thick as her pinky finger and had a slick surface. One of them had come loose from its coupling; sighing, she reattached it. As tempting as it was to begin sabotaging the thing now, she needed to find a part that might reasonably fail and would be complex enough to justify her overlooking it. The nose, simple and straightforward, was not the place to look.

She poked her head inside the cylinders containing the gears and realized that though they looked identical, there were tiny but key differences between them. This was more like it. Suppressing a grin, she began attaching the wrong cylinder to the nose. She'd "discover" the mistake later, make a lot of noise about how stupid she was, and "fix" the thing. One more delaying tactic. She was afraid it wouldn't be enough.

CHAPTER TWENTY-FOUR

Telaine received an early Wintersmeet gift when a fortuitous snow storm came down on Longbourne two days before Wintersmeet, giving her an extra day's holiday from her unwelcome task. Most businesses had given up the pretense that anyone was working. Eleanor told people their laundry could wait a few days, and besides, no one was paying attention to clothes this time of year.

Ben shut down the forge and joined a snowball fight with a handful of young men and women, shouting at Telaine to participate, pelting her with snowballs until she retaliated with a few lumpy ones of her own. Snowball fights were another of the many things she'd never done before coming to Longbourne. Snowball fights, cooking her own food, drinking beer, falling in love.

Disgusted by her inadequate snowballs, Ben tackled her and rubbed her face with snow until she squealed, then kissed her until she couldn't breathe. Definitely another thing she'd never done before.

Aunt Weaver sent the apprentices home early on the day before Wintersmeet Eve. "Happen you don't know our Wintersmeet customs," she said.

"Don't see how I could know, Aunt Weaver," Telaine said, rolling her eyes.

"No need to be disrespectful. Thought you wanted to be told things now 'stead of working 'em out for yourself."

"I'm sorry, Aunt Weaver. Please continue."

"Uppity girl. Well. Tomorrow we clean house. Gets us ready to start a new year, see."

"I do. That's...interesting. I like it."

"Well, I don't so much like cleaning, but it's good and symbolic. Wintersmeet Eve is for families. We eat together and think about the ones who ain't with us."

Telaine thought of Ben, alone in his house. "That would be sad if you didn't have any other family around."

"That's up to you. Then Wintersmeet day you visit with all your friends and exchange gifts. I take it you have gifts?" Aunt Weaver sounded as if she questioned Telaine's Wintersmeet spirit.

"I've made gifts for everyone. Aunt Weaver, what if someone gives me a gift and I don't have one for them?"

"They won't take offense. Wintersmeet gifts is like a thank you for doing something that mattered to the person giving the gift. Sometimes you do more for a person than they do for you. Sometimes it's the other way around. But mostly you know who's giving to you."

"That's good."

"Wintersmeet night is for big gatherings. Your young man leads the chorals down at the tavern. Figure you'll want to be there. Lots of parties and people goin' from one to the other."

"It sounds beautiful. Far nicer than—"

"Don't say what I know you're goin' to say. Not even in here. Don't even think it."

"I thought *you* told me not to get too attached to Longbourne."

"Too late for that. Might as well embrace it." Aunt Weaver paused, then added, in a quieter voice, "Happen you've got a plan for all that."

Telaine hadn't thought about it. She had to go back to Aurilien eventually, but what would she do after that? She didn't have a plan, but it sounded like Aunt Weaver thought she needed one. Perhaps she was right. Could she come back to Longbourne after this was over? It was a daring thought, and one that unsettled her. Something to think about some other day.

The next day they cleaned more thoroughly than Telaine had thought possible. Sweeping and mopping the weaving room, dusting the sitting room and creating great pale clouds that merely settled back on the furniture. Aunt Weaver made Telaine go outside and wave the broom around the rafters of the outhouse, sweeping out cobwebs that drifted around her like strands of gray, sticky clouds.

It left Telaine feeling exhausted, but Aunt Weaver seemed unaffected as she moved around the kitchen making supper. The smell of hot pork roast and buttery mashed potatoes filled the air. "Happen you'd like to get that candle off the high shelf," Aunt Weaver said, and Telaine climbed the step stool and reached up for a fat silver candle in an iron casing. It had been lit many times before, the wax melting down the sides and over the metal holder, smooth and shiny.

Aunt Weaver produced fine china place settings and silverware and a couple of wine glasses, then, even more surprisingly, a bottle of good wine. She served them both, sat down, poured the wine, and picked up her knife and fork. "Happy Wintersmeet, niece," she said.

"Happy Wintersmeet, aunt," Telaine replied.

They ate in silence, and then Telaine cleared the dishes while Aunt Weaver lit the candle. "Family joins us," she said when Telaine sat down again. It sounded like ritual, one Telaine didn't know. "Family binds us. We leave one family to join another. However far we go, family draws us back." She put her hand around the candle, below the dripping wax. "You put your hand over mine," Aunt Weaver said. Telaine did so.

Aunt Weaver closed her eyes. "You never knew your grandpapa," she said in a quiet voice. "He died before you were born, died too young. I'd grieved for him already when I left, because Zara North died and left him behind, but I didn't know I still had it in me to miss my little brother when he died."

She smiled, her eyes still closed. "He was a brilliant, joyful man. When he was young he cared too much for what other people thought and didn't have the sense to know whose opinions he ought care for. But brilliant and joyful. No question what your grandmama saw in him, though they had a rocky road to travel. Wish I'd been there to see them reach the end."

She fell silent, and Telaine sensed it was her turn. "I never knew my mother," she said. She gazed at the candle flame, trying to see images from the past. "She died of lung fever when I was not quite three. But my father was my whole world when I was a child. When she died, he took me to live in the forest he loved so much. I grew up wild and unschooled, without knowing anything but surviving through winter and summer.

"He taught me a lot of things I forgot, later, growing up in the palace. It was like losing a piece of him every time I tried to remember how to tickle fish, or find my way by the stars — I was so young to learn any of that, and maybe he was denying me my mother's heritage, but I think he loved her so much he couldn't bear the places where she'd been. And then he got sick, and I think he knew he was dying, because he brought me back to the palace before the end. I..." She broke off, cleared her throat. "I've never quite forgiven him for leaving me."

They sat in silence, hand over hand, watching the warm silver wax slide and drip over their fingers to the table, waiting for midnight. There was no clock in the kitchen, but there was no mistaking the moment when the lines of power shifted their alignment in response to the solstice, filling Telaine with a rush of energy.

She could feel her connections to Aunt Weaver and Uncle Jeffrey and Aunt Imogen and her cousins for three seconds, and she knew they could feel her presence too. This was how Uncle Jeffrey felt, all the time. She tightened her hand over Aunt Weaver's. She must have been so lonely, all those years...

Aunt Weaver moved her hand away and Telaine pulled back as well. "That's for our dead," she said. "Now for our living."

"I don't understand."

Aunt Weaver sat back in her chair. "Been gone a long time," she said. "Young Jeffrey was no more than two when I left. I resent this magic that keeps me young because I ain't seen you all grow up. Same magic makes it so I can't have children of my own. Certain sure I couldn't have stayed, but if I could... I want to know my family. Tell me."

Telaine's mind went blank. "Ah...Uncle and Aunt Imogen, they don't look like they ought be a match," she said. "Uncle is all about politics and Aunt Imo loves her horses. And I think Uncle is a little afraid of them. Horses. But then you hear them talking and, I don't know, they don't just finish each other's sentences, they have whole conversations where you can't hear them say anything. We've never talked about it, but I can't imagine she doesn't know what his inherent magic is. They don't keep things from each other. That's the kind of marriage I want."

Memories started flowing in from the back corners of her mind. "Julia and I are like sisters. She's near my same age and she helped me get through the first months after my father died. She doesn't use her beauty like a weapon, like I—like the Princess does, and I wish I could be like her. Jeffy, well, he might as well be Uncle's twin in body as well as name..."

She talked herself hoarse into the dim reaches of night, Aunt Weaver listening silently, and cried because she hadn't known how much she missed her family until that evening. She would have to go back to them. As much as she loved Longbourne, she couldn't stay away from her family.

She talked until the candle burned all the way down and flickered out, then the two of them went to their beds. When she was certain Aunt Weaver was asleep, Telaine went silently down the stairs with her bundle of tools and put together a Wintersmeet gift she knew would catch her aunt's eye.

"Lainie Bricker! You come down here right now!"

Telaine bounded down the steps, wearing her most innocent expression. "Yes, Aunt Weaver?"

"You want to explain this?" Aunt Weaver pointed at the sink.

"It appears to be a tap, Aunt Weaver."

"And what is this?"

Telaine made a big show of examining it. "I believe it's a Device for heating water as it comes out of the tap." It was her best creation yet, a slim cuff of brass that slipped over the tap, with fine silver threads on the underside and a motive force the size of a button below the handle.

"I know I told you I don't want these Devices in my home. Certain sure I told you this before."

"You did tell me. Specifically you told me you don't like depending on things that might break down and be unfixable because of there being no Deviser around. And I agree that even though I'm here now, I won't be here for good."

"And yet there's a Device sittin' on my spigot bold as the brass it's made of."

"That's right. Now here's what I'm thinking. This Device is totally separate from your faucet. You don't want to use it, it's just a pretty ornament on the tap. If you *do* want to use it, you turn both handles and adjust the water to be as hot or cold as you please."

When Aunt Weaver opened her mouth to object, Telaine overrode her with, "And I know you have to accept a Wintersmeet gift in the spirit it's intended, and I intend this to pay you back for your hospitality. Plus I want to wash my hair in warm water. So there you are."

Aunt Weaver turned the handle of her old faucet. She turned the Device handle and ran her fingers under the water. "I still have my own ways—"

"—And they've always been good enough for you. Maybe this could be a new way for the new year. Happy Wintersmeet, aunt."

Aunt Weaver began to laugh. Telaine had never heard her laugh before. "You know all you had to do to wash your hair in warm water is boil it and mix it with cold."

Telaine's mouth dropped open. "I never—Aunt Weaver, why didn't you tell me?"

"Wanted to see how clever you were. But I guess you're clever in other ways." She touched the handle of the Device. "If I didn't credit it before, I now know you're definitely my family," she said. "When you get back to Aurilien, tell your grandmama I said tell you the story of how she became Royal Librarian. Certain sure you'll appreciate it."

She held out a pile of knitted fabric in dark green. "Noticed you favor this color," she said. "Spun, dyed, and knitted here."

Telaine unfolded the pile. It was a soft wool scarf. "I love it," she said, and wrapped it around her neck. It hung to her waist. "Thanks, aunt."

Aunt Weaver brushed aside her thanks. "Get dressed and I'll

make flat cakes," she said. "You young people all want to get out and give your gifts first thing before the shine's worn off the new day."

Telaine hadn't finished her meal when someone knocked at the back door. Liam. "Happy Wintersmeet, Lainie," he said, and held out a beautifully carved box that fit into her palm. She opened the box and saw it was lined with dark green silk. Apparently it was her signature color.

"I didn't know you could do this," she said.

"You'll know well enough by winter's end," he said. "I go a bit stir crazy and start carving things until I've got dozens of 'em. Then I sell 'em at the spring fair. You'll see a lot of people doing that. Mistress Adderly does about a hundred of these embroidered pincushions. Don't know how anyone could use that many pincushions."

"Wait here," Telaine said, and ran up to her room to get her box of gifts. She came back and handed Liam a wrapped package. "Happy Wintersmeet," she said.

He tore the wrapping off. "Lainie, you didn't make a watch—" he began.

"It's a stretch, I know, but I didn't have a lot to work with and Aunt Weaver let me raid her store room. I got it working and added something extra." She pushed a button at the bottom of the case and her own voice said, in a tinny peal, *This watch belongs to Liam Richardson.*

He jumped, held the watch out at arm's length, and pushed the button again, laughing at the sound of her voice. "This is the strangest Wintersmeet gift I've ever gotten," he said. "And I definitely think it counts as being made by you."

"That's a relief."

"You want to make the rounds with me? I came here first."

"If you'll wait a few minutes for me to finish eating and put my coat on, yes."

They walked through the tunnels, calling out cheerful greetings to passersby, Telaine with her box and Liam with a basket over his arm that looked almost dainty. All of her tavern friends received some kind of watch—Aunt Weaver was a bit of a packrat—that spoke; Jack Taylor blushed and his friends roared with laughter when the little button produced Telaine's sultriest voice proclaiming *Jack Taylor is a handsome devil*. It was the Princess's only contribution to the holiday.

Out of a caster wheel casing Telaine produced a self-winding seamstress's tape for Josephine, who in return handed her an elegant dove-colored silk blouse. She gave Maida a new tap that measured exactly the amount of beer to pour into a mug, with the promise of more if the first one worked out, and Maida gave Telaine a small keg of her favorite dark beer, brewed by Maida herself. Little Hope got a wooden rabbit on wheels that sped around the floor on its own, with Hope laughing and chasing it, always just out of her reach.

Telaine had thought hard about what to give Eleanor, but in the end, the choice was obvious: Eleanor received the first self-warming blanket, put together from an old quilt from the store room and the last of the copper wire. Eleanor had knitted Telaine a patterned sweater of green and black that was as soft as Aunt Weaver's scarf.

She had expected to see Ben long before she reached his house, which she'd saved for last, but he wasn't part of the crowd thronging the streets. She had to knock on his door twice before he responded, his hair tousled, stubble covering his chin, his eyes bleary. "Lainie," he said, as if surprised not only by her presence on his doorstep but by her existence in general. "What time is it?"

"I gave away the last of my watches, so I don't know," she replied. "Half past ten?"

"Half past—wait a minute." He shut the door. Telaine stood there. She waited for far longer than a minute. She went from curious to annoyed to concerned. What was he doing in there?

The door opened. "Sorry. I overslept." Getting dressed and shaved and combing his hair was what he was doing in there. His eyes looked bloodshot and tired. "Are you all right?" she asked.

"I celebrate Wintersmeet Eve by getting very drunk." He blinked in pain at the sunlight. "Family's not a good memory for me, this time of year. Not my favorite night, and it goes on so long. Ready to go?"

"Where are we going?"

"I have a gift for you, and **it's outside of town**."

She raised her eyebrows at him. "Is it really?"

He closed his eyes. "Can't lie to you. I forgot. I just want to give it to you there."

"Well, yours is right here." She led him into the forge and pointed at the bellows. He squinted.

"I know you didn't make that," he said.

"I treated the leather and patched up a couple of holes, but what I made…is this." She pointed proudly at the Device perched at the spot where the handle met the leather. It had a dial and a button. "Here's what it does." She turned the dial a couple of clicks and pushed the button. The bellows rose and fell, once, twice.

"I watched how you worked it, and saw that sometimes you had to step aside from the metal to make the fire rise," she said when he didn't say anything. "You set it for how many times you want it to pump, and push the button to make it go." He said nothing. "I had an idea for a different way to do it…oh, you hate it, don't you. I'm sorry."

"No. It's perfect. You're perfect," he said in wonder, his eyes not leaving the Device. "Never would have thought of that." He turned and smiled at her. "Come on," he said. He took her hand and practically dragged her out of the forge. She was put out that he had barely looked at her gift, but he seemed so excited about his gift to her…what under heaven could it possibly be?

He led her out of Longbourne toward the fort, to a place where the winds had blown the snow to a depth of only two inches. "Right here," he said. "I wanted to give you your gift out here, away from people. Just the two of us."

He dug in his pocket and pulled out something small, and took her left hand. "Let's see if it fits," he said, and slid a gold ring onto her middle finger. Her wedding ring finger.

"Supposed to be good luck to get betrothed on Wintersmeet Day," he said, closing both his hands over hers, making the ring press into her skin. She looked into his brown eyes and saw her reflection there.

"Marry me, Lainie," Ben said quietly. "Stay here with me forever. Be Mistress Garrett. We can set up a workshop for you next to the forge and I'll put a bigger bed in the bedroom and we can start our own family here."

She felt numb with something other than the cold. "I don't know what to say," she said.

"I was hoping for 'yes,'" he teased.

She leaned into his chest. She wanted nothing more in the world than to say yes. *I never expected this, because I am an idiot. This is where it was always leading. You thought you could have it both ways, but you can't.* She couldn't promise to marry him when he didn't know who she really was. And she couldn't tell him who she really was.

"I love you," she said, her words muffled by his coat.

"What?"

She lifted her head. "I can't promise to marry you," she said. The most awful look came over his face, so she hurried on, "No, it's not what you think, it's because in my family, the patriarch, my uncle, has to approve every marriage."

This was more or less true. King Jeffrey had to approve of his heirs' spouses as new members of the royal house of North, but he'd given in to Julia about Lucas, so Telaine figured he was pretty free with his permissions. "I shouldn't make you any promises when I don't know what he'll say. *And* there are still a lot of things you don't know about my family that might make you change your mind about marrying me."

Ben opened his mouth to speak and she laid her hand over it to still him. "But I can promise you this: if you learn everything about my family, and my uncle gives his permission, and you still want to, you can ask me again, and I guarantee my answer will be 'yes'." She grinned. "And if he doesn't give permission, I will probably run away with you."

Ben smiled from behind her hand. She gently removed it. "I can't say I'm happy about that answer," he said. "Didn't expect anything like that."

"Did I hurt your feelings too terribly? I don't want to be anything but honest with you." *Except about everything else.*

"More surprised than hurt." He turned her left hand over, palm down, and they both looked at the ring. It was a perfect fit. "Suits you," he said.

"I don't know how it fits so well. I didn't know you could even work gold. It's beautiful." It was incised all over with delicate scrollwork. She couldn't begin to imagine how he'd managed it.

"Learned a bit of goldsmithing, back in the day." He removed the ring from her hand and her face fell. He laughed then, a real laugh. "Does me good to see you want to keep it."

"I do. Will you hold it for me? And ask me again when I get back from Aurilien after the snows melt?"

"Certain sure I will." He put the ring back in his pocket. "Glad we came all the way out here," he added. "Didn't tell anyone what I was planning. Didn't want you catching wind of it from anyone but me. Now we won't have to explain why the betrothal didn't come off."

"It did," she said, taking his right arm in both of hers. "Just not the way anyone else would understand."

As they walked back into town, she planned furiously. Back to the capital. Resign her agent's commission. Coerce agreement out of Uncle. Carefully tell Ben the truth and weather out his anger or surprise or confusion until he was ready to propose again, assuming he wanted to. Get married. And, apparently, buy a bigger bed. As long as she could do all those steps in that order, she'd get that ring back.

She groaned. "What is it?" Ben asked.

"Something I forgot to do. It's not important." It was very important. First, she had to stop an invasion.

CHAPTER TWENTY-FIVE

"All right, hold it steady…no, don't let it—*watch it!*" Telaine threw herself backward, away from the steel cylinder that rolled a short distance away, bumping over the hard-packed earth of the keep's yard. "I told you to hold it!"

"Slipped," Private Ormond said. She was sure it didn't matter to him that she'd nearly lost a finger. He was the laziest "assistant" Jackson had given her yet. If he was in on the Baron's treasonous plan, he certainly gave no sign of wanting to advance it quickly.

"'Slipped' is unacceptable," she said, getting up from the dirty, wet ground. Her hip was sore from where she'd landed on it. "Slip again, and the Baron will hear about it."

The soldier swallowed, his eyes wide. "Sorry." He rolled the cylinder back to its original place. Telaine glared at him once more, then stuck her head inside and began bringing gears together to interlock. It was as fussy as trying to get a crowd of two-year-olds all pointed in the same direction. She'd tried wedging the thing, but it rocked no matter what she held it with, and Private Ormond was all that was left to her.

She cursed again, sucked a pinched finger, and resumed her work more rapidly because Ormond looked like he couldn't hold the cylinder much longer, whatever threat she used.

"There. You can let go," she said, and Ormond stepped back, relief sweeping over his dull features. The cylinder held in place, solidly attached to its mate, and that brought the earth mover that much closer to being finished. Wonderful.

She waved Ormond away and began packing up her tools. It was mid-afternoon, but she'd promised the Baron she'd give the manor's hot-water cistern a look. He'd claimed it was behaving erratically, but probably it was just one more thing he'd made up to get her out there. On the other hand, he'd said he'd be visiting the outlying villages that day, so maybe she was wrong about that. In any case, she might be able to get Mistress Wilson to give her supper.

It was a warm, beautiful winter day, and she walked briskly down the valley and through the remaining snowdrifts to the manor. The guards at the door ignored her—well, she was a familiar visitor by now. One of them turned to open the door, then took half a step back when it was opened from the inside and Aunt Weaver came out. She saw Telaine, and an uncharacteristic look of shock passed over her face. "Lainie," she said.

"What are you doing here?"

"delivering an order to the housekeeper."

"But you—"

Aunt Weaver took her by the arm in a firm grip. "How about you walk me home," she said.

"I—"

The grip became painfully tight. "Home," Aunt Weaver said, and towed Telaine down the stairs and across the gravel driveway to the main road, where she released her. She strode off toward Longbourne, not waiting for Telaine. Telaine ran to catch up.

"All right, what was that *really* about?" she said. "I know you don't run errands. You yourself told me that's what apprentices are for. What were you doing in the Baron's manor?"

"I told you. **delivering an order.**"

Telaine stepped in front of her and made her come to a stop. "You were not. What is going on? Does this have something to do with your sneaking out at night, *not* to knitting circle?"

Aunt Weaver eyed her. "You callin' me a liar?"

I'm going to regret this, but it might be the only way to get her to talk. "I have inherent magic. I can hear lies when people speak them directly to me. So yes, I'm calling you a liar."

Aunt Weaver raised her eyebrows. "Young Jeffrey never said a word about that."

"Well, it's not his secret to tell, is it? And he kept yours."

"That he did." She pursed her lips in thought. "Come with me."

They traveled in silence until they reached Aunt Weaver's house, where she dismissed her apprentices, then took a seat at the dining table. "This ain't something I need spread around, not until I'm sure," she said, "but I know now you can keep a secret, and happen you might be able to help, if that magic of yours works the way you say."

"I can't tell if someone's lying if I overhear them talking to someone else, only if they're talking to me. But I've learned how to get people to address me directly, over the years."

Aunt Weaver snorted. "Happen that's a useful skill for an agent to have."

"Certain sure it is."

"Well." She sat back in her chair with her hands clasped loosely in front of her, resting on the table. "You know there've been disappearances recently."

"Yes. Ben said there had been four since he arrived in Longbourne, from all over the Barony."

"There've been seven over the last nine years. All young folks between the ages of ten and twelve, all vanished when they were running errands from home to somewhere a mile or so away. They're assumed dead, lost in the mountains or the crevasse or the forest, but no bodies have ever been found."

Aunt Weaver was gradually losing her strong northeastern accent—stronger, Telaine realized, than that of most of her friends who'd been born in Steepridge as Aunt Weaver had not.

"You think someone's been killing them," Telaine said.

"You're quick. I didn't realize there was a pattern until about two years ago, when I finally got to talking with some of the families. Then I couldn't not see it. I started looking into the disappearances—"

"Why didn't you tell the Baron? Shouldn't he be the one to execute justice?"

Zara glared at her. "If I'd wanted interruptions, I'd have told the knitting circle. And it was nine years ago the Baron came to Steepridge. That's a coincidence I couldn't ignore."

"Is that why you were at the manor?"

"You should hear all of this in order. Stop asking questions. I started looking into the disappearances and realized they'd been happening more frequently as time passed—and that in five of them, Archie Morgan had been in the area a day, sometimes a couple of hours before someone realized the child was missing. Never for long, but again, it was suspicious. Last autumn, after Jenny Butler went missing, I went to the manor one day when the Baron and Morgan were both out and I searched Morgan's room."

"That was incredibly dangerous, if you thought he was a murderer!"

"There wasn't anyone else to do it."

"There was me. I'm *trained* to do that sort of thing! You could have asked for my help."

Zara regarded her with a grim smile. "I didn't want to involve you because this isn't your home. You didn't tell me your business, I didn't tell you mine."

"But—" Telaine sighed. "You're right. Did you find anything?"

"I did." Zara's smile faded. "Four braids of human hair, all lined up in a drawer, and three shorter tufts tied with string."

Telaine's gorge rose. She swallowed twice, and said, "That seems like proof to me."

"Circumstantial proof, without bodies," Zara said. "And I wasn't sure he was the only one involved. He and the Baron live in each other's pockets. I didn't want to accuse Morgan to the Baron and have him dismiss my accusations while Morgan got rid of the evidence. I had a feeling the Baron was more involved than it looked. He...you know how he acts like all of Longbourne is beneath his notice whenever he comes here?"

"Yes."

"The only things he ever looks at are the children. The ones nearly adolescents. And the way he looks at them screams a warning at me every time. So after I looked in Morgan's room, I went and searched the Baron's. Only two doors are locked in the manor. One of 'em's the Baron's office. The other is in his bedroom. But he keeps the key to that one in his bedside table."

"You're more reckless than I imagined!"

"You want to hear this story, or not?"

"Sorry. What was in the room?"

Zara's lips thinned in anger. "Things I wish I'd never seen. Knives. A table stained with old blood. More things I'm glad I can't put a name to." She curled her hand into a fist. "I think Morgan takes the children for the Baron, and the Baron lets him finish them off."

Telaine realized she was holding her breath. "That's impossible. Who would do something like that?"

"Someone who sees other people as things," Zara said. "Young Jeffrey said he suspected him of having...unnatural pleasures, but I imagine this isn't what he meant, or he'd have taken Harstow in charge years ago. It's not the sort of thing you think anyone's capable of."

"You'll need more evidence if you want a court to listen, especially if you're accusing a provincial lord. They won't come search his house on your say-so."

"That's what I was looking for today. Something I could take to prove the Baron's involved. But I didn't get far before one of the servants noticed me and I had to leave. Sorry I escorted you away so quickly, but I didn't want you blurting anything out that would let them know I wasn't there legitimately."

Telaine remembered the manacles and her stomach churned again. "I can look around," she said, "but there might not be any evidence a court would admit."

"I know." Zara clenched her fists together. "I want that man to hang for what he's done. This is my home and I will not tolerate anyone meddling with it."

She looked so much like her portrait at that moment Telaine couldn't help thinking *She's never left off being Queen; she's just got a smaller kingdom.* "Does it have to be for this crime? Because he's guilty of something even worse."

"Can't think of anything worse than torturing and murdering children," Zara said.

"I mean in the eyes of the law." She'd given Telaine her secret;

maybe it was time Telaine returned the favor. "He's a traitor. He's going to open the fort to the Ruskalder and help them invade Tremontane."

Zara's eyes went wide. "You have proof?"

"I do. And my word counts as evidence in court."

"It does. Sweet heaven. He'll hang for that for sure."

"It's why I was so upset about being trapped here for the winter. Uncle needs to know."

"And that earth mover is how Harstow plans to bring the Ruskalder here before anyone below has time to prepare."

"You're quick." Telaine grinned at her great-aunt. "I know. It's not a time for levity."

"Yes, but it's either that or run mad."

They both fell silent. Finally, Telaine said, "I'll investigate the next time the Baron's away."

"No," Zara said. "If you're caught—"

"I'm not going to get caught."

"You're not perfect, Telaine," Zara said, and Telaine experienced a moment of dissociation at hearing her full name for the first time in months. "If you're caught, it could mean your life. At the very least it would mean ruining your mission here. It's not a chance we should take."

"You're right." Telaine banged her fist on the table, then rubbed the pain away. "We have to wait for the pass to clear, and I have to make sure that earth mover can't go anywhere."

"Can you manage that?"

Telaine nodded. "I certainly hope so."

It was full dark, and Zara stood, shaking out her fingers. "Knitting circle tonight," she said, her voice falling into her familiar accent. "Happen you'd like to come along?"

"How can you bear to do something so prosaic after all this?"

Aunt Weaver shrugged. "Sometimes you need the company of friends when the worst is bearing down on you. With that Morgan gone, happen there won't be any more children gone missing, and we can stop the Baron 'fore he does anything else he ought hang for."

"I swear those children will have justice."

"Too late for them. Better hope for justice for the ones he ain't snatched yet," Aunt Weaver said.

After two months, Telaine was running out of ways to stall construction of the earth mover. She had a brief moment of hope when she thought the Device might be too wide to fit through the inner wall gate that led to the pass, but careful measurement said it could pass with scant inches' clearance on each side. Its treads moved smoothly. It had, or would have, plenty of fuel. Aunt Weaver said she probably had less than two months before the last snowfall, plus another month to clear the main pass. She didn't think she could stretch the construction out that long.

She found that the two cylinders' cases were hinged so they could open like a ladybug's shell, giving easy access to their complicated innards after they were connected to the nose, preventing her from sabotaging them in a way that would be impossible to detect. Wonderful.

She was torn, all the time now, between her anxieties about completing the earth mover and her Deviser's joy at completing the earth mover. It was a beautiful piece of Devisery, not only in its exquisite construction but in the beauty of its parts. Someone had cared a great deal about this Device to make it so elegant as well as powerful. It was a shame she couldn't let it be operational.

She decided to run some of the wires through the motive force cluster backwards and weave others in a tight loop before connecting them. The earth mover would work—for a while. Then it would overheat and burn out the motive force. She hated the Baron getting even that much use out of it, but he'd made comments about wanting to see it run before the time came to clear the pass, and she was afraid to make herself look incompetent. It was possible, since he knew her to be excellent at her trade, he might figure out she was making mistakes on purpose.

She didn't think her alterations were terribly obvious, but she was still happy the Baron didn't hover around these days. From what she'd overheard from Jackson, he was making the rounds of the smaller villages throughout the valley. The idea that he might be looking for new victims made her sick. Still, Morgan was gone—she had to cling to that small hope that his absence would make a difference.

Twelve weeks gone. Seven (or more) weeks to go. Telaine took the bulbous "tail" of the earth mover and went out looking for a source. Until studying the earth mover, she hadn't ever tried to contain, or even move, a source, and despite her anxiety she was eager to master this new challenge.

The day was overcast, and the snow was cold and slushy, but she felt wonderful: wonderful because the overcast skies promised another big storm, wonderful because she could spin out finding a source indefinitely. She decided to stay close to home, this time, because of the storm, but there was no reason she couldn't cover the valley as thoroughly as the Baron did, "looking" for a source. She slogged through the mush, wishing her boots were waterproof.

She heard the sounds of a horse approaching, and turned fast to see the Baron bearing down on her, glowering. "Miss Bricker," he said, "what are you doing away from the fort? I'm beginning to question your dedication to your work."

She held up the bulbous tail, grateful to have it with her. "I'm looking for a source," she said. "You know how hard they are to find."

"I believe I have found one," he said. "If you would follow me?" He didn't take her up behind him, but he did keep his horse to a slow enough gait that she could keep up. How could he possibly sense source? He'd said he couldn't! Hadn't he? She couldn't remember anymore. She felt ill. It was too much to hope for that he was only imagining things.

He led her back into town. The sinking feeling was now joined by nausea. He couldn't be going where she thought he was going. He just couldn't.

He was.

He dismounted and led her around the back of the forge; Ben cast a wary eye on them, but kept on working. The high-pitched *tink* of hammer hitting metal followed them through the storm-tinged air.

He waved his hand over the source, *her* source. "I am only able to sense strong sources," he said. "This should be sufficient."

She took a breath. "Milord, this is the source I use to imbue your Devices," she said. "It's the closest coherent source to your manor. I can use it, yes, but it would certainly disadvantage you."

She waited for the Baron to erupt into a rage. Instead, he looked thoughtful. "You might return here for it when the snows have stopped falling, and the earth mover may be used," he said, "and make other use of the source until then."

"That's a good idea, milord, and I think everyone will be grateful you are willing to sacrifice your own comfort—"

The Baron grabbed Telaine's arm and squeezed hard. She let out a pained gasp. The hammer noise stopped. "I grow tired of your constant toadying," he said through clenched teeth. "I admired you because you weren't afraid of me. I feel my admiration dwindling."

Without thinking, Telaine pulled her arm away. "I told you what I thought you wanted to hear," she said sharply. "I thought a man who would sabotage his own Devices so he could have my company was a man who didn't respect me enough to want my true opinions."

The Baron threw back his head and roared his laughter. "Now *that* is the Miss Bricker I have come to admire," he said. The hammer noise started again, quietly now. "You knew all along."

"Yes, milord."

"And you said nothing."

"I didn't understand your motives, milord. Happen you wanted me to play along, happen not. So I kept my tongue."

"Miss Bricker, if I could find a woman of rank with half your personality, I would marry her without another thought. Leave that source. I would hate to deprive you of such a valuable resource. And join me for supper this evening. Leave the tools behind. I simply wish to enjoy your company."

The hammer blows stopped again. "I'm...honored, milord."

"And change your clothes. This supper is a social event." The Baron walked back around the forge house and stood, slapping his gloves into his palm in a slow rhythm. Telaine followed him, trying not to meet Ben's eye, knowing he would explode if she did. "Until this evening, Miss Bricker." He mounted his horse and rode off down the street.

"This evening?" Ben said, laying down his hammer. "Social event?"

"What do you suggest I do?"

"I—wish the snows were over. Wish you were safely down the mountain."

"It's unnerving how I draw the attention of so many crazy men."

"Not going to take that personally."

Telaine laughed. "Other than you."

He leaned over the rail, and said, "Wonder if he realizes he asked you to go up the mountain, through the snow, at night, in a dress?"

Telaine threw her head back and looked at the sky. "Please, heaven, snow before suppertime!"

It did.

Fourteen weeks gone. The earth mover was assembled. The Baron insisted on going out with her every day to search for a source. Telaine judged the season was almost over and he was getting worried about having his Device ready in time. She'd run out of ways to delay him. Once they'd found a source, and she'd imbued the motive forces, the only things standing in the way of the Ruskalder invasion force were the changes she'd made to sabotage the Device.

Fifteen weeks gone. The Baron, curse him, had come up with the idea to collect weak sources and allow them to combine in the chamber. It worked. At the Baron's insistence, Telaine imbued one of the motive forces and showed the Baron how to start the Device. His eyes lit with that frightening passion that could so easily turn ugly. She pretended the Device needed all her attention so she wouldn't have to look into those eyes.

Telaine began the process of charging the motive forces, getting rid of the Baron by claiming to need solitude for the task. She worked as slowly as she could, her mind frantically trying to come up with a way to delay two weeks, a single week longer. The season of storms was nearly over, Aunt Weaver said, but days had passed clear and crisp without a single cloud in the sky, storm or no, heralding that last snowfall.

She left the fort early, weary from the effort of spinning source into the walnut-sized orbs that were the Device's motive forces. She hadn't ever realized how draining the process was, but then she'd never spent so many consecutive hours charging anything, let alone the finicky spheres. Clouds had finally begun gathering that morning, casting a pall over the snowy ground, but she was too tired to be cheered by the oncoming bad weather.

She passed the tavern, passed Eleanor's, passed the forge with no more than a wave for Ben, and went into Aunt Weaver's place through the front door because walking all the way around back was too exhausting.

The loom was unoccupied. Sarah was gone. Alys sat alone at the great loom, making it thump and rattle irregularly. "Where is everyone?" Telaine asked.

"Mistress Weaver went visiting with Mistress Ponsonby," Alys said with a withering look. Glaring at Telaine, even now she had a man of her own and wasn't trying to steal Jack Taylor, was Alys's favorite pastime. "Sent Sarah on an errand."

"You're always sending her out on errands. You should take a turn sometime."

"Youngest apprentice does the running. I did it in my time. So don't come over high and mighty with me."

"And yet you run errands to the tavern all the time. Where did you send her now? Out to Granger or Hightop?"

"Not that far. Just to the manor. Baron ordered a bolt of finest and I sent her off with it."

Telaine sucked in a sharp, horrified breath. "How long ago?"

"Not long. Maybe an hour. Should be back soon."

But she won't be. No. Not another one. And Telaine hadn't passed her on the road, which meant Sarah was already there. There, gift-wrapped and delivered to the Baron because Telaine and Aunt Weaver hadn't told anyone his secret.

The back door slammed. "Aunt Weaver?" Telaine called out.

"Here," Aunt Weaver said, coming through to hang up her cloak. "You're home early."

"Sarah's at the manor."

Aunt Weaver went still. "How long?"

"An hour."

Aunt Weaver turned her glass-cutting glare on Alys. "That's an errand you should have run," she said. "Go home. And I'm not sure I want you comin' back. We'll discuss it tomorrow."

Alys, stunned, gathered her things and bolted. "What now?" Telaine said.

"You'll have to go after her," Aunt Weaver said. "Happen it's not too late."

"We could raise the town. If we'd told someone—"

"Too late for that. And you know well as I do that would just get Sarah killed." She sounded calm and reasonable, but her eyes said everything her mouth didn't. Zara North wasn't used to waiting for someone else to act, and Telaine could see the words being dragged out of her as she added, "I can't do this. You can."

Telaine swept her cloak around her shoulders. "If I'm not back in three hours—call it full dark—come after me. Bring Ben and Liam and anyone else who might be good in a fight."

"That storm'll be here before full dark. You'd better be faster than that."

"I'll hurry." Telaine put up her hood. "Don't worry. I'll be back, and I'm bringing Sarah with me."

CHAPTER TWENTY-SIX

Telaine rapidly went through plans and discarded them as she left Aunt Weaver's house and hurried off through the ditches. Clouds were beginning to gather, good for her earth mover delaying strategy, bad for what she was doing right now. It was late afternoon, perhaps an hour before sunset, but the darkening sky made it feel later. She needed the darkness, but not too soon, not before she'd found Sarah.

She chafed at how slowly she traveled through the snow. Every minute wasted was another minute Sarah might be—she tried not to picture the manacles, the room Aunt Weaver had described, the well-padded walls sealing in the screaming. Maybe she was wrong. It wasn't likely the Baron would take delivery of the fabric himself; he might not even see Sarah. But if he had…if he had, it might already be too late. But she had to try. All her previous justifications disappeared; if they'd acted against the Baron, Sarah wouldn't be in danger. She trudged faster. Her cloak dragged atop the snow behind her.

The manor was only partially lit, but the Baron had to be home. She didn't suppose he would collect his latest plaything and then ride off to amuse himself elsewhere for a few hours. She could see the guards at the door as indistinct blobs; she hoped that was how she looked to them. Actually, she hoped they couldn't see her at all.

She took a wide, curving path around the side of the house, following the tree line, hoping to reach the kitchen door without being seen. Usually the guards were oblivious to everything that didn't happen within arm's distance. She glanced up, and swore. One of them was looking right at her. Now, would he be suspicious if she went in via the kitchen door? She was a tradesman, after all. Telaine cursed again and changed direction. She couldn't risk alerting them further.

She marched up the steps and said, "Good evening," and they let her through. As usual, no one was in the entry. She yanked off her snowshoes and boots and pelted toward the servants' stair.

Telaine pattered silently down the stairs, footwear in hand, and into the kitchen. The kitchen maids shrieked when they saw her, and Mistress Wilson went pale. "Where's the girl?" Telaine asked in a low voice. Mistress Wilson was silent. "Mistress Wilson, this is your chance to help me save one child from the Baron. Where is she? His bedchamber?"

Mistress Wilson shook her head. "Top floor, servants' quarters," she said, and Telaine understood why she was so reluctant to speak. If Sarah disappeared, the servants might be blamed. "Second door on the right from the stairs. We don't know anything. We never know what happens to them. I swear it."

"You could have told someone he'd taken them!"

"Who's to tell? And who would listen to us, accusing our rightful lord?" Mistress Wilson was in tears. "He threatened our families if we said aught about him. There's nothing we can do."

Telaine closed her lips on more recriminations. No sense wasting time chastising the servants, much as she wanted to. "Where's the Baron?"

"Dining room. We've only just served the first course."

That gave her forty-five minutes, based on her previous suppers. "I'll be back. The Baron won't get this one." She put her boots and snowshoes in a corner, snatched up her lock picks, and tiptoed up the servants' stair in her stocking feet, all the way to the top.

She'd never been up here; there had been no reason for it. The stair came out on a long hallway, scuffed from a generation of servants' feet, that looked as if it cut the top floor in half. Plain wooden doors lined the hall in pairs, opposite one another. Telaine felt like sidling along, though it wasn't *that* narrow; she hated the idea of brushing up against anything here, as if every door concealed something evil.

Faint light came in from a window at the far end of the hall. The storm was coming on fast. She jiggled the knob of the door second from the right; it was locked. She went to work with the lock picks, feeling every second as if someone were going to come up the stairs after her. The servants' stair was the only access to this floor, and she was trapped like a bird in a cage, waiting for the cat to pounce.

The seconds stretched out. She was out of practice, and it was going to cost both of them their lives.

The lock snapped open. Telaine opened the door, wincing at the creak, and shut it behind her.

The chilly room, which was about eight feet square, held nothing but a bedframe with a bare mattress and a bedside table. Sarah lay, tied hand and foot and with a handkerchief stuffed in her mouth, on the mattress, dressed only in her shift and barefoot. She had been crying and began to do so again when she saw Telaine. The light from the dirty window above the bed made her look ghostlike, pale and weak.

Telaine whispered, "I'm taking the gag out, but you can't say anything, all right? Nothing." Sarah nodded. Telaine removed the handkerchief and helped the girl to sit up. "I'm going to untie you and then we'll figure out what to do," Telaine said. She removed the girl's bonds in what seemed to take forever; she should have brought her throwing knife with the lock picks. She swore under her breath. She was slow *and* careless. *Stay focused, Telaine.*

With Sarah rubbing her wrists and ankles, Telaine paced and thought furiously. Sarah couldn't walk home dressed like that. She would freeze before they made it halfway back to Longbourne. She couldn't stay in that room, and there was no place else to hide her. If the Baron found out she was missing and went after her—which he would have to do if he wanted to protect his secret—she'd be easy to spot, struggling through the snow.

Telaine looked out the window at the lowering pines. If Sarah could go down the stairs to the kitchen entrance, get to the cover of the trees, she'd be able to follow the edge of the forest back to Longbourne even if the storm came up—but no, she'd still be mostly naked, barefoot, and weak. And Telaine couldn't go with her, because she had to be seen walking out the doors of the manor if she wanted to protect herself from the Baron's rage.

No. Telaine didn't have to walk out the doors. It only had to look like she did.

She tossed her cloak on the mattress and began undressing and tossing her clothes at Sarah. "Put these on," she told the girl, who looked at her in bewilderment. "Do it, Sarah, I'll explain in a moment."

Clad only in her bodysuit and her thick wool socks, Telaine twisted the knob at her neck and heat begin to spread over her body. She folded the corner of her cloak around her elbow and, with a quick jab, smashed the window glass, then picked up a rope and sawed at it with one of the shards until it frayed and split.

She dropped the ropes on the mattress and unlatched the window, pushing it open, then shoved at the snow beneath it to make it look as if something heavy had gone over the windowsill. The window was small, possibly too small even for a person Sarah's size to fit through, and it was a sheer drop down four stories to the ground below, but Telaine hoped it would distract the Baron enough that he wouldn't turn his wrath on the servants.

Sarah looked confused, and afraid, but she put on Telaine's clothes obediently. She was only a few inches shorter than Telaine and Telaine rolled up the extra length of trouser around her ankles. She fastened her cloak around Sarah's neck, wrapped it close around the girl, and said, "Follow me. All the way down. And no noise."

When they emerged from the stairs into the kitchen, Mistress Wilson looked at them both as if they had fallen through the ceiling. The kitchen maids huddled together, eyes wide, mouths shut. "Mistress Wilson, this girl needs your help," Telaine said. "Those guards saw me walk in here. I need them to see me walk out. All I want is for you to walk with Sarah through the doors and bid her goodbye using my name. When you see her reach the bottom of the stairs, come back inside and go back to whatever you were doing. Please, Mistress Wilson, this isn't going to work without you."

"What are you…wearing?" she asked in a faint voice.

"I'll tell you all about it when I see you next, all right? Can you do this, Mistress Wilson?"

The woman nodded hesitantly, then, with a look at Sarah's face, more firmly.

Telaine grasped her hands. "Thank you. *Thank you.* Sarah, listen to me." She took the girl's shoulders and turned her to face her. "Go straight down the stairs toward the road. I left lots of footprints for you to follow. Put on the snowshoes, get on the road and don't stop walking until you reach your father's house, understand? Don't look behind you. Just walk. I'll see you soon."

She helped Sarah put the boots on, then tucked the long trousers into them and, after a moment's thought, wedged the lock picks back into the left boot. The throwing knife was still in the right—it would be useless for what she was about to do. She gave Sarah a hug. "You've been braver than anyone should ever have to be. Now, be brave just a little longer and—go home."

"Let me get you—" Mistress Wilson began, and a bell jangled nearby, making her go white. "That's the last course."

"We have to go," Telaine said.

"Let me at least—surely we have clothes that will fit you—"

"Trust me," Telaine said, "I'll be warm enough. And we don't have time if we're going to outrun this storm."

"Wait," Mistress Wilson said. She went around the corner and came back a few seconds later with a pair of old boots and a worn jacket. "You can't go out there in just those socks. These aren't much, but better than…"

She held the boots out to Telaine. The leather was worn, and they were too big, but Telaine shoved her feet into them as Mistress Wilson and Sarah left the kitchen. She wrapped the laces twice around her ankles, snugging the boots against her skin, and took a few steps. No worse than walking in snowshoes. They'd have to do.

She went around the corner to the kitchen door and opened it a crack. She already knew it was not visible from the front door, but in her dark gray bodysuit and the tan jacket, she felt horribly outlined against the white snow. If the sun hadn't yet set, it was covered by the pendulous clouds that looked as if they might drop their snowy burden at any moment.

She rubbed her hands together, trying to keep them warm. This was the craziest thing she'd ever done. She heard the big door open and Mistress Wilson call goodbye to "Lainie," counted slowly to ten, then made her way as quickly as she could through the snow toward the rear of the manor and the black tree line.

No one cried out after her, so the guards' attention had to be on Sarah. Telaine was probably safe. The guards weren't looking at her, the servants wouldn't dally at the windows, and the Baron's chair faced away from the tall windows overlooking the rear of the manor, though it would be just her luck if he happened to look out as she was slogging past.

She reached the tree line and ducked past the evergreen branches, then stood for a moment, breathing heavily. She didn't have much time—in fact, she didn't have any time to stand there catching her breath. She turned south, trudging through the ankle-deep drifts and dodging branches; it was slow, and awkward, but she had to stay within the trees until she was out of sight of the manor. The storm was coming, and she needed to move quickly. *Dear heaven, please let it hold off until we're both home,* she prayed, and tried to slog faster.

She had no idea how long the route through the trees would take. Sarah would be in greater danger if the storm hit while she was on the open road, but Telaine's path ran through rougher terrain, so not only was it longer than the road, it was slower.

She rubbed her hands together again, then blew on them. *It's so cold,* she thought. Maybe she'd been cocky to reject Mistress Wilson's offer of clothing, but there just hadn't been *time*. She prayed again to ungoverned heaven that she hadn't done something fatally stupid. She remembered how helpless Sarah had looked in that tiny, cold room, and righteous anger surged through her, warming her. They would both make it. They had to.

Though her face and hands were cold, and the boots weren't as efficient a protection from the snow as she'd hoped, the rest of her felt as warm as if she were still wearing her cloak. Warm, but strangely cold at the same time, near her feet. Well, the boots weren't exactly waterproof, and there was a crack in one of the soles, but surely they wouldn't have gotten wet so quickly?

Telaine stopped to feel along her ankles, and her fingers came away damp. She stopped walking and closed her eyes, cursing her stupidity. Of course the bodysuit was wet. The Device was melting the snow as she waded through it, and the thin cotton wasn't water resistant.

She'd known this would happen, it had happened during their testing, but she and Josephine hadn't done anything about the flaw because they hadn't anticipated anyone being stupid enough to wear nothing but the bodysuit while wading through snowdrifts.

Telaine started walking again. There was nothing she could do about it now except stay out of the higher drifts. She had to get to shelter as quickly as possible. She pushed herself harder. *Be grateful you've got the trees, where the snow hasn't piled so high. Be grateful for the suit at all. By heaven, it's cold.*

She slogged along, feeling her ankles go numb and her fingers begin to tingle with cold. *Gloves,* she thought, *gloves that are warm only on the inside, lined with something waterproof so your hands don't get soaked.* This was the most foolish idea she'd ever had, and she looked forward to telling her friends about it while she put her feet up by the fire at the tavern. Even Ben would eventually see the humor, once he got past the part where she risked hypothermia and death to save a life. That was a good thing, wasn't it?

She came to where the tree line made a sharp turn to the left, away from the road and from Longbourne. Now what? She could keep following the trees, but that would take far too long. Cutting across country, trying to keep a straight line toward Longbourne or heading west toward the now-invisible road, was as dangerous in a different way.

Telaine shivered and rubbed her arms, trying to keep her fingers warm. The wires of the Device rolled under her hands. They were sturdier and better secured, thank heaven, than the prototype. It would have to be the trees. She couldn't afford to be caught in the open when the storm arrived. She could compromise by striking out in the open whenever the tree line veered too far away from Longbourne, like now.

She rubbed her arms once more, carefully, and started walking.

The snow was up to her knees now, and so was the freezing cold, and it was taking her forever to slog through it. Her calves were wet; she hadn't been as careful as she'd thought. Maybe she should have taken the longer route under the trees instead. She couldn't feel her nose or the tips of her fingers. This was definitely the stupidest idea she'd ever had.

Then the storm hit.

The world went gray. Wind whipped around her body and howled in her ears. She stood still, not sure how far she was from the forest. She was certain she was still facing the right direction, so she struck out again, feeling ahead until her grasping fingers were stung by thousands of prickling needles lashed by the wind. She clutched at the branch, hauled herself into the shelter of the trees, and stood a moment, panting with fear.

The trees grew thickly enough that the storm's fury was lessened; she even felt warmer, though she was sure that was an illusion. She could move deeper into the forest, find shelter and wait the storm out—

—and end up dead, if this were one of those storms that lasted for days. She couldn't take the risk. She would have to keep moving south, and she would have to travel outside the forest's shelter or she wouldn't be able to see Longbourne when she neared it. *You can't see anything at all in this weather,* Telaine thought, but at this point she had few options left to her. She took a few more deep breaths, made sure the dial on her Device was turned to full, and went back into the storm.

She kept on walking, keeping her mind occupied with plans for retooling the suit, trying not to think about how the cold wetness was spreading. It would need a second layer that didn't become warm, or was waterproof, or both. Something dark loomed up before her; she barely avoided running into a tree and instead knocked its load of snow onto her head. She shook frantically to get it off before it melted.

More walking. She wondered how Sarah was doing. Had she made it home before the storm broke? Had anyone started to look for

Sarah? Had anyone started to look for *her*?

A tugging at her frozen calves told her she'd reached the low rise that ran parallel to Longbourne. She was getting close, though she couldn't tell how much farther she still had to go. Time no longer existed; there was nothing but one foot after another, one step through the snow, then the next. Her suit was wet to her thighs and it was getting harder to feel her legs.

She tucked her hands under her armpits, reasoning that if the suit shed heat like that, she might as well take advantage of it. She ran into a tree and stood hugging it for a moment, afraid she might fall down if she let go. She was so tired.

"Don't stop moving," her father said. "Remember what I taught you. There's nothing to stop you freezing to death but your own two feet."

"I don't remember where our camp is," she told him. It sounded as if he were right in front of her, but the snow was flying into her face so rapidly she couldn't see him as more than an outline that looked more like a tree trunk than a man.

"Don't stop moving," he repeated. "You'll find it, *talaina*, winter flower, but you have to keep walking or you'll find me first."

"I don't understand," she said, but let go of the tree and took a step in his direction, then another. Her father moved when she did, always a few paces ahead of her, and she reached out to him, but he wouldn't take her frozen hand...or maybe he had, and she couldn't feel it.

She started to shake all over and wrapped her arms around her chest to contain the shivering. The wetness had spread above her hips. Her feet were numb now; the only way she knew they were still in contact with the ground was the jolt that went through her knees every time she took a step.

She stumbled over something, a stump or a rock, and landed on her hands and knees. *Have to keep my body out of the snow,* she thought, *it will make me colder.* She wasn't sure it was possible to get any colder. "Papa, help me," she cried, but Owen Hunter was gone, and she was afraid to cry because her tears might freeze her eyes shut, and then she really would be dead. She heaved herself up and, after three tries, made it back on her feet. The world was going darker gray by the minute. She smelled flowers. Lilac...and mint...

It was her source. She was close to the forge.

With renewed energy, she followed her nose until she could plunge her hands into the source, wishing it were warm. Ben's house was...from here, it was to the right, maybe fifty yards away. She'd have to leave the security of the forest and the rise. She turned, stretched her hands out in front of her, and stepped forward, feeling her way like a blind woman.

Just as she'd begun to think she'd missed it completely and was wandering out through the streets, something knocked the breath out of her and she bent double. The forge rail.

She grasped it with her two frozen hands and followed it around the corner, then into the forge. She over the anvil and the empty quenching bucket and groped along the side of the house for the back door.

She held the knob and banged on the door, not sure how hard she'd knocked because her hands were numb. She banged again. No answer. She tried the knob; the door opened and swung inward. The fire was out, the house cold and empty.

Her addled brain panicked. The storm was so powerful it had swept the inhabitants of Longbourne away. Ben had gotten tired of waiting for her and had gone down the mountain himself; he was having tea with her uncle and explaining what the hardie hole on the anvil was for. She was the only living creature in Longbourne, and soon she wouldn't even be that.

She sat in the relative quiet of the open doorway and tried to think. Ben's house was shelter, but she was too numb to start a fire and if she curled up on his sofa, he'd find her frozen to death when he returned. She could barely think, she was so cold. She had stared so hard at the darkness, for so long, she was starting to see specks of light glowing against the background. Or was that a real light? It might be

Eleanor's window.

She stood up, remembering to close Ben's door—he wouldn't want his house full of snow when he came back from tea with the King—and made her way across the forge again. At the rail, she hesitated, then struck out across the great empty space that separated the forge from Eleanor's home.

The glow brightened. It didn't illuminate her surroundings, but it gave her something to aim for. It was so hard to move her legs. Snow crusted her eyelashes and eyebrows and tried to plug her ears, but the howl of the wind buffeted it away. She closed her eyes to keep the snowflakes out—it wasn't as if she could see anything—and took two more steps and ran face first into the side of the house.

A warm trickle ran down her upper lip, and she tasted hot blood. Amazing that she had anything warm left in her. She slid to her left along the wall until she came to Eleanor's door and pounded on it. Her fists were numb. She kept pounding. Would they know it was her and not the wind? She fumbled for the knob and found herself sliding down the door to the ground. *Mustn't stop moving*, she told herself, but her legs weren't listening.

She toppled forward as the door opened and light blazed out. "Who—" someone said, and several hands helped her to her feet. "*Lainie?*" someone else said, and she was lifted and carried into the blissful warmth and light of Eleanor's house.

"You boys, upstairs. You too, Ben. Especially you. Set her down by the fire. Fern, fetch blankets. Marie, get a hot compress going." Eleanor removed the jacket and began unbuttoning the bodysuit, saying, "I might have guessed if anyone was going to try a stunt like wandering around in her underwear through a blizzard, it would be you."

"Where—" Telaine asked, mumbling through her frozen face.

"No talking until we get you taken care of. Sit up for just a moment." Eleanor removed the boots and peeled the sodden bodysuit away from her chest and over her hips until she lay there in her underpants and brassiere and wool socks. She took Telaine's socks and stripped off her soaked undergarments and patted her dry.

"Scoot over onto these blankets. Good. Hope, if you can keep from wiggling, you can cuddle up with Lainie and help her get warm. Take off your dress first." A warm body that did wiggle a little snuggled in against her side. Eleanor tucked several layers of blankets around her and covered her head with a knit cap. "You're going to need this." She lifted Telaine's head and put something warm and dry behind her neck.

Telaine shook so hard she was afraid her teeth might fall out. Hope grasped her across the stomach and squeezed. "Don't be afraid. This happens to lots of people," she whispered.

Eleanor took Telaine's hands out of the blankets and looked at them. "Tuck those under your armpits and leave them there until I say," she said.

She lifted Telaine's feet one at a time. "Fern, do we have some hot water? Get the big pan and mix in snow until it's just more than room temperature." Soon someone lifted her feet and placed them in a burning hot bath of water. She whimpered. "Don't worry, that means your feet are warming up," said Eleanor.

"Ma?" shouted Liam from somewhere far away. "If she's decent, we got a very worried fellow up here wants to come down."

"All right, Ben Garrett, but don't you disturb her," Eleanor warned. Footsteps pounded down the stairs, and Telaine opened her eyes to see Ben's upside-down face in front of her.

"Still alive," she said, and although he began to speak, rapidly and with feeling, she drifted off to sleep.

CHAPTER TWENTY-SEVEN

She woke, confused at how the ceiling was too far away, then after a moment realized she was lying in front of the fire in Eleanor's house. The great room was lit only by the flames in the hearth, making it feel warm and comforting. Her bedmate was gone and her dry, warm feet were under the blankets. Her hands, still tucked in her armpits, were warm and flexible, as were her toes. She thought she had never truly appreciated being warm before.

She stretched, and discovered she was still naked. Her hands hurt when she opened them, and she saw they were covered with scratches and the beginnings of a couple of bruises. Pain, another thing she'd never appreciated, welcome because it meant she was still alive.

Eleanor, doing something at the fire, looked over and smiled.

"Nice to see you conscious again," she said in a low voice. "Everyone's asleep. Past midnight, I think, but I couldn't rest until I was sure you were well." She bent over and wiggled Telaine's toes, making her giggle. "Show me your fingers." Telaine waved them at her.

"Don't mind telling you that you were lucky," Eleanor went on. "Much longer and hypothermia would've killed you. And I don't want to know about that thing you were wearing. Might've killed you quicker."

"It's a design flaw," Telaine said, "and I plan to fix it. It wasn't that wet until I fell down a few times."

"You're well and that's all that matters," Eleanor said. "But I don't understand what you were doing out there in the first place. Didn't even know you were gone."

Aunt Weaver. "I have to go home. Aunt Weaver has no idea where I am."

Eleanor shook her head. "You'd be lost before you took three steps out that door. No way to let her know until the storm passes. Don't worry."

"All she knows is that I left."

"And where did you go, that you were caught by the storm? Even you must have known it was coming."

"I—" She considered her words for a moment. "I think I should wait for Ben and Liam to wake up before I tell that story. Don't want to tell it twice. Or three times."

"Kill me with curiosity," Eleanor said without malice. "You want some porridge? Don't know how hungry you are."

"Very. I missed supper and then I tried to kill myself walking around in a snowstorm."

"I've got some things to say to you about that," Ben said, sitting down beside her. "Mind if I disrupt your patient, Eleanor?"

"Nothing wrong with her now that porridge won't cure."

Ben wrapped the blankets around Telaine more securely and lifted her to lean against him, putting his arms around her. She closed her eyes and snuggled into his strong embrace. "Why aren't you in your own house?"

"Because this storm is like to last four days or more, and it's not right being all alone for that long," Eleanor said. "Happen you start hearing voices."

"I ought to ask you why *you* aren't in your own house," Ben said. "That was a stupid thing to do."

"Don't be too angry. I saved a life today," Telaine said.

"What?"

"Don't bother," said Eleanor. "She says she won't tell the story until Liam's awake too."

"Then I'm going to wake Liam up."

"Liam's already awake because you people won't stop nattering," said Liam, sliding onto the long bench. "What's the story?"

"Porridge first," Telaine said, and the men groaned. She ate quickly, handed off the bowl, and told them what had happened, starting with her having heard a rumor about the Baron being the one who took the children.

"Why didn't you tell anyone? Would've saved Sarah being taken in the first place," Eleanor said.

"I...wasn't sure how true it was." The most despicable lie she'd told, but the actual reasoning she and Aunt Weaver had done included facts she couldn't tell them. "And I thought, with Morgan not there to do the snatching, the Baron might not do it again before he could be taken in charge. I didn't count on anyone walking voluntarily into his trap."

She went on through entering the manor, giving Sarah her clothes, and seeing her head off down the path toward Longbourne before setting off along the forest's edge. When she'd finished describing her journey, her three listeners sat silent.

"That...was brilliant," Liam said.

"It was foolish. And lucky." Ben's arms tightened around her.

"I don't suppose you know if Sarah made it home before the storm hit?" Telaine asked.

Eleanor shook her head. "Didn't even know she was missing. Didn't know *you* were missing. We were occupied getting ready for this last big storm."

Telaine sat up and was restrained by someone who wasn't willing to let her go yet. "The last storm?"

"This is the one. Then we wait for the passes to clear and we're connected to the downside world again." Ben looked down at her, upside down, and made a funny face that Telaine realized was a smile when it was right way round. "And you can make that trip to Aurilien."

"But—" Liam said. "You're still going back?"

Telaine glared at Ben, willing him to stop talking. He might decide her deceptions were too much to take, and how humiliating for him if he had to explain why they weren't getting married after all. But he didn't take the hint. "She needs to see her family, is all," he said.

Liam's face cleared. "Thought you'd get married before that," he said.

Telaine gasped. "Ben!"

"I didn't say anything! We're not even betrothed!" Ben looked as if he wanted to sink through the floor.

"You're not?" Eleanor raised her eyebrows. "You sure have everyone fooled if you're not."

"Don't you think that's something we'd tell people?" Telaine exclaimed.

"We all figured you had your reasons," Eleanor said. "I guess you want your folks' approval first, huh?"

"Eleanor—" Telaine buried her face in her hands. She'd thought it would be an easy secret to keep. She hadn't counted on the observant eyes of hundreds of people all crammed together for the winter.

"We can't be betrothed until her uncle gives permission," Ben said. He'd apparently come to the same conclusion she had, which was that trying to keep this secret was pointless. "So we're not spreading the news. See?"

"Not really," said Liam.

"Yes," said Eleanor. "And I think it's time for all of us to get some sleep. Lainie, I have a dress you can wear, and you can sleep in Liam's bed." Liam protested, but half-heartedly. "You boys get off to the loft, now. Lainie, come with me."

Eleanor's dress was too short and was loose on Telaine in all the wrong places, but it was soft and better than wearing a shroud of blankets with nothing underneath. She slid into Liam's bed and promptly fell asleep again.

One day passed, then another. Telaine became so used to the sound of the storm wailing and beating at the house that she stopped noticing it. She played games with the girls and listened to Ben and Liam and Liam's brother Alex sing, helped Eleanor cook, which she did badly, tinkered with the bodysuit, and sat in front of the fire encircled in Ben's arms, talking quietly into the night. The Baron and his earth mover and the planned invasion were so far away she was almost able to forget about them entirely. Even her anxiety over how Aunt Weaver must be worrying faded, as she eventually accepted there was nothing she could do to change that but wait.

With Sarah safe—and she insisted to herself Sarah was safe—and the earth mover sabotaged, Telaine relaxed and even indulged in some daydreaming. Next winter they could huddle up together in their own house. There might be a baby on the way. She'd learn to cook, or make Ben learn to cook, and she could build Devices all winter and he could do whatever it was he did when he was snowed in. And he wouldn't need to drink Wintersmeet Eve away. The little voice that warned her not to take her future for granted faded nearly to silence.

At around noon on the fifth day Telaine was stirring a pot of soup she'd made all by herself when she realized the sound of the shrieking wind was gone, leaving her with a dull ringing in her ears. Then the younger Richardsons made a scrambling dash for the door, flinging it open and shouting their excitement into the still air.

A drift that had blown against the door fell in and buried Hope, who began to cry, but the others pushed over and past each other and stumbled and danced through the snowdrifts, shouting. The sky was a cloudless blue, not only cloudless but looking like it had never heard of such a thing as a cloud before. Up and down the main street people were poking their heads out of doors and windows and exclaiming that the snows were over and winter was drawing to a close. How they could be so certain, Telaine didn't know, but she prayed they were right.

"I need boots. And a coat," she said. She shivered, standing in the doorway wearing only Eleanor's dress, and reached up to turn her bodysuit Device's knob higher.

Ben looked at her feet, then swept her up and carried her off, shrieking and kicking and laughing, to Aunt Weaver's home, taking her around to the back door and setting her neatly inside.

Aunt Weaver was standing by the fire, stirring the pot, and as the door slammed shut the spoon fell from her hand into the bubbling depths. "Merciful heaven," she said. Then she shocked Telaine utterly by putting her arms around her and hugging her so tightly Telaine couldn't breathe. She hugged her great-aunt back, unable to speak. "I thought you were dead," Aunt Weaver whispered into her ear. "I was never going to forgive myself for letting you go."

"It's all right," Telaine whispered back, "Sarah's safe—I hope Sarah's safe. I had to send her home a different way."

"Tell me the story another time." Aunt Weaver took up another long-handled wooden spoon and used it to fish the first one out. "Hope the two of you didn't get into any mischief, canoodling all alone during the storm." Her voice was rough and she kept her face turned away from them.

"We were at the Richardsons'," Telaine said. "Where do the Andersons live?"

"Down the dressmaker's street and first right, third house on the right. Hurry."

"Wait here while I put on some actual shoes," Telaine told Ben, glowering at his innocent expression, and ran up to her room. Her shoes weren't suitable for the snow, but she didn't have time to find a pair of boots in the morass of Aunt Weaver's spare room.

She bounded down the stairs, two at a time, and raced out the door with Ben at her heels. Snow fell into her shoes and melted, leaving her feet wet, but she didn't stop running until she reached Sarah's house. Then she paused, afraid of what she'd find there. "She's alive," Ben said.

Telaine knocked. After a moment, Sarah answered the door.

They stared at each other, then Telaine wrapped her arms around the girl, who started to cry. "I thought you must be dead," Sarah wept.

"I was afraid you'd been caught out in the storm," Telaine said.

"You want to come on in here?" said a gruff voice. Sarah's mother Susan.

They sat in a drawing room every bit as uncomfortable as Aunt Weaver's. Maybe they were mass-produced somewhere. "Sarah told us everything," her mother said. John Anderson stood behind her with one hand on her shoulder. "We owe you our daughter's life."

"I wish I'd known how to stop him," Telaine said.

"Well, I do," said Anderson. His voice was like the bass growl of a bear. "And I got a bunch of fellows who know how to stop him, too."

"*Please* let the law have time to dispense justice," Telaine said. "I know who to talk to, down mountain, and I promise they'll come after him. Besides, he commands the soldiers at the fort, and his men are well armed. I would hate for any of you to come to grief."

Sarah's father looked as if he didn't think the law's justice would be better than his own, but eventually he nodded. "After the pass clears," he said. "I expect you to be true to your word."

"I will be."

Sarah ran after them before they'd gotten more than a few steps away, carrying a bundle of clothes with Telaine's boots piled atop it. "I found these in your boots," she said, handing over the throwing knife Telaine had taken to carrying with her, to practice, and the flat black package holding her lock picks.

Ben looked at the packet curiously. "What's that?"

"Just a few tools of the trade," Telaine said.

They walked back to Aunt Weaver's in silence, hand in hand. Telaine was adding justice for the Andersons, for all the children, to her plan, and she was startled out of her reverie when Ben said, "Don't know how a man can sit still for having someone do that to his daughter. He's stronger than I am."

Telaine guessed he was thinking about *their* hypothetical daughter, and she wanted to ask him about it, but a tiny part of her still clung to the idea that she shouldn't make those plans until she was safely retired. *You haven't listened to the voice of reason for weeks,* she told herself. *This whole adventure has been one compromise after another. Something's bound to go wrong.*

"Nothing's going to go wrong," she said aloud, and waved away his questions when he wanted to know what she was talking about. She wouldn't let anything go wrong.

CHAPTER TWENTY-EIGHT

The next morning, the main street looked very different. Telaine sat halfway out her window and marveled at the change. People had pitched in the day before to clear the blanket of snow from the street, leaving a half-inch-thick layer now punctuated with footprints. Spaces between the houses and businesses lining the street were full to bursting with packed snow. Longbourne was serious about welcoming in spring as soon as possible.

"They clear the street and the crossroads so's we can have a concert and a dance tonight," Aunt Weaver explained at breakfast. "Only reason we have that gazebo. Happen you can persuade your young man to give us a few solos."

"But the pass still isn't open," Telaine chafed. "I can't settle down for a concert knowing that."

"Don't see how fretting about it will open the pass any sooner."

"You're much calmer than I am. I don't know how you do it."

"I'm seventy-seven years old. Happen I've had plenty of practice."

Telaine dressed warmly, ate, and discovered her usual path around the side of the house was blocked. She would have to use the front door. Outside, she squinted in the bright sun reflecting off the packed snow. The street was more than usually busy with people standing in small groups, talking and laughing. It felt like a holiday. Maybe it was, in Longbourne.

She set off up the street toward the forge, though she guessed Ben wouldn't start the fire today. The sun had melted the snow enough the day before that it had frozen overnight into a thin crust that crunched pleasantly under her boots. She bent down to rearrange her throwing knife, which had slipped slightly and was pressing against the knob of her ankle. She and Ben could go for a walk, and maybe they could have a throwing contest. A walk, and dinner at the tavern…she was going to make herself relax if it took all day.

When she stood up, she saw movement in the distance, a mass of people moving toward Longbourne from the fort. Some of them were mounted. She shielded her eyes from the sun's glare. Those people were marching. Soldiers.

Dread crept over Telaine, and she ducked out of sight behind the general store, as far as she could get with the mass of snow blocking the space between it and its neighbor. Soldiers coming into Longbourne had to be bad.

From her hiding place, she couldn't see anything but people stopping what they were doing and turning to face the soldiers. She heard feet, and hooves, breaking through the crust, and the jingle of harnesses, then she heard a voice that sent an icy spear through her heart. "We're here for Lainie Bricker."

Morgan.

How was he here? Unless—Thorsten Pass was clear. No. Impossible. He had to have found another way back. Rapidly she went over her sabotage in her head—*no*, sweet heaven, if they'd worked out it was only overheating, there was all that snow—

Morgan's lazy voice said, "Where is Lainie Bricker?"

Silence. The people she could see were glancing at each other, their faces impassive. Either no one had seen her, or the good people of Longbourne weren't going to hand one of their own off to a psychopath.

Then she heard a gunshot, and some screams. The Baron said, in his smoothest voice, "The next shot will go through a person instead of that hideous gazebo unless I see Miss Bricker here in front of me in five seconds."

Telaine instantly moved out of concealment, walking forward until she was next to the gazebo, behind the Baron. "Right here, milord."

The Baron turned his head at the sound of her voice, then jigged his horse around to face her. He held a sleek pistol Device aloft in one hand and there was no expression on his face. "Miss Bricker. I believe you've taken something that belongs to me."

He'd found out about Sarah. She thought of Mistress Wilson and ice filled her stomach. "I don't think it was yours in the first place," she said, trying to match his conversational tone.

He dismounted and came toward her. Behind him, Morgan did the same, his feline smile fixed on her and his eyes fondling her body. She kept her attention on the Baron.

"Miss Bricker," he said, "I am the lord of this Barony and what I decide is mine will not be disputed. And I refuse to allow my sovereignty to be challenged by a Deviser with no rank and no power." In an lower voice, he said, "You will not be allowed to take your story down the mountain. I will not waste my time refuting your scurrilous accusations."

"Your behavior says you're worried you'll have to."

The Baron leveled his gun at Telaine. She held his gaze and tried not to flinch. "I won't ask for my property back," he said in a more normal voice. "I'll take you instead. Morgan will be happy to pay you a great deal of attention. I'm sure I'll enjoy watching."

Out of the corner of her eye Telaine saw movement. "No!" she screamed, but it was too late. Ben lowered his head and charged at Morgan, who stepped aside and casually punched him in the jaw. Ben staggered, and Morgan caught him in a chokehold and eyed him as if puzzled by the attack. Then he caught Telaine's eye.

She didn't have time to conceal her horror, her fear for Ben, and for a moment, Morgan looked confused. He glanced again at Ben, then back at Telaine, and she knew the instant he figured it out because his eyes widened with fury.

His arm tightened savagely around Ben's neck, making him arch his back and gasp for air. "*Stop it!*" Telaine screamed, and took several running steps toward them. Then Morgan's usual lazy, sinister expression was back. He kicked Ben's knee, making him drop hard to the ground, and released his chokehold to wrench Ben's arm up high behind his back.

Ben coughed and hacked and tried to jerk away from Morgan's grip. In the next instant Morgan had his knife at Ben's throat, and Ben went perfectly still. "**submit, and i won't hurt him,**" he said with a laugh that had no mirth in it.

Telaine turned away and dropped to one knee in front of the Baron, cold gravel digging into her leg. "I'll go with you if you leave the townspeople alone," she said quietly, her throat closing up. She looked once more at Morgan and saw him turn the blade so the edge rested across the vein. He knew. And he would kill Ben no matter what she promised him.

"Please, make him stop, milord," she added, her hand drifting to her boot. If she did nothing, Ben would die. If she missed, Ben would die. She had one chance. *Dear heaven, if I only hit one thing in my life, let it be this target.* She kept her eyes locked on Morgan's, pleading with him as her fingers gripped the hilt of her knife. Then in one movement she pulled it out and flung it with a smooth overarm motion.

She knew as it left her fingers that it would fly true. Morgan had only just registered what she'd done when her knife entered his eye and drove all the way to the hilt. His one good eye blinked at her, uncomprehending, and he slumped to the ground, the knife falling from his lax fingers. Shocked, Ben raised his hand and touched his neck; his fingers came away bloody from a shallow, long cut.

Telaine couldn't stop looking at Morgan, certain he was playing one final game with her and at any moment he would stand and stab Ben through the heart. She felt numb, so numb that when the Baron grabbed her by the collar and dragged her to her feet, she couldn't resist.

"A murderer as well as a thief," he shouted. "So do I charge you, Lainie Bricker. You will be taken to the fort and held pending trial."

He shoved her into the waiting arms of Captain Jackson, who as usual acted as if he didn't care if she lived or died. Telaine came to her senses and tried to break away, but he restrained her as easily as if she'd been a recalcitrant kitten.

Ben shouted and lunged in their direction, but was grabbed by Liam just before the Baron's shot would have gone through his head. "Anyone who attempts to help the prisoner will be tried as an accomplice," the Baron said. He mounted his horse and stared coldly at the assembled crowd, which had grown quite large. "Captain?"

Telaine gave up struggling against Jackson's grip. She absolutely could not let him confine her. "Everybody listen!" she shouted. "The Baron is the one who took—"

The Baron, who had begun to ride away, turned back and leveled his gun at her. "Bind her," he said in his most vicious voice, cutting across her words, "and gag her. I believe we will have an execution right here. Right now."

Telaine opened her mouth to shout again and Jackson's thick arm went across her mouth. Ben screamed. "Be silent," the Baron said, "or I will silence you myself." Someone grabbed her hands and bound them roughly behind her back, and a none-too-clean handkerchief replaced the captain's grimy, scratchy wool sleeve. She fought back, and the captain kicked her feet out from under her and dragged her to the base of the gazebo, wrenching her bound arms painfully above her shoulders.

This is not how I pictured this ending, she thought with unnatural calm.

The Baron again dismounted and walked toward her. She knelt up and glared at him. He would not see her fear.

He pointed the pistol at her, one of the ones from his collection, *I repaired that one, isn't that funny?* and said in a quiet voice, "I did enjoy your company. A pity I'm forced to kill you." She continued to glare, but wondered, *Should I close my eyes? What's the etiquette for being murdered by a torturer and a traitor?* She kept her eyes open even as she heard the shot. But—that wasn't the Baron's gun, it was too far away...

The Baron looked away, the barrel of his gun pointing up. Telaine threw herself at his legs and knocked him sprawling, heard him curse. Someone landed on him; someone else kicked the gun away; a third person yanked the gag out of her mouth and untied her hands.

Ben pulled her to her feet and enveloped her in his arms, squeezing tightly, putting his body between her and anyone else. She looked up and saw wet trails streaking his face. She laid her head against his chest, feeling his heart pounding as fast as hers was, trying to control her breathing. *I guess I don't have to come to terms with my life after all.*

A confused murmur filled the air, growing louder as the seconds passed. "Let go of me!" the Baron shouted, struggling in Liam's massive arms. Captain Jackson fought Jack for possession of the Baron's gun. And the soldiers, directionless and without orders, brought their gun Devices to bear on the citizens of Longbourne.

Before the soldiers could fire their weapons, another gunshot tore across the clamor. "What is going on here?" a woman's voice exclaimed. Telaine turned around; Ben kept a loose, protective grip on her shoulders. A double file of mounted soldiers, properly dressed and outfitted and looking altogether professional, rode into the town center. Their leader, a fine-boned woman with graying chestnut hair and a major's insignia on her sleeve, held a recently fired pistol Device in the air.

She cast her eye over the gathering and focused on the Baron, who was far better dressed than anyone else. "Who are you?"

The Baron shoved Liam, who had him pinned to the ground, away and got to his feet, brushing snow off himself. "I am Hugh Harstow, Baron of Steepridge, and I am grateful for your arrival, major," he said smoothly. "The people of this town attempted to rebel against my sovereignty, and you can see my men and I are outnumbered. These—" he pointed at Ben, and Telaine, and Jack and Liam—"are the ringleaders. I demand you take them in charge preparatory to trial."

"He was going to kill an innocent person!" Liam declared.

"Hardly innocent. A murderer." The Baron indicated Morgan's dead, abandoned body, its eye still sporting its grotesque ornament.

"The Baron—" Ben began, but the major silenced him with a wave.

"I can see this will take some time to sort out. I'll have to ask all of those concerned to come with me to the fort."

Panic rose in Telaine's chest. This would take too long. If Morgan *had* come over the pass with the earth mover, the Ruskalder army could not be far behind. But there was nothing she could do, unless she could get the major alone—but would the major even listen to her?

"Telaine? *Telaine!*"

At first she didn't recognize her own name. Then, to her dismay, she saw a soldier near the head of the column leap from his horse and run toward her. He was tall, with short black hair and a face she'd known all her life. "Jeffy," she said under her breath. What was her cousin Jeffy doing here?

"Your Highness! Lieutenant North! Return to your position!"

Jeffy ignored the major and barreled down on Telaine. He shoved Ben and sent him sprawling. "Get your hands off my cousin," he growled. "Telaine, what are you doing here? And dressed like a commoner?"

"Cousin? Telaine?" Ben said, staring up at Telaine in confusion.

"What are you saying, Lieutenant?" The major turned her horse and walked back toward them.

"Major, I insist you take these four in charge at once!" the Baron said.

"I thought you were recovering from lung fever," Jeffy said. "Julia's been sick with worry, Telaine, how could you do this to her?"

"Lainie, what's he talking about?" Ben said.

Telaine looked at Ben, then at Jeffy. The major said, "Milord Baron, who killed this man?" and as the Baron opened his mouth to reply, Telaine saw a vision of the future as clearly as if she were there. She saw this argument and confusion growing to encompass all of Longbourne until the Ruskalder came down that road and slaughtered everyone. And there was only one way she could stop that future from happening.

She looked at Ben again, still sprawled on the ground. "I'm sorry," she said.

She stepped away from Ben and Jeffy into a relatively clear space. "Major!" she shouted, cutting over whatever the Baron was saying and causing the major to turn. Her hands were shaking. She took a deep breath. "Major, my name is Telaine North Hunter," she said, so there would be no mistake. "And I am an agent of the Crown."

Everyone went silent. Even the horses stopped moving, as if they knew the magnitude of what she'd done.

"Hugh Harstow, I charge you with high treason against the Crown," she went on. "I charge you with conspiring with the King of the Ruskalder to allow them passage through your Barony into Tremontane. I charge you with the murder of Edmund Clarke and of gross negligence in failing to maintain the kingdom's defenses. I charge you with the torture of seven children of your Barony and with being an accomplice in their kidnapping and murder, and with the kidnapping of another girl. And I charge you with the attempted murder of a member of the royal family and an agent of the Crown." The litany had made her hands stop shaking. The Baron's white-lipped fear gave her great satisfaction.

"You are not—" the Baron said. His voice shook. "You cannot possibly be—"

"Can I not?" This man, this disgusting, prating, hollow shell of a man was responsible for a legion of nightmares. "Harstow, I have spent nine years of my life pretending to be someone I'm not. I am *very* good at my job. You saw what I wanted you to see. You were easy to control, Harstow, and now all I want is to be allowed to witness your execution."

The major said, "You must be the one I was sent to retrieve."

Telaine, caught off guard by her conversational tone, stared at her. It occurred to her to wonder how this troop was even here, with the pass still closed. "Retrieve?"

"My primary mission was to review the fort's defenses. My secondary mission was to find a lost agent and give her all assistance. It was given to me by the King himself." For a moment, pride glinted in her eye. "He also gave me an earth mover to expedite my mission. Is it your Highness, or Agent Hunter?"

Telaine closed her eyes. "Right now, it's Agent Hunter."

"Agent Hunter, what were you saying about an invasion?"

"The Baron was in collusion with the Ruskald King to allow an invasion force through. He sent an earth mover down Thorsten Pass to clear it for the invading army."

The Baron laughed. "Earth mover? Miss Bricker, or whoever you are, you have an overactive imagination. Has anyone seen any evidence of this supposed Device? You have no proof of your allegations. Major, I insist you release me."

"Morgan—" Telaine pointed at the body—"was gone all winter. Major, nobody came up from Ellismere before you cleared the pass, and he didn't come with you. The only place he could have been was Ruskald, and the only way he could have returned is with the Baron's earth mover. And the soldiers all saw me building it. Some even helped. Please, major. My word as an agent counts as evidence in court. This has to qualify."

The major chewed her bottom lip. "I believe you," she said. "How long until the Ruskalder army arrives?" she said to the Baron. He glared at her with disdain.

"The army would have to move more slowly than one person," Telaine said, "but..." She did some calculations and came up with an answer that left her sick and faint. "As early as sunset," she said. She exchanged glances with the major. "What's your name?" she asked.

"Major Anselm. Constance Anselm. Agent Hunter, what is the status of the troops?"

Telaine cast her eye over the assembled soldiers. "What you see here is a third of the troops currently stationed at the fort."

Anselm blanched. "They only have sixty soldiers? For a fort meant to be manned by three hundred?" Her expressive eyes added silently something about the quality of the soldiers in front of her.

"I wasn't kidding about the gross negligence." They stared at each other. "Major Anselm, how many soldiers do you have?"

"I brought a troop of fifty. Supposedly enough to handle any problem you might have gotten into."

"It's not enough," Telaine said. She turned, madly hoping to see more soldiers emerge from the snow, and met Ben's eyes. He'd stood and taken a few steps away from her, toward the crowd of townspeople watching in perfect silence. His expressionless, white face frightened her. It was a look she'd hoped never to see on him again.

"Ben," she began.

"You showed us what you wanted us to see," he said.

"No," Telaine said, hearing her own rash words flung back at her. "No, that wasn't—"

"Just heard you say it. You needed to make the Baron believe you were an ordinary person, didn't you?"

"Yes, but—"

"You lied about who you were. You lied about why you were here."

"I never lied about—"

His voice grew hoarse. "Must've been your lucky day, finding a fool who believed you so completely that he'd love your false self. No better way to fit in than that."

She groped for something to say that would convince him, but all she came up with was, "That's not how it went."

"That sounds like another lie," he said. "We deserve everything you ever did to us for being such fools." He turned and, head bowed, walked away in the direction of the forge. She watched him go, his fists clenched. She felt colder even than the winter air would warrant. Everywhere she looked she saw nothing but angry, dumbfounded, betrayed faces.

Desperate, she sought out friends: Maida, Jack, Eleanor, Liam. None of them would meet her eyes. "Eleanor," she pleaded, and Eleanor turned away, her hands twisted in the fabric of her skirt. The cold threatened to crack her heart in two. She turned away, her eyes burning.

The Baron laughed, a dry, nasty sound, and it turned her pain into fury. She took several swift steps and punched the Baron with more strength than she knew she had in her. His eyes rolled up in his head, and he sagged to the ground. The blow sent welcome pain up her arm, a reminder that she was still alive despite all the evidence to the contrary.

She turned back to the major, who was watching her with unexpected compassion and said nothing about her attack. "The fort is fully stocked," Telaine said, her eyes dry. She'd pay for those dry eyes later. "Weapons, rations, everything. *Milord Baron* meant it all to go for arming the invaders. The new weapons, too, and armor."

"But we need *soldiers*," Anselm said. "It will take too long to bring in reinforcements. The fort will be overrun with only one hundred and ten men and women."

"Don't recall signing up to fight an invading army," Jackson said.

"Excuse me, soldier, but that is precisely what you signed up for," Anselm said coldly.

Telaine made an intuitive leap. "The Baron meant you to die," she said, and Jackson turned to look at her. "He decimated the fort's troops so the Ruskalder could overrun you easily. I don't know what he told you, if he claimed you'd be allowed to join the invaders or something, but you should consider what you know of Harstow, and ask yourself if he's the kind of man who would share power with a scruffy no-name soldier who only has rank because Harstow needed a stooge."

Jackson flinched, and Telaine knew she'd struck home. She added, "You might also remember you could easily be charged with treason along with your master. And, gentlemen—" she included as many of the Baron's soldiers in her gaze as she could—"if you leave this mountain, I will track you down and *I will see you hanged*."

Her voice echoed with a cold fury that promised violence to anyone who challenged her; she heard it, and she knew everyone else did too. The soldiers looked at one another. Jackson came to full attention for the first time since Telaine had known him and said, "Yours to command, major."

A disturbance at the outside of the crowd turned into Ben, carrying his biggest sledgehammer as if it were a willow stick. "I'll help with the defense too," he said, looking at Anselm and ignoring Telaine. "Happen you could use a few more hands."

"I'm with you, too," said Liam. A few voices chimed in, then more and more. Telaine listened to the chorus with growing horror.

"No," she said to Ben, forgetting herself, "you aren't fighters, you'll just get yourselves killed."

He looked at her with such fury she didn't recognize him. "Happen you don't get a say in this," he said coldly. "Get out of here. Go back where you came from. You're not one of us."

Telaine flinched. He turned away, hoisted his hammer over his shoulder, and joined Jack and Liam where they stood with the rest of the townspeople, waiting for the major to direct them. *Why am I not crying?* she wondered, and her own thoughts seemed so remote it was as if someone else were thinking them.

She heard Anselm say, behind her, "There's a garrison east of Ellismere. Fort Canden. We might be able to hold them off long enough for those troops to get here. Sergeant Williams, maybe—"

"I'll go," Telaine said. "You can't spare any soldiers, and I'm done here." She walked over to Morgan's horse and mounted, turning it in a wide circle. "How do I find it?"

"Straight along the road east from Ellismere, no side roads. It's easy to find." Anselm held out her hand and Telaine grasped it. "That was a brave thing you did," she added. "Sorry it turned out that way."

"It was always going to turn out that way," Telaine said. "I just didn't want to believe it." She saw Aunt Weaver in the crowd, looking up at her. Her great-aunt's face was unreadable. *How much trouble did I let her in for?* Not that she could do anything about it. She hoped Aunt Weaver's secret would stay safer than her own. She nodded once at Aunt Weaver in farewell, then turned the horse and trotted away.

Jeffy brought his horse alongside hers as she began heading out of town. "Lainie, did I ruin everything?" he asked. "I only joined her troop two days ago, I asked to be transferred in—it's just that she's a legendary commander, and I wanted…"

He sounded so much like a little boy that she laughed without bitterness. "I'm the one who ruined everything," she said, "and you have nothing to be sorry for. Jeffy—stay safe. Fight well."

"Not always compatible," he said lightly, but his voice shook. She patted his hand.

"I'll send help," she said, and kicked the horse into a gallop.

CHAPTER TWENTY-NINE

She had to dismount and lead Morgan's horse down the mountain road. Though Major Anselm's earth mover had left a wide, obvious trail, it had also left enough snow on the path to obscure any potential hazards.

She forced herself to walk slowly so she wouldn't trip, all the while imagining the defenders of the fort picking their way across the snowy fields, spreading out through the fort, passing out weapons. She pictured Jeffy with his sword he'd never used before, Liam holding one of the new guns, Ben hefting his hammer…she had to stop thinking then, focus on not accidentally walking off the mountainside.

She descended from winter into early spring, a spring still touched here and there by snowdrifts, but spring nonetheless. Daffodils sprouted at the bases of aspen trees, their slim white trunks exclamation points against the evergreen background. *How beautiful the world still is*, she thought in wonder, and could not understand how it could also be so cruel.

No snow remained on the foothills, and as soon as the road was visible, she mounted Morgan's horse and trotted the rest of the way off the mountain. Then she kicked the horse into a gallop. She glanced at her watch. Just past noon. The Ruskalder could be at the fort in less than six hours. She urged the horse faster.

She reached the Hitching Station at one o'clock and scrambled off the horse, thrusting its reins into Edith's surprised hand. The dinnertime crowd filled the tap room, but Telaine got Josiah Stakely's attention by shoving between him and someone ordering a beer. "I need to speak with you in private. *Now*."

Stakely looked at her, perplexed, and finished drawing the man's beer. "Back here, Miss Bricker," he said, and ushered her into the back room. "I hope this is important," he added, frowning, standing with his arms crossed in a forbidding manner.

She took a deep breath. She'd already done it once; how many times could she be damned? "Mister Stakely, I'm not a Deviser. I'm an agent of the Crown and I need your help."

Stakely furrowed his brow at her. "You're a what?"

"I'm an agent of the Crown. A spy. And I need two horses. I don't have any money to pay you now, but I swear I will pay you anything you like for this imposition when I return. *Please*, Mister Stakely, this is more urgent than you can imagine."

Stakely scratched his head. "I don't understand—" he began.

"Mister Stakely, I don't have time to explain. All I can tell you is that I have to get to Fort Canden as quickly as possible, and I need to move at top speed. So I need to be able to switch between three mounts. Can you help me?"

He scratched his head again, his brow still furrowed. Then he turned, and Telaine followed him out of the tap room and into the stable yard. "Edith, Miss Bricker needs two good mounts," he said.

Edith was already deeply involved in grooming Morgan's horse. "Seems she's got one good one already," she grunted. Spittle flew.

"Two other horses. You want to help her saddle up?" Stakely asked her. Telaine held out her hand and shook his vigorously.

"Mister Stakely," she said, "thank you. I promise you'll be rewarded for serving your country."

She and Stakely helped Edith put bridle and lead lines on two horses, not fancy or high-stepping, but good movers who looked like they had stamina. Exactly what she needed. She mounted Morgan's horse and led the other two on a string behind her, trotting through the streets of Ellismere until she came to the road leading out of town. Then she gave her mount its head, and her string of horses set off rapidly eastward.

Telaine became obsessed with her watch. She told herself she would only check it every time she switched horses, but the terrain here was broad, featureless plains, smelling of dust even this early in the year, and there was nothing to focus on, so she would sneak a peek, just once or twice.

As the afternoon wore on, she and her horses began treading on their shadows, which lengthened as the minutes and hours passed until they were thin gray fingers pointing the way to the garrison. The road was well-kept, paved and maintained the way roads between military stations were expected to be. If the troops had to be called out, no one wanted them delayed because of potholes. Telaine stopped watching for hazards and urged her horses on. One more glance at the watch wouldn't hurt anyone.

The setting sun turned their shadows a starkly outlined black, and then it sank behind distant Mount Tendennon, leaving a glow that might have been rosy or golden. Telaine had no time to waste looking at sunsets. She could no longer read her watch face. *A Device that lights a clock face,* she thought, *something soft so it doesn't blind you at night.*

She put it away and concentrated on the road. The light of the half-moon was not quite enough for speedy travel, and she had to slow for fear of veering off over the verge, fear of a horse breaking a leg, and if that happened Telaine didn't know what she would do. She trotted along and tried not to imagine distant screams and war cries. *I hope they give him a gun, that hammer won't do any good until the Ruskalder are so close it doesn't matter.*

She changed mounts again and urged the horses on faster. On her left, the foothills of the Rockwilds, charcoal gray ash-heaps in the starry night; on her right, barren prairie that spread out uninterrupted...no. Something else. Something that sparkled, here and there, with light.

Another half hour, she guessed, and she came to a stop in front of the great wooden doors of the fort. It was little more than a black hulk against the sky. She saw no watchers, no guardsmen at the gate. "Hallo the fort!" she shouted. "Is anyone there?" Had she not seen the lights above the wall, she might have imagined it empty, a shell populated by ghosts.

"Who's there?" someone shouted. A window slid open, shedding yellow light on the ground next to her.

"I am an agent of the Crown and I need to speak to your commanding officer." It was getting easier. And she wasn't dead yet, or destroyed, from saying it. Oh, wait. Yes, she was.

"Can you prove it?"

She wanted to scream with frustration. Instead, she said, "Not from out here."

After a moment, the gate swung open with a hideous groan. She led her mounts inside.

It was smaller than the Thorsten Pass fort, but looked bigger because it wasn't all spread out flat. A couple of soldiers came forward to take the reins from her. She slid down, staggered, and said, "Please care for them. They've worked hard today."

The man who'd spoken to her—she recognized his voice—said, "So. We're supposed to take your word for it that you're a spy. You don't look like a spy."

"If I looked like a spy, I wouldn't be much good, would I?" She didn't look like a spy. She looked, she was certain, like a madwoman, her hair wild, her clothes sweaty and filthy from road grime. "I must speak to your commanding officer."

"Don't be a jackass, Sampson, if she's a spy the commander needs to know," said another soldier, taller and thinner than Sampson. "Wait here, miss." He went up a flight of stairs leading to the top of the keep. Sampson glowered at her as if he expected her to pull out a sword or a gun and attack him. Telaine smiled sweetly at him, or tried to; the corners of her mouth felt tight, as if she had forgotten how.

It took a few minutes for the soldier to reappear. "Come with me, miss," he said, and led the way back to the stairs and into the keep. The crenellated walls and the walkway that ran along them looked uncomfortably like the fort at Thorsten Pass, but the keep was nothing like its counterpart. Where the Thorsten Pass keep had that tall, bleak, depressing central room, the Canden fort was warm and cheery. Its top floor was given over to a strategy room, lit by golden-white Devices and the bright flames burning in a red brick fireplace.

Several soldiers in tidy green and brown uniforms stood in groups of two or three throughout the room. A few, consulting paperwork, sat at a table that would have been more at home in someone's dining room. A surprisingly youthful man wearing major's stripes stood up from the table and came to meet her. He looked as severe as the room looked welcoming.

"You had better be able to back that claim up," he said. "There are heavy penalties for impersonating an agent of the Crown."

"I know," she replied. "I also know you have a protocol for verifying an agent's status." It had never been an issue for her, but she knew it existed. She hoped it was something she could pass.

He pursed his lips and stared at her for a moment. He cracked the knuckles of his left hand, one at a time. "This fort doesn't," he said. "We should." He cracked the knuckles of his right hand. Telaine thought her head might explode from tension.

"What's your name, major?"

"Beckett."

"Major Beckett, let me explain the problem and you and I can figure out what to do about it. At this moment, a Ruskalder army is attacking the fort at Thorsten Pass. The fort is inadequately defended by a force one-third the strength it should be, as well as a number of untrained civilians. I need you to take your garrison up the pass to Thorsten and repulse the invaders. And I need you to do it now."

The major cracked his knuckles again. Telaine wanted to cut his hand off and feed it to him. "I don't think you realize Tremontane is already on heightened alert due to a Ruskalder army massing on the northwestern border. Leaving my post could mean court-martial or execution. I'd need more than the word of a woman who claims to be an agent."

"Major Beckett, the Ruskalder invasion surely overrides whatever orders you currently have."

"I have no evidence *you* aren't a traitor trying to pull me away from my post. For all I know that supposed invasion is going to come from the east instead."

Telaine closed her eyes and bit down on a handful of hasty words before they could escape her lips. "Suppose…suppose I could get you new orders," she said. "Official orders from a source you trust. You'd have to obey those, right?"

"I don't see how you could," Beckett said. He cracked his knuckles again.

"You leave that to me." Telaine rubbed her eyes. "Where's your telecoder?"

"It's broken," the major said.

Telaine stared. "I'm sorry, did you say it's *broken*?"

"We're expecting someone to repair it in two days. The dedicated receiver is still working, but the main Device is down."

She sank into a chair. "Just a minute," she said when the major asked if she was all right. Broken. No tools. No experience. And over one hundred and seventy lives at the fort, not to mention the thousands more living in Barony Steepridge, depending on her to get this major off his ass and up the mountain.

She looked up at him. "Show me your telecoder room."

The two telecoder Devices were in a smallish room on the ground floor of the keep. One, the major explained, could not send messages and was used only to receive official directives, including new orders. The other, a standard Device for sending and receiving, was cold. Every other telecoder she'd used had been slightly warmer than body temperature and gave off a quiet hum. This one was definitely broken.

Thank heaven they didn't send Sergeant Williams. She picked the Device up in both hands. It was surprisingly light. "Be careful with that," Beckett said, putting out a restraining hand. She held the Device out of his reach.

"Don't worry, major, I know what I'm doing," she lied. "Are you afraid I'll sabotage it?"

The major shrugged, lowering his hand. "It's already broken; what more can you do? And, honestly—" he lowered his voice—"I believe you are who you say you are. But I can't violate protocol on one woman's say-so, agent or no."

I will not kill this man. I will not kill this man. Telaine turned the Device over, examining the case. Four small screws fastened the brass plate to its wooden base. "Do you have some loose change?" she asked the major, who gave her a strange look but fished out a handful of coins. She tried one after the other until she found one that fit the slot and then quickly removed the screws. The base popped away too easily, and she almost dropped it before setting it down carefully on the counter.

The wooden base was hollow in the middle, and empty; the wires and gears that made up the Device were connected to the brass plate and fed up through a square hole into the arm of the telecoder. There were a lot of moving parts and a lot of copper and brass wires. Telaine gently eased the rest of the Device out of the arm. Like the earth mover, a thick copper wire the size of her pinky coupled the Device to the arm. She disconnected it and the whole thing slid neatly onto the counter in front of her.

She repressed the urge to despair. She, Telaine North Hunter, had assembled an earth mover without any instructions, and it was far more complex than this thing. *And how many months did it take you to do that?* She began tracing connections, examining tiny gears, using her fingertips instead of her eyes to understand how this Device worked. Gear fed into gear; wires transmitted power from the motive force, which was a disc half an inch wide that, thank heaven, glowed strongly. She had scented no source anywhere near this place and had no time to search for one.

It was going to take forever. Or, worse, she would find the problem immediately and it would be something impossible for her to fix. She closed her eyes to shut out distractions, wishing she could shut out her sense of the minutes slipping by. Had battle been joined yet? Was Ben still alive? She paused in her exploration and waited for her fingers to stop shaking. *Stay focused. There's nothing you can do for him now but this.*

There. A brass gear no bigger than her thumbnail had slipped a fraction of an inch out of place. She moved it, tapped on it to seat it, continued checking the Device in case there was more than one problem. Another slipped gear, and another. What had they done to this Device, shaken it? None of the parts seemed bent or misaligned except those tiny gears; none of the wires were broken.

A thread of hope wound its way into her heart. Surely that had taken mere minutes and not the hours her body told her it had been. She slid her fingers inside the arm and connected the thick wire. Gears moved, the motive force glowed stronger, and she felt the hum through her fingers. She breathed out in relief.

More quickly now, she reassembled the Device, taking great care to seat it into its wooden base without dislodging any more pieces. The major seemed awed. "Is this something all agents learn to do?" he asked.

She smiled. "No, but maybe they should." She reached for the interlocking wheels to set the code for the ultra-secret Device at the palace, then stopped. "Major, here's what I'm going to do. I'm going to send some messages. After that, your receiving Device is going to deliver a message. Don't tell me what its transmission code is. I don't want you saying I somehow found a way to send it a message from this Device. But I have to ask you to back off now. The Device I'm going to communicate with is for agents only and I honestly don't know what they'd do to you if you knew the code."

The major's eyes widened, and he stepped all the way back to the door. Telaine judged that was far enough, and swiftly set the interlocking wheels to the correct settings and sent the "clear all" signal. Then, with a shaky hand, she tapped out a code she'd never used before: agent in distress, immediate response required.

It took less than thirty seconds for her to receive a response, but it felt like forever. IDENTIFY AGENT AND CODE.

Damn it. Of course they'd want to verify her identity, but wasn't her own name good enough for them? AGENT (she had to think hard to remember her number) 15623 CODE WINTER FLOWER. Telaine, *talaina*, the winter flower that grew along the banks of the Snow River in Ruskald. She'd thought using it was so clever, when she was fifteen.

RESPONSE PHRASE WINTER FLOWER

That was harder. It was…what? Right. SUMMERTREE BLOOMS.

Nearly a minute passed. The room was silent except for the sound of her pulse throbbing in her ears, faster and louder than it probably should be. Suppose she'd gotten it wrong? Was there a space between summer and tree? No, her fifteen-year-old self thought it would be, again, clever.

NATURE OF EMERGENCY AGENT HUNTER?

She'd been holding her breath again. RUSKALDER INVASION AT THORSTEN PASS IN PROGRESS REPEAT INVASION IN PROGRESS. FORT IS INSUFFICIENTLY DEFENDED. REQUEST SEND NEW ORDERS FORT CANDEN MAJOR BECKETT. GARRISON TO PROCEED THORSTEN PASS AID DEFENDERS.

She tried to imagine the face of whoever was on duty right then. Her hand shook again as soon as she released the thumbplate. She turned to Major Beckett. "Soon, now," she said. He still looked afraid. Pity the competent Major Anselm hadn't been here instead. No, better that she was at Thorsten Keep. Better for everyone there, probably.

The key began chattering again.

REQUEST RECEIVER CODE FORT CANDEN

She cursed inwardly. CANNOT PROVIDE CODE. KNOW YOU CAN LOOK IT UP SOMEWHERE.

The key went silent. Telaine put her elbows on the counter, linked her fingers together and leaned her forehead on her joined fists. She was afraid to look at her watch again. They might have been in battle for four or five hours by now. Maybe they were lucky and the Ruskalder hadn't shown up until after dark. Would they attack in the dark? Wasn't that a bad idea, military-wise?

What if the military refused to give the agent in the palace the code? What if that agent had to argue with them the way she'd wrestled with Major Beckett? Maybe she should tell the man who she was. Would he respond more favorably to an order from the King's niece? No, she might still be able to keep Telaine North Hunter's name from being attached to this fiasco, as if she could go back to being the Princess after this.

Her eyes were dry and aching, her legs hurt from riding so many hours after...good heaven, it must have been nine months since she'd ridden anything except the back of Morgan's horse.

The key began chattering again. She lifted her head and saw the telecoder wasn't moving. Panic struck her exhausted mind. She hadn't fixed it completely; the Device was receiving messages but not recording them, it was rattling free inside its case, Ben would die and so would everyone else because of her mistakes.

No, that's ridiculous, she told herself, scrubbed the tiredness out of her eyes, and thought to look at the other telecoder. It was tapping away like a merry little woodpecker, to Telaine's eyes as excited about its message as she was anxious.

She stared at it, longing to read the tape but afraid of what the major might think if she did. He was wasted in his current position; he should be guarding the royal family, as paranoid as he was. It wasn't a complimentary thought.

The major took the tape in his hands and read off the message, moving his lips as he did so. "It appears we're going up the mountain, agent," he said. The telecoder fell silent, and he tore off the tape and left the room. After an uncomprehending moment, Telaine followed him.

"Major Beckett, would you mind—" she said, and he glanced over his shoulder at her but didn't stop walking. "For my own peace of mind, could you tell me what happens next?"

They were once again in the strategy room. "I—excuse me," Beckett said, and waved a couple of men with captain's stripes to him. He handed one of them the telecode tape. "We're moving out in one hour. Pass the word. And one of you send telecodes to Forts Blackrock and Dunstan, get them moving along after us. Agent, what's the supply situation at Thorsten?"

Telaine blinked. "Ah—oh, it's got enough weapons to outfit an army, black powder rifles, six-shot rifle Devices, swords, probably other weapons as well. Lots of food and blankets. Some armor."

"Tell the men we're marching light. We'll take advantage of the fort's supplies. You'd better be right about that," Beckett said, rounding on her.

She nodded. "I...inspected the supplies myself."

"Did you? I suppose they have you agents do all sorts of things," Beckett said.

He made as if to leave the strategy room. Telaine stepped in front of him. "Please, major," she said, "I have friends defending the fort. My cousin is there. What will happen now?"

Beckett looked down at her. "You heard me say we'd march out in an hour," he said. "It will take us perhaps sixteen hours to reach the foot of the mountain and another five or six to navigate the pass. We can't travel at full speed or we won't be any good to anyone once we get there. It's a risk, trading weaponry for speed, but if we can't get there before they're overrun..." Beckett cracked his knuckles again. "At any rate, we'll be there in less than a day.

A day. It sounded like forever. "Major Anselm thought they could hold out for a while," Telaine said. Though she hadn't said what "a while" was.

The major's face brightened. "Connie Anselm? She's one of the best military commanders in Tremontane. Your friends are lucky to have her. I wouldn't be surprised if she made general before I do." He patted her on the shoulder. "Let us handle this. You look like you've run yourself ragged."

She nodded. She was exhausted now. Unfortunately, she had one more thing to do before she could rest. Telaine went back to the telecoder room—she should not have left it set to the palace code—and saw a new message had come through for her.

FURTHER ASSISTANCE NEEDED AGENT HUNTER?

She tapped out, wearily, MISSION COMPLETE. REQUEST NEW INSTRUCTIONS.

The reply took several minutes, but when it came, it was only two words:

COME HOME.

Joy filled her before she realized they meant Aurilien.

Finally, she wept.

SPRING

CHAPTER THIRTY

She slept, fitfully, in some soldier's abandoned bunk after the garrison had moved out. They'd left a handful of soldiers behind, none of whom knew what to do with the strange woman who'd blown in like a tornado and left everything scattered behind her. So they left her alone, which was fine by Telaine.

In the morning, she forced herself to eat something she scrounged out of the mess hall and brushed her hair and her clothes. The horses had been well cared for, and she saddled up and led her spare mounts back down the road to Ellismere. She felt as if she were riding backwards, her long shadow shrinking and disappearing beneath her feet. The horses didn't complain when she switched mounts, although they were traveling so slowly she might as well not have bothered.

She reached Ellismere in the early afternoon. Rather than returning immediately to the Hitching Station, she sent a telecode to her bank in Aurilien requesting a banker's draft for fifteen hundred guilders, which she cashed and took payment in notes and some coin. Then she went back to the Hitching Station and forced Josiah Stakely to take five hundred guilders and Morgan's horse as recompense for helping her without question.

She was not in a mood to argue, and Stakely could tell, because his only resistance was pressing a large mug of beer on her and patting her shoulder in sympathy. She avoided the bar mirror, unwilling to see what it was about her he thought deserving of sympathy.

After the drink, she wandered the streets of Ellismere until she found a shop selling women's clothes. This time she couldn't avoid seeing her reflection: she was dirty and unkempt and not at all the kind of woman this store would serve.

She pushed open the door and, before any of the shop assistants could say anything, slammed down a handful of notes on the counter and said, "I plan to spend a lot of money in this store, and I suggest one of you helps me do it."

No one made a single comment on her appearance.

She bought three spring dresses, a bonnet, a bolero jacket, a nightgown, underwear, three pairs of gloves, several pairs of sheer stockings, and two pairs of high-heeled boots. She did not buy any trousers. The so-helpful shop assistants wrapped up her purchases so she could carry them, after which she went to the most expensive hotel in Ellismere.

Telaine headed off the manager's bustling protest about her appearance by demanding a private room with bath in her plummiest royal accent and with a superior sneer. The man, recognizing the eccentricities of the very wealthy, bowed her into a corner suite with no comment. She tipped him ten guilders to be sure.

She bathed and washed her hair without thinking about how wonderful indoor plumbing was. She dressed without admiring her reflection in the full-length, un-cracked mirror. She looked at her dirty shirt and trousers, then kicked them hard into a corner of the room. It was too hard to put her hair up by herself, so she braided it and went to the dining room for supper, where she ate alone.

After supper she went out and bought a suitcase, then returned to her room and packed her new clothes into it. She changed into her nightgown after the sun set and climbed into the beautiful bed with two mattresses, several fluffy pillows, and a down comforter; the early spring nights were chilly. She did not remember dreaming.

In the morning, Telaine went to the coaching station where she could begin the first leg of her journey to Aurilien. The coach yard, noisy and bustling, made her nerves jangle. The idea of traveling with others, people who would want to chat and tell stories and ask about her life, nauseated her. After making some inquiries, she found a coach making a direct run to Aurilien and bought all its fares for the entire journey. She settled into the corner of the coach and watched Ellismere fade into the distance.

The newspapers began reporting on the great victory at Thorsten Pass two days into her journey. Telaine bought a paper and glanced over some of the stories long enough to know that the Canden garrison had arrived in time to push the Ruskalder back and there had been heavy losses. The paper didn't print the names of the dead. She was grateful for that. She threw the paper away and didn't buy any others.

On Springtide, two days later, the coach plodded down Broad Street and turned sedately onto Queen's Way Road, affably moving past other traffic and giving way to cross-traffic. It drove through the gates of the palace, the horses ambling along the wide curving driveway, until it reached the palace steps and the grand front entryway. The coachman hopped down and opened the door to give his eccentric passenger a hand down.

Telaine accepted her suitcase from the coachman's hand, tipped him the last of her money, and climbed the long stairs to the grand front door. No one paid any attention to her as she went through the halls and up the stairs, some gentrywoman from the country come to take care of business in the palace or to participate in that evening's Spring Ball. Not that she had a gown—good heaven, they wouldn't expect her to attend, would they? The idea of dancing and laughing and flirting sickened her.

The guards at the door to the east wing actually stopped her. *Am I that changed, then, that people can see it?* She removed her bonnet and said, "Ensign Worth, don't you remember me?"

His bland guardsman's face went from confusion to recognition with the briefest stop at horror. "Your Highness!" he said. "I'm so sorry—"

"Don't worry about it, Ensign. May I enter?"

The young man bowed nervously and opened the door for her.

Once inside, she didn't know what to do next. It was as if a Device had been making her arms and legs move, propelling her all this way and was now sapped of its energy, its motive force spent. She set her suitcase down and walked into the drawing room.

Julia sat with her back to the door. She was making cooing sounds and bouncing a baby on her knee, making the child giggle. Telaine stopped and tried to swallow the lump in her throat. Of course. Julia would have had her baby a few weeks before Wintersmeet. Telaine didn't even know if it was a boy or a girl. She'd missed so much. She walked forward, unable to think of anything to say. Julia heard her footsteps and turned around, her face so cheerful it made Telaine's heart ache. Her cheerful look faded to astonishment. She lifted the baby into her arms and stood, coming around the end of the sofa. "Telaine?" she said softly. And then, with feeling, "*Telaine!*"

Telaine smiled and held out her arms. "I'm so sorry it took me this long to come home," she said, tears beginning to fall. "I wish I'd never left."

Elizabeth d'Arden had redecorated her townhouse since Telaine had been there last, and now it was full to the brim with backless Eskandelic couches in white and green and a hundred tiny tables at varying heights above the floor. Telaine sipped her tea and smiled at something one of the women, whose name she'd forgotten, said. Time was she'd have remembered every one of the women Elizabeth had introduced to her. Time was she'd have cared.

"You're the talk of Aurilien, your Highness," Stella Murchison said, laying a confiding hand on Telaine's arm. "I can't believe you spent the whole winter in a town practically on the edge of nowhere! Wasn't it too, too awful?"

Telaine giggled. It sounded forced, but then, she was out of practice. "It wasn't so bad," she said. "I do think it was good for my soul, living like a commoner. But did you know most of them still use outhouses? And I had to wash my hair in a *sink*."

Stella gasped in theatrical horror. "I could never do that," she declared.

"But that's not what I want to hear about," Elizabeth d'Arden said. "Tell us about bringing the garrison to Thorsten Pass."

"Oh, you don't want to hear *that* story again," Telaine said. *I don't want to tell that story again, ever,* she thought. She shouldn't have come to Elizabeth's tea party, but she still had an image to maintain.

There had been any number of rumors about where she'd been all those months, and she'd chosen to confirm the one that came nearest the truth, that she'd been pretending to be a commoner in a distant frontier town. She knew most people, when presented with an exciting yet plausible story, tend not to dig for a different truth, and she hoped the truth about her being an agent of the Crown wouldn't come out. The people who'd been present for her denunciation of the Baron wouldn't be leaving Longbourne, and the soldiers at Fort Canden didn't know her as anything but an anonymous agent.

But it was a foolish hope. It was only a matter of weeks, if not days, before the tale would spread.

"Well, all right," she said in reply to the general clamor that yes, they did want to hear the story again. "Obviously I'm no fighter, and the major needed *someone* to fetch the garrison, so I volunteered. I think it was tremendously daring of me, don't you? I rode for hours, all the while knowing our brave men and women were fighting to keep our country safe—oh, but that means I did, too! And I'm so happy we won."

She sipped her tea, then exclaimed, "Oh, Dorothea, I love your dress! I insist you tell me who your couturier is—I swear I won't have one made exactly like it!"

"Well, *I* think you were generous," Elizabeth said. "It's not as if those villagers are our kind of people. I imagine they just stood around while the real soldiers fought."

Telaine indulged a brief vision of launching herself at the woman, shrieking and clawing her eyes out. "I don't know anything more than that the defense was successful," she said. "Would you pass me one of those sandwiches? They're simply divine."

She didn't care for the sandwiches, which were dry; they were just a good way to keep her mouth full so she would have an excuse not to speak. She'd always known the Princess's acquaintances were shallow, but she'd never realized they were thoughtless and cruel as well.

She wished with all her heart Uncle would return from the front so she could resign her commission and…what? She couldn't simply stop being the Princess; it would destroy nine years of concealing her true identity so she could spy for the Crown. But being trapped in this guise for the rest of her life…

She smiled brightly at something Stella said and ate another sandwich. Her uncle would have to have a solution. The alternative was too awful to contemplate.

When the party was finally over, Telaine went back to the palace, passed through her ghastly sitting room with no more than a small shudder, and wearily began to undress before she remembered she should have called her maid to help her. She put on a simpler, more comfortable gown, then stood for a moment staring at her vanity table.

Finally she reached out and opened the drawer, pulled out the false top and looked at her Deviser's gear. It seemed to belong to someone else. She needed to get rid of it. She couldn't bear to get rid of it. She dropped the tray back into the drawer and slammed it shut. She didn't have to look at it. Perhaps in a week, or a month, she'd be ready to give everything away. Someone else would appreciate it.

The Waxwold Theater was unnaturally stuffy, hot and smelling of ozone from the light Devices spotlighting the stage. It made Telaine's skin itch, as if she could rub against her velvet-upholstered chair and shed it like a snake. That might make her cooler.

She scooted the chair back from the edge of the royal box. It wasn't as if it were that high above the floor of the theater, and she wasn't afraid of heights in any case, but she felt everyone was watching her. Maybe it was just that Clarence Darbeneau's latest play was flat and dull, and *she* wasn't watching it. Or maybe she'd gotten used to relative anonymity over the last nine months. She hated the idea of being stared at.

"Stop fidgeting," Grandmama said in a low voice, her lips barely moving.

"It's a boring play."

"Then at least show some respect for the traditions of the theater."

"I can tell you're bored too. You're twiddling your thumbs."

Grandmama's hands stilled. "I am not. And this isn't about me."

The curtains fell, the house lights went up, and a scattering of applause went up from the audience. Telaine clapped absently, her eyes scanning the crowd. She was usually thronged with visitors whenever she went to the Waxwold Theater. Hopefully Grandmama's presence would dissuade them tonight. She wasn't just bored, she was edgy, restless, and she said, "Let's go."

"I can't. Clarence is here and it would hurt his feelings if I left at intermission."

"I suppose you're right." Telaine shoved her chair back farther.

Grandmama eyed her closely. "If you're going to back all the way to the door," she said, "you should move the other chair out of the way."

"I don't like being watched."

"Telaine, is something wrong? You're usually so eager to be off to see your friends."

Telaine tried to summon up an airy laugh, but it seemed so much like work she couldn't bring herself to do more than smile. "Oh, of course! I'm just tired of being asked to tell the same story over and over again. Wouldn't you be?"

"I suppose." Grandmama stood and shook out her silk skirt, figured all over with white roses. "I'm going to use the facilities."

When she was gone, Telaine slumped in her seat. It was harder every day to play the part of the Princess, laughing and flirting as if her whole life weren't shattered beyond recognition. Grandmama knew something was wrong—Alison North was too observant not to recognize a change in her oldest granddaughter—but she was too polite to pry, and Telaine didn't feel like enlightening her.

A knock sounded at the door. "Am I interrupting anything?" Edgar Hussey said, smiling his arch smile. A knot of tension tightened at the base of her neck. Anyone but Hussey.

"Of course not!" she said with a smile, and allowed him to kiss her hand. "How lovely to see you. You can see I'm quite alone."

"Well, you would be, wouldn't you?"

"What do you mean?"

Hussey lowered his voice. "The rumors, of course. Don't tell me you haven't heard them."

The knot drew tighter. "You know I never listen to rumors, Mister Hussey."

"Well, you should listen to this one, because it's about you."

Of course. This was inevitable. She let her eyes go wide. "About me?"

"That you're an agent of the Crown, my dear."

She held her astonished face for a second longer, then forced herself to burst into laughter. "Why, Mister Hussey, how absurd! Me, an agent of the Crown? Do I look like a spy to you?"

"If you were a good agent, you wouldn't look like one, would you?"

"That's ridiculous. Who's spreading these rumors?"

Hussey shrugged. **"who knows how these things get started?** You probably should do something about them, though."

"I haven't the faintest idea how to combat such a thing. You know what rumors are like. But I can't bear to think of my friends believing it."

"You can imagine why they might be so distressed. You might have been spying on them, after all. Fortunately for me, **i have no secrets worth ferreting out.**"

As if his secrets mattered. "I depend on you to counter these rumors wherever you hear them, Mister Hussey," she said, lowering her lashes and looking up at him through them. "I know I won't be able to do it alone."

"you can count on me to defend your honor," Hussey said. "Now, do you—"

The door opened. "I beg your pardon," Grandmama said coldly. "I did not realize you had company, Telaine." Grandmama wasn't any fonder of Hussey than Telaine was, and Telaine envied her freedom to express that dislike. She withdrew her hand from Hussey's and simpered at him.

"I was just leaving, milady Consort," Hussey said, bowing. "Until later, your Highness."

When the door closed behind him, Grandmama said, "You should have given him a solid push out of this box and see if he comes nosing around you again."

"Grandmama!"

"I despise men like him. Your grandfather had a friend—but that's an old story, and not one you'll care about." Grandmama settled herself into her seat. "And I apologize for meddling in your business."

"No, I don't mind. I just—" She couldn't exactly say *I need him to protect my identity.*

Grandmama leaned forward and waved to an acquaintance below. "I understand you're an agent of the Crown," she said.

"I am not," Telaine said automatically, then tried to cover her mistake with an airy laugh. "That's just what everyone's saying. I can't believe how foolish people are."

"They are." Grandmama was looking at her, her eyes narrowed. "Of course it's untrue."

"Do I look like a spy?" Telaine said with another laugh.

"I don't know what spies look like."

The lights went down, sparing Telaine another response. She realized she'd clasped her hands tightly in her lap, so tightly she couldn't feel her fingers, and made herself relax. *You should tell her*, she thought, *she's already guessed*, but the idea made her whole body feel as numb as her hands.

She had to wait for Uncle to return from the front. Let him make the decision. In time, people would forget the rumors if she didn't try to refute them. Unfortunately, since these rumors had truth behind them, it was possible those truths would simply reinforce the rumors until they reached a point where the two became one. But there was nothing she could do about it except wait, and hope her uncle had a solution to this problem as well.

CHAPTER THIRTY-ONE

Telaine reclined on the overstuffed pink sofa in her sitting room, too tired from a long day of socializing to remember how much she hated the room. She had come far too close to breaking character today, when one of the Princess's acquaintances had begun talking about the war as if he knew anything about it, criticizing the defenders of Thorsten Keep for failing to maintain the fort's defenses and not having a unified strategy of attack, whatever that meant. She'd had to leave the room and walk rapidly around the garden to regain her calm. Then she'd left as gracefully as possible and come back to the palace. It was a mark of how miserable she was that this room was a pleasant escape.

Someone knocked on her door. "Your Highness? The King requests your presence in his study at your earliest convenience."

Telaine leaped from the sofa and ran, somewhat awkwardly thanks to her skirt, to the door. "Right now," she said to the astonished messenger when she opened the door in his face.

When she entered her uncle's study, he was standing facing the fireplace, hands clasped behind his back. He said, "If I had known how this would turn out, I still would have sent you."

Tears came to her eyes. "I'm so sorry," she said, "I did everything wrong, it all nearly fell apart because I was so slow—"

Her uncle turned and embraced her. "None of that." He released her, looking into her eyes and, by his expression, not liking what he saw there. He drew up two chairs before the fire and bade her sit. "I know this will be a long story, and I don't think you should have to stand for all of it," he said. "I had some of it from Major Anselm's report, enough to know about your very public denunciation of the Baron, and more of it from the agent who received your telecode about the invasion. I want to hear it all from you, in order, nothing omitted."

Telaine sat and stared at her hands, trying to organize her thoughts. "Why didn't you tell me who Aunt Weaver was?" she demanded.

Uncle Jeffrey's face went still. "So you know."

"I guessed. It was a tremendous shock."

"I thought, if I told you, it would be a distraction. Mistress Weaver's secret isn't a trivial one for this family. She warned me you were likely to figure it out, but it was a chance I had to take. And I suppose on some level I might have *hoped* you'd figure it out. I know it's necessary, but I hate that she's so isolated from her family."

"She was helpful. I wish I'd taken more of her advice." Telaine took in a deep breath and let it out, slowly. "After I arrived in Steepridge, it took me a few days to get the Baron's attention…"

Despite his instructions, she did not tell him everything. She glossed over how she'd become part of Longbourne. She said nothing about Ben or her weird relationship with Morgan or rescuing Sarah. Those things were private, and painful to recall. Leaving all that out made a much shorter story. When she reached the end, having described her race to Fort Canden and the garrison's moving out, she fell silent. It was his turn to ask questions.

"You had no choice but to reveal your identity," he said.

"I didn't think so. It was either that or risk losing precious time or having the Baron weasel his way out of his guilt."

"I agree. That wasn't a criticism. You were incredibly brave."

"No, just incredibly desperate." The memory of Ben's final words to her burned in her heart. She would give anything to have had another option.

"And you think you didn't act quickly enough on the news about the invasion."

"Every time I review my actions, I realize I acted as quickly as possible, and it was just bad luck the storm came in when it did. But if I'd gotten that message out before —"

"You're not thinking about this the right way. You didn't learn about the earth mover until after the pass was closed, so if you'd made it down the mountain before the storm, we would have known about the invasion plans but assumed we had plenty of time to stop them. 'Ifs' can go both ways, you know."

Her spirits lifted. "You're right, I hadn't thought of it that way."

"You didn't say you'd killed a man."

She hadn't expected that to come up. "I—he was going to kill someone, and I had to stop him."

"I was unaware you knew how to throw knives."

"I picked up the skill while I was in Longbourne." Did *every* memory of Longbourne have a memory of Ben attached to it?

"Fortunate for the person you saved. Are you all right? It's no small thing, taking a life, no matter how despicable or vicious that life might be."

"I...sometimes dream about my last sight of him, with the knife sticking out of his eye socket. But I feel at peace with my actions. I saved a good man's life."

"A friend of yours."

"He *was*. I don't think the good people of Longbourne like me much right now. They believe—" she swallowed—"believe I pretended to be their friend so the Baron wouldn't suspect me."

"Didn't you?"

"I..." What was the truth, and what were the lies? "I liked them. Genuinely liked them. Some of them became my close friends, real friends. It's true I wouldn't have been there if not for the mission, but the only one I manipulated was Baron Steepridge. And speaking of him, please tell me the Ruskalder didn't kill him? I want more than anything to see his execution."

"The Baron is on his way here, in shackles. There will be a trial. And you—" the King cleared his throat—"you will be the chief witness against him."

Telaine's mouth dropped open. "But—there'll be no containing the rumors, then! Everyone will know what I am, what I have been. Nine years of espionage...how many people will want my head?"

"Not as many as will want mine," the King said grimly.

"There has to be an alternative," Telaine insisted. She hated the Princess, wanted nothing more than to be free of her, but to do so in such a public way...it would truly be the end of her life.

"Believe me, Telaine, I have gone over the problem with my advisors, looking for some other solution. Harroden will testify, and we can link Steepridge to the smuggling, but your testimony as agent of the Crown ties it all together. This is the only way we can sentence and execute Steepridge."

"But...those letters he sent to Harroden, and the ones hidden in his study! There must be others between him and the Ruskald King!"

The King shook his head. "He never put anything between himself and the Ruskalder in writing. He's going to claim simple incompetence about the fort and deny the other charges of treason. The only certain thing we have him on is his attempt to murder you, and attempted murder is not a capital crime." He smiled wryly. "Now, if he'd succeeded..."

"I almost wish he had," she said under her breath.

The King straightened and stared at her. "You don't believe that," he said.

Telaine shook her head. Uncle Jeffrey lifted her chin so she had to meet his gaze. "You came out of this much more wounded than I believed," he said. "Is there something else you want to tell me?"

Telaine shook her head again. "Maybe someday, Uncle."

"I'm here when you're ready. Or maybe you should tell Julia. You haven't told her the truth yet?"

"I was afraid to. I wanted your advice. Shouldn't the family know now rather than learn about it at the trial?"

"Yes, they should. I'll break it to Imogen. You can tell Julia. Then Imo can decide how to tell the rest. If it has to come out, I'd like it to be on our terms, through your testimony in court." He leaned back and tapped his long fingers on his jawline. "I am sorry I can't spare you testifying. It will not be easy. And you can already guess what will happen after that. But I can promise you that with time, this will fade. Some other scandal will take its place. Is there anything I can do for you? You realize we are all very much in your debt."

Telaine began to shake her head a third time, then said, "Could you get me the casualty list from Thorsten Pass? The...the townspeople? I would like to know whom to mourn." *Is his name on it?*

Uncle Jeffrey covered her hand with his. "Of course."

Like the east wing drawing room, Julia's sitting room smelled of cinnamon and roses. The smell...it was like finally coming home. Telaine reclined on Julia's sofa and rubbed the lavender velvet, smoothing down the nap. It was like petting a kitten. Maybe she needed a kitten. They couldn't be that hard to care for, could they?

"I'm actually relieved to learn you aren't as scatterbrained and—forgive me—shallow as you sometimes seem," Julia said. "I could never understand how you could be so sensible at home and then be so foolish in public. What I also don't understand is why you couldn't tell me the truth. I keep all your secrets."

Telaine looked up from where she'd been watching the baby chew on her watch. Julia had named her Emma Telaine, something that made Telaine go misty-eyed whenever she thought about it. "I couldn't tell *anyone*," she said. "We rarely even share that knowledge with other agents. It's the first rule, the unbreakable rule." *Except that I broke it, and look what it got me.* "It's—you know the saying, how two people can keep a secret if one of them is dead?"

"No, I'm happy to say I've never heard that somewhat gruesome saying."

"Every person who knows you're an agent is one more person who might give you away. Even accidentally. Even if they swear they never, ever would. It's become something of a superstition, with agents. It would have been wonderful to tell you, but I simply wasn't allowed."

"Even so, I'll be Queen someday, and I don't understand how Father could justify not telling me about something I'll have to administer eventually. Suppose he'd gone to war and been killed?" Julia ate a cream puff and tossed another one at Telaine's head. She caught it without thinking. Cream puffs were one of the things she'd missed, along with her family and full-sized baths.

"But it sounded as if the battle on the northwestern front, the

Ruskalder king's overt attack, wasn't. Did the Army actually come to blows with the Ruskalder?" Telaine said.

Julia grinned. "After what happened at Thorsten Pass, Father squeezed some unilateral peace concessions out of the King of Ruskald before our armies had time to clash. Their failed backdoor invasion left us in an excellent position, strategy-wise, because Jannik had committed so many of his resources to it. Including," she said, dropping her voice dramatically, "his eldest nephew, who is his heir. The Thorsten defenders captured him and we'll be exchanging him for, I don't know, everything Ruskald has plus their underwear."

Telaine laughed. "I'm glad it was successful."

"I think so. Father thinks we may have, in his charming phrase, 'neutered' their ability to come to war against us for the foreseeable future." Julia reached over and picked up her baby, then commenced to bouncing her on her knees and making funny faces. Emma Telaine giggled and pulled her mother's hair.

"Julia, you are positively maternal."

"I know. Isn't it wonderful? Motherhood suits me."

Telaine hesitated, then said, "I read about your divorce." She'd avoided the subject when she'd returned, not sure how to bring it up, but now that they were exchanging confidences, it felt like the right time.

Julia paused in the act of bouncing Emma Telaine. "Did you read about Lucas's accident? Wagering he could jump three fences in a row while drunk? Broke his neck over the second one. Killed the horse too." Her voice was emotionless.

"Julia, I—"

"Telaine, whatever you may think, it was his own fault and nothing to do with Father or anyone else. I don't—I loved him, I did, but after the divorce I realized how much more my own woman I am. I don't miss him. I'm not even sorry Emma Telaine will grow up without knowing him. It's a pity she won't have a father, but she has a family. She even has you." She cooed and bounced the baby again.

"I'm sorry I wasn't here for you," Telaine said. "I wanted to be, honestly."

"Yes, and I'm miffed at you," Julia said cheerfully. "Your payment will be to tell me exactly what exotic mission forced you to abandon me in my time of need."

Telaine sighed heavily and smiled at her cousin. "I suppose, if I *must*," she said. "It began when Uncle ordered me to travel to this little town called Longbourne..."

She left Ben out of the story entirely.

CHAPTER THIRTY-TWO

Three days later, Telaine stood at her sitting room window, looking out toward the army barracks that lay beyond the palace wall. Soldiers had been marching in all morning, returning from the front. At this distance they were green and brown insects swarming the parade grounds before receiving new orders. Jeffy ought to be one of them, unless he'd remained in Longbourne... She bit her lip, trying not to remember things best left forgotten. How would the townspeople treat him, the deceptive Princess's cousin?

From down the hall, a familiar voice called out, "Doesn't anyone want to know how I am?"

Telaine turned around fast. Had thinking of him conjured him up? Shouts of "Jeffy!" rang out from the sitting room, echoing through the east wing. Telaine rushed out of her room and down the hall.

Jeffy, his left arm in a sling, fended off family members, laughing. It was so good to see him, alive and mostly unharmed, that her heart felt lighter than it had in days. He met her eyes as she entered the room, and his laughter cut off. "Hope that shoulder doesn't hurt much, coz, because the sling is—" she began.

Jeffy reached out and put his good arm around her, pulling her tight and bending to lay his forehead on the top of her head. "Lainie, Lainie, you saved all our lives," he whispered. "When the Canden garrison burst past us and took the fight to the Ruskalder...it was just in time. I was still sprawled on the battlements because there wasn't a single soldier to spare to carry me down—and I was trying to save another man's life at the same time. Thank you."

She wrapped her arms around her tall cousin and hugged him tight. "I wasn't going to let you die there heroically and get all the glory," she sniffled.

"Did the Baron try to escape? Did you have to hunt him down?" Jessamy asked, bouncing as if he were five instead of thirteen.

"He was a model prisoner," Jeffy said. "Didn't even speak to anyone except to ask to relieve himself. He looks pretty bad, after ten days in the fort lockup and four more on the road."

"He didn't curse or rattle the bars or anything?" asked Mark, sixteen years old and as Army-mad as Jeffy. He sounded disappointed.

Jeffy chuckled. "No, although he was still furious at..." He looked down at Telaine again and released her. "You should have heard him when we put him in the fort lockup, before the attack. No, maybe you shouldn't. Some of those swear words I'd never heard before."

"He's in shackles, so he can say anything he likes," Telaine said. The thought of the Baron in the tiny prison cells made her heart feel even lighter, despite her ongoing dread of having to testify against him in public.

Aunt Imogen entered the room and embraced her son, laying her cheek against his. "And now we're all home again," she said, her Kirkellish accent stronger than usual. "Sit down and let's hear your story."

"Mother! Why aren't you at the front?" Jeffy put his good arm around her and hugged her back.

"Because your father and I tossed a coin and I lost. Though it sounds as if you Thorsten defenders had all the excitement, so I will stop feeling resentful for missing out." Aunt Imogen patted the seat next to her. "I hope this is a long and detailed story."

"Of course. I want you all to appreciate my daring heroics." He winked at his mother. Telaine thought she might be the only one who saw the tremor in her aunt's smile when she looked at her eldest son's arm in the sling. War would never be just a story for her.

Jeffy leaned back and stretched his long legs out. "Major Anselm had a difficult task. Not only defending the fort under strength, but integrating our unit—I'm proud to be under her command, she's amazing—with those scruffy undisciplined louts *and* the townspeople from Longbourne, who were at least willing and fierce. That's an important piece of military strategy: never underestimate someone who's fighting for his home and family."

"Save the military science lectures for later, please?" said Caitlin, rolling her eyes. She was fourteen and rolling her eyes was her default expression.

"Sorry. Anyway, most of them didn't have experience with anything but brawling. A few knife fighters, a couple of men and women who'd served in the military. But those new guns, they don't take much skill to use despite their weight, and the major had a handful of riflemen to use the old black powder rifles, which still have a longer range than the Devices."

"Did you use the new guns? What firing rate do you get? Does the new cartridge wheel cut down on the misfire chance? When—"

"Save the gun chatter for later too, please?"

"Later, Mark. You ought to ask Telaine. I heard she rebuilt more than two hundred of them."

That brought exclamations from her family. "Telaine, where did you learn to do that? I know you've always been a tinkerer, but rebuilding weapons...that sounds like complicated work," said Imogen.

Telaine reddened. "I was secretly apprenticed to a Deviser in the city. For, um, seven years."

That elicited more gasps and exclamations, and then a torrent of questions. Telaine waved her hands at her family. "I know, I should have told you, and I know I say that a lot lately, but I was afraid if people knew about it they'd start taking me seriously, and that could have ruined everything."

"We're not people, Lainie, we're your family," Caitlin said.

"And I think it's unfair you wouldn't even tell *me*," Jessamy said with a scowl.

"It doesn't matter. I've given it up for now. I just don't have the time."

Imogen gave her a skeptical look. "It sounds like an awfully big thing to give up."

Telaine hoped her smile didn't look forced. "I'd rather spend time with all of you," she said, ruffling Jessamy's hair in the way he hated. He ducked away, still scowling. "Jeffy, were you able to separate out the damaged ones?" she asked, ignoring Mark's worshipful eyes. "I was worried about that."

"A few of the Longbourne fellows knew you hadn't finished the job. The major had it sorted out in no time." He hesitated, then added, "They didn't want to talk about you at all. Lainie, I still feel responsible."

"Jeffy, it was entirely my fault. I'm the one who stood up and yelled 'I'm a princess and a spy' without warning anyone. They're entitled to be angry." She had to swallow hard to keep from tearing up again.

"They—never mind. We'll talk about that later. Anyway, the major toured the keep and the fort, and she cursed a lot, then she went up on the wall and cursed a lot more. Whoever built the fort built it too far back from Thorsten Pass. There's over two hundred feet of wall to defend, none of it more than thirty or forty feet high, and that's why it needs so many men; you push back the enemy in one place and he's coming over the wall somewhere else.

"The major's strategy was to hold them off with guns as long as possible, then have teams of two or three each working to defend a section of the wall. We each—the regular soldiers—were partnered with townspeople or the scruffy rejects from Thorsten. No, that's unfair. They stiffened right up when they knew what we were facing. Their so-called captain, Jackson, he turned out to be good at getting his men to fall in line. Jess, would you mind getting me some water or something? I already feel hoarse."

He swallowed some water, then continued. "We had plenty of time to test the new weaponry. Some of those townspeople were naturals. Some of them weren't going to be able to do anything but distract the Ruskalder, but the major said she'd take whatever she could get.

"We hauled stone from the quarry to blockade the inside doors, the ones facing Thorsten Pass—the major cursed about those too, said there was no reason for doors like that in a fortress built for defense. That was something, anyway; we had no shortage of raw materials to fortify the walls. Anyway, we piled stone against the doors as high as we could manage, then we settled in to wait for nightfall. Ate some of those rations the Baron had stored. They were good, for rations.

"We saw the enemy before sunset. There's a sort of plain between the fort and the pass, and the earth mover had cleared most of it, so they had an unobstructed path to the fort and they took it. Remember, they had no idea the plan had changed, so they didn't even bother sneaking, or rushing the wall, they just strolled up until they were in range, and we unloaded a couple hundred balls and bullets into them." He grinned a bloodthirsty grin. "I know war's not a good thing, mother, but watching them run away shrieking made my heart warm."

"My dear son, I rode to battle long before you were born. I know the feeling. And I agree it's not a good thing and as your mother I forbid you to enjoy the heat of battle ever again." Her eyes twinkled at him.

"Anyway. That was the first advance. We shouldn't have been so triumphant, but it had been such an anxious day, and we knew we were outnumbered, so we needed a victory. The Ruskalder retreated through the mouth of the pass and stayed there for a couple of hours.

"It got dark and cold. I tried to make conversation with my team, but they weren't interested in talking—one of them was this big Thorsten soldier, didn't look like he thought about much beyond his next meal, and the other was that friend of yours, Lainie, the one I shoved—"

The blood drained from her face. "Ben Garrett," she said in a quiet voice. Of course it would be him. He was going to follow her around for the rest of her life—no, that was the problem, he *wasn't* going to follow her the rest of her life, she'd just never be able to stop hearing about him.

"He wanted to pretend I didn't exist. I'm not sure if it's because I hit him, or because I'm related to you, but either way he wouldn't talk. I don't know if you've noticed, but I'm a chatty kind of fellow—"

"*We know,*" his family chorused. Jeffy threw a pillow at Edward, the only one of his siblings taller than he; Edward tossed it back.

"— and I thought about asking the major to put me with a different team, you know, in case he wouldn't be able to take direction from me, but I thought that might look like I couldn't rally the troops, even if it was a troop of one. Best decision I ever made, not asking for reassignment."

He has to be alive. Jeffy would have said right away if he'd been killed. She couldn't think of a way to ask the question burning a hole in her stomach without revealing so many things she didn't want to share with anyone, even her family. "Why was that?" she asked, casually, as if her heart wasn't tangled up in his answer.

"Let me tell the story, Lainie," Jeffy said, and she nearly leaped from her seat and throttled him right there. "They came at us again around midnight. I don't know why they didn't wait until morning. Anyway, they had torches and lanterns they set up around the sides of the mountain as you come through the pass, just outside our range. This time they had shields and helmets, so we didn't do as much damage, but we drove them off again.

"And then we did it again, and once more. They had so many men they could afford to waste them on wearing us out. That last wave must have been after full dawn, and we were sagging. Up until that point we hadn't lost anyone, because the Ruskalder didn't have projectile weapons and each time we beat them off before it came to a melee fight. The major had us rotate taking naps, getting food, and she kept her best riflemen watching the pass. There was a wind blowing through the pass, cleared away most of the smoke from the black powder rifles, not that we had many of those. Anyway, we had good visibility during the times between waves.

"They saw movement in the mouth of the pass but they didn't realize what it was until they actually saw them building the siege towers. The Ruskalder only had two, but I don't mind telling you I was terrified. All we could do was watch. Well, all but the major.

"She had the townspeople run out to the sawmill and bring back long, thick poles, and had us carve notches in one end, for something to try to fend the towers off with. Had 'em do some shorter ones in case the Ruskalder had ladders and got that close. We were sweating trying to get all that finished before they came at us again." He laughed. "Thing is, it took so long for them to build their towers we were able to rest up and get our second wind. If they'd kept on throwing wave after wave of men at us, they'd have overwhelmed us by noon.

"So it was maybe three o'clock in the afternoon when we saw the siege towers move. It was a crazy strategy, because they had to haul all that wood up the pass, but it was effective. They were on—" Jeffy shook his head. "The details don't matter. All that matters is the siege towers were slow, but inexorable.

"We had the riflemen and anyone who was a good shot taking aim at the ground soldiers, and the rest of us armed with those long sticks or swords or whatever other melee weapons came to hand. Garrett had a sledgehammer he swung around like it didn't weigh a thing. The Thorsten fellow and I had swords. We were supposed to watch the wall and take care of anyone who got past the stick-men.

"That first advance, though, nothing happened. One of the siege towers got stuck, and the other one, the stick-men were able to fend it off so they had to withdraw. But they were back in half an hour and they'd fixed all their problems, and that's when it got bad.

"We lost maybe thirty people in that second push and had another twenty seriously wounded because none of us knew what to expect or where to focus our efforts. The Ruskalder poured out of the siege towers and then, when those fellows had our attention, more of them came up the walls. It was...carnage." He stopped, staring at something invisible and horrible. Then he shook his head, as if waking himself.

"We—my team—held our ground well. None of the Ruskalder who came up our section of the wall made it over the top. That Garrett—" He shook his head again, this time in rueful admiration. "I'd never seen anyone fight like that. All that anger he—sorry, Lainie."

"It's all right," she said. She clenched her fists, driving her nails into the skin of her palm, trying to keep her composure. *He's not dead. It's not true.*

"Anyway, he had a lot of bottled-up rage, that's all I'm saying.

Anyone he hit with that hammer stayed down, particularly since being hit by it usually meant falling thirty or more feet to the ground."

"What about you, Jeffy? Did you kill anyone?"

"Jessamy, hush."

"I did," Jeffy said, "and I'm not saying it wasn't necessary, but it's not a memory I care to dwell on. Maybe you'll understand some day, Jess, but I hope you never do." He cleared his throat. "Where was I? Right. We lost a lot of people—thirty doesn't sound like much, but it was about fifteen percent of our entire troop, and about fifteen of our injured couldn't fight anymore—but we pushed them back again. Literally, because we got a couple of our sticks in the right place to topple one of the towers, and that bought us more time.

"By then it was late afternoon and everyone was flagging again. The major walked around, talked to everyone, helped everyone find some more stamina. We ate again. Some people napped. I tried to get Garrett to settle down, but he kept pacing that little strip of wall we were defending. He's the one who shouted the warning. I looked over the wall and...there were so many of them. They almost climbed over each other to get up the wall. My team held its ground for a long time, but we were forced back.

"The Thorsten soldier fell first. Sword to the—" He stopped himself. "Sword wound, pretty bad one. He fell off the wall so we couldn't even try to help him. Garrett and I were back to back, and we were doing all right until one of them got me—" He pointed at his shoulder.

"I dropped my sword and fell. It's hazy after that, but I remember Garrett standing over me, screaming like a madman and swinging that oversized hammer of his. I found out later he'd killed six men, right there. The next thing I remember he was on the ground and blood was—I mean, one of those Ruskalder had gotten in a lucky swing, nearly took his leg off at the hip. I was half lying on him, trying to stop the bleeding, and I was calling for help, and then the Canden garrison poured up the stairs and over the wall, and it was all over."

"You saved his life, though, didn't you?" asked Caitlin.

"Only because he saved mine first. There's no doubt I'd have been dead if not for him." Jeffy looked at Telaine, but she was certain her face showed no more than normal interest and concern. Her clenched hand had gone numb. He was alive. He hated her, but he was alive.

Jeffy drank some more water and cleared his throat again. "There's not much more to tell. The Ruskalder army fled down the mountain. We took a few captives, among them the heir to the Ruskald King, who'd been knocked unconscious and couldn't flee. The garrison had someone with some healing talent, saved the direst cases. Saved Garrett's leg, for one, though he won't be using it for a while. Minor injuries like mine have to heal on their own." He grimaced.

"And then Major Anselm assigned me to escort the Baron to prison, probably because she knew my dear family would be worried." He stretched out his long legs and smiled. "You're going to give me special treatment because I'm wounded, right?"

"If by 'special treatment' you mean 'waiting on your every whim,' then no, because the palace healer will come to see you immediately," said his mother, tousling his hair fondly. "But we promise to be grateful to have you back. And now I think you should rest. It's easy to overexert yourself when you're recovering." She stood and gave him her hand to help him rise.

"I won't argue with that," he said. "Ah, Lainie? Could I talk to you for a minute? In *private*, Jess."

They walked a short way down the hall toward Jeffy's room. "I thought you should know," he said. "At the end there, before they sent me away, I talked to Garrett, you know, trying to figure out how you thank someone for saving your life. And I told him...I didn't know what to say, Telaine. I don't understand why you were there or what you did while you were up there, and I don't know if you lied to them or not. I told him I love you and I trust you and asked him if he didn't think he could forgive you for whatever it was." He couldn't meet her eyes. "I think I made things worse."

She put her arm around his waist. "Jeffy, I'm never going to see him again. What he thinks of me doesn't matter. And I love you so much for trying. Now will you stop thinking any of this is your fault? Go rest. Eat good food. Think of how all the girls will want to see your battle scar."

He poked her in the side, making her squeak. "Think how close they'd have to be in order to see it."

"I'm telling Aunt Imo you said that."

She went back to her room to go through the latest pile of invitations. A folded sheet of paper rested on the mantel. She took it, realized it was two pages, and at the top of the first sheet read:

CASUALTY REPORT

Telaine held the papers tight against her chest and, eyes closed, folded the paper into its original creases so she wouldn't accidentally see anything she couldn't un-see. She opened her eyes again. She couldn't do this in this over-gilded nightmare of a room.

She went to her bedroom and sat on her bed, too soft, then on the chair by the window. That was too angular. She went back to her bed and sat, cross-legged, the folded paper squared neatly on the counterpane before her. Before her heart could override her, her hands unfolded the paper and spread it out.

The first page was for deaths. The second was for serious injuries. Both pages bore far too many names. She wasn't sure how many men and women of Longbourne had gone to war, but most of them had not come back unscathed.

She couldn't delay any longer. She read down the column of finely printed names.

Albie Hooper. Mister Fuller's stockboy.

Meg Landry. Longbourne's baker.

Ed Decker. Ben's favorite baritone singing partner and one of the first to be friendly to her.

And then, horribly,

Trey Bradford

Liam Richardson

She found herself crumpled on the floor without knowing how she'd gotten there, sobbing so hard it felt as if she were shaking apart.

Oh, Eleanor. Poor Blythe. She remembered Trey greeting her on her second night in Longbourne, his joy the night of his wedding.

And Liam, Liam who was in almost as many of her memories of Longbourne as Ben, Liam lifting her to put the last touches on her tent of lights, Liam laughing as he pressed the button on his watch and heard her voice teasing him. She pressed her face into the side of her mattress and screamed out her pain. And they had died thinking she'd used them.

She almost couldn't bear to go back to the list after that, but she had to know. She leaned against the bed, weak from crying, and made herself read the rest of the list. Too many friends. Too many she needed to mourn.

She already knew what she'd find, but she turned to the second list. Ben's name was at the top.

"Serious injury," it was titled, as if that were enough, as if people wouldn't want to know exactly what kind of serious injury they should worry about or if it was something a person might die of. Without Jeffy's story, her imagination would have tortured her with the possibilities.

She forced herself to focus on the list. There was her old adversary Irv Tanner. Both the Andersons. At least twenty other people she knew as more than acquaintances. Jack Taylor's name was absent, and so was Isabel Colton's. Small mercies.

She crumpled the pages, then smoothed and refolded them and put them on her bedside table. She went into her bathroom and washed her face, then stared into the mirror to see how ravaged her grief had made her. Her eyes were slightly red and puffy, that was all. It seemed unfair that someone like Liam Richardson could die and that loss didn't show up on her face.

I have to testify, she silently told her reflection. *The Baron did this. He killed Liam and Trey and Ed and all the others. His death won't bring them back, but it might bring them justice.*

The idea terrified her. She had seen trials, seen those pitiable figures sit in front of hundreds of their peers and be questioned and cross-questioned until they almost forgot their own names. She would be unable to hide behind the Princess's mask, and the nobles of the entire kingdom would join Longbourne in hating her, though they would have better reason to do so, since the Princess really had manipulated most of them.

But what else could she do, and retain her honor? She was used to losing things by now. She'd lost Lainie Bricker. She was about to lose the Princess. It seemed she was going to find out who Telaine North Hunter was, because that would be the only identity left to her.

CHAPTER THIRTY-THREE

Graham Belcote's office looked like a tidier version of her uncle's, though the chief questioner for the Crown preferred landscapes in oils and his windows were smaller. Belcote was a small, fussy-looking man whose thin lips and prissy expression concealed a sharp mind and a kind heart. Telaine sat opposite him in a chair whose cushions were too soft to be comfortable and said, "Go ahead and explain, Mister Belcote."

"The procedure is simple," Belcote said. "You'll sit before the grand jury, which includes the King and six randomly chosen men and women of the accused's peers, and tell your story. Then I'll ask you a few questions to clarify what you've said, or draw attention to something I think will be particularly damning. Then the chief cross-questioner will try to show holes or inconsistencies in your statement. After all the witnesses have testified, the grand jury will deliberate and return with a verdict."

"If they find the Baron guilty, how long will it be before he's executed?" Telaine asked.

"The sentence is handed down immediately. For a capital trial like this, it's only a matter of days before it's carried out."

Telaine let out a deep breath. "I'm ready for it all to be over," she said.

"There's nothing for you to worry about. Evan Kirkpatrick is a ruthless cross-questioner, but you don't appear easily rattled."

"I hope you're right. What worries me is that my testimony is going to be the key to the Baron's conviction."

"You're not the only witness. Count Harroden can attest to the smuggling operation."

"But you said the cross-questioner would tear him apart."

"He's weak-willed, true, but we're working with him. Really, your Highness, you've nothing to worry about."

She might not have anything to fear from the cross-questioner, but she could admit to herself in the darkness of her bedroom that she was terrified of facing the public barefaced, as it were. Having the Princess exposed as a spy wasn't as hard, in most ways, as having Lainie Bricker exposed as a spy and a fraud. She didn't care for most of the Princess's acquaintances, though she did feel a pang at the idea of someone like Michael Cosgrove believing she'd made a mockery of him.

But the political repercussions...how many landed houses, how many noble estates, had she infiltrated in her career? How many people would now revile her for stealing their secrets, or assume she'd made such thefts when she hadn't?

She'd had this discussion with her uncle two days before the trial. "I'm still not convinced it's a good idea to admit I've been spying on them for so long," she'd said. "Won't that open you up to a possible rebellion? The fact that you don't trust your nobles, I mean."

"Not in this generation," the King had replied. "Some of them will use it as an excuse to challenge me in the Council, which is a problem I'll deal with, and others will want me to reveal who my other spies are, which isn't going to happen. What it opens me up to is a lot of noise and self-righteous chest-pounding. Everyone spies on everyone else, Telaine, it's not a secret. They all know I have spies. They just won't like the idea that you were one of them."

"I hope this is all worth it. If Harstow gets away with this...I made promises that he'd receive justice."

"It's true, there's a chance he'll be exonerated. All I can tell you is that without your testimony, the possibility of that happening increases dramatically. It's worth the political fallout."

"I know you're right." But she still worried. It gave her no comfort to know the King was dealing with most of this; she would be facing the world naked, without her Princess's mask to hide behind.

The day of the trial, she wore a new gown, fashionable but not frivolous, did her face with the bare minimum of cosmetics, and had Posy style her hair in an elegant fashion she hoped made her look self-possessed and confident. She looked in the mirror and saw, as if for the first time, neither the Princess nor Lainie Bricker but Telaine North

Hunter. Herself.

The assembly hall of the Justiciary, dimly lit with traditional torches rather than Devices, was a steeply tiered auditorium that resembled a funnel, lined with unpadded benches. It wasn't a comfortable place, cold and with a draft strong enough to ruffle Telaine's hair. Despite the torches, which smoked somewhat, the room smelled of nothing, not even the perfumes and colognes the audience surely wore. A plain, unvarnished platform at the bottom of the funnel held seven chairs, ordinary armchairs with no padding, for the grand jury. There wasn't even a throne; the King was one among equals for this, though Telaine guessed his opinion still carried extra weight.

To each side of the platform stood tables, again ordinary ones that might have come from someone's kitchen. The whole thing looked so… 'ordinary' was still the word that came to Telaine's mind. It seemed no one was encouraged to think of the job of determining someone's guilt or innocence as glamorous or deserving of public acclaim.

But it was the chair in the middle of the platform her eye kept returning to. This one was padded, if lightly, and the ends of its armrests were a lighter color than the rest of it, as if people had gripped them tightly and worn the varnish off them over the course of many years. It was where witnesses sat—where Telaine would sit soon enough, to testify of the Baron's guilt and to reveal her best-kept secret. It was only her imagination that it looked back at her.

Telaine looked around when she was led to her seat on the witness row, the lowest tier of seats; she didn't see the Baron anywhere. He would be giving testimony first, but when he wasn't on the stand he had to be isolated, so he could observe the proceedings but not put undue influence on the other witnesses. She hoped she could bear listening to him speak without leaping to her feet and denouncing him again.

It was worse than she'd imagined. The Baron's questioner—not Belcote; legally he couldn't question both the defendant and the witnesses against him—was a smooth-spoken, reasonable man who made the Baron's crimes seem either trivial or nonexistent. Telaine's name didn't come up at all. The Baron was impeccably dressed in a pale blue morning coat and a cravat pinned with the same ruby he was wearing the first time she'd met him. He was poised and calm regardless of how pointed the cross-questioner's inquiries were.

Master cross-questioner Evan Kirkpatrick, a tall man in his early thirties with a strong chin and fierce eyebrows, seemed not put off by this. Telaine had expected Kirkpatrick to rant, try to break down the witnesses with sarcasm and verbal violence, but he simply asked questions until the Baron's self-control cracked and he began answering questions more rapidly.

Eventually Kirkpatrick dismissed him, though Telaine had no idea what he'd gotten out of the Baron, because it sounded as if he hadn't been proved guilty of anything. Probably it was more important what the grand jury made of it.

The Count of Harroden broke down completely on the stand and had to be helped out of the assembly hall. Kirkpatrick looked almost sorry about it. He was definitely a ruthless cross-questioner, and Telaine determined he would not reduce her to tears, or even rattle her composure as he had the Baron's. If the Baron, guilty as he was, could stand up to questioning, she certainly could.

The questioner's assistant called her name. She heard a rustling of sound pass through the audience. Her presence was a total surprise. Uncle had done his work well.

Graham Belcote stepped forward and said, "Your Highness, will you tell this court why you are testifying today?"

She took a deep breath. "Master questioner, I am an agent of the Crown and I uncovered Baron Steepridge's treasonous plot."

There was a moment of absolute silence. Then the room erupted into argument and shouting at her. Voices challenged the King, those words tangled in one another into unintelligibility. The King allowed the furor to continue for half a minute, then stood and walked forward. Silence fell.

"Princess Telaine North Hunter's role as an agent of the Crown is not the subject of this court. She has consented to testify in order that justice may be achieved. Inquiries regarding her status may be directed to the Crown at a later time. Anyone who cannot maintain silence now is invited to withdraw."

No one left. They might be outraged, but they wanted far more to hear what she had to say.

Telaine told her story as rehearsed, which had included practice in not sounding rehearsed, and answered a few questions from Belcote, also scripted. Then Evan Kirkpatrick stood, placed both his hands on the cross-questioner's table, and leaned slightly forward. "Your Highness, how long have you been an agent of the Crown?"

"Nine years. I was forcibly retired about three weeks ago." Quiet gasps, a few murmurs from the audience.

"So you became incapable of performing those duties?"

"A spy whose identity is known is no longer a useful spy."

"Your Highness, you have a reputation as a frivolous socialite. Up until now, in what way have you served the Crown?"

Telaine was prepared for this question. "Master cross-questioner, I am not at liberty to discuss the details of my previous assignments."

"Then speak generally. Explain to this court what kind of agent you are."

Here it came. "I listened to people. I visited homes to investigate rumors the Crown might need to be aware of. I flirted and danced with the right people and avoided the wrong ones. I shone in the foreground so no one would notice me moving through the background."

People started calling out accusations, swearing and shouting. The guards moved through the audience and collected the disruptive. Kirkpatrick waited for the commotion to end. "Do you expect us to believe this background has prepared you to perform the kind of espionage you claim to have engaged in in Longbourne?"

"I have no expectations of this court whatsoever, except that the grand jury discovers the truth."

Kirkpatrick rubbed his chin. "Will your Highness allow me to rephrase my last question?"

"I was not aware the cross-questioner required my permission." A muted laugh ran through the hall.

"I repeat, what training does a frivolous socialite have to perform this kind of undercover espionage? What are your qualifications?"

"Master cross-questioner, I am not at liberty to reveal the details of my training. The King is responsible for determining whether I am qualified to perform a mission. That is, if he sends me, I must be qualified. And with all due respect, sir, the fact that you think me a frivolous socialite only shows how good I was at my job."

She'd said it. She'd confirmed to everyone present that she'd been playing a game, that every interaction they'd had with the Princess must now be revisited and reconsidered. She had discussed this ploy with her uncle, and he'd been the one to insist on total openness. "Trying to conceal this will only make things worse," he'd said. "Better to be honest now and weather the storm. And I think saying it will do you good." He was right.

Kirkpatrick seemed thrown by her answer. It dawned on her she was not only holding her own, she was winning their battle of wits. She reminded herself not to become overconfident. Time enough for that when she was off the platform.

"Your Highness," he continued, "isn't it true your testimony is motivated by a vendetta against the Baron of Steepridge?"

That staggered her. "I beg your pardon, sir, but I think you should rephrase that as a question and not a cleverly disguised statement of guilt," she said, playing for time.

"I beg *your* pardon, your Highness. Do you have a personal animosity toward the Baron?"

"I don't like him much, but then I did have to rescue a twelve-year-old girl he planned to torture and then murder, so I imagine I have some cause." *Take that, Kirkpatrick.*

"Only the Baron's alleged treason is the subject of this court, your Highness, not any other crimes he may or may not have committed. Do you expect us to believe your personal antipathy toward him did *not* influence your testimony against him in the matter before the grand jury today?"

"Sir, I am here to testify to the facts. I have not invented those facts. I have provided the Crown with details that will corroborate those facts. My personal feelings don't enter into it."

"You have been unable to provide documentary evidence of the Baron's collusion with the King of Ruskald."

"Correct."

Kirkpatrick seemed surprised she didn't elaborate. "You don't think that's a flaw in your story? Much of what you've told this grand jury is circumstantial."

"You have the affidavits of the soldiers at Thorsten Pass who saw the earth mover and heard Baron Steepridge claim ownership of it. You have the witness of the citizens of Longbourne that Archibald Morgan was absent from the valley all winter and the witness of Major Anselm that he did not return with them, which means he came back with the earth mover."

"Barony Steepridge has any number of valleys and caves in its mountains. Mister Morgan might have concealed himself there, stolen the earth mover, and used it to allow the Ruskalder access to Tremontane. He need not have been working for the Baron."

Telaine's heart hurt from how hard it was pounding. "An earth mover is enormous, and this one was stored in the middle of Thorsten Keep. He could not have done so without being noticed by the soldiers, all of whom took their orders from the Baron."

"Again, we have only your word for that."

"That's correct, master cross-questioner." Telaine leaned forward in her seat. "My word as an agent of the Crown. Which I understand counts as evidence in court. Why is that?"

Kirkpatrick was taken aback. "I beg your pardon, your Highness?"

"Why does my word count for so much in court, master cross-questioner?"

She'd rattled him. "I didn't know this either," she went on, cutting off the beginning of his reply. "But I think you have to understand what it means that I am here today to testify. From the day I turned fifteen and became an adult, I have been an agent of the Crown. It was my whole life. And I gave it up to sit in this room today and testify of what I have learned. Of the truth." She swallowed. They ought to provide witnesses with water. "An agent's word counts for much because it is the last service she can give the Crown. What are *you* willing to sacrifice your life for, Mister Kirkpatrick?"

Kirkpatrick's back was to the audience, so only she saw him smile, real appreciation lighting his eyes. "Your Highness, thank you for your cooperation. Members of the grand jury, I consider my inquiry closed."

Telaine stood and walked back to her seat. She felt dizzy. She also felt as if she had won, though she didn't know what the prize might be.

The grand jury left the room to deliberate. Telaine gripped both arms of her chair until her knuckles were white. With her testimony complete, she was free to go, but she'd already determined to see this through. The rush of confidence she'd felt facing Kirkpatrick faded, leaving her filled with dread. That was ridiculous. Surely her testimony had made the difference...but Kirkpatrick had made some good points...

She made herself breathe deeply, but not too deeply, calming herself. Out of the corner of her eye, she caught Evan Kirkpatrick looking at her, but when she turned her head, he'd looked away.

The grand jury returned—it seemed awfully soon, and she hoped that was a good thing. She heard a commotion above her and turned to see the Baron being led down the central stairs of the auditorium, this time in chains. He kept his gaze straight ahead as they brought him to the base of the platform.

The King stepped forward. "Hugh Harstow, it is the judgment of this grand jury that you are guilty—" a gasp broke out—"of high treason against the Crown. The sentence is death, to be carried out in three days' time. You are stripped of your title and your lands are forfeit. This inquiry is concluded."

The abruptness of the verdict and the sentencing left Telaine disoriented, as if something were missing. Harstow, no longer Baron, was led out the door to the left of the platform, which led back to the prisons. It was over. No, it was just beginning. But it was justice.

The King caught Telaine's eye and gave her a tiny nod, signaling that she should join him. She followed him out the door to the right of the platform and into the tunnel connecting the Justiciary with the palace. "You did well," said the King.

"Did I?"

"You certainly caused a commotion, but we expected that. No one will look at you the same again. And then there are your peers. They're going to be unhappy with you."

"I'm not looking forward to that. But I think I can handle it."

He patted her shoulder. "Remember you can always talk to me if things get bad."

She nodded, and they walked in silence back to the palace, where Telaine went back to her rooms and sat on the edge of her bed. The Princess was dead, but she'd left behind pieces of her that Telaine North Hunter wasn't sure what to do with. For example, she was engaged to attend Lady Murchison's gala fundraiser that evening. It might be better if she stayed home. *Yes, if you're a coward,* her inner voice said. Telaine clenched her fists. Hiding was not a long-term solution.

Telaine had forgotten how bright the Murchisons' ballroom was: brilliantly white walls, white tiled floor, three sparkling chandeliers overflowing with light Devices to make the walls and floor sparkle. Hiding was impossible. When she was announced that evening, a dead hush fell over the room that made her wish she was a coward.

She stiffened her spine, held her head high, and walked through the crowd, smiling and nodding at people she knew even when they didn't respond. Where to begin? She saw Stella Murchison standing alone, for once, by the door to the verandah, and headed in that direction. "Stella," she said, "your mother has outdone herself this year. It's lovely."

Stella's lips went white and pinched with anger. "Don't pretend to be my friend," she said furiously. "You lied to me and I think you were laughing at me the whole time we've known each other. I hate you, your Highness. I think you should leave." She turned and walked away, her angry footsteps ringing out loudly on the tiled floor.

Telaine felt sick. True, Stella had never been more than a useful tool, but she had liked her enthusiasm and her friendliness. She knew this was the reaction she could expect from everyone she'd befriended as the Princess. She tried to tell herself she didn't care, that the Princess's acquaintances didn't matter to her, but she knew if she could speak to herself she'd hear her own words echo with lies. What if her true friends, like Michael, felt the same?

She refused to cry. She wouldn't let them see that their opinion mattered to her at all. She continued to walk through the crowd, acknowledging people who snubbed her in return, secretly hoping to find one friendly face.

"Your Highness! I suppose I should have expected to see you here," said Evan Kirkpatrick. He held out a hand to steady her; she'd almost walked into him.

"Master cross-questioner—"

"Just Mister Kirkpatrick, when I'm not in the courtroom," he said. He had a lean, angular, handsome face, and it occurred to her that he looked like she'd expected Baron Steepridge to look, back when she'd first met him. "May I get you a drink? Champagne, perhaps?"

She nodded, and he handed her a glass. They seemed to be at the center of a rapidly expanding unoccupied circle. She didn't care. "Are you interested in helping Aurilien's unbonded orphans, then?" she asked.

"I make a donation every year, and then I make it a point to attend the gala and get my money's worth of free canapés and wine." His eyes crinkled at the corners when he smiled, and Telaine smiled back. It was such a relief to talk to someone who didn't hate her. "I'd hoped to tell you I don't think I've ever had a more formidable opponent," he added.

"I feel rather the same way," she admitted. "Was your goal to reduce me to a quivering jelly? Because it almost worked."

He laughed. "Now *that* I don't believe," he said. "I almost laughed out loud when you said you didn't think I needed your permission. I can see why you made such a good agent."

"Thank you for the compliment, sir. And for my part, I can see why you're such a good cross-questioner."

"Please don't judge me by what happened to poor Harroden. I felt almost guilty about it. There's no skill in questioning someone who's so terrified he'll say anything you like to make you stop."

"I could see you felt sorry for him, at the end."

"Did you? I must be slipping. I try not to appear emotionally involved, good or bad. My job is to remain impartial—and yes, I know what you're thinking, I seem antagonistic enough, but a good testimony should be able to withstand my poking at it."

He glanced around. "Your Highness, I'd hate for you to think of me as a villain. Would you care to meet me for dinner tomorrow? I can tell you all about the tedious world of litigation, and you can tell me stories of your daring exploits—those you're at liberty to share," he added with a smile.

"Mister Kirkpatrick, I would enjoy having dinner with you. Shall we meet at one o'clock at the Justiciary?"

"I look forward to it." He bowed, and turned away. Irrationally, she felt as if she'd been abandoned.

She stepped backward and bumped into someone else. "Please excuse me—" she said. It was Michael Cosgrove.

"Your Highness," he said without warmth. "How are you this evening?"

"Michael," she said, feeling afraid, "I never spied on you. Never."

"I'd take your word for it, but I understand agents of the Crown are good at telling people what they want to hear."

"Michael—"

"You know, your Highness, I don't believe you and I have anything to say to one another. If you'll excuse me, I see my husband calling me." He nodded curtly and walked away.

Now Telaine wanted to cry. She blinked rapidly and moved toward the door. These people would *not* see her cry and they would *not* see her run out of here as though she'd been chased away. She walked faster and no longer met anyone's eyes.

She met Julia as she was about to ascend the stairs out of the Murchisons' ballroom. "Telaine!" her cousin exclaimed, and then "What's wrong?"

Telaine shook her head the tiniest bit, hoping to conceal her misery, but Julia looked around at the people deliberately not looking their way, and said loudly, "I'm leaving."

She hooked her arm through Telaine's and led her up the stairs and out of the manor. "Charleton, wait," she called to her driver, who turned the carriage around for them. Telaine climbed into it, grateful for how its enclosing sides and window drapes concealed her from the hateful gazes of passersby.

"What happened? Were they rude to you? Should I go back and have words with Ariana Murchison?" Julia's face was flushed with anger.

"It was exactly as I expected. I just didn't realize how bad it would feel. I don't even like most of those people." Remembering how much worse it had been when the same thing happened in Longbourne was no comfort. "But some of them, I thought, were friends. I don't know why I thought they'd be able to tell I was sincere in how I treated *them*."

"Why not? I always know the difference between people who care about me and people who want to befriend me because I'm the Crown Princess. Or because I'm rich. Or beautiful."

"You know to look for those things. I'm sure most of them are angry with themselves for letting me fool them. It's—it's not easy, feeling like a fool."

The carriage drew up at the steps to the palace and Charleton helped them out. "It will blow over, Father says. You'll see who your real friends are then."

Julia once again hooked her arm through Telaine's and together they ascended the stairs and passed through the white marble dome of the entrance, following the path to the east wing. Her cousin's tall, warm presence comforted Telaine, and she laughed.

"My real friends? You know something, Julia? None of them are my real friends. They couldn't possibly be. They only know me as the mask I wore, the giddy Princess who only cared about clothes and gossip and flirtation. And I'm sick of that mask, Julia, I'm sick of pretending to be someone I'm not."

"You never played a part with me, did you?"

Telaine stopped in the middle of the Rotunda and hugged her cousin. "Never. Don't even think that. I was always honest, as honest as I could be, with my family. But I feel as if it's been years since I knew myself."

"Then you need to rediscover who that person is. And you need to stop caring about how rude all those people are."

"I think, eventually, I'll be able to laugh about how steadfastly everyone didn't look at me. Mister Kirkpatrick's was the only friendly face I saw tonight. Ironic, since he was so antagonistic in court."

"Cross-questioners have to do that, it's their job."

"Well, he was very pleasant. We're having dinner together tomorrow."

Julia squealed and hugged her. "Oh, he's so handsome! Tall and dark and he's got those eyebrows that just, oooh, they're so attractive!"

"What are you babbling about?"

"Lainie, he wants to spend time with you. He's *interested* in you. Don't you think that's exciting?"

A pit opened up in Telaine's stomach. "I didn't know that's what he meant," she whispered. How could she have missed that?

"Well, he did, and you're going to have dinner with him. And honestly, coz, you need something like this in your life. You may think you're putting on a good show, but you've done nothing but mope since you got back from the east."

The pit opened wider. That traitorous voice told her, *Ben never wants to see you again. Do you want to spend your life alone? At least Evan Kirkpatrick is interested in you. You don't owe Ben Garrett a thing.*

"No," she cried, and ran, ducking through the corridors, taking turns at random. She didn't realize she'd unconsciously trodden a familiar path until she found herself in the long hall lined with the portraits of the Kings and Queens of Tremontane. With tears running down her face, she walked along the line of merry or cruel or apathetic faces until she came to Queen Zara's portrait. Aunt Weaver stared back at her down her straight, imperious nose.

"I'm sorry I didn't listen," she babbled through her tears. "I should have broken with him the night you told me to. That little pain was nothing to what I'm going through now." She sat down on the ivory carpet, wrapped her arms around her legs, and buried her face in her knees.

"Lainie, what's wrong? Please don't run away from me." Julia knelt beside her cousin and put a gentle hand on her shoulder. "It's not something about Mister Kirkpatrick, is it, because I was just teasing, you don't have to do anything you don't want to."

"I can't talk about it, Julia," Telaine said, her voice muffled by her skirt. "Please don't ask."

The hand withdrew. After a moment, Julia said, "I told you about Lucas. Every hateful thing he said. I gave you all my secrets and I don't understand why you won't do the same for me. You have to stop trying to do this by yourself, Lainie, I can see there's something eating you up inside but I don't know how to help you. Let me help you."

Telaine lifted her face to meet her cousin's anxious eyes, and all her pain, all her worry, all her guilt turned to tears inside her chest. "Julia—I can't—" she began, then she couldn't speak for crying.

It felt as if the tears were being ripped out of her, leaving her flesh raw, as if she'd never truly cried before in her entire life. Julia put her arms around her and rocked her gently as she sobbed, and as the tears flowed the knot of pain she'd been carrying around began to loosen.

"Shh, shh, breathe now," Julia whispered. "Can you talk about it yet?"

Telaine shook her head. She took a few deep, shuddering breaths, and said, "My face must look a mess."

"Just a little bit. Nothing anyone will care about."

Telaine wiped her eyes. "Julia," she said, "I'm in love."

Julia's eyes went wide. "With whom?"

She took another deep breath. "Ben Garrett."

"Who—you mean, Jeffy's Garrett? *That* Ben Garrett? Oh. *Oh, Lainie.* I'm so sorry."

"He wanted to marry me—"

"Oh, *Lainie.*"

"And now he hates me. And I know, I should be thinking about my future, and Mister Kirkpatrick is a nice man who's interested in me, and I don't owe Ben anything, but it hurts so much to know I destroyed my whole future and I was, Julia, we were going to live in his house and I was going to have a workshop and a bigger bed and—"

"Shh, shh, don't cry. I can't believe you didn't tell me any of this before. Why have you been carrying it around with you all this time? Didn't you think I'd understand, just because you fell in love with someone who doesn't have a title? Your own father didn't have a title. For heaven's sake, Telaine, he was a *Ruskalder warrior.* If the Crown could endure that, I think it can endure your falling in love with a Tremontanan commoner."

"I'm sorry, Julia. It was so tender…it was like I'd been wounded, and I couldn't bear to have it touched."

Julia released her and sat back. "All right. Do you know what we are going to do?"

Telaine shook her head.

"We are going to go back to your room and take off our shoes, and eat cream puffs and chocolate, and you are going to talk, really talk, about what happened in Longbourne."

Telaine had begun to laugh, but that final item drew her up short. "Julia, I don't know if I'm ready—"

"You are past ready. You were past ready before you came home. I think you're taking on way too much guilt over this Longbourne debacle."

Julia pulled her cousin to her feet. "You are guilty of concealing your name and title, and you are guilty of being a spy. But you couldn't *pretend* to be a Deviser, could you? You didn't *pretend* to rescue that little girl. I know you. I know everything you did while you were there came out of your own honest heart, and I'll tell you what else—" she folded Telaine into a giant hug—"I'm jealous of those people for being the first to see what you're like when you're not playing a part. Past time you stopped taking the blame for their inability to see things straight."

Telaine laughed and wiped her streaming nose on her sleeve. "I may have ruined this dress."

"It will wash."

Telaine linked her arm in Julia's. "You know," she said, "I believe it will."

CHAPTER THIRTY-FOUR

Three days later Telaine witnessed Hugh Harstow's execution. It did not give her peace.

Three days after that, Telaine woke with a headache and the remnants of a bad dream echoing behind her eyes. She hadn't slept well since the trial, having isolated herself in the palace so she wouldn't have to face all those people who hated her now. Maybe she should leave Aurilien until the scandal had faded away. The seaside resort in Eskandel she'd contemplated the day all this had been set in motion was appealing.

She rubbed her temples, then the bridge of her nose. No, tempting as that was, she'd been away from her family for so long the idea of leaving again made her heart hurt along with her head. She'd have to ride out the storm and see what remained when it passed.

She dressed wearily and opened her bedroom door on her nightmarish sitting room. All that pink. She hated pink. It was a frivolous, detestable color. The Princess had loved pink. She massaged her temples and closed her eyes. Blue, that was a nice color, sapphire blue like the butterflies she'd once seen in Veribold. Sapphire blue and gold, and light-colored wood, ash or maple. She opened her eyes and looked around. Well, why *shouldn't* she have a sitting room she actually wanted to sit in?

There was a palace decorator, a thin, timid woman who blossomed when she heard what Telaine had in mind. Telaine suspected she didn't have a lot to do most days. She supervised the installation of a wallpaper patterned subtly in pale gold over the pink and white paint and a hardwood floor with a thick golden-brown rug from Eskandel. Telaine chose curtains to coordinate with it, and elegant ash chairs and a long sofa upholstered in sapphire blue to replace the awful overstuffed and over-gilded furniture. The palace carpenters replaced the ugly pink mantel with one of blonde wood that had been rubbed and polished until it glowed.

The process left Telaine invigorated. She energetically decimated the Princess's wardrobe and asked Posy, still doing duty as her maid, to dispose of the unwanted dresses and gowns and boxes and boxes of shoes. She had trouble imagining who might want them. A theater company? A nouveau riche family with lots of daughters? At any rate, they were no longer her problem.

She threw away most of her cosmetics and beauty tools, emptied half the drawers in her dressing table, then went out and bought more Deviser's tools and supplies and put them in the newly available space. Seeing them ranged neatly in what had once belonged to the Princess made her feel triumphant. Cutting her alter ego out of her life hadn't left a hole; it had given Telaine North Hunter space to finally breathe.

But there came a day when she reclined on the sofa in her sitting room and realized she was bored. She didn't miss the Princess's "friends," but they'd made up her entire social circle outside her family, and she didn't realize how much she'd depended on their invitations for her activities. She couldn't throw a party herself, and she didn't like going out because it still hurt to be snubbed in public. She was tired of reading, she was tired of walking in the gardens, and she was tired of having nothing to do.

She sighed and left her room. Perhaps she should go into the city and look for employment. Would Mistress Wright see it as a benefit or a drawback to have it known a Princess was working for her?

Jessamy was kicking his heels in the drawing room. "I'm bored," he announced.

"So am I," Telaine said. "We can be bored together."

Jessamy sat up and glanced around. "Or we can do something else," he said. "Are you an actual Deviser?"

Telaine raised her eyebrows at him. "You mean, do I have the ability, or do I have the certificate? Yes, on both counts."

"Oh." He looked around again, then whispered, "You want to help me with a project?"

"Did you become a Deviser when I wasn't looking?"

"Don't tease, Lainie, I'm serious. Come see."

He led her through the palace to the Royal Library. Telaine had been inside many times, was familiar with the three stories of shelves and the soft carpets that silenced the room, but Jessamy took her to a door she'd seen but never opened. She tried not to laugh at Jessamy's exaggerated whispers and gestures for silence; they were funny, but she knew Jessamy had gotten into trouble more than once for exploring in the library. Grandmama had strict rules about who was allowed into her domain, and where.

Unlike the rest of the Library, these stairs were uncarpeted and looked old. They were probably part of the original rooms Grandmama had appropriated for the Library almost fifty years ago. Telaine couldn't imagine anyone using them. Anyone but Jessamy, that is. They climbed four stories' worth of stairs, which left Telaine breathing heavily. It wasn't as tall as Willow North's tower, but it had to be close. "Jess, is this really worth it? What exactly are you showing me?"

"I found this a couple of months ago, right after Wintersmeet. It was cold and wet and boring outside," he said stubbornly, as if expecting her to criticize his disobedience.

"So what is it?"

"Just wait. I want you to see it before I say anything." He pushed open a door at the top of the stairs. The hall beyond was little more than bare, unfinished wood, with a door standing ajar to the left. Jessamy passed it and went down the hall, which made a left turn not quite at right angles. Telaine followed him until he came to a door that looked like all the others. Jessamy grinned at her. "You're going to be amazed," he whispered.

He opened the door and waved her in. Telaine stopped a few steps inside the door and gasped. Her mouth hanging open, she took a few steps and then stopped again. "Jessamy, this is *incredible*," she whispered.

She stood before a giant chandelier, taller by far than she was and big enough around that she and Jessamy, linking hands, could circle it only if they also had Jessamy's brothers Edward and Mark along. It lay tilted on its side, the massive chain coiled next to it still threaded through the ring on the ceiling from which it had hung. Scatterings of white dusted the floorboards beneath it, something Telaine took for bird droppings until she realized they were flakes of wax. The candle arms still bore most of the wax stubs they had contained when it had been pulled up for the last time.

Telaine climbed onto it and found its arms sturdy enough to support her weight without bending. From that vantage point she could see where the floor had been filled in around the chandelier when it was hoisted and stowed for the last time. Even the winch and the stay-rods were still there.

"I've been chipping out the wax," Jessamy said, "but it takes a long time."

"You want to light this again. Turn it into a Device."

"Wouldn't you?"

"I'm agreeing with you. It's outstanding. Have you spoken to Grandmama?"

Jessamy scowled. "She'd just say no. Besides, I'd rather it was a surprise."

"More surprise to us if we put all that work in and it turns out she doesn't want a chandelier."

"But—"

"Slow down, apprentice. Give me a moment to think." Jessamy glowed in the light of the word "apprentice." Telaine mulled it over. "All right. I'm going to ask Uncle to help us with this. He might know how long the chandelier's been up here…maybe Grandmama doesn't even know about it. And then you and I, my boy, are going to make some light."

With her uncle's approval, Telaine and Jessamy began work. Her uncle's approval was so unqualified she wondered if Julia had told him about her failed love life, and if he too believed she needed something to distract herself. She didn't care. For the first time since denouncing the Baron, she felt joy. Everything else in her life was ambiguous, but you were either a Deviser or you were not, and there was no third ground.

She had to invent a Device before they could even start, a heating tool to melt the remaining wax away. Digging old candle out might have appealed to Jessamy, but even now that she wasn't the Princess Telaine didn't like getting things under her nails.

She found a strong source three attics away, which saved them trying to haul things up and down the stairs without Grandmama seeing them, and using her earth-mover-honed skills she transported it to the chandelier room. She and Jessamy took turns melting wax and washing the brass, something Telaine insisted on when she saw how dirty she was after the first hour.

Later, she went into the city and bought shirts, trousers, and good work boots. Putting them on for the first time gave her a pang of sorrow, but only a little one. Lainie Bricker needed to disappear as much as the Princess did.

Days passed. Telaine fell into what she hoped was a pattern and not a rut. Most mornings she'd steal away, sometimes with Jessamy and sometimes not, to work on the chandelier. They'd managed to keep their activity a secret from everyone except Uncle, even Julia, whose friendly prying into Telaine's business took some work to avoid.

It took six days to clean out the wax and another day for Telaine, crawling over the chandelier to examine it from all angles, to come up with a plan for converting it into a Device. The hollows where the candles went would hold motive forces; she would invent a Device that would plug into those hollows, connect to the motive force, and glow. They would be easy to replace and provide plenty of light for years to come, and if the motive forces died, well, the source to imbue them was right there.

Afternoons she spent with Julia and Emma Telaine, playing with the baby, watching her roll from her back to her stomach and try to crawl. Much as she loved her cousin and her namesake, this was the time of day when she was most likely to become homesick, for as much as she was beginning to find peace, she couldn't stop thinking of Longbourne as home. She thought of Eleanor, mourning her sons; thought of pregnant Blythe, whose child would grow up not knowing its father; thought of Ben, and cut those thoughts off ruthlessly before they could start her crying again. When she caught Julia looking at her oddly, she exerted herself to play and talk and laugh, and if it wasn't completely natural, at least it also wasn't forced.

In the evenings, she spent time with her family, or sometimes attended a dance or a concert. There weren't many of these; it still hurt to be snubbed. She subtly led Evan Kirkpatrick to understand she wasn't interested in him. It seemed she had learned some things from the Princess that weren't poisoned.

Lainie Bricker had been a familiar face at the artificers' yards; now Telaine went under her own name and saw little difference in how she was treated, though one or two craftsmen tried to cheat her now they knew she was royalty.

She explained what she wanted for the chandelier to a woman named Ellen who specialized in working brass, and together they came up with a design for a hollow brass "sphere" shaped like an eggplant, where the narrower end connected with the Device to make the wider end glow. It took several tries to get it right, Telaine experimenting on the Devices in a corner of Ellen's workshop while Ellen worked the brass. She had the idle thought one morning, *I'd like to have my own workshop like this*, and a memory of the forge and watching Ben work came to her so strongly that she had to lay down her tools and squeeze her eyes shut until the dizziness passed.

Finally the day came when the artisan touched the narrow end of the sphere to the surface of Telaine's Device, and they watched the sphere go from deep red through golden yellow to a brilliant but soft white light, while remaining cool to the touch.

"Nice work, Lainie," the artisan said. Telaine had given up everything of Lainie Bricker but the name. Well, it had been Telaine's name first.

"Yours was the hard part, Ellen."

"Not with all those gears and skinny wires it wasn't. How many of these do you want?" Telaine named a figure. Ellen whistled. "That's going to take a while. I can do batches of twenty if you want. Let you go on working 'stead of waiting on me."

"Thanks, Ellen. I owe you."

"You do indeed. I take cash."

Telaine lugged a box of Devices and the first batch of spheres up to the attic and taught Jessamy to imbue his first motive forces. He was so excited he almost glowed brighter than the spheres. "You keep doing that," Telaine said, "while I put together this last thing. Remember, it's impossible to over-imbue a motive force; they just stop taking in energy. So better to take too long than too short a time."

The "last thing" she was putting together was the Device that turned the whole chandelier on or off. Telaine had come up with a Device that was a simple switch with only two settings. She'd embedded an identical Device at the top of the chandelier, out of sight from the ground. Turning the switch to 'off' caused the Device on the chandelier to shift the motive forces enough out of alignment that the spheres wouldn't glow. If for some reason Grandmama wanted to leave the chandelier burning all night long, she had that option.

"All right. That's done. I think we can start installing these things without blinding ourselves. Just don't lose this, or kick it, or step on it, or something," she warned, waving the control Device in Jessamy's face. He snatched it away from her, mock-snarling, but put it carefully on a windowsill out of the way.

It didn't take long to install the first twenty spheres. Jessamy had the honor of testing the control switch. A tiny segment of the chandelier lit up. They cheered, silently, not sure how far their voices would carry, or what Grandmama would do if she heard ghostly voices in her rafters.

Now the work went faster. Telaine would collect their day's batch of twenty and return to install them; the rest of the morning she spent in her sitting room, building more of the tiny Devices. It was almost as tedious as repairing the weapons had been. Jessamy was allowed to watch but not help; he took it well, saying he was already closer to real Devisery than anyone else his age.

Her sitting room became scattered with spare parts and tools, after she decided to set up her shop there rather than her dressing room. The work went faster, but although she had more work space, she still chafed at the limitations imposed by her supply shortage. Every day they turned on the chandelier, and every day the glow spread farther, and yet Telaine wished it might go faster still. She was impatient, all the time, as if she were waiting for something but didn't know what.

A week after installing the first spheres, Telaine balanced a couple of boxes on her hip while she fumbled at the attic door. If she'd left anything behind, she'd...well, she'd just have to make another trip, wouldn't she, because it wasn't as if these Devices would build themselves.

She regretted going to Julia's luncheon party yesterday, since it had cut into her Devisery time and now she had only fifteen Devices and twenty spheres that needed them. Then she felt guilty about that regret. Julia had gone to extra effort to invite only people who didn't hate the Princess, and Telaine *had* enjoyed herself for once. Even so, she was impatient at being behind schedule, even if it was a schedule she'd created for herself.

She set the box of spheres in the corner and spread out a handkerchief on the floor to assemble the Devices on. Jessamy could start installing them when he got there. He had turned out to be an excellent apprentice. She ought to see about formalizing their relationship. No, she ought to see about formalizing a certificate in her own name, and *then* take on an official apprentice. The cheerful idea made the growing heat in the attic more bearable.

She hooked a wire to a screw and tightened both down, set the Device aside and started on the next.

"Hi," Jessamy said, shutting the door behind him. "It's warm up here, don't you think? It's going to be uncomfortable in late summer."

"That's why we're going to finish this before then," Telaine said. She was feeling sticky now, despite not having exerted herself much. She set the completed Device to one side and stood. "I want to install the ones on the underside. They're the hardest to reach and I feel like I've been putting them off too long. Here, see if you can get around there."

The two of them squirmed into position under the chandelier until Jessamy was able to tap a Device into a hollow and seat the sphere Telaine handed him without it falling out. "You sure we can't just roll it over?" he complained.

"It weighs hundreds of pounds. There's no way," Telaine said, panting. Sweat trickled down her neck. She'd have to bathe after this. "I think you can do this by yourself. I'm going to finish the Devices."

Jessamy grumbled, but wormed his way around to the next less-accessible spot. A few more years—hah, maybe a few more months—and he'd be too tall to fit under the chandelier. Well, she could do it if she had to, but that was the point of having an apprentice, you had someone to crawl under things on your behalf.

She started on the second Device and discovered two of the parts were misaligned. She tried to free them with her fingers, applied the miniature wrench with some force, and the tool snapped in her hand. She cursed. "Jess!" she called out. He grunted. "I need you to fetch me a replacement for this from my rooms."

"Why don't you go?"

"Because it's the apprentice's job to run errands. Unless you'd rather keep on with what you're doing."

Jessamy shot out from under the chandelier. So some of those grunts had been for show. "What should I get?" he asked. She described where the tool was, gave him the broken one for reference, and sent him on his way. Then she rolled up her sleeves and took his place. No sense wasting time waiting.

As soon as she was under the chandelier, Telaine wondered why she hadn't gone after the new wrench herself. There wasn't much room, and although she knew the chandelier was immobile—had to be, with all the climbing on it she'd done—she still had the feeling if she breathed wrong, it would roll over and crush her. She couldn't even work quickly without risking dropping pieces that would break or, worse, roll out of her reach and require her to scramble out again.

She pushed her hair out of her eyes. Maybe she should stop and braid it. She tapped in one more Device, seated one more sphere, and slid sideways to the next area, which wasn't so claustrophobic.

She'd begun to wonder what was taking Jessamy so long when she heard him coming across the other attics. "Sorry about that. I got caught by Julia and then I had to take the long way around to avoid Grandmama. She wants to see you, by the way."

"Grandmama?"

"Julia. Guess it's urgent because I heard her tell someone else to find you too. She asked if I knew where you were and I said no, of course, and she said if I saw you to tell you she wants you. So I did."

"Did she say why?"

"Maybe. I wasn't listening."

Telaine groaned. She ought to see what Julia wanted. Her cousin didn't usually seek her out for unimportant reasons. On the other hand, she and Jessamy were behind schedule and she still had three Devices to finish. But if Julia was looking for her...she cursed, then said, "You're not allowed to say those words until you're a full Deviser."

"Yes, Lainie," he said, grinning. "Are you going?"

"I suppose I should. I'll hurry back. You go on installing the spheres, and if I don't come back before you're done, put everything into the box and I'll fetch it later." She wiped her hands on her pants, braided her hair and tied it off with a piece of cord, then descended the back stairs and went looking for Julia.

She came out of the stairwell onto the landing and ran straight into Grandmama, making her drop the book she was holding. "Oh! Sorry."

"What were you doing back there?" Grandmama picked up the book and dusted it off, straightening a few bent pages. "You know those stairs are off-limits."

"I...was following a source." It sounded like a lie even without the echo.

"Hmm." Grandmama tucked the book under her arm. "I'm not going to pursue the question. You always were good at keeping secrets...and now I know why." She smiled.

"I'm sorry I couldn't tell you the truth earlier. I know you guessed, when we were at Clarence's awful play."

"It's all right. I knew you'd tell me when you were ready. I was surprised to learn the truth, of course, but honestly, I was so proud of you I didn't mind that you'd been concealing things from all of us."

"Proud?"

"Of course. You know I love you, but it did make me sad, hearing about your exploits and flirtations. I always thought there was more to you than that. Hoped there was, at any rate. Are you sure you're well? I know it wasn't real, but you did lose half your life."

"Of course. I lost the half I didn't care about. I have my family, I love Devisery, and now I can pursue it openly."

"That's not exactly what I meant. Whatever happened with Evan Kirkpatrick?"

Telaine blinked. "What do you mean?"

"I know he tried to court you, and you rebuffed him. Obviously I don't expect you to encourage someone just because he's interested in you, but you haven't given anyone a chance since you returned."

"I don't know anyone who *wants* a chance, Grandmama. My social life is more or less in shreds. And I'm happy this way."

Grandmama shook her head. "Let me tell you something my father once told me. You're not made to be alone, Telaine. Yes, you're right, the men you know are all wrong for you, but I don't want to see you isolate yourself. Time will pass, and things will be different."

Telaine laughed. "Thank you for caring, but for now I'm happy being on my own. I think it's going to be many a year before I find someone—but I hope you're right."

"I'm always right, dear. Just ask your uncle." Grandmama patted her hand. "Now, I think Julia was looking for you. You might try the east wing."

Telaine searched for more than half an hour without seeing a trace of Julia. For all Jessamy had said it was urgent, it seemed her cousin had disappeared as thoroughly as she must have believed Telaine had. Finally, one of the servants recalled Julia going into a little-used parlor at the far end of the east wing, close to Telaine's rooms but not to much of anything else. Telaine stopped to wash her hands and face and strode down the hall, wondering what Julia could possibly want her for there.

She opened the door with too much force—she remembered incorrectly that it stuck—and saw Julia dressed in morning attire, a cup of tea in her hand, her mouth open as if to say something to her guest.

Her guest, perched on the chair across from her, was Ben Garrett.

CHAPTER THIRTY-FIVE

Her hand on the door knob was the only thing that kept Telaine from falling to the floor. Spots pulsed in front of her eyes, as if she'd been staring at one of her light globes for too long and then blinked. She closed her hand harder on the door knob and willed herself not to faint, or have hysterics, or do anything else stupid.

Julia gasped. "Oh, Telaine, what have you—didn't anyone tell you we have *company*?" She put an emphasis on the last word that, if it were a physical gesture, would have been a sharp elbow to the ribs. Telaine was glad of an excuse to look at her cousin instead of the other occupant of the room.

"No, I heard it from Jessamy," she said, her voice sounding surprisingly normal. *You'd think I'd have some sort of shrieking fit. Or become mute.* "He just said you were looking for me."

Julia scowled. "Trust Jess to miss the most important part," she said. "Really, where have you been? Mister Garrett and I have been chatting for nearly an hour."

"Sorry," Telaine said. "It's a secret. Can't even tell you."

Julia looked pleased with herself. Well, she'd probably brought Ben to this overstuffed, bleak parlor as retaliation for how poorly he'd treated Telaine, as she saw it. Telaine couldn't look at Ben, so she couldn't tell if he'd been intimidated or overwhelmed or whatever it was Julia had had in mind. But Julia didn't have that curling grin she got whenever she'd gotten paybacks on someone she thought deserved it. *Oh, for us both to have the inherent magic of shared thoughts right now.*

"Sit down, Lainie. Have some tea. You look as if you could use it—oh, it's cold, well, you did take an awfully long time." Julia patted the sofa next to herself, and Telaine sat. She could see Ben only out of the corner of her eye; she could not force herself to turn her head. Julia smiled brightly at her, then, terrifyingly, said:

"Well, I'm sure you both have lots to talk about, mutual acquaintances, et cetera, so I'll leave you to it, shall I?"

She stood to go, and Telaine swiveled on the sofa. "Don't feel you have to leave." *Don't leave me alone with him.*

Julia gave her another bright smile, but her eyes were fierce, the equivalent of hands shoving Telaine back onto the sofa. "I do have other things to take care of, Telaine," she said. "Mister Garrett, it was a pleasure, and thank you again for saving my brother's life." Ben said something inarticulate. The door closed. Telaine finally had to look at him.

Aside from being thinner, he looked the same as always. He sat perched on the edge of the couch as if he were a bird prepared to take flight, which, judging by the tense lines next to his eyes, might be the case. He said nothing, just looked at her with that direct, calm gaze she knew might conceal any emotion.

She stood up and walked to the hearth, and looked down at the fireplace. There hadn't been a fire lit in here for...hah, sixteen years. When they'd brought her here just before her father died. What a memory to have right now. "How's your leg?" she asked, unable to think of anything else to say.

"Better. Still hurts some. But at least I still have it." His voice hadn't changed at all either, still that musical tenor. It made her shiver with memory. She was glad she wasn't facing him. Who knew what her face might give away? But what was he *doing* here? He certainly didn't seem happy to see her. How polite did she have to be before she could escape?

"Jeffy said you saved his life."

"He saved mine, so I think we're even."

More silence. He'd always been good at making her work to get a reaction. "I heard about Liam and Trey. How's Eleanor? And Blythe?"

"Eleanor's recovering from the shock. Still shaky and frail, if you can imagine it." He paused, then added, "Blythe lost her baby a week after Trey was killed."

Again she was grateful her back was turned so he wouldn't see her cry. He wouldn't think she was entitled to weep for Longbourne's dead, had told her as much back in the town square. She dragged her sleeve across her eyes before remembering how dirty it was; her face had to be streaked with filth now. She knew there were bits of wax in her hair because they'd never got all the pieces swept up, and she remembered too late that one of her trouser legs had a tear and a bloodstain in it from where she'd knelt on a nail head two days before. "I'm sorry," she said, not sure if she was apologizing for her appearance or trying inadequately to express her pain at her friends' grief.

"They've had the whole town behind them," he said. Was that a rebuke somehow, a warning that *her* support was unnecessary and unwanted? Why was he even here?

"I'm glad," was all she said.

They both fell silent again. The silence bore down on her like a blanket woven of iron and copper wire. What did he want from her? Her embarrassment turned into anger. How much pain was he entitled to inflict on her before it equaled whatever pain she'd caused him?

She thought back on all the long weeks since she'd thrown everything away in Longbourne's town square, how she'd carried that agony with her in her night ride to raise the garrison and all the long way back to Aurilien. How she'd carried it clutched to her heart like a tumor all through the weariness of preparing for trial and through discovering what was left of her life with the Princess excised from it. It was more than enough.

"I can't bear to be in this room another minute," she said, and flung herself away from the mantel toward the door. She looked back at him and saw, for a moment, surprise and fear. It was enough to make her pause. "If you have anything to say, come with me. I just can't hear it in this room."

She opened the door and strode down the hall, then slowed to match her pace to his limping one. *You could run away; he'd never catch you on that leg.* It was too late. They walked side by side, neither looking at the other. It might have been a gallows march.

She went to her rooms like a badger goes to ground, seeking its own safe shelter. Ben looked around with surprise and pleasure. "I like this room," he said. "It's not as uncomfortable."

"Two weeks ago it was worse than the other. I've made a lot of changes."

"Is this your room, then?"

"One of them." Her shoulder blades itched and the back of her neck was sticky. She decided that, Ben in her sitting room or no, she had to change her shirt. "Sit down. You probably shouldn't strain your leg. I have to change."

She went through her bedroom and into her dressing room, closing both doors behind her as if that might keep him from following her. Not that she expected him to.

She stripped off her shirt and her sweat-sodden brassiere, went to the washroom to wash her face and wipe sweat off her neck and from under her breasts, and changed into clean underwear and a new shirt. She brushed the wax bits fiercely out of her hair and braided it up again, then looked at herself in the mirror, holding the brush as if it were a weapon. Whatever he intended to bring to bear on her, she was armored against it.

Ben looked up when she came back in. Again, she saw a moment's fear that turned instantly to surprise and then, oddly, relief. "I thought you might be putting on a dress. Like your cousin."

"I'm going back to work later. No point getting dressed up." *Certainly not for you.*

"You work?"

He sounded so surprised it irritated her. "Yes, Ben, I work. I'm a Deviser. We build things."

Her sarcasm cracked his calm demeanor, though not by much. "That's not...I thought..."

"What did you think?"

He shrugged and turned away. "Doesn't matter, I guess."

Anger rose up inside her again. He came all this way, intruded on her home, and for what? Why couldn't he for once say what was on his mind? She sat on a chair opposite him and massaged her temples against the headache that was trying to build there. "You didn't come all this way just to chat about people who hate me. Why are you here?"

He looked startled. "Nobody hates you."

"Don't they? You all sure gave a good impression of feeling otherwise. Or have you forgotten?" To her horror, tears pricked her eyes. "Ben, *why are you here?* Is your anger and pain so great it can only be eased by telling me, once again, how awful I am? I am *sorry* for what I did. It was selfish and short-sighted and I knew the whole time I had no right to lead you on when you couldn't know who I was. I just—"

She took a deep, shuddering breath. "No. I'm not going to make excuses. I was wrong, that's all, and I don't—"

"No. Stop. Lainie, no." Ben took both her hands in his and clasped them tightly. "Lainie, I came here to ask you to forgive me. Please."

Caught mid-word, Telaine gaped at him. "Forgive *you?*"

"I'm so sorry I said those things to you. That I didn't trust you enough to at least listen to you. I don't like feeling like a fool, and that day…I was angry with myself, and I turned that anger on you. I should never have done that. Not to you. Please, forgive me."

She had to concentrate on breathing, because the spots in front of her eyes were trying to claim her again. "I'm the one who needs forgiveness."

"For what? For being an agent of the Crown, forced to live a lie that turned out to be truth? Lainie, you gave me a false name. You never gave me a false heart."

A tear slid down her cheek. She couldn't wipe it away because Ben was still holding her hands and she didn't want him to let go. "I wanted to tell you," she said. "Truly I did."

"Can't imagine how hard it was to keep that secret." He kissed her knuckles, sending a thrill through her. "Lainie, I love you. I never stopped. Can you find it in you to love me again?"

She smiled through her tears. "I recall someone telling me love's not something you turn on and off like a tap."

He smiled back, that wide, brilliant smile that made her heart turn over in her chest. "I was hoping that was true," he whispered, and kissed her.

She leaned into his kiss, not caring that she was crying in earnest now, tears of relief and happiness. He let go of her hands and pulled her onto his lap so she could hold him close. He still smelled of the forge, a wonderful, familiar smell, and she drew him closer and tried to wipe away her tears without breaking that beautiful, heart-pounding connection. Ben kissed her damp cheek, then her lips again, and she tasted her own tears and laughed. "What's so funny?" Ben asked.

"Nothing. I'm just happy. I missed you so much."

"Sorry it took so long. I was flat on my back for most of six weeks, healing."

"Jeffy told us you'd been wounded. It sounded bad."

"Happen it would've been worse without Major Anselm's healer. Got a nice scar now."

Telaine kissed him again, tracing the curve of his ear with her forefinger. "I'm glad you're here, however long it took."

"It was a long six weeks. Everyone else in Longbourne forgave you before I did. For a while there seemed like everyone in town took it on themselves to tell me how stupid I'd been. Then I started having nightmares that you were never going to forgive me. Didn't help that you came into that awful room looking like you wanted to murder someone and it might be me."

"I was shocked. You were the last person I expected to see."

"I know." He went back to kissing her, sliding his hands across the small of her back. "We'd better be careful. Nice quiet room like this, we could be headed for trouble."

"It's worse than you know. My bedroom is just through that door." She ran her fingers through his hair, making him smile against her mouth.

The door opened. They scrambled apart, awkwardly disentangling themselves to sit upright at opposite ends of the sofa. "*Julia!*" Telaine exclaimed. "Don't you *knock*?"

"Sorry," Julia said, grinning and looking not at all remorseful. "Just wondering where you'd gone."

"Honestly, Julia, we might have been doing anything in here. You should be ashamed of yourself."

"I wish you *were* doing something scandalous. I've never seen two people more in need of sex than you are."

Telaine looked at Ben, whose face was crimson. "Excuse me," she told him, "I have to go murder my cousin." She leaped up and flew across the room toward the door, shoving it slowly closed against Julia's laughing weight.

"Father wants to meet him," Julia panted, "and Mother said to tell you both that dinner will be at twelve-thirty. Ouch." She shoved Telaine back an inch. "But if you *are* going to make use of the bedroom, I could tell her to push it back to one o'clock —"

"Go *away*, Julia!" Telaine shrieked, and slammed the door on her cousin's hearty laughter. She leaned against the door, forehead on wood, and wondered if it were possible to die of embarrassment.

"Now I'm not sure if she likes me or not," Ben said. He was just as red as she felt. She went back to sit next to him on the sofa.

"She approves of you, which is the first step toward liking you," she told him. "You already know the rest of the family is going to like you, because you saved Jeffy's life."

"Can't believe a grown man lets anyone call him 'Jeffy'."

"My cousin Mark will want to talk about your military prowess. I'm afraid I can't stop him. Jessamy — oh no. I forgot about Jessamy. I left him with the project and told him I was coming back." She dug out her watch. "He's probably given up on me by now, but I should go back anyway."

"Can I come along?"

She kissed him. "It's up four flights of stairs. I don't think you'd make it. You can wait for me in the drawing room. It will give you a chance to meet some of the family."

He went from red to pale. "You've got a lot of family."

"You faced the Ruskalder army. How much worse could this be?"

She saw him settled in the drawing room and then flew back to the Library and the attic. Jessamy had indeed gone, but had left the box of parts and tools neatly in the corner. She turned over the half-finished

Device in her hands, hesitated, then set it in the box. She decided never to tell Ben he'd almost come second to a piece of Devisery.

When she returned, he was gone. Julia sat demurely in one corner, doing her needlework, with Emma Telaine chewing on a soft stuffed toy at her feet. The baby sat up when she saw Telaine and reached out her chubby arms, burbling a welcome.

"Where did he go?" Telaine demanded. Julia tied a knot and bit off the loose end.

"To whom are you referring? Oh, the blacksmith? He went off with Father to his study. I expect he's being thoroughly interrogated as to his intentions. I ought to tell Father you were planning to have sex just minutes ago—no, don't, I have a needle!"

She held up her embroidery hoop as if it were a shield, laughing. Then she lowered it, her eyes shining, and said, "I am so happy to see *you* so happy, my dear. It is what you wanted, isn't it? I didn't overstep by throwing you together?"

"You did exactly right, coz," Telaine said, kneeling next to her chair and brushing the soft toy across the baby's face, making her giggle. "And I am wonderfully happy."

"I was going to make him suffer," Julia said. "But it was obvious after only a few minutes that he was already suffering quite a lot. So I knew if you'd talk to each other, you could work things out. I do like him. He's very quiet, isn't he? Or maybe that's him being out of his element." She put away her embroidery and picked up Emma Telaine. "I hope we don't all overwhelm him at dinner. I wasn't thinking about how loud we can all be."

"I think he can hold his own." *I hope he can hold his own.*

"Well, if you need me to sit on any of my more exuberant siblings, give me a nod."

"I think sitting on your brothers at the table would be a bad idea," Uncle said, entering the room. Ben trailed a few steps behind him, looking solemn. "Hard on the digestion."

"You know Mark won't stop talking about guns unless someone muzzles him, Father," Julia said.

"That's true. Come here, niece." Uncle put his arm around Telaine's shoulder and squeezed gently. "I've had an enlightening talk with Mister Garrett, and you'll probably want to discuss it with him. Why don't you take a walk in the garden before dinner? You have a few minutes."

It sounded like a suggestion, but Telaine could tell when her uncle was serious. "All right," she said, and took Ben's hand.

Despite what Uncle had said, Telaine was content to walk in silence with Ben through the royal family's private garden. The roses were blooming, great sweeps of red and pink and gold, and they filled the air with a sweet, tangy scent Telaine wished she could bottle and carry with her, to open some winter day when the snow fell. Finally, Ben said, "Lainie."

"Yes?"

"You set me some conditions, last Wintersmeet. Do you have any other secrets you haven't told me?"

"Well, I'm the heir to a Veriboldan fortune and my mother was a harem—all right, stop tickling me! You know all my secrets now."

"That's good. Let's sit down."

They sat on a marble bench big enough for two in the shade of an elm tree. It was cool and smooth, and Telaine ran her free hand along its surface before Ben took her hand in his.

"Lainie," he said, "I know we're not the same people we were at Wintersmeet. But I certain sure still want what I wanted then. Your uncle's given me his permission, so…will you marry me?"

Telaine smiled and touched his cheek. "I will," she said, "but on one condition."

"Never mentioned conditions before, Lainie. You trying to back out?"

She laughed. "No. Just…promise to take me home."

CHAPTER THIRTY-SIX

They held the wedding on Midsummer Day, in the Library under the giant chandelier. Telaine paid Ellen a vast sum of money to turn out spheres enough that she and Jessamy were able to finish the Device in only four days. Grandmama's eyes when she saw it descending from the ceiling made the long hours, and Telaine's resulting separation from Ben, seem like no burden at all.

He gave her the ring he'd made for her. She gave him her father's ring, a battered circle of white gold Ben had resized during the hours they were apart. She saw her uncle's tears fall as she slid the ring onto Ben's finger and swore to be the strength to his weakness, all the days of her life, and knew he felt Owen Hunter and Elspeth North's presence as deeply as she did.

There were tears from every member of the North family when the King uttered the words, "Telaine North Hunter, do you of your own free will relinquish all claim to the North name and to the Crown of Tremontane, to take the name of Garrett to yourself and to your children?"

She had insisted on it. She loved her family, she assured them, and she would always be niece and cousin to them, but she would never be able to truly be part of Longbourne if she still had one foot in her old world. But her tears only came when she saw the look on her uncle's face that said she no longer registered with his magical senses. She closed her eyes and prayed to heaven she'd made the right decision.

They spent their wedding night in her bedroom, and this time they didn't have to stop.

Two days later they began the journey back to Longbourne in their own hired coach, an extravagance Ben protested until Telaine pointed out that they were bringing back all of her new household fittings and she didn't want anyone else breaking her dishes until she had the chance. She bought plain, simple things, linens and earthenware dishes and stainless steel flatware (sensible, really, not an extravagance), two fluffy pillows and a thick quilt for those long winter nights. New clothes, furniture, curtains and the like would wait until she could buy them at home. Thinking the words made her smile.

In the darkness, that first night, she'd curled up against his side and whispered, "Are you sure they want me there?"

"I told you, everyone else forgave you long before I did. You should have heard them. The Andersons, telling everyone who'd listen that no one needed to hide their identity so deep they'd rescue a girl not even related to them and nearly get killed doing it. Jack Taylor playing with his watch so I had to remember you couldn't lie about being a Deviser. Then, Mistress Weaver—"

"What did she tell you all about me?"

"Just that the King made her take you in because she's your father's half-sister. She got plenty of criticism for that, more when we remembered Owen Hunter was from Ruskald, but mostly people wouldn't say things to her face. There's something about her makes people step quiet because they don't want to be on her bad side. Never seen anyone with that kind of power until I met the King."

"So what else did she say?" Better to cut that line of thought off before it went too far.

Ben put his other arm around her and hugged her close. "She asked how my throat was. Said a little cut like that would have healed right away. Didn't know what she meant at first—I'd completely forgotten about Morgan what with everything else that happened that day. Then I remembered how agonized you'd looked, just before you threw that knife. How when he was dead you didn't look guilty or elated, you looked relieved, like you'd prevented the worst thing you could imagine from happening. Then I knew no one was that good a liar."

"And then you came for me."

"I almost didn't. Kept going back and forth all those weeks between despair and hope. So I started telling folks I was going to the city to get my wife, hoping maybe that would make it come true. Though I nearly gave up when you came through that door like you were looking for revenge. Right then I thought I'd be going back to Longbourne alone, and heaven knows what I would have told everyone then. Good thing for me you said yes." Telaine laughed.

"But that was before I saw this place," he added. He turned on his good side to face her, not that she could see him as anything more than a slightly darker shape against the gray background. "You sure you want to go back? I never realized how much of a shock Longbourne must've been, those first weeks. This is a lot to leave behind. Never felt such a soft bed in all my days."

She trailed her fingers down his chest and lower, making him sigh with pleasure. "I'll miss my family," she said, "and there are some other things I will miss, mostly hot baths and indoor toilets. But I have never felt more like myself than when I was up on that mountain. Besides," she smiled, and did something else with her hands that made him groan, "*this* we can do anywhere."

It turned out she did have one more secret that made Ben sit down on a bench outside the bank to regain his composure. "You have *how much*?" he exclaimed hoarsely.

"I have my mother's entire fortune," she said. "There was something unusual about how she came by it no one's ever explained to me, but it's all mine, free and clear without regard to the North family. Then I'll have a portion of Grandmama's estate when she dies many, many years from now, and that should be quite a lot. Grandmama's good with finances. And I don't want you to say anything about not taking my money, because it was our money the moment you put this ring on my finger. We're not going to live on it, but it will be there if we need it. Or if our children do. And I'm going to use some of it to start our life together. So let me know if you need a new anvil or something, though I don't know how we'd get it on the coach."

He raised his head and gave her that level gaze, then he laughed and laughed until passersby began to look at them both with nervousness, as if hilarity might be catching.

They made the journey in short, easy stages, to ease the burden on

Ben's leg as much as to enjoy their wedding trip. After the first few days, in which they told each other every detail of the time they'd spent apart and Telaine told Ben as much as she could about her life as an agent, they traveled mostly in silence, hands clasped, her head on Ben's shoulder, watching Tremontane pass their coach window. Telaine saw the mountains draw closer, and thought, *Soon, now.*

It was not Abel Roberts' day to come down the mountain, but they had enough baggage they had to hire their own wagon anyway. They sat atop the quilt, which was bundled over crates of kitchenware, and bounced back and forth all the way up the trail. Ben started to look white around the lips about halfway there, and Telaine thought he would need to lie down as soon as possible.

This prompted another thought, and she said, "We never did do anything about that bigger bed."

He smiled at her, though it was clear he was still in pain. "Not a problem," he said. Then he frowned, and added, "Shouldn't be a problem. Guess I could've been clearer with Harkins." Adam Harkins was Longbourne's carpenter.

"Ben Garrett, you sly old thing. What under heaven were you going to do if I said no?"

"Happen I'd change my name and move somewhere far away. Maybe Eskandel. But I figured, you did promise to say yes the next time I asked." His smile didn't quite reach his eyes.

"Isn't there anything I can do to help?"

He shook his head. "Just have to…ride it out." He leaned his head on her shoulder. "Talk to me," he said. "Take my mind off it." She told him stories of her family until the wagon came out of the mouth of the pass and they made the gentle curving ascent to Longbourne.

They drew surprisingly little attention on their way into town. Telaine was preoccupied with Ben's condition and didn't quite know when people started calling out greetings, but a child's piping voice broke through her distraction.

"Lainie, Lainie, you came back!" shouted Hope, running dangerously close to the wagon wheels. "Lainie, why did you go away? My doll stopped working again and you need to fix her!"

"Hope, get away from the wheels," Telaine said.

"Hope!" Eleanor appeared out of nowhere and snatched the girl away from danger. She looked up at the wagon as it came to a stop in front of the forge. "Lainie," she said. "Come down here, Mistress Garrett."

Telaine leaped down and embraced her dear friend, both of them in tears. "I'm so sorry about Liam and Trey and the baby," Telaine whispered.

"I'm sorry I wasn't a better friend to you," Eleanor whispered back.

"Don't mean to sound like an old man, but I think I could use some help getting down," Ben called. Telaine wiped her eyes and went to help, but was clasped about the waist and lifted to one side by Jack Taylor, who gave her a kiss on the cheek before helping her husband off the wagon. "Always nice to see a pretty girl come to town, even if she is married to someone else," he said with a wink. Ben came to Telaine's side, limping, and pretended to shove Jack away.

"I guess they took you seriously when you said you'd be bringing your wife back," Telaine said in a low voice. Greetings and congratulations were coming in from all sides now, and Telaine laughed in joy and relief at the welcome.

Ben put his arm around her, lifted his head and let out that pure, beautiful note she'd heard the night of Trey and Blythe's wedding. The crowd added their voices to harmonize with his, leaving Telaine wondering if she would now be expected to join in. She was about as musical as a frog.

The chord ended. "Thanks for the welcome," Ben said, pitching his voice to carry over what little noise remained. "Mistress Garrett—" A few voices cheered, and Telaine blushed—"Mistress Garrett and I are happy to be home again, and we hope to see you all at our shivaree soon now."

"Tomorrow," said Eleanor firmly. "Just been waiting on you to get back."

"Tomorrow," Ben repeated. "But now I think we'd like to settle in and get some rest."

"That what the city fellows calling it these days?" shouted out someone in the crowd. Laughter.

"I'd tell you what the city fellows call it, but there's children present," Telaine called out. More laughter. Ben rolled his eyes.

Eleanor beat them to the front door. "We thought you shouldn't have to come home to Ben's old bachelor place. He's tidy, but I know he eats over the sink most nights and, well...we did what we could." She held open the door for them. Telaine crossed the threshold and her mouth dropped open.

She'd always liked Ben's neat, small home and in all her plans hadn't thought it needed much renovation. She saw at once she hadn't seen the possibilities. Every surface had been newly sanded or polished or painted. The sofa had been re-covered and the rocking chair had new cushions. The old kitchen table was still there, but the single chair had been replaced by two new ones painted white to match the kitchen cupboards. The sink and stove had been thoroughly scrubbed. A few missing stones in the hearth had been replaced and a new set of fireplace tools sat prominently beside it.

"Lainie," Ben said from their bedroom door. She joined him there and gasped. A new, wide four-poster bed took up most of the space, sporting not one but two thick mattresses. She ran her hand over their smooth linen casings. "It's so beautiful," she said. "Lie down."

"Lainie, they were joking—"

"Lie down before you fall down, Ben. No, take your boots off first." He sat heavily on the edge of the mattresses and she helped him pull off his boots and then eased him around so his leg was in a better position. "You stay here and I'm going to unload the wagon."

"I have to help."

"You have to recover."

"Happen I'll never walk right again."

"That won't be true if you rest more. Journey's over. Time for our life to begin."

She went outside and directed some of her lingering friends in unloading, and tried not to think that there were fewer of them. Time enough to remember lost friends later, at the tavern.

It was fun to arrange things in her own home. A year ago she would have laughed herself sick if someone had told her that today she'd be putting away dishes and figuring out where to store household linens and shouting reassurances to a still-invalid husband. Julia had found in herself an unexpected gift for motherhood. Telaine thought she might have a talent for domesticity.

Having stowed everything, she laughingly shooed her friends away and went back inside to find Ben sitting on the sofa. "What are you doing up?" she asked.

"Got bored," he said. "See how I'm sitting instead of wandering around?"

"I was going to have you move anyway so I could make the bed." She rapidly tucked in sheets and spread the quilt over the mattresses, and chuckled, thinking of her first night in Longbourne and her struggle to fit the sheet to that worn, dirty mattress.

"What are you laughing at?"

"Myself." She sat next to him on the sofa. "Now what?"

"I could make supper." He paused. "You could visit Mistress Weaver."

"Right now? You don't mind?"

"Didn't see her in the crowd. Happen she's waiting for you to come to her." Ben started rummaging in the cupboards. "You rearranged everything. And there's no food in the pantry. Guess we're eating at the tavern tonight."

Telaine went down the street to Aunt Weaver's house and knocked at the back door, then let herself in when there was no response. She heard the loom going in the front room, but not the spinning wheels, and found Aunt Weaver alone at the loom. "Hello," she said, suddenly not sure what else to say.

"Heard you were back. Excuse me for not coming out, but I've got an order to fill by end of this week," Aunt Weaver said, pitching her voice over the noise of the treadles. The shuttle flew back and forth.

Telaine looked around, found a chair, and sat where she could see her great-aunt's face. "I never did thank you for taking me in."

"No thanks needed. Did what young Jeffrey wanted, and not with much grace either."

"You did more than you had to. I'm glad you're here."

Aunt Weaver grunted. Telaine took that as "thanks." "I understand you're still my non-royal father's half-sister," she added.

Aunt Weaver grunted again. "Seemed the best way to handle it. Other options were more complicated."

"Yes, I suppose telling everyone you knew I wasn't your niece would have made them ask why I'd come to stay with you in the first place. And you couldn't say you were related to my royal mother."

"Right." They fell silent. The clack of the arms and the gentler thump of the treadles filled the place where their conversation had been.

"Happen I told you once about my havin' to move around," Aunt Weaver said abruptly.

Telaine nodded. "I remember."

"Told you I moved about every ten years."

"Yes."

"That I'd been here going on seven years. Almost eight, now."

"I know."

Aunt Weaver pursed her lips. "Thought maybe it was time for a change. I could probably stay another ten years before people notice I'm not aging. Longbourne's not a bad place to live."

"Not a bad place to raise a family," Telaine said.

"That too." She stopped the loom and looked at Telaine with those sharp blue eyes. "Happen you'll come by some days, say hello."

"Happen I will," Telaine said.

The corners of Zara North's mouth curled up, ever so slightly, in a smile.

Read on for a bonus short story —
"Night Be My Guardian"

NIGHT BE MY GUARDIAN

The clear spring air carried with it a thousand beautiful smells, pine and flowers and the distant scent of a mountain river. Alison heard it at the edge of her perception, a murmur like that of a palace ball. She closed her eyes and pictured it, the Spring Gala with all those men in pale suits and cravats matching the pastel blues and pinks and yellows of the women's gowns.

How fashion had changed in sixty years. Now they wore thin muslins and laces with puffy short sleeves and low necklines over silk or satin slips with narrow skirts. They'd put so many dances out of style, some of them her old favorites—but then it had been her doing that the corset had gone out of fashion, so she could hardly complain.

"You were always so beautiful, no matter what you wore," Anthony said. She could imagine his breath tickling her ear, hear his marvelous baritone smooth and warm like melted toffee.

"I still prefer trousers to gowns," she whispered back to him. No sense startling the driver, who probably needed all her attention to keep the carriage on the narrow mountain path.

"Even more beautiful with your dress off," he teased, and she smiled at the old joke and wished she could lay her head on his shoulder—but of course, he wasn't there, he was a memory, and a beloved one. She could hear his voice more clearly every day.

"I don't mean this as impatience, but do you know how much longer until we're there?" she asked the driver.

"I think it's another half-hour until the valley, milady Consort," the woman said, "and the man at the stables said it was another half-hour from there to Longbourne. Are you comfortable?"

"As comfortable as these old bones can be," Alison said. Her voice was so creaky these days, like the rest of her. She'd turned eighty-three six weeks before and considered herself fairly hale for such an old woman, even if her joints creaked as much as her voice did and her formerly smooth skin was dry and wrinkled as old paper.

Jeffrey had been horrified when she proposed this trip, but he of all people knew why she had to make it. "I'm surprised you didn't do this earlier," he'd said, "fifteen years ago."

"Fifteen years ago my granddaughter didn't give me an excellent excuse for the trip," she'd replied, "and I've kept this secret too long to risk revealing it, even now. The Norths are strong, but no sense stirring up scandal."

He'd shaken his head, but hadn't argued further. Imogen had been more aghast even than her husband, and Alison wondered if she suspected there was more to this trip than the desire to see Telaine and her family in their own home. But she was still Alison North, with a will of iron and the determination to see things through, and now here she was bouncing up the pass toward Steepridge.

It was actually a fairly comfortable ride, less jolting than the Device Jeffrey had imported from Eskandel that drove you around the city without horses. It was a novelty, a child's toy, but Alison had observed how easily it handled, how it didn't leave piles of dung wherever it passed, and predicted Tremontane was seeing the birth of a Devisery that would change it forever.

"We've seen so many changes," Anthony said. "I wonder what changes our children will see."

"What changes they'll make," she said quietly. "Telaine has already made a name for herself, even in her little village. When she gets her hands on that Devisery...imagine this trip made twice as fast. She already keeps the passes clear in winter."

"I've seen them all through your eyes. They're quite the legacy."

"Yours and mine."

She napped in the spring sunshine and woke when the carriage's pace changed, became less bumpy and faster, and sat up to look around her. Now she understood what Telaine had fallen in love with. If she'd come here fifteen years ago, she might have stayed herself. Green grass stretched out in both directions, coming up against the darker green of evergreens in one direction and the silvery coins of aspens in the other.

The sound of rushing water faded somewhat, but in the far distance she could see a thread of white water spooling down the face of a mountain that still had snow on its peaks. Mount Ehuren was visible beyond that, its darker gray stark against the pale blue sky. The road wound on through the gentle rise of the valley, branching off toward unseen villages elsewhere in the barony. "Stop," she told the driver. "I want to stretch my legs, then ride on the seat with you."

"Are you sure you'll be comfortable enough, milady Consort?"

"If I'm not, it will pass, and I want to see Longbourne on my own terms."

She needed the driver's help to emerge from the carriage, tottered around until she had full control of her body, then climbed up onto the seat and held on to its edge as the carriage continued along the road.

"You might take my arm instead of that splintery seat," Anthony said. She smiled, but didn't reply. Ahead, she could see the sun glinting off the blue-gray slates of roofs. Longbourne. It grew up around them, outlying farms becoming houses and then the two-story businesses that lined Longbourne's main street.

The horses' hooves went from thudding on hard-packed earth to ringing out with the same sharp taps they did on the stone-paved streets of Aurilien. Telaine had written with great excitement about the paving of Longbourne's streets four years ago, how it had replaced the gravel. Alison had tried to imagine the life her oldest granddaughter lived now, she who'd been raised wild and then tamed into a society belle, or so they'd all thought before she was revealed as an agent of the Crown. No wonder she'd thrived here.

The carriage came to a stop near the forge, where the sound of metal tapping metal and a hot crisp smell of glowing coal said Ben Garrett was at work. The forge was attached to a two-story house, which in turn was attached to a shorter building with large glass windows that would let in enough light for the most precise, finicky work. A couple of men standing at the forge rail turned to look at the newcomer, idly curious. Of course they'd have no idea who she was. The driver helped Alison down. "Where shall I take your bags, milady

Consort?"

"Would you wait for a few minutes?" Alison said. She approached the forge rail, where the two men's expressions had grown confused, as if they couldn't believe what they'd heard. She nodded politely to them, leaned on the forge rail, and said, "Might I have a moment of your time, master blacksmith?"

"Just a—" Ben said, then turned around fast, tongs in hand. *"Milady Alison!"*

"Hello, Ben," Alison said. It had taken most of a year to convince him to stop calling her *Milady Consort*, as if they weren't related at all. "Surprised?"

"Of course! *Lainie!*"

A small black-haired girl with extraordinary blue eyes that always made Alison catch her breath came running out of the house. "Ma's in the workshop," she said in that lilting northeastern accent that sounded like music. Her eyes went round. *"Grandmama!"* she shrieked, and threw herself at Alison's legs, making her totter.

"Zara, be careful," Ben said. "Go tell your ma who's here."

The little girl ran off. "She's grown," Alison said.

"Going to overtop me and Lainie both someday," Ben said, pushing his light brown hair from his brow. "No question whose grand-niece she is, either."

"It breeds true, the North good looks," Anthony said. "I wonder if Telaine knew that when she named her."

"No question at all," Alison said.

The workshop door opened again, and Telaine Garrett came out at a run. "Grandmama," she said, hugging Alison. "You shouldn't have come all this way. Was it a comfortable trip? You should bring your things inside, we've got room—"

"Actually, I thought I'd stay with my old friend Agatha Weaver," Alison said. "She knows I'm coming."

Telaine's eyes went wide. "I can't believe she kept it a secret from me!" She laughed and shook her head. "All right, actually I can. Of course you would—" She stopped and glanced over her shoulder southward. "Happen you wouldn't want to come upon her unawares and expect her to put you up. But I think she'd be happy to see you, awares or not."

"I hope so," Alison said. "But I'll have supper with you, if you don't mind."

"Not at all. Ben's cooking tonight, so it'll be edible. Do you—"

"Yes, I'd like to see Agatha now. Will you show me where she lives?"

Telaine linked her arm with her grandmother's and led her down the street, the carriage following slowly behind them. Alison observed her covertly. She'd seen her and, later, her family once a year every year since her marriage, when they came to stay at the palace for a few weeks, but she'd always wondered if Telaine was different when she was at home.

She sounded different, for one, dropped the cultured accents she always used, probably by habit, in the palace. She'd put on weight since she'd had her three children, which was as well because she'd always been too thin, just like her mother. Her walk was every bit as confident as it ever was, but there was something about it here in Longbourne that was different. It said this was *her* place, that she was a part of it as if she'd lived here her whole life. It warmed Alison's heart to see her so happy. If only Julia—but that was a worry for another time, and Alison was about to step into the past.

Telaine took her around the back of a long, low building that had an upper story half the size of the lower one, with three windows ranged across it. She pushed open the back door without knocking. It opened on a tidy kitchen with a pot of something that smelled delicious bubbling over the fire. In the distance Alison heard clattering and rattling and the faint whir of a spinning wheel. "Aunt Weaver, you have a guest," Telaine called out, and led Alison out of the kitchen and down a short hall into the great central room of the house.

A young woman and a slightly younger man sat at spinning wheels; the young man turned to see who'd entered and let go the puffy wool in his hand, which the wheel, spinning on its own, swallowed up. An enormous loom filled the back of the room, clattering away, but its movement slowed and then came to a halt as the woman behind it let her hands and feet fall idle. Alison felt as if she'd sprouted roots that went through the floorboards into the earth and kept her from moving, kept her from falling, as the weaver left the loom and came to greet her.

Sweet heaven, she looked just the same. Older, maybe—she appeared to be in her mid-thirties—but the eyes, sharp as diamond, the black hair like Anthony's, the firm chin and the look that said *You had better not be wasting my time*...how under heaven had she ever fooled *anyone* into believing she was an ordinary woman?

Mistress Weaver's expression was placid, but her voice was sharp as she said, "Maris, Jonathan, you're excused for the day. I ain't seen my friend for...a long time, and happen we've a lot to talk about."

Maris and Jonathan wasted no time in tidying up their work places and running out the front door, shouting happily at their freedom. "Aunt Weaver," Telaine began, then looked from one face to the other, slipped her arm free of Alison's, and said, "I'll see you at supper. You're invited, Aunt Weaver, if you want." She left the room, and soon Alison heard the faint sound of the back door shutting.

Alison looked at Mistress Weaver. "It's been a long time," Anthony said.

"It's been a long time," Alison said.

"Sixty years," Mistress Weaver said. Her blue eyes glittered. "A lifetime."

She blurred in Alison's vision. *"Zara,"* Alison said, and went toward her sister, arms outstretched, as Zara did the same, and they clung to each other, weeping, though Alison didn't know if it was joy or sorrow at how fate had robbed them of those sixty years.

"You haven't changed," Zara said.

Alison laughed through her tears. "Because I've always been wrinkled and white-haired and limped from a broken hip that never healed right?"

"Your eyes are the same," Zara said, pulling away to look into those eyes, "and you still walk like you own the world."

"Like you're about to take on the whole damn world at once," Anthony said in her ear.

"I never really believed in your inherent magic until now. It's impossible to comprehend, when the last time I saw you you had most of your face blown away."

"By you. Thank you."

"I had nightmares about it for weeks. Thank heaven Anthony and I had each other. Was it worth it?"

Zara's eyes went distant. Alison wondered what she was seeing. "I imagine sometimes what would have happened if we hadn't killed me," she said. "I picture young Jeffrey wasting his life, waiting for me to die. All those children becoming nothing more than hangers-on at court. Telaine never becoming an agent, never finding her heart here.

"I won't say it wasn't hard. But I had love—I doubt I'd have found that if I'd stayed Queen—and I've made a life and I even got to see my descendants grow up. Though I thought about murdering Telaine when she gave that child my name. Said 'I thought she should have a little of my favorite relative's spunk' and I near burst into tears right there. Never tell her that."

"I wouldn't. And she does. Have spunk, I mean. She's the terror of the palace whenever she visits. The only time I see her quiet is when she's in the Long Gallery looking at her namesake's portrait. Who knows what she's thinking?"

"Probably that her Aunt Weaver looks uncommonly like Queen Zara North," Anthony said. "She knows it's time to move on and can't bear to. But I can hardly blame her for that."

"I wish I could have come sooner," Alison said. "But that was just one more sacrifice."

"It was," Zara said, "but I'm glad you've come now. Let's get your things inside. And then we can talk."

There wasn't much time before supper to talk. Zara showed her the room she'd be staying in. "Fitted it up with a better mattress," she said. "Used to be this old, thin thing with hardly any padding to it. Put Telaine on it her first night in Longbourne, see what she'd do. Not a word of complaint. I'd been expecting fancy manners and demands for special treatment."

"Even when she was pretending to be a brainless socialite, haughtiness wasn't part of her character," said Alison, lowering herself onto the bed. It was soft and welcoming and she thought about pleading tiredness and taking a real nap, but that wasn't what she was here for. "She's her father's daughter, down to the bone. There's very little of Elspeth in her."

"She says it skipped a generation and appeared in young Julia," Zara said, leaning against the bedroom wall next to the dressing table and idly running her finger over the mirror's rim. "The child does take after her great-grandmother, except for the eyes."

"Who knows how these things come out in the blood? Owen doesn't look like any of his maternal relations. Ben's never said the boy looks like anyone on his side of the family. Though he doesn't talk about them much."

"Doesn't talk about them at all. He's hiding something, but Telaine won't dig for it. Says it's his business and none of hers."

"She seems happy."

"She is." Zara stretched. "I'm going to pull supper off the fire and put it in the cold room. Won't hurt it to be heated again tomorrow. Then we can see what Ben's come up with tonight."

Alison had to work hard not to be appalled at Telaine's relatively primitive living conditions. How long had it taken her to adapt to this small house, with its plain furnishings and little rooms and the narrow staircase that led up to where the children slept?

"You're a bit of a snob, love," Anthony said. "Would you have complained at all if I'd asked you to leave the palace and live in the forest with me?"

She shook her head, then smiled at Ben when he asked if anything was wrong. It was true, she was accustomed to luxury. She watched her granddaughter swipe a cloth across her three-year-old daughter

Julia's face, making the child laugh. *It's not about the furnishings,* she told herself, *it's about who shares them with you.*

After supper, she brought out presents: an old book of folk songs for Ben, a newly printed schematic for the Device that propelled Jeffrey's new toy for Telaine, picture books for Julia and Zara, and a huge encyclopedia of Tremontanan animals for eight-year-old Owen, whose eyes gleamed when he saw it. "You remembered, Grandmama," he said.

"Your grandmama has never forgotten anything to do with books in her life," Telaine said.

"I'm afraid I'm a bit single-minded in my interests," Alison said, "but it's such a joy, matching people with books they didn't even know they needed."

"You don't mind if I spend all night in the workshop again, do you?" Telaine said, teasing Ben, who put his arm around her waist and pulled her close for a kiss. "Well, all right then," she said, breathlessly.

"Pa, sing for us," Julia said. She climbed onto her father's lap and turned the pages of his book.

"One of these?" Ben said. "I think I need some practice." But his hand stilled hers, and he ran his finger down the staves of music on one of the pages. "Or…happen not."

They settled in around the fireplace while Ben stood before them, moving his lips as he ran through the words of the song. "Good thing for me my voice has changed some since I was young," he said. "More a baritone than a tenor, these days."

"Still the most beautiful voice I've ever heard," Telaine said.

"Zara's going to follow his example, you know," Anthony said. "She's only five and you can hear it in her voice."

Alison said nothing, just watched Ben as his stance shifted and he began breathing rhythmically. Did Telaine know her husband was a classically trained opera singer? He'd never given any hint of being more than just a man with a gift for music and a love of folk songs. But Alison had attended many concerts in her day, most of them against her will, and in her boredom with the music had turned her attention to the singers, observing how they stood, how they moved, the way they held their chests and throats and lips. Ben Garrett might not have taken up the profession, but it wasn't for lack of either talent or training. Well, if Telaine wasn't interested in ferreting out her husband's secrets, it wasn't any business of Alison North's.

"I've heard this song before, but it never had words, not that I knew anyway. It's an old lullaby that's supposed to come from the time of Haran, back when we still worshiped gods," Ben said. "The words are in—is this Kantnish?"

Alison took the book from him. "An old dialect of it. I can't read it."

"Well, whoever wrote it down translated it into something we can understand. Couldn't sing it else." He closed his eyes, took in a slow breath, then held the book where he could easily read from it, and sang.

Now the day is over,
The sun, it dips into the sea.
It burns a path along the waves
That bring you back to me.

The stars will be your blanket,
The moon will paint the grasses blue,
The night will be your guardian
'Til I come home to you.

Then rest you on your pillow
Within your cradle, slumber deep.
I'll watch o'er you 'til morning comes
As peacefully you sleep.

The last notes of the song floated away, leaving silence behind. Ben lowered the book. "I liked it," Julia said.

"That was beautiful. You can tell it's an old melody, can't you?" said Telaine.

"Don't know how good a translation it is, but it feels sad." Ben held the book so little Zara could look at it. "Thanks, Milady Alison."

"I knew you were the right one for it." She tried to hold back a yawn. "Excuse me. I'm more tired than I thought."

"You should sleep," Telaine said. "And tomorrow I want to show you everything. The lake is so beautiful this time of year."

"I'm looking forward to seeing it. Goodnight, children."

She hugged them all, then walked the short distance to Zara's house with her sister. Sunset came early in the mountains, and the snows on the top of Mount Ehuren were tinged faintly pink from the rays of a sun that had already dipped beyond the western peaks. To the east, stars glittered against the indigo sky, more than anyone could see in Aurilien, which glowed in the light of a million Devices every night. "How much longer will you stay here?" she asked.

Zara didn't respond. She stayed silent until they reached her back door and entered the kitchen. "Until the first snows fall. Can't afford to stay longer. Been here too long as it is."

"I can see why you wouldn't want to leave."

"Never hated this magic so much as I have these last two years. I almost wish she'd never come here. It hurts like hell, leaving 'em all behind, but..." She reached into a cupboard and took out a bottle of wine. "I say we get drunk and tell old stories. If my heart's goin' to break, I want it to break in company."

She lit a dozen candles and they sat at the kitchen table, talking and laughing and even crying, but just a little. "Doyle never gave away the secret," Alison said. "I miss him sometimes—he died about twenty-five years ago, probably from all the drinking. I thought he'd outlive me." She took a swallow of wine. "I thought a lot of people would outlive me."

"I wish I'd been there for you when Anthony died."

"It was horrible. Waking up to that, him lying there so...it's still hard to remember. It was a long time before I could think of him without crying."

"I never wanted to hurt you, love," Anthony said.

"I know," said Alison.

"Know what?" Zara said.

"It's nothing." Alison yawned again. "I think I'm ready for sleep now."

They climbed the stairs together, and at the top, Zara embraced her. "I'm glad you came," she said.

"So am I," Alison said. "Good night, Zara."

Alison sat on the bed in her nightgown, watching the stars. *The stars will be my blanket*, she thought. Would it be a warm blanket, or a cool one? How would it feel to be decked in those lights, wrapped in them so you took their brilliance with you wherever you went? She leaned out of the window and looked up the street to where lights still burned in the house by the forge. Did they still look up in wonder, or was all this beauty just a commonplace for them?

The sky was growing darker; there was no moon to ruin the brilliance of all those twinkling diamonds. It felt as if heaven were drawing closer, though no one knew what it looked like or where it was, just that it was bound to earth by the lines of power and populated by the dead. When she was a young child, she'd seen her grandfather's body before his burial, and for months afterward she'd pictured heaven as full of motionless gray people. Now the idea of heaven held no fear for her.

She lay back in the bed and closed her eyes. It was a good mattress, nearly as good as her bed at home, but she hadn't slept well for weeks. Possibly it was something that happened as you got old, needing less sleep. Some nights, she sat up reading, or walked through the Library tidying up, but mostly she lay awake in her bed feeling guilty that she couldn't sleep like a normal person.

The wine was relaxing her body but not her mind, which went around in fuzzy circles touching on half a dozen things she had to do when she returned. Possibly it was time for her to resign as Royal Librarian, spend more time with her family, but that would only give her fewer things to fill her nights with. And her body might have slowed down, but her mind was as sharp as ever, thank heaven.

Her circling brain began to slow as she drifted closer to sleep. The faint scent of pine tickled her nose. Maybe she should close the window, but it smelled so good, and the coolness of the air relaxed her further. *Finally*, she thought, and slept.

It felt as if she'd only slept for minutes when something woke her, a sound she couldn't remember upon waking. She knew immediately she wouldn't be sleeping again anytime soon, cursed under her breath, and sat up. There was no point lying there staring at the ceiling, so she dressed and went carefully down the stairs, not wanting to light a lamp and possibly wake Zara, hoping she wouldn't trip and fall and break her damned hip again. Bright moonlight came through the kitchen window, enough to help her avoid the table and its single chair. *Oh, Zara. How lonely you must be.*

She stepped out into the back yard, which looked pale and barren despite the new growth of spring sprouting around the edges of the sheds. The high creaking sound of she had no idea how many crickets filled the air, an invisible choir singing a series of notes all in the same key. A breeze brushed her face, bringing with it the now-familiar scent of pine and the unexpected smell of water. There was a lake, or a river, somewhere around here, and she wanted to see it.

It wasn't hard to find the road that led westward out of Longbourne toward the smell of water, but the road tapered off as it entered the forest of evergreens and then vanished, and Alison stood at its end and contemplated the woods. She ought to go back, but for what? More hours lying awake in Zara's spare room? And it wasn't as if she could get very lost out here. She left the road and continued walking, following her nose. A tune came to mind, and she hummed along, though she couldn't remember the words. It was beautiful, and fitted the night perfectly.

It was much darker beneath the trees, dark enough that she had to feel her way between the trunks. It took only a few minutes for her to realize this had been a bad decision. She stopped with her hand on the rough bark of a pine tree whose branches brushed the top of her head and thought about turning around. *No, you'll just get confused and end up wandering these woods until morning. At least if you move forward you'll end up lost somewhere interesting.* That didn't make much sense, but the idea of finding the river, or the lake, had taken hold of her, and she knew she was looking for an excuse to keep going.

Feeling her way, conscious of the dangers of falling and injuring herself here in the dark, she kept moving. The cool, damp breeze came to her now and again, leading her in what she hoped was the right direction. With every step, that hope turned into something more certain, until she was walking quickly, knowing her path as surely as if it were picked out by bright daylight. She breathed deeply and let the smell of clear water fill her lungs. She was nearly there, she could feel it.

She came out of the woods so abruptly she almost fell over, having anticipated more trees where there were none. And there, spread out before her, was a vast black lake that glittered under the moonlight with hundreds, no, thousands of tiny waves stirred up by the breeze. Short grass covered the ground between her and the shoreline, which was shrouded in rushes that remained still despite the wind.

The smell of water filled the air, but now it was mingled with the green scents of growing things that surrounded the lake, hidden by the rushes. The sound of crickets was quieter here, she didn't know why, and the low bass rumble of bullfrogs joined the choir. It was so beautiful it made her heart ache. She felt as if she could hear the tune now, as if it wound itself around the high thin creak of the crickets and the deep, echoing beat of the frogs. It was so familiar, and yet she still couldn't remember where she'd heard it.

Movement off to the right drew her eye. Someone stood about a hundred feet away, near the shore, someone who wasn't more than a black smudge in the moonlight. He, or she, stood almost motionless, and for a moment Alison thought it must be a stub of a tree trunk, burned and broken—but no, it was definitely a human figure, and although Alison couldn't make out a face, she was certain the person wasn't looking at the lake, but at her.

The whole scene seemed odd somehow—surely the moonlight

should light up the person's features? — but then this whole night had taken on a surreal quality. What had possessed her, and it did feel like possession, to leave her bed and go wandering in a strange land at what must be nearly midnight? She must be more drunk than she imagined.

She began walking toward the figure. Part of her considered that it might be dangerous, that whoever it was might not be friendly, but she was eighty-three years old and death no longer frightened her, if it ever had. And perhaps this person had been drawn to the lake the way she had, and maybe knew something about what that impulse was, and why it had taken hold of her.

The person didn't move as Alison approached, though she was still convinced that he — she was close enough now to see it was male — was watching her closely. She was also, irrationally, convinced she knew him, though the only man she knew in Longbourne was Ben and he wouldn't stand there silently waiting for her to reach him.

She couldn't understand why she couldn't see his face clearly. It was as if the moon was moving to put him in shadow, trying to deceive her. It made her angry, though she knew it was ridiculous to be angry with the moon. So she turned her anger outward, toward the silent man. "Who are you?" she said.

In response, he whistled a phrase of the tune. "Who do you think I am?" His voice was unfamiliar.

"I have no idea. Why did you come here?"

"Who do you think I am?"

Alison's temper flared. "I can't even see your face. If the moon — "

She stopped. There hadn't been a moon before, just the starry blanket over Longbourne. And this moon was too bright, too large, and it lit everything except the stranger's face. Alison looked back toward the woods. Nothing of Longbourne was visible, but she was absolutely certain that if she were to retrace her steps, she'd never find Longbourne again. "Show me your face," she said.

The man turned, and in that moment she knew who he was, and before he could do more than say her name she flung herself at him, throwing her arms around his neck and sobbing, "Anthony, Anthony, I didn't know!"

His arms, those familiar arms, went around her waist, and then his lips were on hers with a passion she had never forgotten, gentle and insistent and offering her his whole heart if she'd only do the same. She smelled the spicy scent of his cologne and felt the faint roughness of his cheeks, and her forty years of loneliness vanished, swallowed up by the lake.

Anthony brushed tears from her eyes, kissed her forehead, then drew her into his embrace while she cried, not knowing whether she was happy or confused or grieving all over again. "It's forever now, love," he whispered to her. "Forever, and past forever."

"Were you speaking to me, these last weeks? Was that real?"

"No. But it is now."

"I woke up that morning, and you were lying there—"

"I know. I'm sorry you had to endure that. It hurt so much knowing you were suffering and I couldn't comfort you."

"It doesn't matter now. You won't leave me again?"

"Never."

She heard the music again, and this time it made sense: the old lullaby Ben had sung, now filling her with joy instead of sadness. "Is this why I came to Longbourne? To make one last goodbye?"

"I don't know. There's a lot about this place no one understands. Like why earth is as invisible to us as heaven is to them. Or what we leave heaven for, when it's time. We only know there's no more pain, no more sorrow, just ourselves and our loved ones until we, too, pass beyond. Together this time."

She stepped away and clasped Anthony's hand, and saw instead of the wrinkled, blue-veined, age-spotted claw she was used to, firm, smooth skin. He, too, was young, as young as he'd been when they first met. It pained her a little that he wasn't the forty-five-year-old man whose memory she'd carried all these years, but she'd have been just as happy if they'd both been eighty. "When does that happen?"

He shrugged. "When it's time. Whenever that is. When we

decide." He tugged on her hand. "Come with me. There are so many people who want to see you."

"Just a minute." She turned to face where Longbourne would be, on earth, and took in a deep breath of green-scented air. "You won't hear this," she said quietly, "but it has to be said. You won't be lonely forever, Zara. And we'll wait for you. However long it takes."

Her words floated away into the distance, and the lullaby came back to her, so quiet it was impossible to tell who was singing it, or to whom. *Promise*, said the wind, and Alison held Anthony's hand and let it follow her all the way to the mountains and beyond.

ABOUT THE AUTHOR

Melissa McShane is the author of the novels of Tremontane, including SERVANT OF THE CROWN and RIDER OF THE CROWN, as well as EMISSARY and THE SMOKE-SCENTED GIRL. After a childhood spent roaming the United States, she settled in Utah with her husband, four children, three very needy cats, and a library that continues to grow out of control. She wrote reviews and critical essays for many years before turning to fiction, which is much more fun than anyone ought to be allowed to have. She is currently working on the next Tremontane novel. You can visit her at her website **www.melissamcshanewrites.com** for more information on other books and upcoming releases.

Made in the USA
Middletown, DE
04 December 2018